Astrid Cooper

Georges France Photography

Astrid Cooper has been active in s.f. and fantasy fandom since 1978, she has edited and published over one hundred 'fanzines'. She has also been published in novellas, short stories, non-fiction and writes for science fiction, fantasy and historical magazines. She has studied Medieval History at University and uses this knowledge to add depth to the fantasy worlds that she creates.

When Astrid isn't writing her spare time is absorbed by: free-lance editing, presenting workshops, reading for national writing competitions and restoring antique china. She is co-ordinator and editor for the Australian Network of Futuristic, Fantasy and Paranormal Romance Writers.

Astrid lives and writes in Adelaide, South Australia. She says her aim is to provide readers with strong, imaginative stories with plenty of romance, but without the 'bodice ripping' cliches.

Crystal Dreams

ASTRID COOPER

JB BOOKS

JB Books
is a trademark of
Life on Paper *Publishing*

First published 1997 in Australia by
JB Books
PO Box 115
OAK FLATS
NEW SOUTH WALES
AUTRALIA 2529

ISBN 0-9586998-3-6

Typeset in 10 pt Baskerville
Printed and bound in Australia by
Griffin Press, Adelaide

This is a work of fiction. All characters
in this book have no existence outside
the imagination of the Author.

Acknowledgements

Dreams do come true: the publication of this
book proves it.
I wish to especially thank
The S.A. Writers' Centre for their support,
Dorothy Boyd, Patricia Mullen,
Helen McKerral and Debra Milsom
for their friendship
And to Bruce for his encouragement.

And to Julie Bauer for daring to dream ...

Glossary

Ban-druidh (*ban-drooy*) witch, sorceress.

Ban-laoch (*ban-loch*) amazon, heroine.

Bothan (*bo-han*) cottage.

Breacan an fhelidh (*breckan an fela*) belted plaid.

Claidheamh mor (*clyiv mor*) claymore, a great
       sword, broadsword.

Coimheach (*koy-ach*) foreigner, stranger, alien.

Companach (*comp-an-uchc*) male companion,
       friend.

Deamhan (*joun*) demon.

Dubhlan (*doolan*) defiance, challenge, the name
       of Connal's horse.

Ghraidh (*gra-igh*) darling.

Gradhag (*gra-dhag*) dear little one, pet.

Gradhmhor (*gra-gh-var*) greatly beloved.

Graidhean (*gra-yen*) a beloved person.

Tighearna (*tee-urnu*) district chief, lord.

Tiodhlacadh (*tee-ulucu*) a funeral.

Chapter One

League Station 12, Zeta-Iridani Quadrant.

"I know I *doona'* have an appointment, ye rusty bag of bolts. But I havena' come half way 'cross the galaxy fer nothing. I demand to see ye Mistress!"

Wondering if the *infairnal* machine understood, Connal glared at the sensor box attached to the metal wall. Running a hand over the door, his fingers drummed against the lintel as the seconds passed in ominous silence. He doubted his ability to force entry to the apartment. Much too dangerous to try. At all costs he had to avoid any League entanglements - save one.

The purple crystal in the centre of the box flickered ...

"This is Liandra Tavor." An impassive female voice emanated from the glowing gem.

"I must see you immediately."

"My consultations have ended for the day. Please come back tomorrow, I -"

"Tomorrow will be too late! 'Tis a matter of life and death, and not one for the discussing, unless we be face to face!"

Her sigh, again coming from the crystal intercom, was laced with fatigue.

"Very well. Please make yourself comfortable in my office. I'll be with you as soon as I can."

The door slid open. Squaring his shoulders, Connal strode forward. With a soft hiss the door sealed behind him.

He stared in shocked disbelief. Outside, the austere metal corridors of League Station, within ... so beautiful. Like being inside an opalescent rainbow of lilac, silver and gold, the walls and ceiling were awash with light. With colour. In the centre of the room, like stalagmites, a formation of seven clear crystals, pivoting upon a base of gold, stretched to the ceiling. Their surfaces refracted every colour.

His boots almost sank to the ankles in the thick carpet mottled rose and green; like the heather fields of home. *Home.* Connal's gut churned. Would he ever see home again?

He paced the confines of the room. No doors. Even the entrance was now hidden behind the swirling colours coalescing over the walls. With every circuit the chamber became smaller; claustrophobic. Obviously, the room had not been built to accommodate a person of his height. He had only to stretch up his hand to touch the ceiling.

"How long am I to be kept waiting?" he demanded of the room.

"I'm sorry. I had retired for the day, so if you wish to see me, you must wait until I'm ready." Her reply came from another box-sensor on the wall.

"Damn it! I will wait. But not forever!"

Slowly, he unfurled his fists and took a long, steadying breath. He coughed, his lungs rebelling against the sharp, metallic tang of the artificial atmosphere. *Arran's Mercy! I am going to choke to death. If this so-called air doesna' kill me, this infairrnal suit will!* Connal tugged at the collar of his overalls, only to find that once he had removed his hand, the fabric resumed its strangle-hold.

Out - he had to get out of this place before he suffocated.

He dragged a hand through his hair. Leave with his business unfinished? How could he face more of Fianna's tears?

In four strides, Connal reached the end of the room, halting before the narrow glass cage. He had seen it before, yet paid it no mind. Now, as a distraction, he watched the eel-like creatures as they frolicked in the turquoise water. *Poor beasties.* What honour was there in keeping a species in captivity solely for decoration, or amusement?

Reaching out, his fingers did not meet a hard surface, but plunged into the scene, disrupting it. Not a cage, an image ...

Scent wafted around him, sweetness tinged with musk. His skin goose pimpled. He was no longer alone.

Whirling into a defensive crouch, he grabbed for his dagger. Damn it! Not part of his disguise, he had left his weapon behind. He focused on a swirl of silver material, the fabric parting to reveal slender legs, a thigh. Undeniably female. Slowly, he straightened.

Connal stared.

The woman's hair was green. Oak-leaf green. Wide and wary, her sapphire eyes regarded him.

He forced a smile. "I am sorry if I startled you. You shouldna' sneak up on a man."

"How may I help you, *Maer*?"

Connal's body clenched. Her voice, like honey, flowed about him, through him, sweet and slow. "You are the Dream-Weaver?" he asked hoarsely.

Her eyes narrowed. "I am *Counsellor* Tavor," she said. The honey had gone, in its place was ice.

"Thank you for seeing me," Connal began.

"You did say it was a matter of life and death." Her smile did not thaw the frost in her eyes.

The intensity of her gaze disturbed him. It was as if she was probing him, stripping off the layers of his disguise. Stripping him naked.

"I *doona'* like to be stared at," he hissed.

"I don't mean to offend. You're strange to me. Even your speech. My translator knows every League dialect, but it's having the *Stars* trouble translating your language into Standard."

As if to emphasise her words, she held out her wrist. Connal's eyes flickered over the silver, gem-studded bracelet. Another alien contraption!

"Aye, well. I must have picked up an accent. I have been out of League circulation a wee while." Not exactly a lie.

"Obviously for some time. Your suit is an old style."

Connal quirked a brow at her. She flushed

"I'm sorry. It's my work to notice these things."

His frown made her drop her gaze from his. He took the opportunity to study her. Younger than he had expected. Her skin seemed unnaturally pale. Perhaps she never left her artificial world to experience real sunlight? A surprise that she looked so human, so obviously a woman. Her silver gown clung to her, subtly hugging, highlighting the slender - for his tastes, too slender - feminine curves beneath. Around her waist, which his two hands could span, she wore a woven gold belt. Her delicate beauty surprised him. Yet underlying her fragility, something else. A woman not to be trifled with, he read that in the firmness of her full pink mouth, and the determined set of her jaw.

Connal swallowed against the tight dryness of his throat. He could not have foreseen this, not in a million years. His temples throbbed in unison with the beat of his heart, and the more he gazed at her, the more the blood pounded in his veins.

She be a witch, an alien witch. Remember that. Remember who ye are! But looking at her, made him forget - *Arran's Mercy*. It suddenly felt hot in this room! Again, his fingers snaked into the collar of his overalls.

"Are you ill, *Maer*?" She took a step towards him, hand held out.

Connal waved aside her concern. Damned if

5

he would allow her to touch him. *Doubly damned.*

"I am well, Mistress."

"You are certain? I can call the med-tec -"

"No."

She regarded him for long moments, the silence punctuated by the hammering in his chest.

"Then, shall we begin the consultation?" she asked. "Please be seated."

She motioned to a corner, empty save for a slim crevice in the wall. Without waiting for him, she went to the opposite corner and seated herself, reclining on nothing, as far as Connal could see.

He followed her example. Something soft moulded itself to his buttocks. An invisible alien device touching the private extremities of his person - *By Arran!* He jumped up. "I - I prefer to stand." Connal retreated to the far wall and leaning against it, he regarded her with arms folded across his chest.

She clasped her hands demurely in her lap, watching him. "How may I assist you?

He frowned at her. Once more her voice had assumed its silken texture, the professional's voice, geared to lull and cajole. "I need your help in locating my missing *companach*."

Her delicate brows drew together as she stared at her wristlet translator. "I don't understand this word."

"Kinsman," Connal interpreted.

"It might be better if you were to see the Justiciary. A lost citizen is -"

"Is he lost? I said missing. To my mind, there be a difference."

She presented her hands, palms up, in a gesture he did not know. His eyes narrowed as he saw the trembling of her fingers. All to the good, if she was afraid of him.

"The translator seems to be malfunctioning. I'm not being difficult, *Maer*." She raised her gaze to his. "It's just that my last client was very demanding. I am feeling quite weak. It would be best if I see you tomorrow -"

"No. By then, 'twill be too late."

"Do you think your friend is in danger?"

"You tell me."

"Very well, I'll try. Have you something which belonged to your friend? I need it to focus my search."

Connal snapped open the fastener of his breast pocket and drew out the gold pin, shaped like a thistle. Frowning down at it, memories came rushing back. Boyhood, manhood memories. Bittersweet, the pain sliced through him as he remembered.

"May I have it, please?"

Reluctant to touch her, reluctant to have her touch something of his world, he hesitated.

"I can be trusted, *Maer*. I am a fully registered counsellor."

His brows raised skeptically. Slowly, he placed the brooch in her outstretched palm.

"What is your friend's name?"

"Garris."

How well she played the game. No indication from her that she recognised Garris' name. Almost he could believe in her innocence. Almost.

Her fingers closed over the jewellery. Bowing her head, she concentrated on her hand. "Hear me, Garris," she whispered.

Connal grimaced. Her pronunciation, without the Caledonian burr, butchered the name of his kinsman.

Minutes later, she drew in a shuddering breath and looked up at him. Her fatigue was evident in the tight line of her mouth.

"I can't focus. Others have handled this so much that the auras are blurred. One is stronger than them all. Connal ... a man named Connal, owned this brooch before."

The hairs on the back of his neck rose, as a chill swept down his spine. "I gave this badge to Garris. That much you see clearly, Weaver. What more?"

"Nothing."

"I havena' come this far to be thwarted by one such as you. Are ye not a professional?"

She sighed. "Even professionals can't do the impossible, *Maer* Connal."

"I did not give you leave to use my name -" With difficulty, he bit back his anger. "Is there nothing you can do, *counsellor*?" The word caught in his throat.

"I can try a deeper search."

"Then do so."

"I'll need your assistance."

He nodded, curtly. "What must I do?"

"Come with me." She stood up and walked towards the far wall.

He stared in amazement as part of the wall dematerialised around her.

"Maer?" She beckoned.

Connal strode after her, the wall solidifying behind him. Like the room outside, this one also shimmered with colour. At its centre, a separate compartment had been formed by a canopy made from swathes of silver and lilac silks hung from the ceiling. She drew aside one of the curtains.

By Arran! This was her bed-chamber! He stared at the crystalline four-poster bed. It seemed too delicate to be anything more than a decorative piece, with its rainbow-tasselled cushions and matching coverlet. But one thing he had learned since arriving in League territory - nothing was as it seemed. Damn, that he had to deal with these aliens and their blasted machines! He wiped damp palms on the backs of his thighs.

As she sat on the bed, the strands of crystals hanging between the posts oscillated, sending spirals of colour coruscating across the walls. The lights seared, weaving inside his skull. Sickening.

"What is it ye are doin', Weaver?"

"My name is Liandra."

"That I know."

"Then why don't you use it? It's almost as if-"

"Aye? *As if*?"

"As if you have an aversion to calling me by

9

name. You don't like me to use yours. Is this a trait of your race?"

"Your questions have no bearing on our business. I ask again, Mistress. What do you do?"

"Because I'm so depleted, I must use my bed to augment the dream-search. It's the only way I can find Garris, since you aren't prepared to wait until tomorrow."

"Continue, then."

"You must lie beside me. Together we'll enter the dream-scape. It's quite painless; quite safe. My computers will monitor us."

"Computers! I have no faith in *infairrnal* machines. Such got me into this mess in the first place!"

Her dark brows arched skyward. "Normally, I would try to accommodate your wishes -"

"I am sure you can be *vairrrry* accommodating," Connal said. "There is no other way?"

"No."

Slowly, Connal lowered himself onto the bed. Its surface encased him in softness and warmth, like the body of a woman ... Savagely, he quashed the thought. He watched as she drew out two caps of crystalline mesh that were attached to the bed by fine silver cords. Connal jerked his head away as she held out one of the caps.

"What are ye' doin' now?"

"This is a dreamer's cap. We need them to join, to make the transference. Don't be afraid."

"I am not."

"No, of course not." She smiled.

"What will happen when we make this transference?"

"Very little. You may see an image of Garris, perhaps even of yourself. You won't be a participant because I'm only going to do a first level dream-search. You'll only observe."

"I do not understand."

"When we enter the dream-dimension, your subconscious creates focal points, familiar images, drawn from your own life experiences. Just like your normal dreams. The only difference is that it is I, not you, who controls the dream we are to undertake."

"Have I no say in what occurs?"

"We'll be able to converse. Your input is vital to the success of our search. Now, may I affix the cap?"

"Aye. Best get on with it, before I change my mind."

Smooth fingers brushed aside tendrils of hair from his forehead. Leaning over him, she fastened the cap to his head. Connal gritted his teeth, as her fragrance washed over him, through him. Her woman's warmth whispered against his flesh. His body broke out into a sweat. Her touch, soft, yet burning, ignited the knot in his stomach, so that it erupted, like fire to engulf his every cell. The witch was casting her spell over him. It would not work. *Would not!* Connal kept his eyes firmly on the ceiling as she lay

11

down beside him.

"Now, think of Garris. Clearly. Yes ..." she whispered.

Lights whirled around him, scents, voices singing, sweet and high. "I am going to be sick," Connal muttered.

"No, *Maer*," she said. "It's a normal reaction. It'll pass quickly."

He watched as slowly the ghostly image of a young man began to solidify...

"Kinsman!" Connal shouted. His friend's face was gaunt, ashen, his brown hair dishevelled and dirty. "Garris, what has happened to ye?"

"Remember this is not your friend," her voice intruded. "I'm using his image to focus my search."

"But he looks so -."

"Your visualisation is unusually intense. In the real world, you and he must share a strong bond."

"Aye. Else I would not be here."

"Now, don't interfere, I need to concentrate." She paused. "Garris, look at me."

He turned hesitantly. Fearfully, he glanced back over his shoulder, into the hidden recesses of the dream-dimension.

"Garris. Listen to me. No other!" she commanded.

Connal saw his friend's image shudder, wavering to near transparency, so torn was he between her call and that other which held him.

Then he vanished.

"I'm sorry," she said. "That's all -"

"Not by a long measure, 'tis not all! I have been polite in the asking, now, enough of your games, witch. Garris risked everything to come to you. He has disappeared. I know you be involved. I want my kinsman back. No tricks. No lies."

"I don't know what you're talking about! What are you hiding from me?"

"If you be the professional, read my mind. 'Tis what you do, is it not?"

"No!" She sighed. "I'm too tired. I must end the dream."

"Not yet, we havena' ..."

Against his will, she led him up, towards the light.

Connal felt his awareness return to his body resting against the soft cover of the crystal bed.

An instant later, he was wrenched back into the dream-dimension. This time the transition was violent. Winds tore at him as he plummeted down a long, dark tunnel that seemed to stretch to infinity. Finally, his momentum slowed as thick billowing mist enshrouded him. Ahead, Connal saw his own image rise up out of the fog, trailing thin fingers of mist which eddied about his body as he strode forward. His black cloak flapped around his body with the wind of his speed.

Instinctively, Connal put out his hands to avoid the collision. As the dream-image fragmented, Connal felt pain slice through him, like a knife twisting in his gut, dismembering him. He cried out with the agony of it. Red stars exploded in his skull.

Connal came to his senses, lying face first against something cold and moist, like snow. Icy mist coiled around his body. Shoving back the wet hair from his eyes, he pushed himself to his knees.

"What is happening to me?" Connal yelled. No longer the spectator, he was inside the dream. A participant. Feeling, hearing, tasting ...

He struggled to stand, hampered by the clinging folds of his cloak. *Cloak?* He quickly glanced down. His disguise had gone. Beneath his cloak he wore his plaid and a thick shirt open to the waist. At his side, sure enough, his trusty knife.

Arran's Mercy! Stop this at once! His thought vibrated through the dream-scape.

"I'm not doing it!" she replied, her voice a faint whisper. "We've entered the deepest level, where the boundaries between dreams and reality become blurred."

"End this dream!"

"I'm trying. Wait there, I'll come to you."

Minutes passed, then a whirlpool of colours appeared before him. Slowly, they took on shape and substance. The witch solidified a few paces from him. He watched as her eyes took in his transformation.

"Who are you?' she demanded.

"I be the one to ask the questions, Weaver!"

Taking her shoulders, he shook her once. Her hands pressed against his bare chest. At her touch, molten fire pooled in his groin. He groaned, not from pain, from a deeper, intimate agony, the hard reality of which pressed upward against her.

"No!" she cried, pushing at his hips.

"I want this finished," Connal hissed.

"I'm trying."

"Do better than try, witch, else -"

A rainbow shimmered around him. Connal found himself in yet another shadowy dream-place. He laughed, his whole being alight, alive to a woman's presence. He held out his hand and to his amazement it was the witch who went to him quickly, willingly.

Only ... not she. Dressed in a Caledonian robe of russet velvet, her long hair flowed down her back like a river of rippling silver.

"Something is corrupting our sharing," she said. "We must escape, or perish! Concentrate on returning to your real body."

The dream-scape flickered, then returned, more solid, more real. Her fear washed over him, cold and sharp.

"You are touching my mind!" Connal cried.

"It's the dream-link. I've never experienced this ... It's almost as if something is holding me prisoner. Are you -?"

"No, witch. I like this less than you. I canna' stop. I dinna' want this - *Ach, no!*"

His arms enfolded her in a tight embrace which he knew, from their mental rapport, made her heart beat frantically. Not from fear. From desire. Smiling, he lifted her against the taut expectancy of his fevered body. His lips brushed against hers, softly sliding, savouring, sampling her sweetness. Slowly, slowly, he increased the pressure of his kiss, parting her lips. His tongue plunged into her mouth, entwining sinuously, stroking ...

She twisted her head away. "This is wrong!" she shrieked. "I can't. *Mustn't.*"

He felt her wrestling against the dream. She pushed hard against his chest. The dream held them both captive.

Swinging her up into his arms, he carried her through the mists to another dream-place, where he deposited her gently onto a pile of thick, soft rugs which lay before an open fire. With infinite care, patience, tenderness, he teasingly removed every item of her clothing, before he, too, was naked, his body pressed to hers.

"No! Stop!" she demanded.

"Too late for that, Mistress. Ye must finish what ye start."

Fingers snagging gently in her hair, he drew her head back to expose her neck to his mouth and tongue. His lips traced a path of hot moisture across her silken skin. Skin with an aroma of musk. Pungent. Intoxicating. Skin that burned and shivered with hot expectation. Expectation of him!

The sweet agony, the tension inside his

head, in his body, spiralled out of control. His mouth descended to one of her breasts, to the nipple, teasing it, bringing it to a hard nub.

"Please," her voice, a faint murmur.

"Please ... what, My Lady *Ban-druidh*?" His husky whisper caressed, as his fingers fanned over her body. "*Please* ... that I stop, or *please* that I continue?" He raised himself on an elbow to smile down at her.

"Don't call me Lady Witch. My name is Liandra." She laughed.

Its sound, like gentle music to his ears. He felt her hands curl into his hair as she arched her body to accommodate his questing mouth. Lower and lower. He found her centre. She gasped as his lips and teeth scrolled and teased. As his fingers gently probed her, she moaned like one possessed. On and on he carried her, her heat spilling out over his hand.

Enjoined by the bed, by the dream, Connal experienced her responses amid his own. Such intensity, it took his breath away. He could not stop, nor could she. She took him with her as her climax came, ripple upon molten ripple. On and on they both travelled, until she plummeted, drawing him with her over a deep, dark chasm that exploded into brilliant, searing light.

"Connal," she whispered, reaching up to cup his cheek. He pressed his face into her palm, his lips caressing, his tongue coaxing, inflaming.

He groaned as her hand touched his rigidity, a finger tracing along the length of his shaft, stroking, teasing. As her hand clasped his nest, he thickened painfully.

She laughed up at him, her eyes dark and triumphant. "Come to me, Connal. At last. Be one with me."

Ice seeped into his heart and loins, returning a small measure of sanity. "Arran's Mercy, no!" He prised her fingers from his tumescent flesh.

"No?" she cried.

"I am master, here, witch. Your spells have no power over me." He hurled himself into the darkness, and she followed.

"Connal, wait!"

He kept his distance. "I want Garris. Now, witch!"

"Please - Oh ... *No!*"

She skidded to a halt, fear on her face. Terror so profound that Connal reeled away from it.

The dream-scape shivered as he strode towards her.

"Something's wrong! Go, Connal, back to the light. That way!" She turned and ran.

Something tugged at him, drawing him backwards. An explosion of light, her scream shattered the dream.

Connal awoke to find himself pinned against the bed. Wearily he opened his eyelids. She lay atop him, her body wedged between his wide-spread legs.

"Witch, enough!"

No response. The coldness of her body seeped into his. Quickly, but gently he lifted her away, and stared down at her ashen face. Tears coursed down her cheeks. Flinging off his dreamer's cap, he jumped from the bed. Disoriented, he staggered, clutching at the bed post until the room stopped its pitching.

Connal reached down and shook her shoulder. "Mistress?" She moaned weakly. He tore off her dreamer's cap and she screamed.

Instantly, the room was filled with high-pitched chiming.

"Arran's Mercy! What now?"

Desperately, Connal wrestled the curtains aside and found its source, a sensor box embedded in the wall, with a jewel in its centre flashing red. He ripped the crystal from its mounting. It came away, burning his hand. The beeping did not stop. More chorused the original, a cacophony of noise, unrelenting from every sensor. How long did he have before someone came in answer to the alarms? Not long enough to have his answers. Not long enough for him to get away, undetected.

There was nothing for it. He had to call his ship. Connal dug into his thigh pocket and drew out the pencil-shaped com-link and flipped open the top with his thumb.

"Dougall!"

No response, just static.

"Dougall! Are ye' there?"

"Aye, *Tighearna*."

"There has been a change in plan. Do those *infairrnal* sensors pick up everything within a six foot radius of my signal?"

"Aye, lord."

"Then shift it all, now."

"Are ye demented?"

"Do it! And once I am on board, head for home. Maximum speed. Get me out of this alien menagerie!"

Chapter Two

En route between the stars

" Is she going to die?" Connal asked, looking down at the witch's pale face.

"No. My medicine has stopped the convulsions," the old woman said. "However, it was a close thing, *Tighearna*. Lucky for her, you insisted I accompany you."

"I thought Garris might need your ministrations, Katrine. I did not expect you would be tending an alien, instead."

Katrine smiled. "I am confident there will be no lasting effects from her seizures. She shall soon awaken."

"No. I want her sedated until we reach home."

"Four days asleep? Is that wise, my lord?"

The plan was never wise, he thought grimly. Four days! Time to decide what is to be done. Time to recover my wits after my foray into enemy territory. "She cannot be allowed to see our world, our secrets," Connal said.

"Is it not too late for that?"

He flinched, for Katrine's voice held a tinge of accusation, and truth. "If everything goes well, her remembrance of me will become part of her dream." He dragged a hand through his hair. *If* everything goes well. So far, nothing had gone to plan. And in the process, he had damned near killed the witch by tearing the dreamer's cap from her head. The instant of severance from her bed, she had screamed, and then her seizures began.

Bringing her on board ship, the corridors and then his cabin had echoed with her cries, until Katrine had silenced them with her concoctions.

"*Tighearna*, you look tired. Perhaps I should prescribe a sleeping potion for you?"

"No. Katrine, thank you for your service. Best leave me now."

Katrine shook her head. "I must see to her other needs, now that she is over the worst."

"No!" Connal snapped. "I want no other contaminated by her person, or possessions. I shall watch over her. You may monitor her progress when you bring the sedatives. Only then."

"I have been a healer for fifty years. I do know what I am about."

"I have no doubt of it. Still, I must do what I must."

"As you say, *Tighearna*." Katrine said, tightly.

Connal watched her mixing another potion. Turning away, he strode to the porthole. With arms on either side of the window he stared out. Stars, red-tinged, streaked past as the ship hurtled through the abyss between the constellations. One star beckoned. Home, still so far distant. How he hated the dark and cold of space! Cold and dark, like that dream-place. His hand curled into a fist.

"It is done," Katrine said, stiffly.

Connal turned wearily back to the cabin. "Thank you. Now, leave me, Mistress."

Collecting her medicine bag, Katrine went to the door. As it slid open, she glanced back.

"I am all right," Connal said, waving aside her unspoken concern.

"I have been the family healer since before your birth. I know when you are *all right* and when you are not."

"Away with ye!"

Connal waited until the door closed behind her. Steeling himself, for what he had to do, he stalked over to where the Dream-Weaver lay asleep on his bunk. Though still pale, her cheeks had gained a faint pink hue. He frowned. No, it was not a natural flush. He gently stroked her cheek and mouth. Coloured by some artificial means, like her mint hued eye-lids. Obviously permanent, for despite what she had been through, her make-up had neither smudged, nor deteriorated. Unlike her hair. Still green, but now diminished to a shining copper-green. He much preferred her dream-state silver tresses.

The dream ... His body throbbed, tensed and pulsed in remembrance. He grimaced. How fortunate he wore his proper clothes. No one could witness his arousal. Different, though, if he had been wearing those *infairrnal* League overalls. The fabric moulded itself to the contours of his body, so snugly in places, a man could keep no secrets. Mentally, he shook himself. Too long, he had delayed the inevitable.

Bending forward, Connal fumbled with the snap ties of her gown. His hands trembled so much! In the dream, disrobing her had been so easy. In reality, damn near impossible. Finally, the material parted. One pert breast, with an erect, rosy nipple confronted him.

He hesitated. Undressing an unconscious woman was an invasion of privacy. But if he did not, Arran knew what League paraphernalia her clothes, or jewels might contain. Her actions might have rendered her undeserving of his chivalry, yet no woman, not even an alien whore, would be treated less than honourably while she was in his custody.

Drawing the coverlet over her body, his hands then laboured beneath to remove her clothes. Even though he could not see, he could still feel feminine curves, thighs, ankles, legs; all igniting, tantalising.

Arran's Mercy! His throat constricted painfully, so he could hardly breathe. He took her hand and unfastened her wristlet translator. Gently prising her fingers apart, he tugged at her opalescent ring.

It would not budge. Her fingers, fine-boned, delicate, curled against his. Long nails, coloured green, gently pressed into his skin. Connal frowned at her hands. Hands that had never seen an honest day's work. Hands that plied an art as old as time. Hands that had cupped his manhood. His body pulsed and hardened. Even in her drugged sleep, it seemed she still wove her magic.

"Not on me, witch," he said, startled by his throaty whisper. Connal carefully leaned forward and slickened her ring finger with his tongue. Her skin tasted of honey and spice. Slipping the ring from her, he resolutely returned her hand beneath the quilt.

Connal stuffed her belongings under his arm and turned to leave. He glanced back over his shoulder. What would her waking bring? Tears or rage? Rage, more like. He had sampled her passion in the dream and it stood to reason that she would have a temper to match. Well, then, so did he.

"You be in my Castle the next time you awaken, witch. You shall rue the day you crossed the will of Connal MacArran."

Chapter Three

Castle MacArran, Caledonia.

Something wrong ... Snapping open her eyelids, Liandra's horror amplified as she found herself in a deathly still, enveloping darkness. She came to her knees, fighting against the panic. Had to get out. Frantically, she crawled across a soft, spongy surface. Something clung to her body, hindering her by folding itself around her legs. Hurling herself away, she fell through a sleek, soft barrier to crash onto a cold, hard surface.

Cold? She heaved herself away from the floor, in that instant realising she was naked. Clothing or its lack, was of no concern to her. Without the enviro belt attached to her robe, she was at the mercy of her environment, for the first time in her life. She didn't like the thought, not one bit! Where was she? Liandra stared in disbelief.

The room before her was empty, except for the canopied bed upon which she had awoken. Swallowing against the lump of fear in her throat, she sent a telepathic probe outwards. Her mind responded sluggishly. She had been drugged! Turning her senses inwards, she sensed the foreign substance swirling in her veins. She tasted the drug's bitter residue in her mouth. Apart from the narcotic, her body seemed normal.

More forcefully this time, she probed outwards. Not illusion, this room. Reality. Or perhaps the drugs were confusing her senses? The chamber appeared to be made from huge chunks of blue stone, the ceiling cris-crossed by intricately carved wooden beams. Muted light filtered down from a lump hung from the centre of the largest joist.

Stone and wood! Both weak and unreliable. No race used such primitive building materials. Would the stone and wood come crashing down upon her? Her heart beat tempestuously in her chest. Calm, keep calm. She drew in a trembling breath. Another. And the smell. She sniffed cautiously. A floral aroma. Not unpleasant, just strange.

Cold numbed her toes and heels. She flung herself back onto the bed, rubbing her stinging feet. Hugging her arms around her body, she telepathically probed every wall. The only door remained closed to her testing.

A prisoner. Liandra shivered with cold, and fear. Slowly, as the drug in her body dissipated, her memory returned, though her fuzzy mind held an array of confusing images which made no sense. Connal ... he had come to her for help ... looking for Garris. They had lain upon the crystal bed. The dream-search. *Dreams ...*

Liandra's skin tingled with the memory of her *sharing* with Connal. That had never happened before. If some being required counselling which included sexual therapy, then she referred them to a sensualator. She'd never allow herself, or her image, to be used as a client's substitute dream-lover. Sex was well known to her, in a dispassionate, theoretical way.

Being twenty-five and still unpartnered appalled her friends and colleagues, for Asarians considered celibacy an unnatural state. Though there were exceptions. Her father had not experienced the Asarian love-call until the age of thirty-three years when, again defying tradition, he had taken a human woman as life-mate. Liandra had never felt the need to mate. Her work kept her fully occupied, and satisfied. She knew she wasn't sexually frustrated, why, then, should she react so to Connal in the dream?

Time enough to sort that problem out. First she had to escape her prison. And that meant confronting her captors - when they presented themselves. What possible motive could any have in kidnapping her? It was just conceivable, it had happened before, though many generations in the past, when Asarian Weavers first ventured forth from their home-world. Viewed as an exotic novelty, some were captured, held prisoner and used by powerful individuals for their exclusive entertainment.

Seven Stars! That was a long time ago. No League member would do that now. Surely not! Liandra shuddered. If this were the case, she would resist and die, death being more preferable to a nightmare life as a dreaming vessel for the private amusement of some perverted being.

Liandra waited. It was the only thing to do. After pulling back the curtains which hung around the four posts of her bed, she sat on the edge of the mattress, counting every stone to keep her mind from wandering. To no avail. She wanted answers, an end to her solitude.

And what about her foolproof monitors and servitors? How could each one have failed? And her dreamer's cap, her bed ... The tools of her profession were more than mere instruments, they were part of her, and always nearby. Now, she could not catch a hint of the vibrations from her bed. What if someone, something, was touching it? That would be akin to having her own body violated. She shivered uncontrollably. Closing her eyes, she began the ritual litany to calm body and mind.

It seemed only moments later that Liandra started out of her trance, sensing someone close by. Jumping to her feet, ignoring the icy floor, she came face to face with a woman of about her own age, dressed in clothes similar to the robe she had worn in the dream-state ... before Connal had expertly teased it from her body!

The stranger's attractive face was framed by

red hair that curled freely about her shoulders. With eyes dark and wary, the woman edged backwards, rattling the crockery on the tray she carried.

"Where am I?" Liandra demanded. "Why have I been brought here?"

The young woman shook her head, and held out the tray offering its contents.

Liandra reeled away in disgust. Though hungry, no power in the universe would make her touch a thing! It might be drugged. Even worse - it looked like *real* food. Things which had grown, lived. Her stomach knotted at the thought.

"I demand to know where I am!"

No answer, only a look of puzzlement. Perhaps the creature was a simple servitor, incapable of speech. Liandra closed in on her, and the woman stepped back until she was trapped against a wall. Running a hand over the smooth cheek which suddenly flamed red, Liandra caught the terror and indignation.

"I'm sorry, *Maera*, I didn't mean to offend," Liandra said, gently.

The young woman dropped the tray and raced away to cower behind a bed post.

Behind Liandra, something hit the wall with a resounding crash. She whirled about to see the silhouette of a man standing in the doorway. His fury lashed out at her.

"Connal?" she whispered.

"What goes on here?" he demanded.

His grey eyes, as cold and as hard as Santarian steel, flickered over her. To Liandra's amazement, his cheeks flamed red. Not with anger. With embarrassment. His emotions lapped at the periphery of her consciousness, before she hastily blocked them.

Snapping his gaze away from her, he focused his attention on the woman beside the bed. "Fianna, were not my orders specific enough? No one, *no one,* save myself is permitted in this room. What are ye doin' here?"

"I ... I came to see if the ... the lady was hungry," Fianna stammered.

"Since when do you lie to me, Mistress MacLeod?"

She blushed furiously. "I... I came to ask the lady about my Garris, *Tighearna.*"

"The truth sits better on your lips, Fianna. Now, away with ye!"

She hesitated, glancing from Connal to Liandra.

"Or is it a punishment from me, you be wanting?"

Fianna fled to the door, closing it softly behind her.

Liandra swallowed against the tight dryness in her throat and chest. "Is it really you, Connal?" she asked, hesitantly.

For he was not the man she remembered from her apartment. Now, as in the dream, he wore the same oddly-fashioned striped skirt ... kilt. *Kilt?* Liandra wondered at the strange word

31

invading her thoughts. The kilt reached to his bare knees. His long legs, below the knees, were covered by a thick, knitted material, his feet encased in soft, ankle-high boots. Over his shirt, he wore a silver-studded sleeveless jerkin of some unknown material ... *leather* ... that was the fabric; the word sprang into her mind. Leather! From some dead animal! She shuddered. What civilised individual would wear the skin of a once-living creatue? Connal's severe hair braid was gone. His blue-black hair loose about his face and shoulders amplified his handsome features, though the firmness of jaw, the way he stood - they were as she remembered from their first meeting. Unbridled arrogance. Distasteful and intimidating.

His eyebrow quirked at her, but Liandra forced her gaze to hold his.

"So you are awake," he said. "Immediately weaving your witchery on my people. How did you coerce Fianna? She has never disobeyed me."

"Get out of my dream, Connal. I want to be awake! Free -"

"If it were a dream, then I would be calling it a nightmare This is reality, Weaver. You are here, at my bidding. At my mercy."

She disregarded that for the moment. "I would prefer it if you called me Liandra."

He regarded her, trying to ignore her nakedness. With chin raised in defiance, she returned his gaze. He gritted his teeth. How could she be so unaware of herself? He dragged a hand through his hair. That tightness in the pit of his stomach, and lower, had returned, and with it the hot, light-headedness.

"Damn it, have you no shame?" He tore the coverlet from the bed and hurled it at her. "Cover yourself, then we talk!"

"But -"

"Do as I say!"

Liandra wrapped the quilt around herself and eyed him defiantly. "*Maer* Connal, how is it that I understand you? My translator -"

"While you were brought here, I had you tutored subliminally in my language. No time for you to learn my language from first hand experience. For what you and I are to discuss, I want no misunderstandings. I have no faith in the translating ability of any mechanical contrivance."

"You've drugged me, too. What else has been done to me?"

Connal's lips tightened into a thin line. "Nothing! My word on that."

"How can I believe you? You who have resorted to kidnapping ..."

Connal took one step towards her and stopped. With difficulty. "Have a care before you accuse me, woman! My word is my bond. Unlike that dehumanised rabbit-warren you call home, where no creature can be trusted to deal fairly with a man!"

"Coming from you, that's ironic. You haven't

dealt fairly with me. You tricked me."

"You tricked yourself," Connal snapped. His smile was as cold as space. "I treated you with consideration, not that you deserve such, being what you are!"

"And just what am I?" She arched her brow.

"A woman common to all."

"Yes."

"You do not deny it?"

"Why should I? I'm proud of my profession. I received my calling when I was five years old. My father trained me."

"Ye *father*?"

"Men who become Dream-Weavers are among the most skilled of my profession."

Connal clamped his mouth shut. Bad enough women whoring, but men ... Unthinkable.

Liandra stared up at him. Like silver laser bolts, his eyes bored into her. What did he see that made him look at her with so much distaste? She drew the coverlet protectively around her. "Did you remove my clothes and jewellery?"

"I had the dubious honour." Almost, he had said *pleasure*.

"Why?"

"Nothing of the League is what it seems. I wanted none of its taint upon you, when we talked."

"What is it we must discuss, *Maer* Connal, or is your name just another deception?"

"'Tis my name. Do not use *Maer* again!

Shallow League pleasantries have no place here. Anyway, 'tis you who are the deceiver, not I. You have been brought here, so that I can find my clans-man, Garris."

"I can't. The dream-search showed you that, surely? Where am I? I demand to know."

"Ye be in nae position ta make ainy demands o' me. What haivve ye done to Garris?"

Liandra frowned at him. "Please, calm down. When you're angry, your words burr and distort so much, that I can't understand, even with the subliminal tutoring."

Connal jerked his hands onto his hips. "What have you done with Garris?" His speech was cold, staccato.

"I've done nothing -"

"Do not add lies to your litany of wrong-doing, woman!"

"I never lie."

"Is that so?" His voice was distant, unbelieving.

Liandra folded her arms, her fists balled. How she wanted to beat her frustration against his wide chest. Wide, *half-naked* chest, she amended. She didn't want to touch him ... ever. She drew in her breath, calming her anger.

"Will you please tell me what it is you truly want?" she asked.

"For some reason I cannot fathom, Garris went off world to seek someone, the dream-weaver Liandra Tavor. You are she."

"And that's it? The reason for kidnapping me? I've never seen or heard of this Garris until you came to me. I'm telling you the truth. Believe me."

"I do not."

"Why would I lie?"

"I, not you, ask the questions, Weaver. You have frightened Fianna with your witchery. Be warned! I am a fierce protector of my kin-folk. As Fianna is one such, you will not harm her. If you do, you will answer to me. And be assured I am not a forgiving man."

"I've never hurt any being," Liandra whispered.

Connal glanced down at the tray and its spilt contents. "How difficult you make your stay will depend upon your behaviour. Please me and I am prepared to grant you as much courtesy as I can. Displease me and ..." He shrugged, leaving the threat hanging heavily in the air between them. "Was this not to your liking?" Connal asked, again staring at the broken dishes. "Used to your synthesised chaff no doubt. Well, you will get none of that here, Weaver, only proper food such as man was intended to eat."

Again, that deadly gaze of his swept her body. Liandra felt he had stripped her naked. Not that she had any inhibitions in that regard, she was half Asarian, after all, but this man, in every way, made her ill at ease.

"And eating proper food might do ye some good. Put some meat on those bones of yours," he added.

Liandra raised her chin. "There's nothing wrong with my figure."

He smiled tauntingly. "I suppose no one has ever had the courage to be so familiar with you. I am a man, in every respect, so your sorcery has no hold over me. Remember that. Now, Garris."

"Back to him are we? I could deny it until the moons of Vesnar turn purple, and still you wouldn't believe me. So what's the use? You say I'm supposed to have met this Garris. Why? Did he need a counsellor? Have you none on this world of yours? Just where am I, Connal?"

"This is my estate. I am *Tighearna* of County Arran. Caledonia is the name of this world."

Liandra frowned. "I know every League world, I don't recognise -"

"We are not of the League."

"Pardon?" Her heart turned in her breast. If he spoke the truth, she was far from home, a long way from everything she knew. No one to whom she could appeal for sanctuary. Rescue, out of the question. The slow smile which played across Connal's tightly drawn lips did nothing to dispel her fear.

"Aye, Weaver. So now you begin to see the way of it. Indeed, you be far from home. So if you co-operate with me you can be quickly returned. If not - "

"And if I do not?" Liandra asked, with a toss of her head.

"It doesna' bairr thinkin' about."

"Already it doesn't bear thinking about. I

swear to you, Connal, I have never met Garris before our dream-sharing. I couldn't make out his features, even then. Does he look like you?"

Connal's eyes narrowed. "I grow tired of your intrigue, Weaver. Well you know Garris is smaller than me, his brown hair shorter, he has a scar on his left arm. I daresay you were close enough to notice that. Your... counselling revolves around that infernal bed of yours, does it not?"

"Just what have you done with my belongings?"

"Your clothes are near by. I brought the bed in case you required it to find Garris."

"I need my computers and servitors."

"We have none such here."

"You are joking. Everyone has them -"

"Everyone of the *League*, Mistress."

"To live without machines is madness."

"We only use machines in the direst circumstances."

"How did you manage to smuggle me out of my apartment, undetected? Station security is infallible."

"You cannot replace a man's honour or loyalty, with bolts and circuitry."

"That doesn't answer my question," Liandra snapped.

"Does it not?" Laughing, he strode to the doorway. "I shall leave you awhile to ponder your fate. A word of advice to you, Weaver! Next time, do not be so disdainful of Fianna's cooking. Because, for the moment, your belly will be growling with hunger. That might teach you some humility and manners."

"I've been the one drugged. Kidnapped. Insulted! It's not me who needs to be taught a lesson! You have treated me dishonourably."

Liandra heard the sharp hiss of his indrawn breath. Slowly, rigidly, he turned to her. Their gazes clashed across the room. His fury washed over her. Cold, murderous fury.

"What do your kind know of honour?" His low, frigid voice made her shiver.

"More than you, it seems," Liandra retorted.

"Enough, Mistress!"

As he strode up to her, she retreated until she felt the cold stone against her back. She tried to evade him, but Connal placed hands against the wall on either side of her. His maleness beat against her, as his scent, a curious musky freshness, stole over her. Worse, a thousand times worse than deadly laser shields, the bulging muscles and naked flesh of his arms formed the confines of her prison. She hugged her arms about her body, to make herself as small as possible, so that his skin did not touch hers.

"Understand this, well!" He took her chin in a crushing grip, forcing her to look at him. "My patience does have its limits. And you are perilously close to reaching it."

As Connal towered over her, Liandra's mouth went dry, numb. He could do with her what he willed, his height and strength more than a match for her. Though fear coiled heavily inside her stomach, she couldn't let him know how afraid she was.

"What are you going to do? Beat me?" she asked, hoarsely.

He grinned. "What an interesting possibility. However, be thankful that here a man is considered less than a man if he must resort to violence to earn the respect and obedience due him, especially from a woman. At least it is so, under ordinary circumstances. You, Weaver, are far from ordinary."

As Liandra opened her mouth to speak, Connal placed a finger against her lips. He leaned closer. Her heart skipped a beat. He was going to kiss her and that was only slightly preferable to a beating. Lifting a tendril of hair from her forehead, he rubbed the strands between his fingers, a bemused expression on his face.

"No!" She tossed her head away, freeing her hair from his touch. "How dare you!" she whispered huskily.

"Oh, I dare very much." He stepped backwards. "I intend to find Garris. Be very careful! Do not defy me again. I will return this eve, when I expect to find you in a more reasonable mood. Until tonight ..." With one more gaze which stripped her to the bone, he turned on his heel and strode to the door, slamming it behind him.

Liandra sagged weakly against the wall. Her body trembled with rage, and more. His liberties, his nearness, had caused her body to flush with warmth, to tingle with ... *Seven Stars!* She, who had never know the touch of any lover, for no creature had ever aroused her, now found her senses reeling from a man who was a ... a cruel, ruthless ... Words failed her and she had a hundred languages at her disposal in which to describe him. And she could not! Every word that came to mind was too inadequate.

Liandra paced the floor. "Think! Think!" The walls echoed her cry. *Until tonight* - his ultimatum. *Stars* knew what he was capable of! She would have to think of something. Fast. Until tonight. How long did that give her? Well, whatever he had in mind, she would be long gone before he returned.

Connal tore open the heavy wooden door to his apartment and kicked it shut behind him. The swords on the walls rattled in their mountings.

You have treated me dishonourably. Her reproach stung all the more, because she had the right of it. Damn that woman! Worse - damn him for reacting! To her accusation. To her. Truly, doubly damned.

Though his flesh crawled with the memory of the dream they had shared, his memories were tinged, not only with revulsion, but desire. *Desire!* He could not credit it. Against his better judgment, spurred on by his anger, he had, again, touched her, felt the soft smoothness of her skin, the silken texture of her hair and smelled, again, her curious, sweet scent ... that perfume which invaded his every cell ... his memories and his dreams - *Arran's Mercy!* It had truly been desire.

Desire for a woman who gave her body as easily as she gave her dreams. And he wanted no part of a woman like that. His body was playing the traitor. He, who was always cool, was anything but since his expedition off-world to seek out the Weaver. After that, nothing had been the same! *He* had not been the same!

Shrugging himself out of shirt and jerkin, he kicked off his shoes, peeled off his hose and tore off his kilt. Clothing flew about the room. He left each item where it lay. In the bathing-room he ran a long, cold bath.

Slowly, he lowered himself into the water, its iciness quenching the fire in his loins.

"Now I be immune to your spells, witch -" He groaned, as the image of her pale, slender body rose up before his eyes. His blood thrummed. Not again! Exasperated, he ran a hand through his wet hair. She had been unashamed, standing before him unclothed, while he, *he* was the one disconcerted by *her*, when normally, the sight of a naked woman caused him no embarrassment.

Was she truly a witch who had cast some spell over him? Well, whatever she had done it would not work, he vowed. After all, he was Lord MacArran and that counted for much.

Still, he had to admire her courage. Most

women he knew would have thrown themselves on his mercy, begged and cried. Pleaded. Not the Weaver. Instead, she had challenged him, lied, feigning innocence. Her defiance surprised him. The woman ... Liandra ... he liked the sound of her name. He rolled it around in his mind, practising it, pronouncing it as she had done.

"*Liandrrra.*" He started out of his musings, as the walls echoed with his fevered whisper. He had spoken her name aloud!

What was he going to do with her? Liandra was not easily intimidated, he had discovered that much. Somehow, he would have to convince her, by fair means, or foul, that her only option was to tell him the truth. All of it!

Why go off-world, Garris, without so much as a by your leave to your lord, or even a word of explanation to Fianna? Connal knew if he had such a lady as she, to call his own, by Arran, he would not be leaving Caledonia to seek out the dubious pleasures of the dream-weaver whom he had kidnapped.

Aye, kidnapped! Connal frowned, tearing fingers through his dripping hair. The methods he had employed to bring her to Caledonia might not be honourable, still to get to the truth of the matter he would risk more than the indignation of one dream-weaver. At least his people would not openly censure him. A *Tighearna*'s word was law. He did not have to explain to any of them. No doubt, though, knowing how his tastes ran, they would be speculating as to what he was going to do *with* her. Except they would be wrong. He wanted none of her, though the memory of her exquisite body against his during that accursed sharing had haunted his dreams since returning to Castle MacArran. He forced the images from his mind. He had other problems, besides a missing clans-man and an alien woman to worry about.

The Council. They might not be so understanding. *Blast them, too!* This was clan business, and he would not brook any interference, no matter what! No matter from whom! *I would defy every League World for you Garris ... what a fine pickle you have gotten me into, this time. And no mistake!* Connal frowned.

A few hours on her own, to mull over her predicament, and he would try again. Persuasion came in many guises, and he would have to call upon the experiences of a life-time to understand her and secure her co-operation. At least that was the plan, though so far, he had failed miserably.

Until tonight. Her reaction to his threat had been fear, more defiance and an insult that cut too close to the bone. He had always thought no Leaguer had the stomach for a good fight. Yet, her actions proved otherwise.

He laughed. Matching wits against her ... the contest might prove interesting. But no doubt as to the victor! He would never be bested by any green-haired alien witch!

Chapter Four

Liandra heard a metallic jingling, followed by a scraping sound coming from outside the door. With heart hammering, she leaped from the bed, drawing the coverlet to her chest. Slowly, she let out her breath as Fianna entered, carrying another tray laden with dishes.

Liandra's stomach gurgled at the prospect of food. She was hungry enough to eat anything. Well, almost, until she caught sight of the steaming bowl of the Seven Stars knew what!

"Lady... please." Fianna's voice, a mere whisper, held a hint of fear.

In answer, Liandra held out her hand in what she hoped would be interpreted as a gesture of appeasement. She smiled, trying to alleviate Fianna's obvious distress, and the younger woman smiled back hesitantly.

"I'm sorry if I frightened you before, *Maera* Fianna." Liandra frowned, sensing that the young woman was trying to summon the courage to speak. "What is it you would say to me?"

"Please ... lady." Fianna paused, drawing in a ragged breath. "I know not why my Garris

45

went off-world to you ... only tell me that my *gradhmhor* is safe and well."

"Garris is your beloved?" Liandra asked.

"My husband," Fianna said firmly.

"Before I met Connal, I'd never heard of Garris, of Caledonia. All of this." Liandra glanced about the room. "Believe me."

"I ... I do." Fianna bit her lip. "Is there nothing you can do? Connal -"

"He insists I'm to blame for Garris' disappearance."

A ghost of a smile from Fianna. "Aye, Connal's a stubborn man, especially when he thinks he is being crossed by a woman." She gasped, her eyes wide. "I say too much, Connal will have my hide if he knew."

"I don't understand," Liandra said.

"'Tis probably just as well," Fianna replied and turned away.

"Wait, *Maera* -" Tentatively, Liandra rested her gaze on Connal's kinswoman. Fianna's hazel eyes registered shock and fear as the contact was made and held.

"I'm sorry, to abuse you in this way, but Connal's threats leave me with no alternative," Liandra said. Carefully, she placed a palm to Fianna's temple, and felt the wild pulse beat. She ushered the woman backwards to the bed, gently nudging her down upon it, and sent her into a deep sleep.

Liandra quickly removed Fianna's bulky robe and struggled into it, finding, as she had anticipated, that the clothes were too big for her. *Skin and bone*, Connal had called her. He'd pay for that insult! She smiled grimly as she imagined what she might do to curb his arrogance, to exact revenge for what he'd said and done to her. Revenge? Such a contemptible thought. No civilised creature retaliated violently against another's wrong-doing. But she wanted to - *oh, how badly*! Her palms itched at the prospect. Disconcerted, Liandra suppressed her thoughts, save one. Escape.

After tucking the bed cover around Fianna, Liandra went to the door. It wouldn't budge. She hunted through the gown for any locking contrivance, and found a set of curious metal objects in one pocket. Holding them in the palm of her hand, she concentrated, *reading* them. The devices, which she had mistakenly thought were trinkets, were actually keys, something with which to release her from her prison. Finding the correct key, she inserted it into the lock, and peered out through the crack in the doorway. Casting her senses outward, she touched only inanimate objects.

The wide stone passageway was decorated with tapestries and weaponry. Swords and knives ... *Seven Stars!* These were weapons which hacked and pierced, cut and maimed. She had seen similar items in the Terran museum. Then, as now, she marvelled that anyone could consider an array of weaponry to be decorative.

Liandra slipped out of the room, into the

deserted corridor. She crept forward, hugging the wall of the passageway. It appeared to go on for miles. And Connal had the temerity to call her home a rabbit-warren ... *dehumanised* he had said. How typical of his arrogance, that he expected every dwelling to be outfitted for the sole requirements of one species. The huge space platform where she made her home was capable of sustaining life and providing comfort for the diversity of League members using its facilities. No one race had an advantage over the other. Connal would -

A heavy, furious heat burned in her heart at the mere thought of him. *Seven Stars!* Asarians did not think this way. Revenge. Violence. Could it be possible that exposure to such a primitive as Connal was acting as a catalyst to bring out some volatile Terran traits, inherited from her mother, that up until now had lain dormant? Yes, that was the answer. It was Connal's fault.

"Damn him!" She paused, shocked, by her vehement cursing - a barbarian's cursing. She must return to her own world and exorcise these archaic emotions from her being!

For perhaps ten minutes, she stole along the deserted passageway. Then, just as she considered retracing her steps, she came to a landing. Immediately she jumped back into the shadows where she could observe, undetected, the length of a wide, carved wooden staircase which led to a large hall. Men and women bustled around long tables, arranging food and drink, laughing and chatting as they worked. The women wore long gowns similar in style to the one she wore, while the men were dressed in shirts and kilts. Draped across the chest of each man or woman was a wide sash of material, the same as Connal's kilt - garish red, green, yellow and silver stripes against a black background.

Hastily, she crossed the landing to head down another passageway. Moments later, she jolted to a sickening halt as bright light temporarily blinded her. *Windows! For the Seven Stars sake!* These people relied on windows to illuminate their homes. The transparent material from which the windows were made was patterned and tinted, so that the sunlight cast a rainbow-coloured mosaic on the floor. Beautiful, almost like home.

Her chest constricted painfully and tears pricked her eyes. Home. Would she ever see home again? She ran a hand over her eyes. Lingering in the corridor and weeping over her predicament would not help. Steeling herself, she went to the tall windows and peered out over the expanse of Connal's house. Made of blue-grey stone, it resembled ... what was the word? *Castle.*

Liandra recalled the place where her mother had taken her, as part of her history education. The Terran castle, over a thousand years old, had been restored and then held in stasis to protect it from the ravages of time.

Where that ancient castle had been dark and dismal, Connal's larger dwelling was beautiful. Turrets and towers stretched to the sky, while wide columned balconies ran the perimeter of the structure throughout its many levels. Below her, a dizzying drop to green forested lands, which stretched far into the distance. Escape from the castle would be very difficult. Perhaps impossible? No! She wouldn't even consider it!

Hugging the wall, she trotted along the corridor, heart hammering, fearful of discovery.

Other windows allowed her glimpses of the estate. She paused to look down at the luxurious gardens, blazes of colour as hundreds of bushes, flowers and trees complemented one another. In their midst, fountains sparkled and shimmered in the bright sunlight.

Men's voices and heavy footsteps echoed in the corridor ahead of her. Stumbling against the hem of her gown, in exasperation she lifted the cumbersome thing to her knees, and retreated up a narrow flight of stairs. Up and up she ran, until her breathing became laboured. Then, mercifully, the last step. She lost her footing and sprawled onto a dark floor. Dragging herself to her feet, she fled into the first room she saw.

She skidded to a halt. Weapons of every description decorated the walls, although a few heavy tapestries alleviated the rows of ancient killing tools. A huge metal machine stood in the far corner. Man-shaped, without any body features, it towered over everything.

Liandra froze, terrified that the robot had sensed her presence. Or was it deactivated? It hadn't moved. No light issued from its metal head to indicate that it was aware. Tentatively, she reached out with a telepathic probe and found ... nothing. Hardly surprising. It was a machine. Still, she should be able to sense the circuity, some power. It appeared dead.

Liandra let out the breath she had been holding. Creeping forward, she touched the metallic monster, enthralled despite herself, by the intricate etched patterns over the robot's formidable torso. The machine was a functional item, but like everything else she had seen in the holding, functionality had not obliterated the need for every thing to be pleasing to the eye. Grudgingly she admitted that it said much for a culture who made even the most practical item elegant, though this was at odds with what little she knew of primitives.

Leaving the robot, she carefully opened the next door and paused, even more shocked to see that each wall was covered with shelves containing books. Real books, like she'd seen in the Terran museum.

Strewn about the room were large rugs and resting upon each were wing-backed chairs covered in green velvet. Brightly patterned, tasselled cushions lay against the back of each chair. Large panes of tinted glass allowed natural light to illuminate the chamber.

But of all the wonders she had seen, it was the fireplace that fascinated her. For the wood and flames were merely an illusion to please the eye, the warmth came from thin wires cris-crossing the back of the hearth. She stretched out her cold fingers, puzzled to find this level of technology in such a barbarous place.

Going to the window, Liandra despaired. She was in one of the highest levels of the castle, and hundreds of feet below a river cut a thickly wooded valley in two. The forest stretched as far as the eye could see in every direction. There appeared to be no towns or any other sign of civilisation. She would have to try another corridor, and another vantage point.

Retracing her steps, Liandra reached the corridor. She heard voices, Connal's unmistakable above the others. She stepped back, just as he appeared around a bend in the passage. Leading him, straining on a leash, was a huge, shaggy brown beast.

She sped into the library, only to find the door leading from it was locked. *Trapped!* With no other place to go, she jumped onto the wide window ledge and hid behind the thick folds of curtains, just as the library door opened. Holding her breath, she closed her eyes, willing him to go away.

Connal's laugh, a humourless sound, made her shiver. "Witch, come out from where you hide."

Liandra played dead, like the robot in the other room. A square snout thrust itself between the curtains. Slowly, the beast opened its mouth to reveal rows of large, very pointed teeth. Liandra screamed as the monster raised its head to her, fangs almost touching her arm.

"Come out, now, or my hound will rend you limb from limb."

Liandra didn't need prompting. Shakily, she parted the curtains and peered down at Connal. He stood in the middle of the room, hands on hips, legs planted wide apart.

"Come here, at once!" The voice fairly crackled with suppressed rage.

"No." Liandra pressed back against the window as the hairy monster pressed a cold, wet snout against her foot. "Your monster will kill me ..."

"Obey me, and I will call him off." Connal paused, eyeing her warningly. "Fergus, heel!" The creature obeyed him instantly and came to sit at his side. "Now, Mistress, come here, or I will drag you out. Your choice."

With a wary eye on man and beast, Liandra jumped from the window embrasure.

Connal strode up to her, grasped her by the shoulders and shook her until she was giddy. He set her down on her feet and Liandra stumbled backwards, grasping a curtain to stop herself from falling.

Regaining her balance, she glared at him. This barbarian needed to know that brute strength would not subdue her, no matter what he did.

Connal watched as she tossed her head angrily, chin high, eyes blazing, a deadly sapphire assault. She still defied him. Unexpected. Intriguing. Despite himself he had to smile. "Is that the way of it, *ban-druidh*?" he asked. "Be careful when you lay challenge to MacArran. Know the stakes you play for are very high."

"I consider my freedom a very high stake, indeed!"

Connal threw back his head and laughed.

Liandra's hands balled into fists. "How dare you make light of my situation. It's no laughing matter!" *Stars, I'd like to slap that smile from your face and ...* What she wanted to do ... no Asarian should dare contemplate, but it might *feel* good, just the same!

"You are nothing but a barbarian!"

Connal drew in a long breath. His eyes darkened, extinguishing all trace of humour "I do not like to be called a barbarian."

"And I don't like to be called *ban-druidh*."

Connal grimaced. "If you are going to speak my language, please do it the courtesy of correct pronunciation."

"For what you've done to me, expect no courtesy -"

"Then in that regard we are even. Expect no consideration from me for your actions. You escaped your chamber by witchery. Be warned! You will not do so again. Now we must talk, and how considerate of you to choose to come to me." He inclined his head in mock gallantry. "However, you have made a great mistake in leaving your chamber."

"Really?"

"Yes, really," Connal mimicked. "You have seen more of my world than I intended."

"I don't understand."

Connal folded his arms. "Once you had revealed Garris' whereabouts, I would have returned you to the League, little wiser about me, or Caledonia."

"And now?"

He regarded her silently. The situation might still be salvaged. She had no idea of Caledonia's location. He could return her home. What little he knew of Liandra, her curiosity and determination would insist on answers. No doubt she would search, probably have the League launch an investigation, but he and his people would remain hidden. Safe. No real damage done.

"Connal?" she asked. "What are you going to do with me?"

"Co-operate, and you can go home. Fergus." He gestured to the beast. It trotted up to Liandra, using its massive head as a lever to prise her from her corner. She stumbled after Connal as he unlocked the door leading into the adjoining chamber.

Liandra paused, regarding this new turn of events with alarm. Her heart clamoured in her breast. For in the room she saw a wide bed, much larger and heavier than the one she had lain upon. She didn't have to be telepathic to know that it was a man's bed.

Connal's bed.

She turned to him, silently accusing, wary as he strode towards her, his grin predatory.

"First things, first, *ban-druidh*! Talking is on my mind - at the moment. Be seated."

He absently waved her to a high-backed chair beside another illusionary fire. At her reluctance to follow his direction, he whistled to the hound and it herded her forward, baring its teeth if she faltered.

Tentatively, much like the time Connal tried her seating arrangements in her apartment, Liandra lowered herself onto the proffered chair. It wasn't so bad ... even comfortable, in a curiously *primitive* way, of course.

He poured some golden liquid into a long metal flute and held it out to her. Liandra shook her head.

"Still insisting on this childish fast? I grow bored with the display. However, I think that, as with all things, I will be the victor in this game you have chosen to play."

"I wasn't aware it was a *game* you and I played, barbarian."

Cold fury cramped his gut. He suppressed it with difficulty. Slowly, he sipped his drink, eyes measuring her over the rim of his cup. Damned if the witch would goad him. He had to deal with her calmly. He could not allow her, again, to incite him to anger ... arouse him to other things.

"I warned you once that if you harmed any of my clans-folk you would be sorry. The mind-control, such as you used on Fianna, will not be tolerated -"

"I didn't touch her mind. It's unethical -"

"Spare me your counsellor's morality." Connal glowered at her.

"If I do read minds, then I would have seen your deceit back h ... home."

Hearing the tremor in her voice, Connal frowned at her. At last, he had found a chink in her armour! Dishonourable to use her home-sickness as a lever, but what other choice did he have? Steeling himself against any softening of his resolve, he cleared his throat.

"Understand this, Mistress. If you be-spell any of my people again, in any way, you shall be sorry. I want your assurance you will not use any of your alien witchery upon any in my house."

"You insist I'm a liar, then surely any assurances I give will be false, too?"

Connal's brows drew together. "For your sake, do not bandy words with me! You are at my mercy. I should punish you for your treatment of Fianna." He paused. "However, I might be in a forgiving mood, should you decide to co-operate fully with me."

"And what form of co-operation do you require?" She glanced uncertainly at the bed.

"I am not so desperate for a woman that I would spend myself upon you. Perhaps the dream you gave me was a glimpse of your skill. However, 'tis something I have no wish to relive in the flesh, so to speak." He grinned and again casually sipped his drink, his relentless gaze never leaving her face.

Liandra squirmed in embarrassment. Her heart thudded against her ribs. Curiously, though, gone before she could examine it closely, a sensation ... of loss ... something almost akin to disappointment.

Disappointment, that this barbarian would not force himself onto her? That was ridiculous. *Seven Stars!* Maybe she was losing her sanity. She savagely quashed her thoughts, save one. How to gain her freedom.

"Mistress, your behaviour defies logic. You have only to tell me the truth and gain your freedom."

Liandra drew in her breath, and studied him professionally. "*Maer* Connal, are you telepathic? Again, you've just given voice to my own thoughts. Use your psychic talent to see I've had nothing to do with Garris' disappearance."

"Arran's Mercy! I have no such ability. I do not wish to touch your body, let alone your mind! Just the thought of it is abhorrent, I -" He drew in a long, steadying breath. "Now, an end to this charade. Tell me what I want to hear and you can go home."

58

Liandra stared down at her hands linked tensely on her lap. She felt light-headed, floating, as if she was no longer a creature of substance but of shadow. She swallowed convulsively, recognising the tell-tale warning signals.

Her Asarian heritage made it impossible to maintain an argument for long. If she wasn't careful her body would shut down temporarily to avoid further confrontation. She sighed, realising she had only one option. To gain a respite from Connal, she must lie. It would give her the time she needed to recover her wits and discover what had happened to his friend. If she helped him locate Garris, Connal would return her home.

"As you say," she whispered, her eyes downcast. "Garris came to me ... for help."

"What kind of help?"

"That is privileged information. I can't reveal why a being comes to me. My loyalty is to my clients."

"Very well. Continue."

Keeping her eyes averted, Liandra spoke quickly. "Garris undertook some therapy. He seemed to be happy with what I did for him. I gave him some further instructions, and exercises to do when he returned home. He left immediately after he paid me and -"

"How did he pay you, Weaver?"

Liandra's face flamed in indignation. She caught his innuendo as clearly as if he'd spoken it. "I am not a sensualator, *Maer* Connal."

"How did Garris pay you?"

"A ... as do all my clients, in credit tokens."

"Liar!" Connal hissed.

Liandra glanced up at him, seeing the thin line of his lips. At the sound of his master's angry voice, the hound, which had been lying before the fire jumped to its feet, growling. Liandra pressed back in her seat, as the creature's glowing yellow eyes focused on her.

Connal set his goblet down on the table beside him and leaned forward in his chair.

"Indeed, I would feed you to Fergus, only you would make a sorry meal. My hound is a fussy eater. Now, an end to your lies, woman!" He captured her gaze in silent challenge, daring her to continue her deceit. "Garris did not come to you for counselling. He certainly did not pay you for his visit in coin, or credit. We have neither the liking nor the need for such, nor for that matter, anything of the League. Try again, witch. This time the truth." Connal regarded her icily.

"Why do you have an aversion to everything the League has to offer? Our technology -"

"The League can give us nothing we on Caledonia cannot provide for ourselves, without the need to resort to dehumanising machinery."

"Is that so? How was I brought here, if not by star-ship?"

"Perhaps Caledonian magic?" Connal smiled grimly.

"Now it is you who are lying."

Connal's knuckles showed white, starkly protruding where he gripped the arms of his chair. He drew in a ragged breath and it was with difficulty, Liandra saw, that he exerted an iron will to calm the anger within. Yet, his fury was tinged with scorn and revulsion. *Revulsion? Seven Stars - why?*

"Have a care, witch. No one calls MacArran a liar and lives to brag about it."

"You keep telling me you have nothing to do with technology. If that's so, what about the fire? That is a clever piece of science. Anyway, I have further proof that you are the liar and when I prove it, you can apologise to me. Well? Have you nothing to say? Are you afraid?"

"I am not afraid of an under-fed *ban-druidh*! If you can prove me a liar, then I shall apologise. But what will you give me in return, should you fail to find me guilty of your charge?" He raised a taunting brow. "Show me your evidence, *ban-druidh*."

"I'm not a witch."

"I will be the judge of that."

Tentatively, keeping her eyes firmly on the hound, she rose from her seat.

"Where do you go?" Connal snapped.

"The proof is in the other room. Or are you going to acknowledge -"

"I concede nothing." He pushed himself up from his chair and strode after her.

Liandra stalked to the robot. "See. Here is my

61

proof that you have been tormenting me." She didn't say *lied*. That might enrage him again, and she wanted him placid. As placid as a barbarian like Connal could be. Her smile of triumph gradually faded as she saw the bemused look on his face.

"And what evidence is this?" he asked. "If I did not know the right of it, I would say you were on the receiving end of one of your spells."

"As beautiful as it is, this robot -"

Connal threw back his head and roared with laughter. Liandra regarded his reaction with uncertainty, and growing alarm.

"This thing you call a robot, is none such! 'Tis a suit of armour."

Liandra mouthed the curious word. The heat of embarrassment, and rage flooded through her as Connal continued to laugh.

Still chuckling, he pulled off the robot's helmet and showed it to her. "See no bolts and circuitry. Do you understand what it is?"

"No."

"In battle, long ago, our enemies wore armour as protection. This suit belonged to our foe. When my ancestors raided his castle, this they seized, among other items. Eventually, it came into the possession of Arran. Ever it has been in my family as a trophy, a symbol of victory, for no Caledonian worth his salt would wear such a cowardly thing. We arm ourselves with only those weapons as you see on my walls.

Just as lethal as any League blaster, but more elegant. With them a man may measure his strength and courage through his prowess, rather than by killing anonymously with an indiscriminate coward's weapon such as your kind carry."

"Beautiful though this armour is, it's still barbarous ... as are you!"

"You call *me* barbarous because my preferred weapon limits me to hand combat - a test of skill and courage? Whereas your more *civilised* way is to blast a man out of existence from so far away he can not tell from which direction danger is threatening. I think I have the right of it, Mistress. And you have failed to prove me a liar."

"To me this armour looks like a robot. It might have..." She was making it worse, drowning in her own words because she didn't have the good sense to admit her mistake. "You could still be ... lying. This might have been a robot, you could have stripped out the insides...." Her voice trailed away, her protestations sounding ridiculous even to her own ears.

"Aye, I could have, but 'tis nothing more than a suit of armour. And you owe me for falsely accusing me of lying."

"Very well, I apologise."

"Not enough, witch."

Liandra squared her shoulders. "And what manner of *apology* do you want?"

Connal grinned wolfishly. As his eyes roved over her, Liandra endured it, although inside

63

she seethed, hot and cold. Red rage. Cold fury. Only her sense of justice kept her silent. She had wrongly accused him, so she must accept the consequences. Or, at least try.

"Well?" she asked. "Do what you must. Get your beating over with. Or do you intend torture?"

Connal's eye brows arched skyward as he took in her stance. She was poised for flight, despite her brave words. How galling he found it, to instil fear in a woman, yet he must, to keep Liandra off-guard. She must not suspect the truth that he never punished any transgression with violence. She was canny enough to use that knowledge against him. In his experience, there were other ways, often more enjoyable, to curb a woman's waywardness. And while she might be an alien, she was *all* woman. And his body knew it too, in that moment, in the tightening of his muscles, the rush of blood through his veins. If he satisfied that curiosity now, then maybe he would be able to put the memories of their dream-sharing behind him. He strode up to her and gripping her by the shoulders, raised her to her toes.

"My punishment is a suitable one which, doubtless, you have experienced many times in the past." His lips slanted down upon hers, crushing, savouring, drawing her protest into his mouth.

Liandra struggled against his kiss. She felt his fingers snag into her hair, holding her still.

As she squirmed even harder to be free, he wrapped his arms around her, imprisoning her. His body leaned intimately into hers, while his mouth continued its savage plundering.

How long his torture lasted Liandra did not know, only that the furious assault did not lessen. Finally she admitted defeat. She leaned into his strength as he had his way with her. Only then did his kiss become less fierce, almost, but not quite, tender.

She clung to him for support as her legs, her whole body, began to tremble, as if he were draining the life from her. Light suffused her body, flowing in her veins like a heady drug. Almost pleasant, his arms so strong about her, his pulsing warmth merged with hers. His thighs pressed to her legs, his arousal hot and hard against her. Seven Stars, this was more erotic than any dream.

"*My Lord!*" a woman's voice intruded.

With a whispered curse, Connal put Liandra back on her feet. For a moment she swayed as her legs refused to take her weight. She stared up at him, saw his bewilderment and contempt, and before it was swiftly suppressed, she caught his desire. With his face set in rigid planes, he turned away from her.

Liandra took the time to regain her composure. She put a trembling finger to her tingling mouth which still bore the imprint of the pleasure and pain of his caress. Pleasure from a barbarian's kiss? Inexplicable! Improbable!

"So, the *ban-druidh* does cast a spell, even on you, My Lord."

"Not so, Jenna. I chasten her."

"May all your chastisements with me be so enjoyable."

"*Ghraidh,*" Connal said. "What is it you want?"

Liandra looked from one to the other. He had called this beautiful, dark-haired woman, *darling*. Was Jenna his life-mate?

Cold fury washed through her. As a means to punish, Connal had kissed her, embracing her like a lover. Only there was no love, no tenderness in his action. Nothing but a callous violation. Her chest tightened. With shaking hands, she smoothed her matted hair.

She watched as Jenna stepped up to Connal, her body moulding against his. He stared down at her with a mixture of disapproval and ... something else which Liandra did not understand.

"Is my Lord so sorry that I saved him from that one's wiles? Fianna told me how she bespelled her. Even a man such as you, my Connal, needs rescuing from time to time."

"Aye, but I think it was the *ban-druidh* who needed the rescuing, not I. See for yourself, she looks sickly."

Jenna's smile was forced, her blue eyes cold and harsh as Liandra met her gaze across the room.

"I have almost finished my business with the witch. I thank you for your concern. Now away with you."

"But ... My Lord."

"GO!"

Casting a venomous eye on Liandra, Jenna turned to leave, but it seemed not as quickly as he expected. Connal's hand swept in an arc, slapping her on her bottom.

Jenna squealed, though it had the desired effect. She ran to the door. Pausing a moment, she glanced over her shoulder. "I enjoy your chastisements in the privacy of our bed-chamber, My Lord, but I draw the line at displaying such before the likes of her!"

The door almost broke from its hinges as Jenna slammed it behind her.

Connal's cheeks burned. Damn Jenna! And damn him for what he had done to her. He had never smacked her before. Why now? Especially now! Flustered, he ran a hand over his eyes.

Turning to Liandra, he saw the horror on her face and steeled himself against it. If the witch feared him, then so much the better. Maybe, then, she would co-operate with him, so that the muddle his clans-man had caused could be resolved with little fuss and with little injury to his world, and to MacArran honour - if that were possible. His gut felt like a coiled spring as he regarded her. "Now, *ban-druidh*, where were we?"

"I believe I was apologising to you."

Connal grinned. "Aye, I wish all apologies to me were so ... pleasant."

"Save that for your life-mate," Liandra said, dryly.

"My...?" Connal chuckled. "I have none such. Even so, make no mistake about Jenna. More possessive than any wife, she will be after your blood for what you just did to me."

"I was a victim in what just occurred, not the perpetrator."

Connal laughed. "The distinction would be lost on Jenna."

"Then, if I must defend myself, I'm not without protection."

Connal's frown was ominous. "Practise your witchery upon any in this castle, and you answer to me! Now, we were discussing Garris, and you cleverly distracted me."

"I told you what you wanted to know."

"I want the truth."

"When I told you the truth, you didn't believe me."

"My *companach* is not a liar. He went off-world to find you -"

"Are you so certain?"

"Aye."

"Very well. I accept that he intended to seek me. Have you considered the possibility that something may have happened to him, without my involvement?"

Connal's raised brow was her only answer.

"There is a way I could convince you," Liandra said.

"Go on."

"We could use my bed, for another sharing. We would both learn the truth. That I promise."

"And as before, have you ensnare me in some dream? I think not," he said coldly.

"I had nothing to do with that dream. I liked it even less than you, but what other way is there?"

"Perhaps I could beat the truth out of you."

"Oh," Liandra whispered.

"Despite your opinion of me, I am not a cruel man," he said, frowning, as he watched her hands twisting together.

"I beg to differ on that score, Connal."

He leaned against the wall and studied her. "And if I agree to this sharing? How long will it take? How soon can you be ready, Liandra?"

She stared at him, momentarily taken aback at his sudden change of mind and more besides. His accent made her name sound so very different. She liked the way he rolled the 'r' - almost like a purr. Mentally, she shook herself. She had to deal with this man in a professional way!

"I must check my bed. You say my monitors were left behind?"

"Aye. Do not worry about them. I can find suitable replacements."

"I need time to recover my energy."

He nodded. "I will see that Fianna tends you. How -"

"You are not going to agree to this ridiculous scheme?" Jenna demanded from the doorway.

Liandra saw Connal's face tighten in anger.

"I thought I told you to leave," he said, coldly.

"You did. I stayed nearby in case you needed me ... again. Your voices carried."

"You mean you were eavesdropping," Connal corrected.

Jenna shrugged. "I forbid this, My Lord."

"*Forbid?* Woman, do you forget to whom you speak?"

"No, but I think you have taken leave of your senses."

"They are mine to take leave of if I want." Connal smiled.

"You may think this a laughing matter, My Lord. I most certainly do not."

"There is nothing to concern yourself with, *Maera* Jenna. I am fully competent in what I do," Liandra said. She stepped back in alarm as Jenna sprang forward, her hand raised.

As quick as Jenna was, Connal was faster. He interposed his body, protecting Liandra from the assault. He grasped Jenna's arm and propelled her backward.

"Understand this well, *ghraidh*. This one is under my protection. No one may harm her. She answers only to me. Is that clear?"

Jenna stared wide-eyed up at him.

"Is that clear?" Connal repeated and she nodded. "Now, leave. I -"

"And what of the witch?"

"For the time being, she stays with me."

Jenna pursed her lips. "Just think on this, my Connal. Your mother would turn in her grave to see you consorting with a woman whose hair is green! 'Tis hardly fitting that she be your paramour, my Lord MacArran!"

He strode swiftly after Jenna, but she fled the room, the door slamming in her angry wake. Connal turned to Liandra, his face grim. "You have made one enemy today, Weaver. Not the least enemy you have here, I think."

Liandra glanced uncertainly up at him as he joined her side.

"I will give you a day to rest. After that I will undertake the sharing with you, and then, by Arran, there will be an end to this deception."

"I look forward to its conclusion with no less delight," Liandra said dryly, and to her amazement Connal laughed long and hard.

"Come."

"Where are you taking me?"

"Back to your room."

"No!" Liandra pulled back from his grasp and in exasperation he ran a hand through his hair.

"Would you rather stay here with me?"

"That would be preferable. Please, I can't tolerate the other place."

With eyes narrowed, he studied her. "Why are you so afraid?" he asked.

Had he picked that up from her? Liandra frowned. Surely he must be telepathic.

"An answer if you will, Weaver, and swiftly, or I shall return you to your chamber."

"It's because of what I am. A dream-weaver you called me. I am that and much, much more.

It's in the nature of my kind to live with sound and colour. Remember the decor of my office? I have different sensory requirements. To be deprived of any of them will cause illness, even death. I'm not being difficult, it's how I am."

Connal cupped her chin, tilting her head. The eyes which regarded her were a softer grey. Was it a hopeful sign that he believed her?

"Aye, then I am sorry. I did not know," he said gently. "We have little knowledge of any off-worlder, let alone one such as you. We have no desire to interact with any *coimheach*."

"Yet you went to the League seeking my help, even though I am ... what did you call me ... a foreigner?"

Connal smiled grimly. "I had no other choice. Would that the circumstances have proven otherwise, for it galls me to ask aid of any *coimheach*. You are the first off-worlder to grace my Castle, but Arran's Mercy, you shall be the last! While I might grant you the liberty of different accommodation, do not mistake my consideration for a change of heart. You are still my prisoner and I intend to have my use of you, Weaver. Come." His fingers bit into her arm as he propelled her down the corridors, his pace so fast that she had to trot to keep up with his long strides.

Now she could sense he was angry again. His shifting emotions were difficult to track, even more difficult to understand. And she was going to dream-search with such an unstable man?

Seven Stars. After what happened the first time, what might occur the second time they dream-shared?

Still, once done, Connal would know the truth and she would be free. Though all things considered, her freedom would be bought at a very high price. Freedom ... an ache deep within, a longing, gone before she could examine it ... a feeling that she did not want to be free.

Ridiculous! This planet could offer her nothing. Soon, she would be back among civilised beings who knew how to treat one another with courtesy and respect, so very different from the man who even now was branding her flesh with his fingers, indifferent to her suffering. Surely she wanted to leave this madness behind? She glanced up at him ... *Connal MacArran, you are nothing more than a barbarian!*

One day, she promised herself, she would look back on this incident, see it as an adventure. Maybe even laugh about it. Though, at the moment, there was nothing funny in her predicament. And that her fate rested entirely on the benevolence of a man like Connal MacArran ... well, it boded ill for her.

Finally, Connal stopped in front of a door and opened it. He waved her ahead of him. "I trust this will meet with My Lady's approval," he said.

As Liandra took a step forward, Connal grasped her wrist, halting her. With a calmness she was far from feeling, she forced herself to look at him.

"Be warned, Liandra. Fergus shall guard your door. He will tear out your heart if you leave this room without my permission."

Without waiting for her answer, Connal stepped back. With an ominous thud the door closed.

Once more, Liandra found herself alone. In darkness.

Chapter Five

He's tricked me again! But as her eyes grew accustomed to the gloom, she saw a fine sliver of light penetrating the room through a gap in the curtains.

Rushing forward, she drew back the heavy drapes. Sunlight beating fiercely through paned, tinted windows, cast a coloured lattice-work on the walls and floor.

Kneeling on the window embrasure, Liandra stared down. She could see the entire length of one wing of the castle as well as the manicured gardens and the land beyond the castle walls.

Turning, she viewed her new chamber. Beautiful, and definitely not a male abode. The decorations were unmistakably feminine, softer, more ornate, without a single weapon adorning any of the walls. Although spotlessly clean, she sensed that no one had lived within its four walls for a long time. Silently, she thanked Connal for his generosity.

Even as her thoughts softened towards him, she hardened her resolve. He had granted her request for different accommodation from practicality, not kindness. He needed her well and capable of performing the dream-sharing when he required it.

Remember - you're his prisoner, not his guest!

Drawing back more curtains, she discovered a doorway that led out onto a wide balcony. Locked. Hardly surprising, for Connal would make sure she remained in his castle, until he had finished with her. Liandra shuddered. What might he do to her, and how long would she remain in his custody?

She strode about the chamber, impulsively testing the heavy wooden door, that led into the room. Suprisingly, it wasn't locked. Opening it cautiously, she saw Connal's monstrous animal in the corridor. It jumped to its feet, its large mouth opening in a snarl.

"It's all right, Fergus," she said, shakily. "I'm not trying to escape."

She left the door open and in alarm, watched as Fergus trotted forward to settle his great body down on the threshold of her apartment. As she moved about the chamber, she could feel the creature's gaze on her.

Another door led off her bedroom. She inspected the bathroom with its taps and unfamiliar contrivances. It was better than she had hoped. Not up to League standards, but certainly not primitive. Liandra experimented with every fixture before returning to the main chamber. In dismay, she noticed Fergus had inched his way further into her room.

Liandra heard Fianna's voice in the

corridor. Moments later, she appeared at the doorway.

"Fergus! Get out of the way!" In response, the hound settled his head firmly between his paws. "You be the most stubborn beast I know!" Fianna cried, stepping over the dog's prostrate body.

Liandra's smile faded as a huge man with curling red hair and beard joined Fianna's side. His wary brown eyes fixed her to the spot; his forearm muscles rippled as he flexed his fingers over the handle of his knife. Perhaps a silent warning to her? She stepped backwards, retreating to the relative sanctuary of the opposite side of the room.

Fianna dumped a bundle of clothes on the bed. "The *Tighearna* thought you might have need of these."

Liandra glanced down, surprised to see that among the items Fianna had brought were several of her favourite garments, stolen - like herself - from her League apartment.

His selection was more than a lucky guess. While Connal MacArran would deny it, maybe he was not even aware of it, Liandra was certain his random choice resulted from some telepathic ability.

"I have brought you some other things, as well."

Fianna held out more items of clothing, which included a heavy woollen shawl. "The nights can grow chill, Mistress. You will be pleased to have this, I think."

Liandra quickly sorted through the clothes.

"Thank you for your kindness, but see here." She held up the gold girdle, still attached to her counsellor's robe. "This is my enviro belt. It responds to my environment, so no need for bulky clothing."

"Truly? What a marvel!" Fianna said.

Liandra stroked the opalescent gown she'd been wearing the day Connal had first come to her. How long ago that now seemed!

"Connal was most specific in his orders to me. You are to eat and rest. Is there any particular food I can bring you? He said your tastes are different to ours."

"When Connal abducted me, he didn't think to bring my food?"

Fianna bit her lip. "No. However, Castle MacArran's kitchens are extensive, the best on Caledonia. I can bring you almost anything."

"I don't suppose you have *dennamaz* or *tansred*?"

"What are they?"

"Liquid supplements. They're what I normally consume."

"Only such? No real food?"

Liandra frowned, trying to draw the impressions of Caledonian food from the recesses of her subconscious. She shuddered at the array of 'delicacies' that flashed before her eyes.

"Nothing which has lived, no creature of flesh and blood. I refuse to touch that, whatever Connal says."

"Very well. Will you take tea, also?"

"Tea?" Liandra asked, and immediately the

image of some steaming liquid came to mind. "I suppose."

"Good. There is one more thing." Fianna edged to Liandra's side. "Dougall, your guard, he is not as ferocious as he looks. However, he shall ensure that you do not leave your chamber."

Liandra glanced over Fianna's shoulder and saw Dougall sitting on a chair outside her door.

"He cannot be touched, as you did to me," Fianna said.

"For that I'm sorry. Was Connal angry with you for allowing me to do that to you?"

"I did not *allow* you to do such, Mistress."

Liandra smiled. "I could never put the sleep on you if you didn't have some empathy for me."

Fianna nodded. "I suppose I did feel sorry for you. As for Connal -" She laughed. "Over the years, I have weathered many of his angry moods. Do not ever touch me like that again."

"I won't."

"Good."

Liandra sorted through the toiletries and other items Fianna had brought. The name of each item flashed through her mind. *Soap, toothbrush, shampoo ...* on and on in a confusing parade. She quickly hunted through her clothes.

"What is it you seek?" Fianna asked, gently.

"My ring. It isn't here."

"This was all Connal gave me. If you like I can ask him for you?"

"Thank you."

Fianna gently touched Liandra's arm. "I will try and make your stay here as pleasant as possible. It must be very difficult for you to accept what has been done."

"Save your sympathy for someone who deserves it!" Jenna swept into the chamber, her rich red robes billowing about her. "I do not know why you show her any compassion, Fianna. 'Tis quite probable she bedded down with your Garris."

"I've never had any man," Liandra said.

"Only in your dreams, then? I doubt that very much. Still, whatever the truth, you would be enough to turn the stomach of any man. *My* Connal has not been the same since he returned from off-world."

"You have an acid tongue, Jenna. The *coimheach* is our guest."

"Do you take her side, over that of your own sister?"

Liandra looked from Jenna to Fianna, not understanding. How could two sisters be so different, in looks, in temperament?

Jenna's face darkened in fury. "'Tis only I then, it seems, who is not smitten by this alien bitch! I grant you anything you like, Fianna, she plied her trade on your Garris. Why would he forsake your bed for hers, unless ...?"

"Please do not!" Fianna burst into tears.

Liandra moved to interpose herself between the two as she saw Jenna's triumphant, malicious smile. "*Maera* Jenna, you -"

"What goes on here?" Connal's chillingly calm voice intruded. He strode into the chamber. "What mischief are you causing now?" His steely eyes rested on Liandra.

She flushed, outraged. "Why do you immediately assume I'm to blame?"

"She did not start it, *Tighearna*," Fianna said.

"It ends here, and now! Is that clear?" Connal looked at the women, each in turn, his cold gaze resting on Liandra.

"I have no wish to cause trouble," she insisted.

"No wish? Perhaps. Yet trouble seems to find you."

"That's only too true," Liandra said. "You arrived at my apartment door."

At that he almost smiled, but caught himself in time, Liandra saw. He turned to his kinswomen. "The witch and I have plans to make. Leave us."

While Fianna scurried away, Jenna was slow to obey.

"I am in no mood for your games, Jennie. Get you gone!"

Connal stared down at the clothes on the bed, noting the additional items which Fianna had, on her own initiative, supplied to the *bandruidh*. He nodded. To be expected, Fianna's heart was too soft, too soft by far, to deal with his unwelcome guest.

He turned back to Liandra. Her eyes regarded him warily. By Arran! He felt a flash of irritation that she regarded him thus. No matter who she was, he did not like to be the cause of her dismay. But, he reminded himself, he had deliberately set out to subdue her by hinting that if necessary he would inflict violence upon her to ensure her co-operation. What a tangled web he had spun for himself!

"I trust this chamber is more to your liking?" he asked gently.

"It is. Thank you for your consideration."

"Is there anything else I may bring to make your stay here ... less traumatic for your alien sensibilities?"

"Do you mean that?"

"Aye."

"There are two things. The door leading outside is locked. I'd like to walk in the open, I find these four walls very difficult to bear."

Connal folded his arms and eyed her shrewdly. "Not looking for a chance to escape, are you?"

"Escape? Where would I go if I did leave this castle? There's only wilderness."

"You have the way of it, Liandra. Wilderness, it is. Not to my people, of course, because we are skilled woodsmen. Even so, we enter it with caution. A woman such as yourself, who knows nothing but controlled, sterile environments, would quickly die of exposure. I will see to it that Fianna brings you the key. And the other?"

"A small thing. When you found me, I was

wearing a ring. It's not among my belongings."

Connal's throat constricted. That ring and the memories it invoked. He swallowed down hard. "I remember it," he said. "It must be in my chamber."

"My mother gave me that ring. I'll be very upset if it's lost due to your interference - "

Connal smiled, bleakly. "I have a lost kinsman to worry about, more important, by far, than a trifling ring."

Liandra sighed. "So we're back to Garris?"

"Come with me," Connal said, and before she could move, he had taken her arm in that fierce grip of his. He propelled her to the door.

Liandra managed to wrench her arm free. "Must you always treat me so roughly? You've already given me bruises, you callous barbarian."

"I have what?" he demanded. He reached out and pushed up one of her sleeves.

She saw the look of scepticism turn to a frown as he viewed the red welts on her skin.

Reaching out, he cupped her chin, tilting her head, so that she had no choice but to look into his eyes.

"I did this to ye? For that I be sorry, witch," he said. "Perhaps I underestimate my strength, or are your kind so fragile? I apologise to you. It shall not happen again. Please, come with me."

Gently, but firmly he placed a hand under her elbow and escorted her to the open doorway. Immediately Dougall and the hound jumped to their feet.

"Where are you taking me?" Liandra asked.

"'Tis a surprise."

"I've had quite enough surprises recently, thank you!"

Silently, he ushered her down the passage. Glancing back, Liandra saw Dougall and Fergus following, at a discreet distance.

Connal pushed open a door and waved Liandra ahead of him. The concern at where she was being taken and for what purpose fled the instant she saw her crystal bed.

With a delighted cry, she rushed forward. The bed's familiar vibrations were a welcome respite to the alien emanations of Caledonia. She rested her cheek against one crystalline post and closed her eyes, letting the swirling vibrations, caressing with sound and colour, enter her mind and soul. How long she remained like it, she did not know, only Connal's hand on her shoulder, brought her back to the present.

"Thank you for keeping it safe." She smiled up at him, and their eyes met. For the briefest moment, he returned her smile, before his face hardened, before his mouth turned down.

"I am not a barbarian to destroy the property of another, however alien." He tentatively reached out a finger to stroke a crystal. "It be warm."

"Yes."

He frowned at it, then at her. "Is the bed fully functional? Will it, will you be ready for what must be done tomorrow?"

Liandra nodded, not trusting in her voice to answer, for she knew it would betray her foreboding. She didn't want to dream-share with him again, yet what other choice did she have?

"Good. What else will you need?" Connal asked.

"I suppose it's true that all my equipment was left behind? I always have a monitor when I dream-share, so that I don't become lost in the dreams."

"How is that done?"

"The computer watches over me, as well as my client. If we go too deeply, then it brings us back to a light sleep. If there's danger, it will awaken us."

"It didna' work too well before!"

"No," Liandra whispered. "I don't know why."

"Every machine has its limitations." He paused. "I will have one of my people perform this task. I will not, again, entrust my life to the whims of electronic gadgetry."

"And I don't feel comfortable having a stranger look upon me in the dream-state. Besides which, none of your kind could possibly be skilled in monitoring."

"Is that so?" Connal raised a taunting eye brow. "My people have the ability to do everything, and more besides, than a mere machine."

Liandra shrugged. "Why do you have such a

distrust of technology? It's illogical, almost bordering on a pathological phobia."

Connal smiled, grimly. "Do not try your counselling on me, Mistress. I have very good reasons for the way I think. If you wish to believe I am mentally deranged, so be it. 'Tis true, perhaps? Who else but a mad-man would kidnap a Dream-weaver from under the noses of her incorruptible League servants?"

"Who else, indeed, but a mad-man," Liandra said. Though she meant it as a stinging rebuke, Connal laughed at her rancour.

"I will escort you to your apartment, now. Come away from the bed. It remains here, under lock and key ready for the morrow."

He returned her to her bed chamber, firmly closing the door behind him as he left.

As pleasant as her new apartment might be, Liandra still felt as if the walls were crowding in on her. She waited only moments before she scurried across the room and opened the door wide. Once again, she saw that Dougall and Fergus sat outside on guard duty.

Minutes later Fianna arrived, carrying a tray laden with food. Liandra suddenly realised how hungry she was as she looked down at the dishes.

Fianna smiled, and gently touched Liandra's arm. "Connal said you were not to be left alone, so you shall suffer the presence of Dougall and that hound while you are our guest. Set aside your fears. Whatever he says, Connal will not harm you. No one in the Castle will."

"I'm not so certain about that," Liandra said.

"And for my sister's behaviour, I apologise." Fianna grimaced. "Her tongue is sharper than any dagger. She sees you as a threat and that makes her doubly dangerous."

"A threat?" Liandra asked. "In what way?"

Incredulously, Fianna regarded her "She is jealous of you, and what you and Connal have shared. 'Tis true when she said that the *Tighearna* has not been the same since he returned to Castle MacArran."

"That makes two of us!"

Once Fianna had gone, Liandra sat at the table and inspected the food. She stabbed at it with her fork, tentatively tasting a morsel. Its sweet warmth soothed her mouth before she slowly swallowed. She forced herself to eat only a little, just in case the food reacted against her metabolism, causing sickness. Medical facilities on Caledonia would no doubt be basic. She had no desire to find out, first hand, just how primitive!

With her hunger alleviated, she felt weariness descend. She needed to sleep, to prepare herself for the next day and what it might bring. Stretching out on the canopied bed, she grimaced at its hard surface.

At home, she was used to the anti-grav. cushioning of her crystal bed, its warm lights spinning a cocoon around her body, as she floated on a mattress of air. On Caledonia she had only a cold, unyielding bed. The thing was *impossible!* More like an ancient torture device than a place to sleep.

She pushed herself up from the bed and went to the window. Caledonia's single moon cast a strange purple-blue light on the brooding mist-enshrouded countryside. She drew in her breath, for it was beautiful, in a wild, alien way.

Liandra knelt before the fireplace and experimented with the controls, so that the 'fire' flickered amber, red and orange. She brought her pillow and quilt to the hearth and covered herself, watching the flames, hoping that the lights and colours would bring comfort and sleep. She was so tired, living on her nerves for too long. Although the sleep she desperately craved was a long time in coming, when it did, it seemed only a few minutes had passed before a voice violated her sleep.

"Ban-druidh?"

The word echoed in her mind, and she tried to ignore it, thinking Connal's gentle voice a dream. A memory. When the warmth of a hand cupped her shoulder and turned her, Liandra started awake.

Connal knelt beside her. With a cry, she dragged herself upright, drawing the quilt to her chest.

In a blur of speed he hurled himself to his feet, hands on hips. "You have no need to fear me. What is it you do before the fire?"

"Trying to sleep," Liandra said. "What do

you want?"

He laughed. "Most women I know find early morning a bitter-sweet thing, depending upon whom they find in their bed when they awaken. Fianna tried to rouse you from slumber. She could not. Fearing you were ill, she summoned me. And I find you like this. Why? Was the bed not comfortable enough?"

"I'm used to something different. This chamber is oppressive."

Connal glanced around, eye brows arching skyward. "'Tis one of the finest apartments in the Castle. It belonged to my mother."

"I'm not ungrateful, Connal. But I'm used to my own bed, it lulls me to sleep with its sounds and colours. A dream-weaver must have such to maintain health."

"And by the look of you, your sleep was not restful. Well, that makes two of us."

He turned on his heel and stalked from the room. Liandra noticed he did not close the door.

She struggled to her feet, cringing as she felt sore, cramped muscles. Longingly, she thought of her rejuv. chamber. It would have soothed away her aches and pains. Now without it, she would have to tolerate her discomfort. Somehow.

She heard the voices of men in the corridor outside, and Connal's above them all giving instructions.

Moments later four men staggered into the chamber, between them they carried her crystal bed. They carefully placed it down and looked at Connal for more directions.

"Where would My Lady like her bed?" he asked.

"By the window, please."

"As the Lady says."

The men positioned it as directed and then, their work done, they studied her curiously before Connal dismissed them. Obediently, they hurried from the room, though each man cast a backward glance, to catch their final glimpse of her.

"Thank you for this consideration," Liandra said, stroking the bed.

Connal shrugged. "I -"

"Fergus, get out of the way! Connal, do something with this beast of yours!" Fianna stepped over the dog, who had once again, positioned himself in the middle of the doorway. She ushered in two girls who each carried a tray of food.

"Put them on the table, and be off about your work," Connal said.

The servants hastily retreated from the chamber. They paused to take a long hard look at Liandra, before they scurried away.

Connal chuckled. "My people are curious to see, for themselves, the green-haired *ban-druidh* Jennie has told them about."

"I'm not comfortable being the centre of attention." Liandra frowned at Connal. She was a novelty. If their positions had been reversed and Connal was a 'guest' on her home-base, there would be many women - and some men - who would want to get more than a second look at such an exotic creature as Connal MacArran. She wondered what he would make of such notoriety. As images of his discomfiture passed before her eyes, Liandra had to smile. Seven Stars, she'd love to see that day!

"I like not the way you smile, *ban-druidh*. What are you about?"

Liandra blinked and drew her mind back to the present. "I was thinking about home." Not exactly a lie.

"The sooner you help me, the sooner you will see it. As we have plans to make, I thought you and I could breakfast together."

He motioned her to the table and awkwardly Liandra sat down on the chair he held for her. Once she was seated, he sat opposite, eating quickly.

She nibbled at a small piece of toasted bread with a thin spread of jam. It was delicious! She kept her gaze downcast on her food, conscious of the way Connal studied her. His silence was most disconcerting. She sipped her tea, finding that of all the things on Caledonia, this liquid was, by far, the nicest thing she had encountered.

Connal sighed deeply, contentedly, and leaned back in his chair. She put down her cup and regarded him.

He raised a quizzical brow. "Is that all you intend to eat? You will fade away before my eyes, *ban-druidh*."

"Unlike you, my appetite is small. Besides, I have no way of knowing how this ... poison will react to my metabolism. They are primitive nutrients."

Connal laughed long and hard. "Do not let Fianna hear you speak thus about her meals. She would be much insulted."

"I don't intend to tell her. Do you?" Liandra raised a delicate brow and Connal grinned at her.

"One MacLeod after your hide is more than enough for you to handle."

"One ... what?"

"MacLeod. Fianna, like Jennie is from clan MacLeod. Their family is affiliated to me."

"You didn't come here to reveal your family tree," Liandra said. "What did you want to discuss with me?"

Connal stretched out his long legs. "I would say much."

From inside the pouch - the *sporran* - which hung at the front of his kilt, he pulled out a thin, oblong package. As Liandra concentrated on it, the word 'envelope' came to mind. Connal placed the envelope in front of her and she regarded it and him curiously.

"We found this two days after Garris disappeared. His letter to me explained where he had gone. That was how I knew where to begin my search. Open it."

Liandra carefully did as she was told. "This is made from paper!"

Connal's eyebrows shot skyward. "Aye."

"I've never touched paper before." She regarded the smooth, fragile surface, which was decorated with bold scrawls of dark ink. "Garris wrote this?"

"Aye."

She traced a finger over the script, *sensing*. Like the piece of jewellery Connal had given her, it was also confused. "So many people have handled this letter, I cannot focus on any aura."

But there was something else. Something dark. Sinister. Then it vanished, though Liandra shivered as the legacy of that feeling stayed with her. Her imagination, surely?

"I thought the letter might help, for the dream-search," Connal said.

"I need something which no one but Garris has touched."

"I will see what I can find." Connal frowned. "What make you of the letter?"

Liandra turned the paper in her hand, studying it from every angle. "I've never seen anything like it before, except in the museum on Terra."

Connal pursed his lips. "You know of Terra, do you? Earth is the name I know it by."

"So it was before it joined the League. My mother is Terran. She took me there as part of my education."

"*You* are an Earther?" Connal's brows drew together in a measuring frown.

"Why does that shock you?"

"I had not expected you to be human."

93

"*Human* is such an arrogant word. Every sentient being calls itself human. In every League language, *human* means civilised. It doesn't denote origin."

"I stand corrected. And your father is also Terran?"

"Asarian."

"I have little knowledge of this race."

Liandra stared at him, her turn to be shocked. "Over two hundred years ago, Asarian weavers ventured forth from their home-system to search for sentient life. From their journeys and subsequent meetings with other beings, the League eventually formed. How is it that you don't know this? Every civilised world -"

"Caledonia is not a *civilised* world," Connal said dryly. "Or have you forgotten?"

"How could I, when the evidence of it is constantly before my eyes?"

"Please do not provoke me, Liandra, especially so soon after breakfast!" He studied her deeply "I am curious. You say your mother is human ... forgive me, I should say Terran. How primitive of me to forget! And your father is Asarian. Whom do you resemble?"

Liandra wondered at Connal's sudden curiosity. Previously she had the impression that he had no wish to know anything of her, and the less he had to do with her, the better. Now he was asking for her life history. She much preferred this interrogation to his usual shouting and taunting. Perhaps she could humour him awhile longer.

"Asarians aren't so different from Terrans. In some ways I'm like my mother. My best traits, I inherited from my father."

"And your worst traits? Where do they originate?" Connal teased.

Refusing to be baited, Liandra shook her head.

"You have not answered my question," Connal said.

"There've been so many, to which do you refer?"

"The letter. What make you of Garris' words?"

Liandra frowned down at the paper. The words swam before her eyes. She couldn't understand, not even the subliminal tutoring could aid her. "I don't know. I can't read them."

Connal's eyebrows arched skyward. "Cannot or will not?"

"Can't," Liandra said. "My computer -"

"Say no more! And you dare call me barbarian? At least I am able to read and write. I do not rely on some *infairrnal* machine to think for me. Give me the letter." He snatched it out of her hand.

"It's not what you think, Connal - "

He waved her to silence. "Spare me your explanations. I shall read it for you.

Castle MacArran, Caledonia 12th day, 8th Month, Year 709. Tighearna."

Connal glanced up at her. "That's me, in case you've forgotten.

Tighearna When you find this letter, I will be off-

95

world. I have sought the services of Dream-Weaver Liandra Tavor. Do not ask me why, because in my own mind I am not certain why I must see this coimheach, only that I must. Garris."

Connal looked up at her, to see that she was still listening, before he, again, dropped his gaze to the paper. "And to Fianna a post-script.

"Forgive me, *ghraidh*, I could not tell you in person where I go and why."

He flung the letter down on the table. "Well?" he demanded, studying her.

"It's a mystery to me."

"And to me," Connal said. "No Caledonian ventures off-world without a damn good reason, and certainly not without his lord's permission. He most definitely did not have my leave to go. As far as I know Garris had no motive to see you. I am bewildered by his knowledge of your existence."

"There are few Dream-Weavers in the League, so if someone needed to find me they would have no difficulty. Because of our rarity, my skills are well known throughout the hundred worlds."

"I did not know I was host to a celebrity." He inclined his head mockingly. "I am honoured to have your company and expertise at my finger-tips."

Liandra glared at him.

"Tell me this, Mistress. Where do beings go who need the professional help you offer, but who cannot, for some reason, employ one such as you?" Connal asked.

"They would go to Space Med."

"Who?"

"Not who, what. The League offers a medical service on every world. Computers and androids can generally help most cases."

Connal grimaced. "I would not trust my well being to any creature which is not flesh and blood. And I would not want *counselling* from any agency that considers a computer a viable alternative to good old-fashioned doctoring. 'Tis beyond me why any would want to seek out a mechanical contraption for any reason!"

"I don't understand you!" Liandra said.

"One thing I am curious about, *ban-druidh*." Connal eyed her shrewdly. "You said you have parents. From what I hear of the League, there would be no place in their scheme of things for parenting, as we on Caledonia understand it. Children are artificially created, that is the truth of it. Yes?"

"We of the League have choices. Most parents prefer matrix-surrogacy as it's more convenient. *Seven Stars!* I couldn't imagine the other biological way, it's barbarous."

"Life artificially created thus would have no soul, surely? No love -"

"That is where you're wrong, Connal. All children are conceived in love, no matter how it is done. What about those beings who are not able to produce a child, whether because of genetic incompatibility, or sterility? Would you render them childless simply because of some ridiculous aversion to technology? The League has ethical standards to ensure life is revered in its many forms, no matter how they might be conceived."

Connal frowned. "And what of you, counsellor? Were your parents similarly detached during the time of your creation?"

"My mother and father mind-touched with me as soon as I attained consciousness. Within moments of my conception I knew how much I was loved."

Connal swore. For once Liandra's knowledge of Caledonian was inadequate to meet the translation of the words he hissed.

"Now I know why the League has no stomach for fighting ... soul-less cowards."

"How is it you think you know so much of the League? You've told me often enough that you have no dealing with any alien."

Connal smiled grimly. "I study the ways of my enemy very closely."

"The League is not your enemy. We are a peaceful confederation of more than one hundred star systems joined -"

"Enemies come in many guises. The League 'tis the opposite of everything we Caledonians hold sacred. Your science has even perverted the begetting of a child. And so, 'tis my belief that a man from the League has forgotten how to please a woman, unless he takes some damn pill, or he be hooked up to some electronic contraption, such as you have on your bed."

Though Liandra had no experience of men, she knew that for many, what he had said was true. She chewed her lip and glancing up, saw Connal's triumphant smile.

"Do I have the right of it Counsellor Tavor?"

"And I suppose you consider yourself an expert where pleasing women is concerned?"

He grinned. "They have not complained."

"From what little I know of you, Connal MacArran, a woman would not dare make a complaint to you."

Connal laughed. "My women dare very much. By our mutual pleasuring they are granted more liberties than some of them truly deserve. Why this sudden interest? Are you curious to sample what it is you have been missing - a real man?"

Liandra gasped. "I would rather die."

"Oh, you would not die of the experience, Liandra," Connal's voice had taken on a seductive, throaty quality. "That I promise you. You would even enjoy it. For once, a man worthy of the name!"

Liandra jumped up, and stepped backwards. "Of all the pompous, insufferable things to say. Just keep away from me!"

Connal came to his feet, laughing. "I fully intend to, *ban-druidh*. Save your *counselling* for your clients!"

"You make my profession sound disgusting. I'm not ashamed of what I am, nor what I do."

"You should be."

"I bring relief -"

"Truly? Well, I found none such in your bed and your dreams, Mistress Tavor! Your profession 'tis repulsive to me, and especially so, because I am forced, once again, to seek the services of mind-touching alien witch -"

"Why ... you ... arrogant barbarian!" She reached out and grabbed the first thing her fingers touched. Before she knew what she was doing, she hurled the teapot at Connal.

As quick as she was, he was quicker. He ducked as the pot sailed within inches of his head, to shatter against the wall a foot or so from where he had been standing. Hot liquid sprayed in every direction. Caught in the shower, Connal's linen shirt was spattered with tea.

He strode forward. "*By Arran!* Ye shall pay for that you, you -"

"*Ban-druidh?*" Liandra suggested, retreating quickly to place her bed between herself and Connal.

"I am quite capable of thinking of suitable names to call you, woman!" He lunged at her. "Come here, at once!"

"No!" Liandra dodged around her bed, keeping Connal always at a safe distance.

"Give in and accept your punishment, or I will make you even sorrier when I eventually catch you!"

"I refuse to lie down and just let you do what you wish."

"Who said anything about lying down? No

bed is a suitable place to inflict a punishment."
He dodged around the bed, and Liandra eluded
him. "Come here, damn you!"

"I want none of you Connal MacArran. Keep
your distance!"

"You will not be *having* me, *ban-druidh*! Of
that you may rest assured. I prefer my partners
to be willing, to purr with delight as -"

"You're despicable!"

"I?" Connal laughed and lunged forward. She
twisted away, her sleeve tearing in his grasp. All
he had to show for his manoeuvre was a strip of
fabric in his fist, when what he really wanted was
a pale, slender neck, which he could wring.

Again, Liandra twisted away from Connal's
charge. "Only a primitive resorts to violence!"

"As you say, Liandra. 'Twas you who threw
the teapot."

She paused. By the Seven Stars, he was right!
She *had* started the fight!

And that moment of lost concentration was
her downfall, she realised as Connal flung himself at her, caught her, and brought her down
onto the bed. For a moment she stared up at him,
not understanding. Even though his action had
been quick, he had been careful, and used only
enough of his formidable strength to capture her
without causing any harm.

"Get off me, you oaf!" She squirmed against
him.

Her robe hitched up to her thighs, his kilt
bunched around his thighs, she felt his naked,

tensile flesh against her. For a moment she stared up at him, as he stared down at her, his eyes dark and tempestuous. Only the sound of their quick, shallow breaths broke the sudden silence in the room.

One of his hands slipped beneath her, cupping a hip, drawing her body to his.

"Liandrrra ..." His mouth hovered a fraction from hers. "*Ban-druidh -*"

The last word spoken not as a taunt, but intended as a caress.

"I am not a witch!"

He drew back from her, his eyes no longer a sultry, mysterious black, but as harsh and as cold as space.

Indignation flooded through her, her body chill as the look in his eyes. "Release me!"

"Not until you apologise."

"Never!" she snapped, writhing beneath him, trying to buck him off.

As they wrestled on the bed, they rolled close to its edge, teetered on the brink and then fell in a tangle of bodies and quilt. Somehow in the moment of time it took for them to reach the floor, Connal turned her, so that she landed on him rather than on hard stone.

The pain of contact made him grunt, and for an instant his hold lessened. Liandra seized the opportunity to beat her fists against his chest. In one fluid movement he drew her wrists together and pinned them with a hand above her head, while rolling her onto her back, his body straddling hers.

"Stop this. You're nothing but a savage!"

"Aye, if that is so, what then might be the next move by this *savage* ?"

Liandra closed her eyes. "Please ... don't."

"Do not what, *ban-druidh*?" Connal panted above her.

"Whatever it is you have planned, I'm sure it'll be unpleasant, like the first punishment you inflicted."

"You did not enjoy my kiss?"

"It was disgusting."

"Savages are disgusting, Liandra."

"So they are. How careless of me to forget. Get off me!"

"'Tis a pity, for you make a very appealing mattress."

Connal chuckled and still holding her firmly by the wrists, he dragged her off the floor. He stood behind her, and keeping her arms pinned at her sides, his thighs pressed into the back of her legs. He forced her to walk to the wall.
"Observe your *civilised* handiwork," he drawled.

Liandra flinched away from his lips, so close to her ear. She stared at what she had done. Tea and tea leaves stained the wall and fragments of the teapot littered the floor.

"Dougall," Connal called. Almost immediately the door opened.

"Aye, My Lord?"

Liandra saw Dougall's eyes widen in shocked surprise as he viewed the chamber's disarray.

"I want you to have a servant bring a bucket and cloth," Connal ordered.

"Aye, My Lord."

Minutes later a young girl deposited the items by the doorway.

"Thank you, Karra. Now close the door and be off."

"Aye, My Lord."

"How well they all say *Aye My Lord,*" Liandra accused.

"As you shall, in time."

"Never! You are no Lord of mine, Connal MacArran."

"How well you say my name. I would, however, prefer it done a little less sharply, and somewhat more melodiously if you expect me to answer you."

"You will never hear me purr your name as your other women have done."

"Will I not?" Connal chuckled. "We shall see. Now, for your punishment."

Suddenly Liandra was free and she rubbed her injured flesh. Though he had not hurt her, she made it a ritual cleansing to dispel the taint of his hands upon her.

Connal carried the bucket and cloths and deposited them at her feet. "You have made an unsightly mess in this chamber, and now you will make amends. Begin."

"Begin what?" Liandra looked at him, confused.

"Clean the walls, the floor, everything which

is sullied with tea. Later I will bring you my shirt and you shall clean that, too!"

"I won't. I'm not a servitor."

"You shall." Connal glanced down at the bucket. "I am waiting."

"You'll wait forever, for I'll not do any such thing as clean. It's intolerable!"

"No stomach for honest work, eh Weaver? My people have no such qualms, much better to wash and clean than earn a living as a ... *counsellor*. I will not leave this room until you have cleaned it to my satisfaction. The sooner you begin, the sooner will I be gone. Or are you refusing to obey me because you enjoy my company so much?" He raised a sardonic brow.

Liandra glared at him, turned her back and stalked to her crystal bed. With arms folded, she sat down. Connal flung himself into a chair, his long legs stretched out in front of him.

Minutes passed slowly, and Liandra began to fidget under his direct, glowering scrutiny. Inwardly, she cursed him, using the worst expletives she could. The tongue of Caledonia was very rich in such words.

"Must you stare at me so?" Liandra asked, finally. Connal merely shrugged, his gaze firmly on her. She sighed. For a time she was able to use her skills to remain detached from him, but little by little the silence in the chamber eroded her control. Even her bed was not its usual haven. Like herself, it was out of its depth, robbed of power by the brooding savagery of Caledonia.

A light knock sounded on the door and Fianna popped her head through the crack.

"We are not to be disturbed, under pain of death. *Not for any reason!*" Connal snapped.

Fianna's eyes were as round as saucers as she looked from him to Liandra, then to the wall and its stain. "As you say, My Lord." The door was very carefully closed.

"You have your people cowed into submission by your brutality. I hope you're proud of that fact," Liandra said.

The only response from him was a tightening of those lips. He was camouflaging his fury amazingly well. She could only catch a faint emanation of his true emotional state.

The silence between them stretched into minutes, an hour, another. Never once did his stare waver from her, though Liandra had long since tired of the contest. She counted every stone making up the walls, the floor, everything she could see to keep her mind from focussing on the man in the chamber.

How long was he going to sit there? *For as long as it takes,* came her inner response. He would not be the one to back down. His authority was on the line, not to mention male ego, something she had never experienced before.

If she capitulated, she would never be allowed to forget it. More was at stake here than just punishment. She would have preferred something that was quickly over. Hours in silent confinement with Connal MacArran was the worst punishment Liandra could imagine. And as the afternoon dragged on, the room began to grow darker and darker.

She swallowed against her rising panic. She'd told him she could not stand the dark, now he was, doubtless, deliberately using her fragility to torment her. It was one thing to reject his authority over her, quite another to allow herself to become disoriented, and ill because of the mess from one teapot. Her inner senses screamed a warning.

"Very well," she said, weakly. "What is it I must do?"

"Clean the floor, the wall, everything which has the mark of tea upon it."

Liandra rose with as much dignity as she could and stood beside the bucket. "How?" she asked. "My servitors -"

"Are not here now, so get water from the bathing room, and bring it back."

"How shall I carry it?"

"In the bucket." He threw his hands heavenward, shaking his head in exasperation.

Liandra did as she was told and when she returned, the chamber was illuminated. *Thank the Seven Stars for that small mercy!*

Connal reclined in his chair, arms behind his head, watching her. He had the good sense not to smile at her, Liandra thought, as she glared at him.

"Dip a cloth in the water, and wash."

Liandra pursed her lips, and tentatively

began her task. It was appalling, but to take her mind from the work, she pretended that the surface she was cleaning was Connal MacArran's face. She'd wipe it to oblivion!

When she stole a glance at him, he was as she had seen him before, only now there was a triumphant smile on his arrogant, handsome face! For a moment she felt like hurling the contents of the bucket over him. What punishment might that action incur? It did not bear thinking about.

"You are going to rub a hole in that cloth if you are not careful, Liandra."

She gritted her teeth as she heard his laughter. "'Tis your ugly face I am washing off the walls," she said, and then paused, horrified. Her accent was now Caledonian. She heard Connal draw in a long breath, but she continued scrubbing the floor on her hands and knees. Straightening her aching back, Liandra paused.

"Do you consider the task finished?" Connal roamed the room, inspecting her handiwork. "Passable, but only just." He raised her to her feet. "And perhaps next time you will remember this punishment, before you dare raise your temper and your hand against MacArran."

"If you incite me again, you'll receive more than a teapot aimed at your head."

"I warned you once before not to challenge me. Or do you enjoy the punishments I hand out? If that is so, I can be very accommodating."

"I'm sure you can be *vairry* accommodating." Liandra's tongue rolled the 'r' like a native Caledonian.

Connal smiled at the memory of the time in her apartment when he had said much the same to her. He swallowed to release the tight dryness in his throat. "I have missed lunch and supper through your childish actions, so I will take my leave. Later, I shall return to supervise the washing of my shirt."

"Don't expect me to be here waiting for you."

"By Arran!" Connal strode towards her and pinned her against the wall, his hands on her shoulders. He stared down at her for long minutes.

Liandra held her breath, wondering what would be done to her for this latest transgression.

Chapter Six

Connal took her by the arms and lifted her off the ground. He shook her once, before releasing her.

"By Arran! You are a thistle beneath my kilt, and no mistake! I wish I did not need you to find Garris, else I would send you off-world so fast, your head would spin."

Connal stepped back from her. To Liandra's horror, he shrugged himself out of his shirt, and hurled it at her. Only reflex made her catch it.

She stared down at the garment, in half a mind to fling it back at him. Even as the thought crossed her mind, she saw his grey eyes narrow in that now familiar, silent challenge of his.

"Well, get it over with! You've taunted me long enough, and now you intend to rape me. Go ahead, but I warn you -"

Connal laughed, a cold, hollow sound. "You dishonour me! And I like it not! No Caledonian forces himself upon any woman. I prefer my partners compliant-"

"You'll get none such from me," Liandra snapped.

"I want none such from you! Come."

Once again, Liandra found herself propelled against her will, this time to the adjoining bathroom. His terse instructions were specific. While he sat back and watched, Liandra scrubbed his shirt, her thoughts dark as she worked. One day she would make him pay for every insult. How, she did not know, only that she would!

"See *ban-druidh*! The little experience you have of domestic chores and already your cleaning skills have dramatically improved. Practice makes perfect, Liandra."

She drew in a ragged breath. "Rest assured, Connal MacArran, this is the first and last time I clean anything, especially your clothes."

"That sounds very close to a challenge, Counsellor Tavor. And you know how I respond to such. Do not provoke me, else you will suffer more punishment. Perhaps you enjoy my discipline?" He raised an enquiring brow.

"Why, you ... you!"

"Lost for words, Mistress? 'Tis a good sign." He laughed. "I will be away then, for my long-delayed supper. All your work has no doubt given you an appetite. I will have another meal brought to you and this time I expect you to eat more than just enough to keep a bird alive."

"What I eat and how much is none of your concern."

"That is where you be wrong! I want you strong for our dream-sharing." He reached out and cupped her chin, forcing her to look at him. "And you will not be starving yourself just to spite me."

Collecting his soggy shirt, Connal stalked from the chamber. Liandra slammed the door after him, and sent a cushion flying across the room before silently venting her fury on the closest pillow to hand. She threw herself on her bed and pummelled its unyielding surface. Tears of rage welled up in her eyes. Angrily, she blinked them away.

What was happening to her? Always in control, she rarely cried or showed anger. Why should these emotions suddenly surface in such a disgusting, strong, uncontrollable flood? She chewed her lower lip. Connal was to blame.

Her counsellor's empathy had taken control of her emotions and actions, reducing her to his level, so that she could deal with him. So that he understood her. She was reacting to Connal in the only way he could comprehend. For the first time in her life she cursed her abilities which now rendered her so receptive to Connal's barbarity. How was she going to control her outbursts?

Yet, it was more than that. To be fair to him - though the thought appalled her - it wasn't just Connal's fault. She was part Terran and her mother's blood flowed in her veins. Connal was just the catalyst who had brought her Terran genes out of hiding. She had spent a lifetime in denying them, now they were free and

tormenting her - their revenge for her sup-
pression. Hadn't her father hinted as much,
many times in the past? That it was dangerous to
deny oneself? He enjoyed his wife's unique
temper. The only time they met as ardent equals
was when they came together as lovers. Asarians
were passionate about their mates - to the
exclusion of all things. Had she inherited that
aspect of her father's heritage? So far she hadn't
experienced the Asarian love-call. She had
always thought she had escaped it, but there had
been moments just recently around Connal
when she had felt her blood stir in spite of
herself.

Liandra groaned and pressed her face down
into the pillow. What was she going to do? *Fight
it - that's what*. The last thing she wanted was a
man - any man - especially one who was a savage.
She had to resist. Survive, somehow, and leave
Caledonia and Connal; leave everything far
behind.

Once home, she would return to normal. Or
would this abhorrent experience forever leave
its mark on her psyche? At such a terrifying
thought, tears ran unchecked down her cheeks.

Liandra woke to the light knock on the door and
moments later Dougall strode warily into her
chamber. Behind him, a young girl carried a tray
which she placed on the table.

"With Lord MacArran's compliments,"
Dougall said, backing out of the room. The

serving girl scampered after him.

Despite her hunger, Liandra tried to ignore the aroma of food. Before she knew what she was doing she had lifted the lid of the tray, staring down at the meal which Connal had sent.

Well, she wasn't going to starve herself. Besides, she knew that if she did follow through with such a childish act, Connal would undoubtedly force-feed her. Her dignity had taken more than enough battering, it was time for a new strategy, so while she ate, Liandra considered her options.

After her third cup of tea and a delicious wedge of fruit tart - amazing how food could put a different perspective on things - she felt renewed. Time to attend to more of her needs. Her skin itched. What she had post-poned could not be put off any longer.

She experimented, again, with the bathroom fixtures, finding through trial and error how to work the shower. She grimaced as the warm water trickled through her fingers. This experience was not going to be pleasant, she thought, stripping off her robe.

Stepping under the spray of water, Liandra shuddered. A few minutes later, she had grown used to the sensation, made doubly interesting by the lather of scented soap which took some of the tired ache from her body.

She attacked her hair, finding it an almost impossible task. It snagged and more than once she mouthed a Caledonian expletive as her fingers knotted in the wild tangle of wet hair.

How, in the Seven Stars, did the women of Caledonia manage? Again, she thought fondly of her servitors. Now, without them, she realised, for the first time in her life, just how totally reliant she had become on her mechanical aides.

Leaving the bathing-room, Liandra threw a shawl around her body, and opened the door.

Dougall sat in his chair against the far wall. At his elbow he had a small table laden with food and drink. A young man beside him, was laughing, as Dougall spoke. They were immediately silent the moment Liandra stepped from the chamber. She stood uncertainly in the corridor, water pooling around her feet.

"Och!" The young man said. His eyes widened as he took in her every detail.

"Control ye-self, Colin!" Dougall snapped at his companion.

"*Maer* Dougall?" Liandra said.

"Aye?" He came stiffly to his feet.

"I need help."

"Och aye?"

"*Maera*... Mistress Fianna. Would it be too much trouble to send her a message, at your convenience? Please. I need her assistance."

Dougall frowned, his eyebrows bristling.

"I realise my accent is strange," Liandra said. "Can you understand me?"

"Aye, lass, that I can." He turned to the young man. "Colin, do as the lady bids."

Colin nodded and backed down the corridor, his eyes never leaving her. He nearly tripped over his own feet.

Dougall swore, exasperated. He turned his gaze on Liandra, his thick eyebrows drawing together in a fierce scowl. "I would be getting back in your chamber if I were you, Mistress. The air be chill and you are not ... well ... decent." A flush raced across his wide cheeks.

Liandra glanced down at herself. Since she saw no intimate flesh exposed, she wondered what was wrong with him.

"*Mistress Liandra!*" Fianna's shrill voice echoed in the corridor. She hurried forward, Colin at her heels. Another young giant, grinning from ear to ear, appeared at the end of the corridor.

Dougall stalked down the passage, waving his arms. "Be away with ye, or I will be taking a birch to both your backsides!"

Silently, Fianna ushered Liandra into the chamber and firmly closed the door.

"What were ye thinkin' of, Mistress Liandrrra?" Fianna said.

"Why are you angry with me?"

"*Why* ...? Arran's Mercy! You canna' stand half naked in the corridor, with the men ogling you like that! The castle will be gossiping with this latest news. You mark my words, Colin and Angas are notorious."

"I don't understand."

Fianna threw her hands heavenward. "Aye.

116

I forget you are not one of us." She drew in a deep breath. "Colin said you wished to see me. Why so?"

"My hair!" Liandra ran a hand through her dripping, tangled curls. "'Tis a disaisterrr." She frowned, for her own speech had taken on a Caledonian accent.

"What did you use on your hair?"

Liandra led Fianna into the bath-room. "This," she said, taking up the sticky cake of soap.

"Soap is for the body." Fianna drew down two containers from the shelf. "This lotion is for washing hair, and this for rinsing, to keep away the tangles."

"What are these for?" Liandra asked, sweeping her hand over the jars and bottles that Fianna had given her. Not knowing what else to do, she had placed them on the bath-room shelves.

"Lotions for cleansing the face. Have you no experience of such?"

"At home, I bath in a cubicle of light, where impurities are removed from my body without the need for soap and water. My servitors see to everything. I just lie back and relax."

"Truly?" Fianna regarded her in amazement. "I would like to see that. You do not have water on your world?"

"Of course. When I lived with my parents on their estate, I used to swim in the lake. There the water's trillian-gold. It didn't feel like this, and it never wet me."

Fianna's mouth dropped open. "You come from a place of marvels, that is certain. Now, sit."

Liandra did as she was told and allowed Fianna to gently administer to her.

"Oh ... by Arran ... your hair, Mistress Liandra!"

"What's wrong?"

"'Tis changing colour. Before my eyes, it is! What have I done?"

Liandra tossed her hair back from her face and regarded herself in the mirror. She grimaced. "The water's reversing the colour I programmed into it."

Fianna's eyes were huge in her small face. "And this silver I see, 'tis your natural shade?"

"Yes."

"I like it better than the green."

Fianna carefully dried Liandra's hair, began to comb out the tangles, though the pain of her ministrations made Liandra flinch.

"Sorry I am, Mistress," Fianna said. "Next time you know what to do, but if you ever need my help, with anything, at any time, you have only to ask."

"Thank you. I would prefer it if you called me Liandra. I am not a Mistress."

"That would please me."

"But not me!" Connal's voice thundered behind them.

Both women started in shock and turned to him. They flinched at the anger in his eyes.

"What is it ye are doing, Fianna?"

Haltingly, the young woman began her explanation. As Liandra listened, Fianna's soft voice trailed away to a whisper. She watched the line of Connal's lips grow even tighter. His grey eyes turned a stormy black. Trouble for her, again, Liandra thought. How well she knew the tell-tale signs.

"Leave me," Connal said.

Fianna hurried to obey. Once the door closed behind her, Liandra turned accusingly to him. "What is it you do to your people that makes them fear you so?"

Connal folded his arms. "They have a healthy respect for me, 'tis all."

"I don't call it *healthy,*" Liandra countered.

He shrugged her accusation aside. As he studied her from head to toe, Liandra pulled the shawl closer around her body, wishing she was more properly screened from his penetrating gaze. Up until that moment she had never been discomfited by her body - nude or otherwise.

"Downstairs, the men are eagerly plying my two young clansman for every intimate detail of my ... guest's appearance. What possessed ye to stand naked in the corridor?"

"I wasn't naked. I wore this."

"It leaves little to the imagination, and my clans-men are very inventive. For your own sake, do not ever do it again, Liandra. My men are only flesh and blood. I do not feel like punishing any transgressions which you will cause by appearing like this before them."

"If your men as so carnally inclined, don't hold me culpable."

"I am not in the mood for your provocations! If ye canna behave in a seemly manner, then I will have ye locked in your chambers like an errant child. Though, as I see, child ye *airre* not."

Liandra drew the shawl tighter to her body. The action revealed more flesh than it hid.

Fascinated, Connal watched the spectacle. Slowly, he drew his eyes away from her shapely legs. "Why did you send for Fianna?"

"I needed her help. Because of your abduction, I'm without my servitors -"

"What a tragedy! You are now forced to rely on yourself to see to your daily needs. Perhaps this experience might teach you a lesson."

"It has already done that, Connal MacArran," Liandra snapped.

"Oh, aye?"

"Never to open my door to a stranger who cannot speak League Standard."

Connal threw back his head and laughed. Furious with his indifference, Liandra turned her back on him and stalked away. She picked up her comb and began to run it through her hair, wondering how Fianna could manage the task so easily. Her fingers were all thumbs.

"You are but a child," Connal said, taking the comb from her hand, before she could protest. "Let me." He seated her on a chair before the fire and stood behind her. Gently, he proceeded to untangle every knot in her hair.

"You do that very well, Connal MacArran," Liandra said, surprised by the husky tremor in her voice.

"Years of practice." Connal laughed.

Liandra rolled her eyes heavenward. How many times, and with how many women had he performed just such a task, no doubt as a preliminary to other, more intimate forms of foreplay? At that thought, her throat constricted painfully. Her breathing became rapid, to match the pace of blood flowing in her veins. The man was a walking contradiction of emotions and behaviour. Totally unstable. The League males of her experience were cultured. Predictable. But in their refinement they lacked vitality and spontaneity. Whatever Connal's failings - and Stars knew he had many - she could admire his proud individuality. His uniqueness.

The comb ran smoothly through her hair, and the warmth of his body so close to hers, melted her ice-cold flesh. His presence swirled all around her, through her. His fingers rested on her shoulder, searing her skin, while his other hand expertly tooled the comb.

Connal glanced down at her. The comb slid easily through her hair now cleared of every tangle. He fought the urge to rub his cheek against the silver hair, to inhale its scent. He would not be able to keep up the pretence of hair-combing for much longer. And why did he want to? His gaze slipped lower, along her thighs, slowly travelling all the way down to her slender ankles, back up her body to the swell of one breast beneath the loosely held shawl that covered her nakedness. In response to her, the blood began to sing in his veins. He closed his eyes and swallowed down, hard, determined not to fall victim to this alien witch's spell. *Or was it already too late, Connal MacArran?*

"When I first saw you in your apartment ... I had never before seen a woman with green hair. Now 'tis fading."

His voice was a husky whisper, so low, that Liandra felt certain he had inadvertently spoken his thoughts aloud.

"It's not my true colour," she said.

The combing shivered to a halt. "What did ye say?"

"I said green is not the natural colour of my hair."

"If that is so, why change it?"

"Because I don't like it."

"What I see beneath the green, 'tis the colour of starlight. Many women I know would be pleased to have such."

"If they had the technology at their disposal, they could alter it to any hue they desired. People should be allowed choices. My servitors indulge mine."

"A woman who wishes to change the beauty of her natural appearance, the more fool she," he retorted.

"I only -" Liandra pursed her lips. How could she reveal the truth to him? That the reason she kept her silver hair disguised had nothing to do with vanity, but practicality.

The curious and the deranged often pursued Asarian dream-weavers, to experience their legendary mystic sensuality. Her uniquely Asarian hair had been camouflaged since her first unfortunate experience at the age of twelve. She hadn't suffered physically from the man's ardent curiosity. Her security servitor had been able to incapacitate him. She'd been badly frightened, but nothing more. The memory of that encounter had made her wary. She had never revealed her true self to anyone. She could not tell Connal this. He was a stranger, and no one except another Asarian could understand.

"You be very quiet, Counsellor. Perhaps, because, I have the right of it? Do you easily change your appearance to accommodate the tastes and fancy of your clients?"

She turned to him. "My style is for my pleasure only. Not yours, nor any other! Mine, alone!"

Connal smiled his disbelief. "How many other Liandras are there? How does any man know which one is the real she? Perhaps even you no longer remember."

"I haven't forgotten whom I am."

"I have a feeling that by the time your visit to Caledonia is over, you are going to learn much more about yourself than you ever expected."

As his knuckles brushed over her shoulder

and down one arm, she shivered. Not from horror, or disgust. From pleasure. Pleasure from a barbarian's caress. She loathed everything about him, yet she wanted more of his touch.

Fight this, now, Liandra! You must for your sake as well as his!

Because if she allowed more physical contact, even if her rational half didn't want him, sometimes things happened which were beyond one's control. She'd been careful in the past to avoid relationships. But Connal's savage masculinity had managed to infiltrate her in ways no other male, no matter how gentle, had ever managed. She closed her eyes and when she opened them again, he stood before her, a strange, faraway way look on his face.

He took some of her moist hair and caressed it between his fingers, his gaze holding her prisoner. "The green hair was becoming, but the silver ... that I much prefer."

"I'm so pleased to have your approval," Liandra said, finding to her shock, that her voice was a throaty whisper.

He chuckled. "You will never have my approval, *ban-druidh*. That I promise you."

It was with visible effort, Liandra saw, that he pushed himself away from her, and without a backward glance, strode to the door. It closed behind him. Liandra sagged against the chair, wondering why it was so that whenever he left her, it was as if some invisible prop had been removed. His absence was preferable to his presence, wasn't it?

Liandra did not dare to answer that question. It was dangerous for her to be near him. And they still had to dream-share. They were playing with fire.

Chapter Seven

"Mistress?" Fianna asked.

Turning from her bed-chamber window, Liandra smiled. Behind Fianna, Connal strode into the room.

"Is everything prepared?" he demanded.

"Yes," Liandra said.

"You are certain this is safe?" Fianna asked, twisting her hands together. "I could not bear it if you were also lost to me, Connal."

"We know what we do, the witch and I. We shall find him, *ghraidh*." He gently touched her hand.

"There is no danger for you, Mistress?" Fianna asked.

Liandra smiled reassuringly. "This is my profession. Trust me."

"I am not certain I can do this," Fianna whispered.

"For someone new to the role of dream-search monitor, you are surprisingly adept. I trust you, *Maera*."

Fianna grimaced.

"You will not fail us," Connal said.

Liandra checked the crystal alignments of her

bed. When she glanced up, she saw Connal's eyes narrowed as he regarded her. That grey gaze of his was most unsettling, as was his frown.

"Is something wrong?" Liandra asked.

"Aye. Everything. I find your choice of clothing most inappropriate."

"And I find your Caledonian women's clothes quite impossible. Suffocating, in fact. But you're safe with me Connal MacArran, I'm not a sensualator."

"So you keep insisting, though you dress like one."

"How would you know?

"I have a healthy imagination."

"Truly? Is your interest objective, or personal? Perhaps you need the help of a sensualtor? I can refer you to one if that's the case."

"I need no therapy in that, or any regard!" he said, indignantly.

Fianna touched Connal's arm. "I have great foreboding of this plan. Garris would not want you to risk your life for him, *Tighearna*."

"I owe him my life, many times over. That you know. Now, no more foolishness. Please do not cry. You know how I hate the sight of a woman's tears. Besides, think you a bed can hold any fears for me, Fianna? *Tsk*! You should know me better than that." He laughed.

Liandra ground her teeth. The man was full of sexual innuendoes that made her uncomfortable. Doubly so, because very soon she was going to be sharing her bed with him, and the intimacy and passion of their last dream-sharing had rocked her to the depths of her being. With great effort, she put her fears to one side, lest they interfere with her work.

"Just remember, Fianna. Should any of the crystals darken, you must call us back. Otherwise we'll become forever lost in the dream-state."

"If I must awaken you so, I will not harm you?"

"Greater danger if you don't."

"But the last time you almost died!"

"Fianna!" Connal snapped.

"What do you mean I almost died?" Liandra asked.

Both Connal and Fianna avoided eye contact with her.

"I be sorry, *Tighearna*," Fianna whispered.

Connal ran a hand through his hair. "'Tis all right."

"What are you talking about?" Liandra demanded. "If you don't answer me, I won't perform the dream-search."

"Tell her, Fianna," Connal said.

"I ... spoke to Katrine."

"Katrine?"

"Our healer. She went with the *Tighearna* when ... when he abducted you. She told me how ill you were, that you nearly died."

Liandra frowned. "I was?" She turned to Connal.

"Aye. At the end of the dream, I removed your dreamer's cap. You screamed and then went into convulsions.'

"You could have killed me!" Liandra whispered.

"I didna' know removing the cap would effect ye so." Connal said huskily.

"But Liandra, do you not recall? Katrine said you near screamed down the walls before she managed to sedate you." Fianna said.

"I was in brain shock. I'm glad I don't remember it." Liandra shuddered. Very few Asarians weavers who had been torn from their dreams survived the experience. She had been lucky. Especially so, given that Connal and his healer had no way of knowing how to treat her. Pure blind luck had saved her. Liandra closed her mind against what might have been. She had to concentrate on the present. "And is that why you're afraid to monitor me, Fianna?"

"Aye."

"If the dream goes badly, you must take the two main crystals from the alignment. That will bring me back from the dream without danger. Just don't touch my dreamer's cap."

"I ... I understand."

"We rely on you, Fia," Connal said. "Dougall is outside if you need him. His orders are to admit no one to this chamber, unless you ask it. I want no interference when Liandra and I are together." He held out his hand. "Now, Fianna, give me the *claidheamh-mor*."

Connal passed over a heavy leather scabbard to Liandra. Shuddering in disgust, she slowly drew the great sword from its sheath.

"This belongs to Garris. Can you get your focus from it?"

Liandra sat down on the crystal bed, holding the sword. She picked up several auras - Fianna's and Connal's. But Garris's vivacity was stronger - unaffected arrogance tempered by an individual humour. Overriding everything was an all-consuming love for Fianna. That unique resonance would make it easy to home in on its owner.

"*Ban-druidh*?"

"I can see him."

"Let us get this over with, Counsellor Tavor."

Connal reclined on the coverlet and waited patiently while Liandra fitted the cap to his head. Once he was ready, she lay at his side, pulled on her bejewelled dreamer's cap and closed her eyes.

As always the swirling lights and sounds quickly dragged her down into the dream-dimension...

The cold and darkness were a surprise. She willed the light and warmth to come to her, and they did, reluctantly, as if some other force was controlling her dream. And that was impossible.

"Liandra?"

"Here, Connal."

He slowly joined her side, his image solidifying beside hers. "Which way?"

Liandra carried Garris' sword, only in the

dream-state it was no longer an object of metal, but pulsing light. It thrummed with Garris' distinctive vibrations.

"He's in this direction."

They entered another dream-dimension where the purple sky was threaded with rivulets of silver and gold. The ground beneath their feet became a pale green, shimmering like a carpet of emeralds which stretched in all directions as far as the eye could see.

Garris? Liandra sent telepathically.

"Who is there?" he responded, weakly.

"Wait -" Even as Liandra called out, she sensed the distance grow between them.

She and Connal followed him across the landscape, not walking, just flowing. They covered enormous distances in the space between two heart beats. A strange way to measure it, Liandra thought. She heard Connal laugh in response.

"This landscape is of your making?" he asked.

"Yes. Do you like it?"

"I much prefer Caledonia."

"Is this better?" she asked. The scenery twisted in on itself. They now walked across rolling green and purple fields.

"'Tis still not as vibrant as home. Thank you for the consideration. Does it take much for you to maintain this illusion?"

"Yes."

"Then do not do it for my sake. Conserve your strength for what lies ahead."

"As you wish."

Liandra allowed the dream-scape to revert to the colours of her crystals, though here and there she could see a sickly green taint that had nothing to do with her. As she tried to focus on it, it retreated.

Though they walked for hours, Garris remained distant. Even the emanations of the sword she carried were weaker.

"I need to rest," Liandra said, tiredly. She imaged a low stool and sat down upon it.

Connal paced up and down, the ethereal substance of the dream-state swirling around him like a cape.

"Must you do that? It's very distracting."

"I like not this place! And the waiting sets my teeth on edge. How much longer?"

"Garris is far away. It's difficult to reach him. Please try and keep still."

Liandra bent her head and concentrated, slowly slipping into a deeper state. She probed and called, over and over.

Connal sat back on his haunches, his every nerve tingling with a warning he could not understand. By Arran, he did not like this! Not one bit. And the witch ... He glanced away, though ever his eyes, as if by their own accord were drawn back to her. He tried to ignore the way her gown clung to the contours of her body, highlighting and emphasising her sweet curves.

Aye, she was enough to drive a man to distraction! How could he find her so comely?

She seemed so unaware of her beauty and the effect she was having on him. *Damn her!* She must know. She had told him she was empathic, the skill being necessary for her work. So she must be aware. She was teasing him - that was it! As a woman well versed in the art of seduction, she knew what she was doing. Only too well ! How many clients had she in the past? Connal swore beneath his breath and impatiently tore fingers through his hair.

"What's wrong?" Liandra asked.

"Nothing."

"You're angry and confused."

"How do you know? Are ye reading my thoughts?"

"It's more sensing your feelings. Our minds are united by my bed and the dreamer's caps."

"If we be so connected, why ask what it is that worries me? Read my mind and have your answer, *ban-druidh*!"

"I told you before I never share my mind with another, unless that one is willing. None of my profession would consider doing such a thing."

Connal folded his arms. "Is it not a little ironic to have ethics in this regard when in other respects you do not?"

"I don't know what you mean. We haven't got time for this, Connal. Will you tell me what's wrong? Your worry is disrupting my concentration."

"Why do you always wear such clothes that

leave little to the imagination?"

Liandra glanced down at herself. She smiled, thinking what he would say if he should see her dressed in her usual clothes. If he was disturbed by this gown, he'd have a seizure if he saw her in her body-fitting suits. She gasped as her clothing suddenly transformed itself into a Caledonian creation; long, voluminous and totally impractical!

"Much better," Connal said. "Now you look like a lady."

"How dare you!"

Liandra struggled against his imaging, surprised by the strength of his control. For a time her robe was Asarian, then as Connal gained the upper hand, her clothes became Caledonian. They battled hard for mastery of the illusion.

"Connal, stop what you're doing. This is my dream."

He laughed, slowly relinquishing his imaging. Moments later, Connal found himself robed in a trailing Asarian gown, which left much of his chest bare. It flowed around his body, teasing and caressing in a sultry seductive manner, almost as if it had a life of its own.

"*Ban-druidh!*"

"Two can play at the game you started, Connal MacArran. Now you look almost civilised."

"Release me, at once!"

She smiled up at him. Allowing her imaging

134

to fade, he reverted back to the barbarian she knew ...

"I would prefer that you not call me a barbarian. 'Tis a wrong you do me."

"I'll stop calling you barbarian if you stop calling me *ban-druidh*."

Connal shrugged. "You do not like my epithet? It does become you."

As she glanced up at him their gazes met. For a moment there was something in the turbulent grey depths of his eyes she had not seen before. A knot formed in the pit of her stomach, and tension spiralled outwards in an all-consuming tide which left her weak and trembling. She drew in a sharp breath as the memory of Connal in the Asarian gown came to mind. Why choose to dress him in the traditional bonding robe? Its style suited the delicacy of an Asarian male, but it looked totally incongruous against Connal MacArran's masculinity. She hadn't imaged it on purpose, it had just happened, though she hadn't decorated his face with the stylistic paint of a bond-mate. She almost smiled at the thought, wondering despite herself what he would look like if she did.

"Are you ready to resume your search?" Connal's steady voice drew her thoughts back. Once more he had assumed the facade of a man in control, though Liandra knew it for a deception. His inner turmoil reached her in a clear, strong assault.

He held out his hand and she allowed him to

raise her to her feet. They headed towards the shining gold horizon, and it was only a long time later that Liandra realised Connal still held her hand. For once she did not mind his touch. His warmth and strength were comforting in a place which normally held no apprehension for her.

Liandra came up against the black void as if she had slammed into a solid stone wall. As she staggered back Connal steadied her.

"What is it, Liandra?"

"Something ... I've never encountered before."

Liandra concentrated and probed deeper. Its vibrations were weak. *What in Seven Stars was it?*

"What be there?" Connal followed the direction of her gaze.

"A shadow. I believe it's a machine of some sort. It's ... Almost as if it exists simultaneously in the real world and here. I don't understand, because machines can't enter the dream-state." She glanced at Connal. Something fleeting ... his hastily blocked thought. "Do you know what this is?" she asked, suspiciously.

"How could I? I canna' even see the *infairrnal* thing!"

She heard someone ... a voice calling ... and even as she concentrated, the spectral-sword in her hand flared into life. Unable to control it, she was dragged away, her hand wrenched from Connal's grasp.

"Connal -" she cried and he lunged forward

to help her. Too late.

Out of control, she plummeted down a long, black tunnel. She closed her eyes against the sickening motion. Finally, her descent slowed. Halted. She felt the presence of another and opened her eyes.

"Garris?" she whispered.

He stood from where he had been crouching in the darkness. His shirt hung in filthy tatters about his chest that, like his arms, were criss-crossed with dozens of tiny scratches. She hastily blocked away his fear.

"I'm Liandra. Connal and I are here to help you."

"Arran's Mercy! Con, are you truly here?" Garris demanded of the darkness.

Moments later, Connal struggled to materialise beside her. "Liandra, do not leave me behind again! 'Tis my kinsman we are seeking." His image shivered before solidifying. "Garris -"

"Get away while you still can ... not safe ..." Garris choked out. His outline wavered and disappeared.

"Garris, where are you?" Connal shouted. The dream-scape rippled.

"I do not know..." His reply, the faintness of his voice was testimony to the distance between them. "They have -"

"Stay, Garris. You must obey me!" Liandra tried to bind him to her, though the force of her command hurt every nerve in her body. She was so close to finding him ... so close ... she mustn't fail this time! Then all about became sickly green-black. She cried out in alarm as the dream-claymore was torn from her fingers. She commanded it back. It almost returned to her outstretched hands. With a sound like breaking glass the shadow-sword dissipated into a thousand shards of light.

She was hurled backwards, the dream-state mists, reflecting her pain, were tinged red. She struggled against the force drawing her down. As she plummeted through the dream-scape, she felt the life-force tearing from her. Quickly she built a light shield around her body to impede the drain. For how long and how far she fell, she didn't know. When she finally came to her senses she lay sprawled on the ground. Wearily she raised her head.

"Connal?" Silence her only answer. About her, she felt a consciousness. "Who are you?"

"L..L...iandra."

She knew that voice. "Jalinda?"

"Danger, Liandra!" Jalinda cried.

"Jalinda?" Liandra gasped in shock at the form which slowly solidified before her. Jalinda's once beautiful face and body were now emaciated, her life-force very weak.

"I'm captive here, Liandra. You must escape -" Her image shivered into nothingness.

"No, wait!" Liandra rushed after her, on and on, trying to hold Jalinda to her. Her friend vanished into the mists.

Liandra carefully probed outwards, and caught the faint vibrations of other Asarian minds. Like Jalinda, their auras were also wrong; twisted, distorted, fearful. Some were close to death. Alone, she could not help them. Connal, where was he?

"Here, *ban-druidh*."

He emerged from the mists, and without thinking Liandra rushed into his arms.

Momentarily taken aback by her action, his arms tightened about her as he caught her fear and sorrow. Gently, he stroked her hair. "Do not be afraid," he said. "What happened? Where's Garris?"

"I'm not sure. The dream-scape is wrong."

Connal held her out at arm's length. "You know little, Weaver. Why? This is your dream!"

Liandra shook her head. "There's something else here fighting me for control of it."

"What be here with us?" With eyes narrowed, Connal glanced around.

"When you and I entered the dream-search back in my League apartment, just at the end, I sensed something. It's here, again, this time stronger. But when I try to focus on it, it disappears." Liandra shuddered and sank to the ground. "It's draining me."

Connal knelt before her and took her hands between his own. "You be as cold as ice."

A little distance away, a fire blazed into existence. Liandra felt Connal lift her into his arms and carry her to it. "You did this?" she asked.

"This be my dream, too, so I can make whatever I wish appear." He knelt with her before the fire and wrapped his arms around her body, holding her close. "We must find Garris."

"I've lost his sword." Liandra sighed and marshalled what little strength she had. "I'll try to re-gain my focus."

"Later! Rest for now."

"I-"

"No, Liandra, listen to me! A warrior knows his limitations and accepts them. Better to rest awhile than fail later when the battle's fought merely because you were too impatient or arrogant to admit your limitations."

"I'm not a warrior."

"You fight like a warrior in your own way." He smiled tenderly. "We Caledonians have an old saying ... *it is not known what sword is in the sheath till it is drawn*. For you, 'tis very apt. Before this dream you kept your valour hidden. You fight valiantly. Now, rest! Please."

She leaned against him, and he shifted his body to accommodate her more comfortably. She closed her eyes, content to feel him against her, feel that powerful male aura which blazed strong and clear about him, and his scent ... of herbs and musk ... it coiled into her every cell. Now who was weaving a spell? This time it was Connal MacArran. And his was a very potent magic. As old as time ... It felt so good to have his warmth and strength all about .*Too good*. She didn't want this dream-search ending like the other -

"I will not be falling into your dream-spell again, *ban-druidh*," he whispered against her ear. "If you do not trust yourself, then trust me. I can control myself." He laughed gently.

"Meaning I can't? Even if I wanted to *share*, in my present state, I haven't the energy to spare."

"Then I be safe!" Connal laughed. He rested his cheek against her head. Her perfume, which had haunted him with such alluring intoxication, flowed around him. As he breathed deeper, its sweetness spiralled down through his body, causing his muscles to clench, the blood to sing in his veins. Another of her spells, a charm to coax and tease her clients? He was certain, though, it was her own body scent, not some artificial redolence. Unlike any other woman he had experienced.

He smiled at that. Of course she was not like any other woman he had known. How could she be? Liandra was an off-worlder. An alien witch who was also a warrior. His initial surprise at that discovery, was now replaced by pride. Pride, that she fought so tenaciously to locate Garris, when he had believed no League member had the stomach for true battle. A mystery and a contradiction, his *ban-druidh*!

HIS ban-druidh? She would not like to think of herself as his, though it brought him a curious satisfaction. He rubbed his face against the silken texture of her silver hair. Hair the colour of star-light ...

Liandra started awake to the sound of someone calling her name. Strength tempered with gentleness held her close. Against her cheek she felt the slow, rhythmic beat of a heart.

The summons came again, a familiar, feather-soft caress. "Liandra?"

"Father!"

Connal turned her in his arms to look at her. "What is it?"

"My father sends for me." She struggled to her feet and probed far out into the dream landscape. "Where are you?" No answer, just swirling dark mist.

"Can I help you, *ban-druidh*?"

"Give me your strength."

"You have it," Connal said, holding out his hand to her.

She smiled and cupped his hand between her palms. "I mean mind to mind. It's the only way."

"I canna' do -"

"Connal, please. Oh ... *No*! Don't!"

A green-black cloud swirled around her. It severed her mental shield, and plunging inwards, raped her consciousness. Hatred coiled itself around her. She fought against the psychic invasion. In response, relentless malice pierced her mind. She dropped to her knees, holding her head, trying not to cry. The assault intensified. She heard screaming. Her screaming. Dimly she felt Connal raise her into his arms.

"Damn it, whatever ye be!" Connal shouted

at the cloud. "Fight me if you will, leave her alone. By Arran you shall pay for every hurt done to her! End the dream, Liandra. End it now!"

Liandra sent out her command to the bed, and the mist swirled with a shimmering oscillation of colours. Her mind touched the familiar crystal emanations. Almost she could reach the source. She cast out as strongly as she could, trying to follow the rainbow-hued path home. She caught a glimpse of her real-world self and Connal lying on the bed, bodies entwined. Fianna sat beside them, monitoring.

Liandra felt herself wrenched back into darkness. Something was there beside her. Again, like electrified tentacles, it attached itself to her aura, sucking out her life force. She flung up her strongest mental barrier. "No! Get out!" she screamed.

A triumphant, chiming sound, like perverted laughter, echoed in the darkness as she collapsed on the ground at Connal's feet.

Crouching protectively over her, he addressed the void. "'Tis a fight ye want then, is it? Then come to me and get it!"

Through her tears of pain, Liandra watched as his image blurred, then solidified. Still dressed in his linen shirt and kilt, over all he wore silver-studded leather tabard, at his side a long dagger and in his hand a claymore. He brandished it in the mist.

"It's useless, Connal, you can't fight that way."

"Have ye given up, then?"

"No, dammit, I haven't. I never give up. You should know that!"

"Aye." He hunkered down beside her, his sword across his knees. Gently, he reached out to caress her cheek. "Just who, or what, do we fight, Liandra?"

"I'm not certain. I only sense its terrible hatred."

"If it can feel, then 'tis alive, our enemy?"

"I -"

"L...iandraaa..." A male voice echoed about them, and the dream-scape pulsed.

"What be that?" Connal demanded.

Even as he spoke, he spun around, sword gracefully arcing through the air. Liandra marvelled at his fluid speed.

"Liiianndraa."

"Father. Here. Over here."

She reached out and touched her father's consciousness. Other Asarian minds added strength to his sending. The colours of his aura eddied around her, caressing, energising, before it was wrenched away, to be replaced by darkness and distress.

"Liandra?" Connal frowned at her. She raised her eyes to meet his. He felt something. A fleeting touch. Definitely not his imagination, he sensed her fear and fatigue.

"Connal, the dream-dimension has been corrupted. We're trapped here!"

As he went to take her into his arms, to comfort her, to give her strength and courage, he hesitated. She did not enjoy his touch. He must try other means to rally her.

"Try again, damn you! You said you are a professional - then prove it! So far all I have seen from you is a lot of wailing. You are ready to admit defeat before the battle's even begun. I told you no Leaguer has the stomach for a good fight. I have the right of it, *ban-druidh*!"

"Why, *you*!"

Her anger burst forth in a blinding surge that she directed through the haze. It slowly parted. She felt the emanations of her real-world body. Just a little further and she would be able to merge ... The searing touch exploded into her every nerve. She suppressed her cry as she struggled against the force that pulled her back. She must fight. *Must*! When she opened her eyes, she found herself in Connal's arms. His cheek rested against her head.

"Sorry, Liandra," he said. "For causing you hurt. That last attack touched even me." He lifted her into his arms.

"What are you doing?"

"Taking you to safety."

Liandra watched as he concentrated on the dark mists. Slowly it gave way to reveal a cave in the side of a heather-clad hill. He gently deposited her at the entrance and moments later a small fire sprang into life.

She glanced down at it, then up at him. "You dream-image very clearly."

"Thank you for the compliment." He reached

out and cupped her cheek, his fingers gently caressing. "We need to marshal our strength. I do not know about you *ban-druidh*, but I am famished. I am going to conjure up some food. And you?"

"I'm not hungry."

"Suit yourself."

Connal sat cross-legged by the cave entrance and ate. She watched him for a time, the hollowness within her growing every minute. She thought about nourishment, and a long glass of blue liquid solidified in her hand. She drank it down in one gulp. It did little to ease the emptiness inside.

Connal eyed her shrewdly. Again, he could sense her foreboding. It matched his own. He kept a tight rein on his thoughts, in case she picked up his concern. She had more than enough to worry about, without his fears adding to hers. "Try a little of this," Connal said, holding out some of his food.

"What is it?"

"Blueberry tart." He grinned ruefully. "My favourite. I will become as fat as Dougall. 'Twill be my undoing. Unless, of course, a green-haired *ban-druidh* gets me first."

"My hair is now silver," she retorted.

"Aye, 'tis, though doubtless if you had your way it would soon again be green."

Ignoring his teasing, she tentatively, took a piece of the tart and bit into it.

Connal watched her, a brow raised in silent

enquiry as she finished.

"It has a certain ... appeal," she said.

He laughed. "High praise from you, indeed! It would not hurt you to say you enjoyed it."

"Very well, I enjoyed it. Are you satisfied?"

"And I thought your acid tongue might be improved by the sweetness from the tart. Tsk!"

Liandra smiled. Connal's teasing had dispelled her melancholy, at least for a moment. Now, as she glanced around, the gloom descended upon her, again. She paced up and down, probing the darkness, finding that everywhere she quested the barriers were erected so that no thought could reach her, nor could she escape. She shivered. "It's getting cold."

The wind began to howl around them, and they retreated further in the cave. Heavy rain pelted down, before turning to hail. Great chunks of green ice crashed against the cave's entrance.

Connal imaged a thick fur-lined cloak which he wrapped around himself. He drew Liandra back against his body, enfolding them both in the warm mantle.

"Let it alone, Liandra," he said, as he felt her summoning her strength to counteract the dream-scape. "Whatever it is that produced this tempest, if we ignore it, maybe it will go away."

"But -"

"Let it be, I say!"

"If that's what you want," she said.

"Aye, 'tis."

The storm did not lessen with the passage of time, if anything it became worse. The noise grated on her nerves. How she needed some peace and quiet, or something to take her mind from the violence outside. Connal's arms around her were comforting, but it wasn't enough.

"Connal?"

"Aye?"

"May I ask you something?"

"If you wish."

"The oaths you use, by Arran, Arran's Mercy. Who is this Arran?"

"Why so curious, now?"

Because I need to hear your voice. It's soothing and melodic. But she couldn't tell such an insufferably conceited barbarian that. "Please, I'd like to know."

"Arran was the first Caledonian. It was he who gave us our laws, our way of life."

Liandra nodded. Every world had its creation mythology. "He's a god then?"

Connal chuckled. "No, a true man. I am from his line, in direct descent, hence I have the right to be called MacArran. MacArran means Son of Arran. I am his only living heir. Dougall -"

At his silence, Liandra turned to look up at him. "Yes, you were going to tell me more."

Connal grinned ruefully. "Dougall gets nervous. 'Tis his age, I tell him. He berates me for my tardiness in taking a wife and producing an heir, or heirs more like. As the last MacArran if something should happen to me, the line ends. He, like the rest of my people, is afraid I will not do my duty."

"And why are you so remiss in your responsibilities?"

Connal laughed. "I have yet to find the right woman. Arran's Mercy! If I have to wed, at least let me find a wife I can ... tolerate. To join solely for the sake of producing an heir is monstrous. Though in the past, it was so. Blood-lines were considered of paramount importance."

"You have Jenna." Her own words caused her heart to turn in her breast.

"Aye, I *have* Mistress MacLeod. That is pleasure and ..."

"Yes?"

"No, *ban-druidh*. 'Tis my business and I do not ever speak so freely with any as I have done with you. Let a man keep some secrets."

"Of course."

"And what about you, Liandra? No husband to keep you at home and stop you plying your trade across the galaxy?"

"No life-mate would ever consider imposing their will on their partner. Is that how it is on Caledonia? A partner is not free to pursue their calling?"

"It would depend upon the profession. Most women are content to be wives and mothers."

"So, on your world a man may have a career,

149

a woman may not. How typical!"

"There is nothing more important than caring for a husband and family."

"I've never met anyone so intractable."

Connal laughed. "'Tis the pot calling the kettle black!"

She smiled to herself and began the ritual to purge her mind and body of all thought. Thanks to Connal, she was feeling better. Now, she needed to rest. She'd relax for a few moments...

How long she slept, she did not know. She came slowly awake finding herself pressed against Connal's body. He lay asleep, one of his legs thrown casually across her knees, his body wedged intimately into her. Slowly, tentatively, she reached out and stroked his cheek.

How much gentler he looked, younger, now that sleep softened his features. She brushed back the wild array of hair from his face and shoulders. Running her fingers through the raven mane, she marvelled at its soft texture. She traced a thumb over his cheek, over his lips. He was beautiful, this arrogant barbarian. *If only* ... she snatched back the thought as it rose to her consciousness. Too late, though, for the blood began to thrum in her body in an exhilarating tide which she had never wanted nor ever experienced until Connal MacArran had entered her life.

Eyelids snapped open.

Liandra smiled as his eyes focused on her, at

first steel-harsh, then softer grey, tender, once he realised it was she. He made no move to extricate his body from hers, and as Liandra snuggled even closer against him, letting his warmth flow into her, his arms tightened about her. His fingers stroked her bare back.

"*Ban-druidh.*"

"Yes?"

He sighed. "'Tis nothing."

He wanted to tell her something, she could feel it. Perhaps it was her turn to humour him. "Garris called you Con. I haven't heard it used before."

Connal smiled. Mentally and physically attuned in the dream-state, Liandra felt his reactions as keenly as if he had spoken them aloud. Not for her, she knew, but for Garris, Connal's aura glowed blue, the colour of love. It nuzzled against her own body-field in lapping strokes. Then it receded, but the remnants of it left her inflamed. Did Connal know what he had just done? She fought against the urge to return his intimate caress.

"You haven't answered me, Connal," she reminded him.

When he spoke his voice was husky. "Only Garris has the right to use my shortened name. He and I grew up together. I was fosterling in his father's house."

"You lived apart from your parents?"

"'Tis often the way for the son of a *Tighearna*. Besides which, my father and I were not close."

"Why?"

His thoughts and emotions surged through her. Bitterness. Sorrow. Hurt. A boy's confusion at the rejection by a father whom he idolised. Such treatment must have tempered him, his independence coming at a very young age. Sorrow coursed through her, her desire very real to cosset this man whom love had not touched.

Connal laughed gently. "Spare me your sympathy, *ban-druidh*. My foster-father loved me truly. And as I grew older, I had affection from other quarters."

She caught images from his memory. Faces of girls and women flashed before her eyes. He had sampled many sweet moments in his youth, and as a man. In response there was a sharp pang of envy, a reminder of her own life spent without a partner. No Asarian love-call to inflame her.

"And what of your parents? Where are they now?" Liandra asked.

"My mother died when I was five. My father never recovered from it. When I came to manhood, I finally understood his rejection of me. I was very much like my mother, so ever I reminded him of his loss." Connal smiled grimly. "My father and I had just started to heal the rift between us when he was killed in an accident ten years ago. At the age of twenty-three, I did not want the burden of clan leader. Fate decreed otherwise."

"Fate does have a way of going against one's wishes," she said wistfully, running a finger over his cheek.

Connal smiled, and placed his hand over hers. He kissed her fingers. "Now, if you will, there are other things we must do besides talk. Because I have a feeling that if we lie here much longer, this dream-search may end like our first. Neither of us want that."

"No," she replied. Though if it was the case, why did she feel the severing so keenly when he lifted her gently, but firmly away?

Connal struggled to his feet. "The wind has died down," he said looking out across the bleak landscape.

Liandra joined his side, smoothing down her crumpled gown. She felt terrible, and no doubt looked just as bad. Her flesh itched and her hair ... it must be in hundreds of tangles. She could rectify her appearance in the blink of an eye, except that would be a waste of energy. She needed every iota of strength for what lay ahead.

"What must we do to escape this prison?" Connal asked.

"Alone, I'm powerless."

"What about your father? Can you reach him?"

Liandra concentrated. "No," she said, finally. "It's as if he doesn't exist."

Connal raised a dark brow. "There must be something we can do?"

"There is a way. You won't like it."

"Go on."

"To reach Fianna, I must supplement my strength with yours. However, I'm not going to be able to help Garris."

"First things first. Garris will not be thanking us if we become ensnared in this place. How can you gain my strength?"

"Mind to mind."

Liandra saw the tightening of his jaw, the harshness of his eyes. He tried to hide his dismay from her.

"I do not have the skill to do what you ask."

"You don't have to, I can take what I need. It's the only way."

"I like it not!"

"It'll be nothing worse than a dream-sharing. I know what I'm doing."

"'Tis disgusting, the thought of something, someone, touching my mind."

"Is it the idea you find disgusting, or me?" she asked, her voice a whisper.

Connal frowned at her. He stroked the back of her hand. "No, Liandra! How can I explain? To you such skills are second nature, to me ..." He shook his head. "'Tis abhorrent to any Caledonian."

"You don't have to be afraid, I won't try to read your mind. It's only your mental strength I need."

"I prefer a good, honest fight, rather than all this! Are ye certain 'tis the only way?"

Liandra nodded.

"Then get on with it, *ban-druidh*!"

She made Connal sit before her. Reaching out, she cupped his face between her hands and concentrated. Deeper and deeper she went. She felt Connal's strength, the outer limits of his mind, and retreated from that powerful masculinity. Tentatively she returned, and drawing on his strength, she propelled her thoughts outwards, probing the darkness for time uncounted.

Connal heard music like the tinkling of crystals. Like a sultry mantle, purple, silver and gold lights swirled in and around him. Her musky scent permeated his every cell. He breathed in deeply. Gently, so very gently, he felt her touch his mind. He gasped in dismay, forcing himself not to pull away. Perspiration trickled down his spine. Her mind caressed, then retreated. Carefully, she drew strength from him. His gift flowed to her in the colours of the MacArran tartan.

This isna' so bad. Enjoyable, almost - Connal gasped at his own thoughts. Liandra's laughter flowed over him, like warm honey.

Minutes passed. Slowly, the mists parted. The ghostly silhouette of Castle MacArran loomed up ahead. Together they plunged through the structure, coming at last to Liandra's chamber. They saw the real-life Liandra and Connal upon the bed. Fianna was leaning over them, trying to rouse them from their sleep.

"Fianna! Bring us back! Remove the crystals.

Now!"

She did not respond.

As Liandra tried to send a more powerful summons, a bolt of pure agony sliced through her. Instantly their link was severed. Both she and Connal cried out in agony as they found themselves, once more, back in the dream dimension.

"Give us the Asarian. You and your kinsman can go free." A dozen voices demanded in unison.

"What the -" Connal began. He bit back his cry as minds washed over him in silent, intimate probings. Then he was discarded, considered of no worth. But they sent him pain just for the pleasure of inflicting it. He shuddered, sickened to the depths of his soul by their touch, by their cruelty.

Liandra stared into the void. The green-black cloud swirled through the dream-scape. Voices whispered, just on the periphery of her hearing. "Who are you?" she demanded.

Again, the hatred lanced, like burning needles. It drank her essence, all that she was, her every thought. But in that attack the enemy's defences were down. She now knew what she faced.

"They're aliens!" Pain enveloped her. She staggered against Connal. His arms around her supported and steadied.

"*Coimheach*?" His eyes, as dark as midnight, pierced the sickly green mist.

Liandra drew in a gasping breath. The alien

consciousness retreated from her, to hover just on the edge of her thoughts. They hadn't given up the fight, merely withdrawn to taunt her, that much she could understand.

"Now I know why I couldn't touch them, they're so different from any other life I've ever encountered."

"Is it they who hold us prisoner?" Connal asked.

"Yes. But why?" Liandra focused every ounce of energy on her probing. She sensed them, saw them for what they truly were. Their surprise at her intrusive inspection battered against her, then without apparent effort, she was flung aside.

Garris' image wavered before them. "*Tighearna.* 'Tis the woman they want. Give her to them and you and I can go free."

"I will na' bandy words with ye. Ye are not Garris, for he is no coward to buy his life with that of another. Did ye hear that, *deamhan*? I will na' be buying my life, or Garris' with the life of another."

"Fool!' the alien minds grated.

"Aye, 'tis glad I am to be called that! Better a fool than a mind-touching coward."

Hideous laughter echoed in his mind.

"You should have given them what they wanted," Liandra whispered.

"Do you value your life so little, *ban-druidh*?"

"No. Two lives for mine, it seems a fair exchange."

"Not to me."

"Listen to the Asarian!"

"Aliens! Arran damn you!" Connal's anger flamed outwards, igniting the dream-scape for a moment, so that it burned scarlet and orange.

Caught up in that all-consuming rage, Liandra shielded herself as hurtful blows were exchanged, parried backwards and forwards between Connal and the minds of their captors. She was lifted and then dragged back and forth as they battled over possession of her. Pain seared her body like fire. Something grasped her arm, nails raking her skin.

"Give us the woman. Give us the woman!" alien voices chanted.

Connal placed Liandra behind him, his body shielding hers, while his sword swept before him in a powerful arc, that scattered the darkening mist. "Get you gone, ye *deamhans!*"

The enemy screamed. Liandra felt their hold on the dream diminish. Just a fraction. They drew back in a silent measuring of their new opponent. Then the attack began in earnest.

Bolts of blazing green light flew towards Connal. As he twisted away Liandra imaged a laser-shield around his body. The beams bounced off the barrier and fell to the ground, dissipating in a sickly green-black fire.

"My thanks. You saved my hide, *ghraidh*."

For a moment his figure fluctuated between dream-state reality and nothingness. Liandra cried out, thinking that the aliens had somehow managed to abduct him. Then he returned, solid. Real. A new Connal. Liandra stared up at him. Towering over her, dressed in his battle-armour, he made a formidable opponent for any creature.

He smiled "Does this meet with my lady's approval?"

"You look like a robot."

They both smiled at the shared memory.

"Why the armour? You told me once that no Caledonian would wear such a cowardly thing."

"Desperate times, Liandra, require desperate measures. Besides, I had the feeling this was the right thing to do."

As she probed outwards, she sensed the darkness retreating. Colours swirled around her. Cyclonic winds buffeted them. The green-black alien taint streaked away.

"Give me your hand, Liandra." Connal cried.

Just as her fingers grasped his, she was yanked away.

Abandoning his suit of armour, Connal pursued her. He caught up to her, dragging her back into his arms.

Their auras flamed red. Pain ripped through them both. They were falling ... falling into a dark chasm where no light or sound existed and she screamed over and over ... She clung to Connal for sanity. For life.

Chapter Eight

Hurt ... hurt so much. Hurt to breathe. To think.

She rested on something warm. A heavy weight across her back held her so tight she couldn't move. She struggled to consciousness to find herself clinging to a body. Such strength, it swirled around her. So unique. So welcome.

"Connal?" Her throat felt raw. She looked down at his pale face. Slowly he opened his eyes.

He smiled gently. "You are all right, *ghraidh*?"

"I've been better."

"'Tis proud I am of you, Liandra. You fought like a Caledonian wild-cat."

She smiled. "I assume that's a compliment?"

His lips sought hers, and she leaned into his kiss. His hands feathered inquisitively over her. When the tip of his tongue touched hers, she gasped, allowing him deeper access. She drew strength from him, from his kiss. It warmed her starving senses.

"Tighearna?"

Connal snapped his head sideways, his mouth instantly leaving hers. His momentary tenderness, was now replaced with tension.

Liandra felt him draw away from her; mentally and physically.

"Y ... you are here? Truly?" Fianna asked. Her face was gaunt, ashen.

Connal glanced at Liandra. "Is this another accursed dream?"

"No."

Connal gently lifted her away and swung himself over the bed. He rested at the side, head in his hands. It was only then that he noticed the blood staining his shirt. He was not wounded ... then whom?

He turned to see Liandra lying limply on her bed. Where moments ago she had been clinging to him, returning his kiss with passion, now she looked unto death. Leaning over, he drew her into his arms. She came unresisting.

Her gown hung in tatters. One sleeve had been totally shredded. Her arm bled profusely from seven furrows, as if some beast had used its talons against her.

"Liandra, ye be hurt. Why did ye not say? Fianna, have Dougall fetch Katrine. Quickly! *Ban-druidh,* take from me what you need. I am not afraid of your sharing."

Liandra closed her eyes and accepted his gift, drank in his strength and warmth. A little renewed, she glanced down, just becoming aware of the stinging pain in her arm. "Not right," she whispered. "Injuries sustained in the dream-state ... don't carry through into the real-world ... unless ..."

Connal smiled grimly. "'Tis a lot of incredible things have become reality of late! What were you to add? Unless - what?"

"Unless, somehow, the creatures have managed to penetrate the real-world. It's possible. There was some force tearing at the dimension."

"What you speak is gibberish to me."

"There's a belief that the fabric of space and time is multi-layered and that it's possible to journey from one dimension to the other. League science has been trying to achieve it for years."

"And you are saying these creatures have done so? That the dream-state we entered was more than just imagination? I cannot believe it."

"A mere dream could not do this to me. I think that where we were was a place between dream and reality."

"Arran's Mercy! Garris is there. How can I reach him?"

Connal pushed himself up from the bed, his muscles angrily protesting. He felt so weak, like a new-born babe. Yet tinged with the weakness was anger, revulsion, a myriad of other emotions swirling around to leave him unsteady on his feet.

Returning from her errand, Fianna handed Connal a goblet of wine. He drained its contents in one gulp.

"You were gone so long," Fianna said.

"How long?" Liandra asked as she struggled

to sit upright.

"Two days."

Connal swore beneath his breath.

"I thought I had lost you ... both of you," Fianna choked out. "After Garris' sword disappeared, I thought you would be taken from me at any moment. I could not wake you."

"And ever you remained at our side, *grahmhor*?" Connal gently touched her cheek. "I chose you well for the task. It must have been very frightening. 'Tis proud I am of you."

He brought a goblet of wine to Liandra and forced it between her chattering teeth.

"You asked for me, My Lord?"

Liandra turned at the sound of the new voice. A middle-aged woman stood by the doorway.

Connal beckoned her forward. "Quickly, Mistress, see to my guest."

"Who are you?" Liandra asked, pulling away, as the elderly woman bent over her. She had more than enough of strangers touching her.

"'Tis all right, Liandra. Katrine is my most trusted healer. She will see to your injuries."

Liandra reached for one of the crystals on her bed. "My bed can heal -"

"No! You shall not use this *infairrnal* contraption again. No telling what might happen if ye do. No! If you continue to argue, I will confiscate the bed. Now, lie still and let my healer aid you."

Katrine soothed her flesh with an ointment which smelled of herbs, then she bound

Liandra's arm in linen.

"Whatever you put on my arm, it's stopped the pain, Mistress Katrine. I'm doubly in your debt. Fianna told me you saved my life, before -"

"'Twas my duty." Katrine smiled, and turned her attention on Connal. "You must rest, *Tighearna*."

"I am well."

"You look unto death to me! Stubborn! You have always been so."

Connal managed to smile. "I will rest in awhile. Have someone send food and drink for Liandra and me."

"Aye." Katrine collected her healer's paraphernalia and hurried from the room.

Liandra forced herself upright in the bed. She still felt weak, and the room pitched and spun before her eyes. That was hardly surprising after what she had encountered.

Fianna stepped closer, and touched Connal's arm. "Were you able to find my Garris?"

"Aye," Connal said. "He be a prisoner."

"Oh, no!"

"As to where, I know not. Say by what, not whom. The creatures -"

"I do not understand."

"Neither do we. Not fully."

Connal explained what had occurred in the dream-state. Fianna's face remained impassive, though the more he spoke, the paler it became.

"Then there is no hope ..." Fianna bent her

head and Connal drew her gently against him, letting her sob into his shirt.

The pitiful sound tore at Liandra's senses, activating her counsellor's empathy. But something held her back. They might resent her alien interference in what was a private matter between Connal and his kinswoman. Liandra chewed her lower lip, torn between conflicting loyalties.

Connal held Fianna at arm's length. "I shall find him, *ghraidh*. That I promise you. I will follow -"

"No! You shall not place yourself in peril for Garris. He would not want it of you. Promise me your foolishness is at an end!"

Connal smiled, gently wiping the tears from Fianna's cheeks. "I must do what I can."

"You have already done more than enough." Fianna cast a meaningful glance towards Liandra. "My Lord -"

"Fianna, I know what I am about. Trust me."

"That is what Garris said, and look what happened to him!" Fianna shrugged herself free and turned away.

"Although I don't understand the circumstances which led Garris to the dream-dimension," Liandra said, "I do know that the aliens have used him as a lure to bring other dream weavers, besides myself, into the dream-dimension."

Connal stared at her. "You be certain?"

"As much as I can. I caught some of their

thoughts before-"

"Then Garris and I, we are to blame for all this mess?"

"It's just fate which brought you to me. They would have trapped me at another time."

Liandra watched as Fianna and Connal exchanged glances. "What is it you're not telling me?" she demanded.

Connal ran a hand through his hair, and refused to meet her eyes

A light knock on the door, and it opened slowly. With eyes averted, serving girls left trays of food and drink on the side table. Though they dared to look questioningly at Connal, his scowl sent them scurrying away.

Connal placed a tray on Liandra's knees.

"I'm not hungry," she said, trying to push it away.

"Just a little, Liandra. For once, humour me. Please."

He held out a spoon and she took it reluctantly. Swallowing the broth, its warmth hit the icy hollow in her stomach. Quickly, she dipped the spoon again, eating heartily, her appetite almost matching that of a Caledonian.

"I gather it meets with your approval?" he asked.

"Mmm," Liandra replied.

For a moment Connal watched her in amusement before he turned and attacked the steaming meal on his tray. Later, Fianna served them tea. After the second cup, Liandra felt her strength returning.

Connal eyed her shrewdly. "We have plans to make, Liandra. When you are well."

"I'm fine. Truly."

He raised a disbelieving brow. "I know you better than you think. Our sharing was most enlightening. Stubborn you be when it comes to your duty. I can respect that, except yours borders on folly."

Liandra smiled. The dream-search had been a surprise for her, too. Moments of intimacy and pleasantness, all overshadowed by the horror they had encountered. Curiously, at such a perilous time, Connal had been a tender, yet fierce protector. She looked at him as if through new eyes. It had been his indomitable barbarian strength that had kept the aliens at bay. Something that with all her experience, she had been unable to accomplish.

"The aliens are powerful, Connal. They took Garris's sword from me in reality, as well as in the dream. Should they find a way to infiltrate our space, they intend to invade. That much I learned from my sharing with them. But they're not strong enough. Not yet." Liandra chewed her lower lip. "I must warn my father."

"He was in the dream, so surely he must know as much as we."

"I don't know that. For the moment, the aliens are trapped in the dream-dimension. They must be contacted and helped."

"*Helped*? I would be sending them to oblivion -"

"No! They are entities, and mustn't be hurt. My father will know how to help them."

"And how do you propose to reach him?"

"Connal you must return me home -"

He sighed deeply, tiredly, dragging fingers through his dishevelled hair. "I cannot allow that."

"What?"

"'Tis my fault you be involved in this whole business. And now you have been hurt defending MacArran. 'Tis my duty to protect you. My honour -"

Liandra smiled. "That's very sweet of you, Connal, but I can look after myself. Truly! My father is the administrator of Asarian dream weavers. He's much stronger than me. Together we can assist these beings -"

"In explaining everything to your father, you will mention Caledonia."

"Yes. Already he's aware of you. He saw your dream-image."

Connal sucked in his breath. "Does he know my origins?"

"No."

"That is how it will remain."

"I don't understand."

Connal mentally braced himself for what was to follow. "I cannot allow you to return to the League, Liandra."

She stared up at him. The only sound in that suddenly still, cold room was the drumming of her heart in her ears. "Don't joke with me,

Connal."

"'Tis no joke, *ban-druidh*! For centuries Caledonia has remained isolated. Our world is shielded from discovery by outsiders. It galls me to realise that it was I, Garris and I, who have betrayed our people. But only to you, and to keep our whereabouts a secret, you must remain here."

"I will not." Liandra bit down her hysteria. *Calm ... calm ... deal rationally with him.* "More than this world is at stake, Connal. Already the aliens have imprisoned several Asarians. They'll die of their captivity. Even if you don't care about them, what about Garris?"

"Believe me, Liandra, I want none of your colleagues dead. Your father has been in the dream-state, so he knows of the menace. He can deal with it, effect a rescue. And I shall attend to the problem of Garris."

"I can't just do nothing, when my friends are fighting for their lives. I have to help."

"There be nothing you can do."

"I don't know Caledonia's location. If you return me, I swear I won't reveal anything about you."

"Circumstances have altered, Liandra. Before, I fully intended to release you once you found Garris, now I cannot. The risk - the consequences. I am sorry."

"*Sorry?* You conniving, lying barbarian! I've done everything you've asked and more ... endured your insults and savagery because you

169

promised that if I helped you find your kinsman you'd return me to my world. Well I have. And now you refuse to keep your word. Liar! I won't stay! I won't." Liandra stood up shakily from the bed.

"She has the right of it, Connal," Fianna said, gently. "You cannot keep her a prisoner forever. Besides the Council - "

"The Council will agree with what I do. Are you taking her side over mine? Your *Tighearna?*"

Fianna's pallor took on a grey hue. "Do not ask me to choose Connal."

"I think you have already made the choice, Mistress MacLeod."

Connal's kinswoman burst into tears.

"Leave her alone, Connal!" Liandra shouted.

He ran a hand across his eyes. Suddenly he felt so tired. "See you the danger? You have been but a few days on Caledonia, and already your influence has robbed me of someone who has been loyal to me all my life. If you were to leave, my world would be open to invasion by more insidious forces than the aliens we have battled. Loyalty would be divided and traded for the baubles of League science. I am responsible for you, Liandra. Your residence here will no longer be that of a prisoner. I can grant you much as my guest."

"*Guest ... prisoner.* What's the difference? But understand this, I will not stay here. I will return to my home."

"How so, *ban-druidh*?"

Liandra tossed her head, ignoring her weakness. The pain in her arm throbbed anew. "I have ways and means of reaching my father. If not physically, then mentally."

Connal frowned. He strode up to the bed. Before Liandra could stop him he had removed the four main crystals. "When you told Fianna about the workings of this contraption, 'tis a good thing I listened. I know by removing these you cannot enter the dream-state again, though your bed will be available to you for your other purposes. Forever more, these crystals remain with me."

Liandra flew at Connal, her fingers clawing at his hands. He held the crystals high above his head and with his other hand he kept her at bay.

"Liar! Thief! Give them back to me, at once!"

"Take these, Fianna, and get you gone!" Connal dropped the crystals into her hand while restraining Liandra.

Fianna fled to the door. She paused and turned imploringly to Connal.

"Go!" he shouted.

With a sob she raced away.

Furiously, Liandra tore herself free from Connal's grasp. "Return my property at once! Damn you!"

"No! I will not have you endanger your life, nor betray my people by your witchery."

"Why - you!" Liandra hurled herself at him.

Connal dodged her flailing fists. She beat

ineffectually against his chest. Taking her hands between his, he held her gently, but firmly.

"I am sorry, Liandra. 'Tis my people I must consider first and foremost. I did not know it would come to this. Truly. Believe -"

"Everything about you has been a lie!"

He frowned down at her. "Have a care, Liandra. I will suffer your temper and your insults this once, because I be to blame. However, do not overly try my patience."

Liandra wrenched herself away from him. As she paced the room, she saw Dougall and Angas hovering in the corridor, their eyes wide and disbelieving at the spectacle before them.

"What are you staring at?" She slammed the door in their faces.

"Hold *thairre*, woman!" Connal strode up to her. Taking her by the shoulders, he shook her once. "Understand this well! 'Tis my doing and mine alone which keeps ye here. Vent your anger on me if you must, but never upon my people or ye will regret it!"

"What more can you do to me?"

"Carry on as you have and find out."

"I'd turn you into a Slevian slime worm, only that's too good for you!"

Connal grinned.

"You won't find it so funny when I wither you on the spot!" Liandra cried.

"Where are your counsellor's ethics, now?"

Her hand arced towards his cheek.

Lightning fast, Connal intercepted the blow. Liandra found her hand held by his in a surprisingly gentle hold.

"I will not tolerate your violence, *ban-druidh*! No woman raises her hand against me. This time I forgive you. See?"

He raised her hand to his lips. Liandra stared as he tenderly kissed her knuckles. She shivered as his warm lips grazed her skin. She gasped in fury, in indignation. Heat raced through her body, dissipating her anger, replacing it with a more powerful emotion. Desire. Though she went to tear her hand away, his fingers curled even tighter around her.

"How dare you!"

"Always dare much, Liandra. You never know what you might reap." He smiled smugly. "I see you are somewhat pacified by my caress."

She pursed her lips. Humiliated and furious with him - with herself - Liandra tore free from his grasp and fled to the bathing-room. Shakily, she locked the door.

Think ... must think. Calm ... calm. No use, for once her training could not dispel her fury, her rage fuelled by her inexplicable reaction to his caress. Rage at herself for allowing that response. Rage at him for daring to touch her in the first place. She barely controlled the urge to smash every object in the bathing-room.

How long she angrily paced the confines of her prison, she did not know. A knock on the door startled her out of her frenzy.

"Come out, Liandra. You have sulked long enough. Come out now, or I will break the door down."

Liandra eyed the door in alarm. Her anger retreated in the face of his threat. She knew he would break it down in an instant. Arguing with Connal MacArran was not the way. She would have to outwit him.

Besides, if Connal had to force his entry to the bathing-room, he'd be in a fine temper. It would make dealing with him even more difficult, perhaps dangerous. He might do something unimaginable to her. Slowly, tentatively, she opened the door.

"Come out. You and I need to talk," Connal said.

"Talk about what? You've already determined what's to become of me. What can I possibly say to change your mind, barbarian?"

He smiled grimly. "I like it not that you call me barbarian. 'Tis you who are the savage. When have I ever raised my hand to you as you have tried to do to me?"

"I was provoked beyond endurance."

"As I have been, on many an occasion. Even so, you have never experienced any punishment such as a man may give an errant woman. Think on that a moment." He folded his arms and frowned at her. "As a guest of MacArran you shall want for nothing. You will be happy, here, that I promise you."

"By the Seven Stars! Do you think this barbarous place could make me happy?" Liandra swallowed her anger. She was an experienced counsellor, so the sooner she started acting like one the better. "Connal, why do you fear discovery of your world?"

"'Tis not something we discuss outside the clans. Perhaps one day I will be able to explain." He paused. "You have saved my life, and that is a debt MacArran pays."

"Then make recompense by returning me home, I won't reveal -"

"If that were only true. Perhaps I can trust you. But others? Word of us would eventually spread. The curious would besiege us. No, this is the best way."

"Best, for whom? What can you possibly hope to gain by keeping me prisoner?"

"Caledonia's freedom."

"In exchange for mine? Back in the dream-state you would not trade my life for yours and Garris'. What's the difference now?"

"Obviously a great deal. The loss of your freedom, for the sake of an entire world? Yours is a small price to pay."

"Because it's *me* who's doing the paying - again!" Liandra ran a hand across her face. "You can't remain forever isolated. It will be only a matter of time before the aliens infiltrate this space. You must get help."

"From the League? I think not. We on Caledonia have ways and means of protecting ourselves. We will fight this menace on our own terms. We have existed without League help in the past. We shall do so in the future."

"The League has so much to offer. What do you truly fear?"

"Contamination. An end to our culture. We have witnessed it before."

"Where? You know so much about us, or so you think. How so? You've kept yourself in isolation, or is that a lie, too?"

He frowned. "'Tis sorry I am that you believe me a liar. Although our world is shielded, we know what occurs outside our star system. We study the ways of our enemy. What we see, we like it not."

"The League is enemy to no one. Member planets revere the diversity of life. I've told you this before. We would never try to destroy your uniqueness. That would be a crime too great to contemplate!"

"What about the aliens we encountered in the dream?"

"They're different."

"And will you always be able to guarantee that another species would not try to do to us what was done to us in the dream?" Connal demanded.

"What do you mean?"

"The violation of our minds."

"The League has codes of conduct - "

"We govern ourselves by loyalty and honour. Our way is different to yours,

Liandra."

"Not so different as you would discover, if you truly took the time to understand. Believe me when I say you have nothing to fear from League discovery."

"I cannot risk losing all that we are, just on your word, Liandra. I am sorry. When you think on this, you shall see I have the right of it."

"The moons of Vesnar will turn purple before I think as you, Connal MacArran. I will not remain here. I - I'll escape."

He sighed deeply. "How will you leave? How can you find your way home without knowing from where it is you start?"

"I'll find a way."

"That is a hollow threat, childish in the extreme."

Liandra flung her hands to her hips. "You can't keep me prisoner here."

"How you live among us is your choice, Liandra. Prisoner or guest?"

"My father will look for me. He won't give up until he finds me." Liandra paused. "At least let me send a message to my parents to say that I'm well. After what happened in my dream-search they will fear the worst."

"I cannot risk even that, *ghraidh*. I am sorry."

"Do not ever call me darling, again!" Liandra paced the confines of the room. "You'll be sorry for what you do to me, barbarian."

"That sounds very much like a threat, Liandra. You know what I say to such."

"I will find a way to escape your tyranny. You'll pay for every insult. That's a promise."

She picked up a cushion and hurled it at him. Another and another sailed at his head. Ducking the projectiles, he retreated to the door.

"When your mood is more agreeable, *ban-druidh*, I will return and we can talk more sociably."

"Get out, and stay out! I'll never speak to you again - you lying barbarian."

Connal smiled grimly. "I can wait for as long as it takes for you to see my point of view."

"Your wait will last an eternity. I never want to see your ugly face again."

"Tsk! And I thought you liked me. You woke me with your caress when we dream-shared."

"That was before you revealed your true self. It was a moment of weakness, which you'll never see again. You'll live to regret what you've done to me."

"There is nothing I like more than a good challenge. I look forward to the contest." Connal laughed. "Call me when your temper has improved. You behave like a shrew, your screaming hurts my ears."

The door closed behind him and Liandra raced to it. Locked in, again. Blinking back the stinging tears of rage and desperation, she sagged against the door.

Calm down ... think!

Somehow, she would escape the Castle. There must be a way. Could she appeal to some higher authority? Fianna had said something about a Council. As in the League, perhaps Caledonia had a place where all leaders met for discussion and legislation. She would find out where they were and make them see reason and perhaps bring some judgment down upon Connal's arrogant, autocratic head. Abduction, imprisonment ... surely even such a barbarous place as Caledonia had laws against such? Connal MacArran would live to regret the day he came to her door. Of that she was certain!

Liandra's optimism lasted a matter of seconds. There were flaws in her plan. To put it into action, how long would it take? Days? Weeks? How many others would the aliens kidnap and destroy in the time it took her to make good her escape from the Castle?

Liandra shuddered. She knew the answer even before she allowed it a voice. She would have to use her bed for a dream-sending. Her father would have sensed the aliens already, but how much did he know of their intentions? Alleron Tavor might be the most powerful dream-weaver, but even he could become entrapped in the dream-state because she knew he wouldn't give up searching for her. She would have to contact him to explain what had happened. And that was going to be doubly difficult if she couldn't reveal the existence of Caledonia. She had other worlds to think about, other lives. Caledonia's secrecy might be sacrificed. What other choice did she have?

Wearily, Liandra ran a hand across her eyes. She didn't want to face that dream-scape again, but she had to. Somehow she would have to recover her crystals and send a message. Seven Stars, how she wished there was some other way. And she would have to be careful. If Connal knew of her plans he'd ... well what he'd do to her, she didn't want to think about!

Connal leaned back against the door of Liandra's apartment and drew in a deep breath. The exhaustion which he had held at bay was finally overtaking him. Willing his muscles to obey, he pushed himself down the corridor. Dougall intercepted him.

"I suppose you are going to add your protests to Fianna's and the Weaver's?"

"The women do have the right of it, *Tighearna*. And you know how it is with a woman's scorn. They will not forgive you ... not in a long while. The witch especially."

"Aye." Connal smiled ruefully.

"Is Garris truly lost to us?"

"No, by Arran! When I have rested I intend to follow his trail again. 'Tis the least I can do."

Dougall grasped Connal's forearm. "No, never again, *Tighearna*! The things I heard coming from the apartment, when you and the witch were a-dreaming. It near curdled my blood. You canna' do this! 'Tis madness. The Council -"

"Is to blame for our predicament. They

overrode me last time and look what happened.
Henceforth, I will not be seeking their say so in
any of my decisions."

"My Lord -"

"Enough, I say! Look to our guest. Give her
some time to recover her composure and then
have one of the women keep her company. I
have the right of it when I say my face will not
be too welcome for awhile in that chamber."

Dougall grimaced. "The alien is somewhat
spirited."

"She is certainly that!"

Connal strode down the corridor, his
thoughts awhirl. Aye, the witch had spirit that
would make a Caledonian proud. If only there
was another way. He liked it not, keeping her
against her will. What other choice had he? In
time she would become reconciled. He would
make sure of it. He had brought stubborn
women around before. It might be worth every
difficult moment ahead to see Liandra subdued.
Compliant even? He smiled at that. He could
not imagine her so.

Still, for the moment he had more significant
tasks to perform; finding Garris the most
important in a growing list of problems. How
had everything gone so terribly wrong, in such
a short time?

His original plan had been so simple. All so
simple! But look what had happened. She had
turned his world upside down, pitted one loyal
kinswoman against him already ... not to

mention Jenna. Arran's Mercy ... what was a man to do?

Besides, the thought intruded, after what they had shared on the crystal bed, would he have been truly content to let her leave, just like that? He had not loved Jenna since his return from off-world. He had tried, yet for the first time in his life his body did not reciprocate passion, no matter how skillfully Jenna had enticed him. He had wanted none of his Jennie. And why? The witch was to blame! He knew it. So did Jenna.

He could not deny it, he was curious about Liandra. Surely this was not the reason he was keeping her prisoner, to sample first-hand, in the real world, the delights they had dream-shared?

No! Impossible! It was Caledonia that he was thinking of, not himself. How could he even consider bedding an alien whore? *If only* ... He cut off that thought instantly. No going back. For good, or ill, he had decided what was to be done.

But that tight coil in the pit of his gut, why did he feel that worse was yet to come?

Chapter Nine

The insistent scratching on her chamber door roused Liandra from her misery. Her only break from solitude had been the dutiful ministrations of Katrine to tend her wounds, and the serving girls who brought her meals. Liandra forced herself to eat, knowing that if her plates were returned unsavoured, Connal would hear of it. No doubt he'd force feed her. She'd suffered enough indignities at his hands.

The scraping came again. Cautiously, she opened the door. Fergus' massive frame knocked the door aside. The hound planted a cold, moist snout against her hand, prodding her until she caressed his head. Satisfied, Fergus lay down in front of the fire, watching her with his huge amber eyes.

"Well, you've made yourself at home. Pity I can't do the same thing," Liandra muttered.

Turning, she saw Dougall sitting in the corridor, though as her eyes met his, his gaze fell to the floor. Liandra strode up to him.

"*Maer* Dougall. I was wrong to be angry with you. I apologise."

Dougall glanced at her and to her amazement,

the man's cheeks flamed red with embarrassment.

"You have the right of it, Mistress, to be so incensed. In your place I would have torn the *Tighearna* limb from limb." He chuckled.

Despite herself Liandra had to laugh, too. "I did come close to it."

He pulled out the chair on the opposite side of his table. "Will you sit and take wine? 'Tis the best MacArran vintage, Connal's recompense for my solitary duty outside your door."

"Are you going to be my guardian for -" Liandra bit back the word. She wasn't going to say 'forever'. That would be admitting defeat, and she was far from vanquished. She wasn't going to stay very long on Caledonia, not if she had anything to do with it!

Dougall raised a bushy red brow. "The *Tighearna* is a good man, Mistress, though I doubt at the moment you would think it. Still, of all the lords, he is a man worthy of the name, and his position."

"I disagree."

"Aye. In time you will see I have the right of it."

Liandra groaned inwardly. *Insufferable smugness. Did every Caledonian man suffer from it?* She slowly sipped the wine. Never had she tasted its like. Its warmth spread through her body, relaxing the tension in a curious way.

"I haven't seen *Maera* Fianna for days. Not since the dream-search. Is she about? I'd like to speak to her."

Dougall shook his head. "She be in mourning,

and so, not the very best companion, I would think. You will have to make do with my company for a wee while."

"In mourning?"

"Aye. Her Garris is gone."

"I know that, I -"

"I mean he be dead, Mistress."

"Dead? Are you certain? When I left him he was a prisoner. Frightened, yes, but still alive."

"While you kept to your chamber, Connal ... followed him, again. There was no sign of his kin-brother."

Liandra frowned. "How could Connal follow him?"

Dougall shrugged. "For that you must ask the *Tighearna*."

"I intend to. What of Fianna? Could I see her, perhaps? I'm a qualified counsellor, I can give assistance in times of grief."

"Come, then."

Liandra followed Dougall down to the end of the passageway. He tapped lightly on a door, before carefully opening it.

"I will wait outside," Dougall said, retreating to the corridor.

Stepping inside, Liandra reeled back from the melancholy within the apartment. "Fianna?"

No response. She probed the darkened chamber to find her friend lying on her bed. Creeping forward, Liandra looked down at Fianna. The woman radiated pain and distress.

"Fianna."

"Go away."

"I won't. What are you doing to yourself?"

Fianna rolled away, covering her head with a pillow. "My Garris is dead, so let me alone."

"How do you know he's dead?"

"Connal -"

"Connal can't possibly know that."

"He does. I did not even have a chance to say good-bye to my *gradhmhor*." Fianna dissolved into sobs and Liandra let her cry out her misery before sitting down beside her on the bed.

"Tell me what you mean about saying good-bye."

"He went off-world without a word to anyone. Only that wretched letter. What did I do wrong that would make him leave Caledonia ... without word? I thought Garris loved me."

"In the dream-state I could catch his love for you. It was very strong."

Fianna turned to her, propping herself up on an elbow. "It was? But -"

Liandra frowned. She caught the word 'Jenna' echoing in Fianna's mind.

"No matter what anyone says, Garris loves you. Along with the sword, I used Garris' devotion to you as my focal point."

"Truly?"

"I'm sure Garris had some driving purpose behind what he did. You can't blame yourself. He didn't tell Connal where he was going, either."

"I know."

"Will you come with me?" Liandra asked.

"Where?"

"I wish to help you. I can only do that in my chamber."

"I do not understand."

"Then let me show you. Please. And staying here alone without food or drink, is only hurting yourself and those who love you."

"Connal said the same thing. What would he know?" Fianna whispered.

"Well, for once he and I agree on something."

Fianna smiled weakly, pushed herself up from the bed, and silently followed Liandra out into the corridor. Dougall escorted them and resumed his seat outside the chamber.

Gently Liandra took Fianna's arm and led her to the crystal bed.

"I want you to lie here. Sleep, *Maera* Fianna. You need to sleep."

"Cannot," she said. "The dreams ..."

"Will only be pleasant for you I promise. Now close your eyes."

Liandra sat beside Fianna on the bed, monitoring her as she slipped quickly into the healing state. It would be an easy thing now to probe Fianna's mind, to learn the answers to her many questions. Liandra recoiled from the monstrous thought. By the Seven Stars! To even contemplate doing such went against everything she held sacrosanct. Was she so desperate to escape that she would violate another creature as she had been violated in the dream-state? No, her freedom would not spring from such a despicable act! Better to remain a prisoner, forever, than to break the confidence Fianna had in her.

Liandra gently stroked Fianna's cheek, sending soothing, healing thoughts by combining images and words with her own special talent.

Connal strode into Liandra's chamber and stopped dead in his tracks. What witchery was before his eyes? His anger evaporated as he saw the gentleness on Liandra's face. He listened to her soft, lilting song. Presumably Asarian, not that he could understand. What might she be singing? He would give much to know. Never before had Liandra looked so vulnerable, so gentle. There were more facets to the witch than he suspected. By Arran, she be such a mystery!

"What is it ye are doing?"

At the sound of his voice, he saw her whole body go rigid. When she slowly turned to him he saw the mixture of anger and distress in her eyes, on her face. Connal tried to ignore it, knowing he was the cause. Realisation brought more pain, more anguish to him. He swallowed down hard, frowning at her as she stood up, chin raised, ready to do battle once more.

"Fianna was on the verge of nervous exhaustion. I couldn't let my friend suffer so. I'm healing her."

"For that I thank you. Fianna would not be consoled, no matter what I, or anyone did. There is no danger from the bed? What about those creatures?"

"I'm only using a healing state. You've seen to it that I'm not able to use my bed for any in-depth dreaming."

"I thought perhaps you might have a trick or two up your sleeve."

"My gown doesn't have sleeves."

No, he thought. *Your* gown *does na' have much to it at all!* "'Tis a figure of speech, My Lady *Bandruidh.* Meaning, I suspected you might be hiding something from me, perhaps some powers I have not yet seen."

"You've rendered me powerless by robbing me of everything."

Connal raised a quizzical brow. "Not quite."

His innuendo made Liandra blush.

"How long will Fianna sleep?" Connal asked.

"When she needs to awaken she will. It may take hours, or days." Liandra regarded him. "She told me you sought Garris again. How did you do that?"

"I followed the path Garris took."

"How?"

"As I already have told you, we of Caledonia have our own magic, which I will not reveal to you."

"And Garris?"

"Nothing, not even an image, as if he never existed. Now ask me no more. I am here to take you on a tour of my castle. I will not tolerate your hiding in this chamber any longer."

"I prefer to remain here. I don't want to see you ever again."

As she turned away, Connal strode up to her and took her lightly, but firmly by the shoulders. He made her face him.

"Let us make peace, *ban-druidh*! Nothing will be gained in maintaining this discord."

Liandra swallowed her arguments. To escape Castle MacArran she would have to gain access to the estate and she couldn't do that keeping to her own apartments, as much as she desired it.

She sighed. "I suppose it's inevitable."

"Come, then. Will it be all right to leave Fianna alone?"

"Yes, she only sleeps and dreams."

"What dreams have you given her?"

"Ones to renew. She will be able to say goodbye to Garris, as she wished. This she must do before she can begin her own healing process."

"My thanks for that, Counsellor. Fianna's heart is too soft by far. I thought she would sicken with sorrow."

"She would have. I've stopped that. It will take time for her to heal. Do Caledonians die when they lose their life-mate?"

Connal frowned. "No one dies from a broken heart."

"Then your kind are very lucky, Connal MacArran."

"What do you mean?"

"There are some League species who, like Asarians, will wither and die if their soul-mate expires."

Connal's eyebrows arched skyward. "Truly?" He glanced at the crystal bed. "I have a question for you. Would it be true to say that people, your League members, might prefer to live out their lives in dreams, where no hurt can touch them? Is there danger of such?"

"Yes, that's why only those qualified and licensed may practice dream-weaving. If a client becomes too dependent on our services then that being is counselled in other ways, by other facilitators. For some, the dreams can be an irresistible lure."

"And what about you Liandra? Can a counsellor such as yourself become addicted to the dreams?"

She shook her head. "If I exhibited dependency on my dreams, I'd be de-registered. Only the best Weavers may act as Counsellors." She flushed as she saw his taunting brow creep upwards. "Don't misunderstand. I'm not being conceited. It's merely a statement of fact. I am what I am. I do what I do very well."

Connal grinned. "Aye, I can vouch for that. Are there creatures in the galaxy who might wish to corrupt your skill for their own stimulation?"

"In times past, Asarian weavers were hunted throughout the star systems and enslaved for the perverted delights of their captors. Dream-weavers kept in captivity do not function well after a time. They eventually die. Every League member knows that, so we are free to roam the galaxy, without fear."

Connal frowned. "Then I shall have to ensure, Counsellor, that the conditions of your residence here are not so harsh they will make you sick."

"There is no chance of that."

"Oh?"

"My incarceration may be primitive, but it's far from intolerable. You've adequately provided for my needs."

Connal grinned, a self-satisfied look if ever there was one!

"At last I have a compliment from you."

"Savour it well, barbarian. It's the first and last you'll get from me."

He threw back his head and laughed. "Come." He held out his hand.

"I will walk with you as you wish, Connal, but do not touch me."

"Tsk! And I thought you had mellowed towards me."

"Never!" Liandra snapped.

"*Never*?" He smiled his disbelief. With a theatrical bow he waved her ahead of him.

Connal glanced at her as they walked down the corridor. By Arran! Liandra was full of surprises and contradictions. One moment gentle and kind, and the next, screaming and spitting like a wild-cat. Her profession confused him, too. For the benefit of her clients she bedded frequently. Even he, a stranger, had been allowed such sweet intimacy that the memory of it had captivated his dreams ever since. Was his experience of her in their dream-sharing how it would be in reality? After experiencing a dream-coupling would a man or woman be ever satisfied, again, by a real-life bedding?

He studied her sadly. She would never know what it was like to be loved by a real man without the need of dreams, drugs or a crystal bed. Dreams were just that ... dreams. Real love-making, even with an inexperienced woman, was far better than any exotic, erotic dream.

Though if true, why was his sleep fraught with fantasies amid the memories of Liandra's sensual dream-touch? She was an alien witch, and as such was out of his reach. Must be beyond his desire. That being so, why was it so difficult to exorcise her from his mind? To keep his imagination at bay, he needed a distraction. Work. That was the answer. And in time what they had shared would fade. Love ... women ... memories, they were all transient things. Even his most intense relationships had faded with the passage of time. So it would be with the *ban-druidh*.

"I will concede this, Connal, you have a beautiful home. You must be proud of it," Liandra said as she walked beside him.

"Aye. It has grown over the generations. Each *Tighearna* puts his distinctive mark on the castle."

"And what do you intend?"

He shrugged. "I have yet to decide. Would you offer some suggestions?"

Liandra shook her head. "Your scheme will not work."

"Oh?" Connal asked, trying to maintain a facade of innocence. He flushed all the way to the roots of his hair as her dark brows arched delicately above her piercing sapphire eyes.

"You seek to give me some task, so that it distracts me from my predicament."

"I canna' be that transparent?" He grinned. "Work heals many hurts, Mistress. I shall have to think of some other ploy."

"Nothing you do will -"

"So certain of that, are you?"

"Yes."

Connal laughed.

For an hour he led her on a grand tour of his home. He pointed out places of interest, explained the objects adorning the walls, not just the weaponry, but other artefacts, both ancient and modern. As they walked in the castle, Connal's people greeted him warmly and casually. There was an easy familiarity between them which traversed the normal social hierarchy of such a primitive culture. Though such did not extend to her, Liandra realised, for as they regarded her they grew wary, even though Connal introduced her to every person they met. She committed all faces and names to memory.

"I know this Castle is very different from what you are accustomed to," Connal said. "Is there anything I can do to make your stay more comfortable? I can give you all save your freedom, Liandra. You are free to walk the castle and its grounds."

"Dougall is still outside my door."

"'Tis not a permanent arrangement. I do not want him wasting his time as your guard. I have had my pax-man there for your own protection."

"My protection?"

"Mark me well. No one will harm you. I feared you would do some harm to your self or others." Connal paused. "You did threaten to turn me into a worm, and to wither me on the spot."

Liandra bit back her smile. "I haven't the power to re-arrange molecules. Besides, Asarians are not a violent people. We are only passionate -"

"Yes?"

"Nothing. You wouldn't understand."

"Maybe I might surprise you."

"You've done that often enough."

Connal laughed. "Then the score is even, *ban-druidh!* I am curious to know what Asarians are passionate about."

"Their mates, to the exclusion of everything else."

"What about your Terran half? I know that species is given to violence and other un-pleasantries."

"You refer only to their bad qualities. Though they have many faults, Terrans have much good in them. How is it you claim to know so much, given that you keep yourself in isolation?"

"I told you before, we closely analyse the ways of our enemy."

"How?"

"I will not reveal clan secrets to you."

Liandra frowned at him. "Will you truly allow me outside, unguarded? I've seen the gardens from my apartment. I'd like to walk there."

Smiling, he held out his arm. She flinched away.

"Habits die hard, Liandra, I am not taunting you. 'Tis the custom on Caledonia. When a man walks with a woman he offers her his arm, as a mark of respect."

"How can you say you respect me, when you've treated me so -"

"Liandra..."

She heard the weariness in his voice and quickly turned to study him with professional eyes. "You are near to exhaustion, Connal."

"Do not concern yourself with me."

He ran a hand through his hair and she followed the path of his fingers. Today he wore his hair loose about his shoulders. She much preferred it to that severe braid of his. During the second dream-search when he had slept beside her, she had touched his hair. The emotions which that simple action had provoked! She closed her mind against the memory, in case it ignited a similar response in the real world.

"Connal, you aren't well." As her hand rested

on his forearm, she felt the muscles tighten beneath her fingers. "You're tired -"

"Do not cast your witch's eye upon me. I am all right."

"You haven't been sleeping," Liandra said.

"Who is to blame for that?" he asked, looking down at her.

Liandra met his gaze. Surely he hadn't been losing sleep over her? Seven Stars, why? Did Connal MacArran have a guilty conscience where she was concerned? She could not believe it!

For a moment neither of them moved and then he sighed deeply. "I will show you the gardens. They are the best on Caledonia." His voice contained a husky tremor. "Do me the courtesy of taking my arm."

"Only for the sake of courtesy."

"Aye, what else?" He grinned.

Connal escorted her down a long flight of stairs. Together they crossed a gigantic hallway whose entire length on either side was decorated with bright tapestries and other Caledonian artefacts and weaponry. Though everything had been built on a grand scale, it wasn't frightening, or intimidating. Neither was it musty nor gloomy, unlike that Terran museum she had visited.

Liandra paused beside the gigantic, metal-studded wooden doors. Sunlight streamed down onto her body. She breathed in deeply, reeling from the hundreds of different scents and sights that greeted her.

"Liandra, are you ill?"

"No, it's just a shock after so long inside."

"Can your kind truly die if left in isolation and darkness?"

"Yes. That's why some Asarians had already died in that dream-place."

"Aye, it was enough to give me nightmares."

"Have you, since our return?"

"Aye."

No sleepless nights from a guilty conscience after all! The realisation stabbed at her, bringing a twinge of sadness. And she had thought him capable of remorse as far as she was concerned. She almost laughed at her naivete.

"Connal, if you'd allow it, I can help you to dispel -"

"No! I am quite capable of looking after myself. Let me show you the stables, they are the best on Caledonia."

Once more taking his arm, Liandra walked beside him across a wide courtyard and into another lofty building. Inside, empty stalls lined the length of each wall. Connal went to a wooden barrel and drew out a handful of white cubes which he placed in a small bag he took from a hook on the wall.

"We let the horses run in the summer, 'tis only in winter we see them confined at night in the stables."

"Horses?" The image of a beast came to Liandra's mind.

"I will show you."

Walking side by side, they emerged from the stables to a field which stretched far into the distance. Creatures - horses - grazed the grass. Connal whistled and in the distance a black horse raised its head. Liandra heard it cry out and with head and tail held high, it streaked across the field, coming to a halt before Connal. He caressed its muzzle, blowing his breath into the horse's flared nostrils.

"This is Dubhlan. And well-named he is," Connal said. "He challenges me at every opportunity. Much like yourself, Liandra. Still, over the years the horse and I have overcome our differences. As I hope you and I shall in the future."

Liandra rolled her eyes heavenward and Connal chuckled.

"What is the monster doing?" she cried as the horse stretched out its head towards her.

Connal blocked her escape. "Dubhlan will not hurt you. One day I will take you riding and show you my county. And you can make up your mind whether County Arran is the most beautiful on Caledonia ... or not."

"You will allow me to see the rest of your world?"

"Eventually."

"How?"

"I do not understand."

"You have no air cars."

"We ride our horses."

"*Ride* them!" Liandra looked at him aghast.

"Aye." Connal laughed. "I like nothing more. He be the fastest horse in the county."

"How can you ride this monster?"

"'Tis easy, *ban-druidh*. When saddled you ride on its back. By the use of reins you direct the horse. I can teach you if you like."

"No, I would not abuse a creature in such a way."

Connal frowned. "There is no abuse. If a creature be ill-treated 'twill not respond, except with fear and violence."

"Much like me."

His brows drew together. "You have not known mis-treatment."

"Have I not?"

"Most definitely not."

Liandra laughed at him. Slowly a grin replaced his frown.

"You were teasing me," he accused.

"I?" Hesitantly holding out her hand, she allowed Dubhlan to nibble her fingers.

"'Tis a greedy monster you be!" Connal said. He dug into the bag and drew out one of the white cubes. "Here, like this." He placed it on her flat palm, and still holding her hand he held it out to Dubhlan.

The horse gently took the gift and chomped it quickly, whiffling against her palm, looking for more. Liandra couldn't credit it that such a huge beast could be so gentle. Dubhlan rubbed his head against her body with such force that she stumbled against Connal.

Laughing, he steadied her. "You are honoured, Liandra. He usually shows affection only to myself and the stable-master."

Connal smiled. So, even Dubhlan fell under the witch's spell. Instead of anger, he felt strangely pleased that his horse favoured her. Jenna was afraid of the 'black rogue', as she called him. On the rare occasions she went with him for a ride in the countryside, Dubhlan remained aloof, except when she got too close and then she had to quickly move out of range of the horse's teeth.

"I have many horses in my stable. I could find you a placid mare to ride."

"No thank you."

"I will not press the matter. But I hope you change your mind."

Connal took her elbow. In silence, they retraced their steps across the courtyard. Going through a stone arch, Liandra gasped in shocked surprise as they entered the gardens that she had glimpsed from her windows.

It was an intoxicating mixture of sights and scents; the bright colours of flowers, their perfumes combining with a wet, earthy smell. She had experienced similar on her father's estate years ago. Since leaving her parents, she had lived in one austere environment after another. Maybe when she returned home she would install a conservatory. Her League apartment had a back room she'd never fully utilised.

She suddenly realised how she missed her Asarian home ... and her parents. And that led to other things ... the aliens. Her friends trapped in the dream-state.

"What is it?" Connal's fingers on her arm made her flesh leap with a life of its own. She frowned down at his brown fingers, in stark contrast to her pale skin.

"I was just thinking of home."

Connal withdrew his hand immediately, as if she were white hot. "That League rabbit-warren?"

She caught the disgust in his voice. "No. My home on Asaria. I left it years ago to pursue my career elsewhere."

"Why?"

"I just wanted to see more of the galaxy. I wasn't content to live among my people. There are some Asarians who travel. I was one of them. I enjoy meeting new beings, and seeing new things."

"There is much for you to see on Caledonia."

"Really?"

"Aye, if you could but open your mind to the possibility." Connal smiled. Perhaps there was some neutral ground upon which they could meet as ... as what? As friends. Equals. He frowned down at her. Was it possible she could ever forgive him for what he had done? For, he realised, having her pardon was very important.

Liandra moved away and went to the first bush in what was a long row of similar plants growing along the length of the castle wall. She breathed in the sweet perfume of one large red bloom. "We've nothing to compare with this on Asaria. What is it?"

"A rose." He smiled at her. "Have you finally found something here against which the League cannot compete? 'Tis a wonder you managed to tell me so, and not choke on your words."

"The truth never hurt anyone. I always speak my mind."

"So I have noticed." Laughing, he bent down and removed a small knife from a sheath in his boot. Before Liandra could protest, he had cut the stem and handed the flower to her.

"You shouldn't do that Connal. You've killed it."

"It will last a few days in water. Take it as a gift from me."

Liandra breathed in the rose scent. "At home we keep our flowers in stasis, their fragrance is duplicated -"

Connal snorted. "Does the League have nothing real about it?"

"Of course. It's just that we respect all life. It's a crime to kill a beautiful thing for the sake of admiring it. However, thank you for the gift."

They walked side by side down the avenues of manicured gardens. The sights and sounds, the colours, and scents nourished Liandra's starved senses like a heady drug.

They came to the end of the garden and through the gateway she saw vast green fields and orchards. In the far distance were hills and further still, the dark snow-capped mountains. Everything was tinged a faint, blue-purple. The haze lent a mystical quality to the land, softening all with its subtle hue.

"What is that flower growing in the fields?" Liandra asked.

"Heather. 'Tis the emblem of Caledonia. I will have someone fetch a sprig for you."

"Thank you." Liandra twirled the rose between her fingers and gasped in pain as something bit her. Glancing down she saw the droplets of blood on her finger.

"Thorns. I forgot to tell you about them," Connal said.

Liandra studied the sharp barbs along the length of the rose's stem. The pain in her finger became secondary, as Connal took her hand to examine the wound. Liandra swallowed against her dry throat as his hand continued to hold hers - ostensibly to look at her injury, though as more time passed, she suspected he cupped her hand for other reasons. She liked the feel of his warm skin against hers. Liked it too much. Reluctantly, she pulled her hand away.

"May I come to this garden when I wish?" Liandra asked.

"It is for all my people to enjoy."

But I'm not one of your people, she wanted to scream. She forced herself to keep silent. She appreciated Connal's kindness in showing her his home, although as always he had an ulterior motive. This time, to show her that Caledonia was not barbarous, that there were things in the Castle and its grounds with which she could identify.

If it weren't for the circumstances which had stranded her on Caledonia, she might almost be content. She had never known true contentment. All her adult life she had constantly been on the move, looking for something, that even when she questioned herself, could not put a name to what she sought. Now, here, of all places, she felt something very close to finding that elusive, unidentifiable something for which she had yearned. Seven Stars, *here*. It was unthinkable.

"There is one thing I would ask of you, Liandra." Connal's deep voice purred its way into her consciousness, drawing her back from her thoughts.

"Yes?"

"When you walk in my Castle, or its grounds, please robe yourself properly. As I said before, men are only flesh and blood. If you find Caledonian gowns distasteful, then at least wear the plaid shawl Fianna gave you. It is my own personal tartan. It identifies the wearer as being under the personal protection of *Tighearna* MacArran."

"Very well."

Connal smiled. He opened his mouth to speak, but the crunching of gravel nearby alerted him to another's presence. He turned to see his Castellan, standing indecisively at a distance.

"Ranald?"

"I need to speak to you, *Tighearna*."

"Aye."

"Privately, if you will."

"I'll wait for you by the fountain," Liandra said. Reaching the far end of the garden, she stood watching as the two men talked. A few minutes later, Connal resumed his place at her side.

"Business, I am afraid, *ban-druidh*. I must be away. Still, there is no reason for you to return to your apartments. Stay here for as long as you wish."

"I'd like that."

"Will you need an escort back to your apartment?"

"I can find my way. Asarians have a keen sense of direction."

Connal laughed. "What about your Terran half?"

"It's always under control."

"*Always?*" he asked with a meaningful raise of his eyebrow.

"Except when I'm provoked beyond endurance."

Again Connal laughed, and she decided that she liked the sound of his laughter very much. Perhaps too much. Suddenly, this man was a stranger to her. Gone was the grim-faced barbarian. Now for a short time she had seen him gentle, happy. Relaxed. Almost a civilised gentleman.

She watched Connal stride swiftly away. She had never noticed before how his kilt hugged his lean hips, and now as he walked, the garish material swayed back and forth allowing a glimpse of lower thigh. Seven Stars! She swallowed down hard. That kilt of his! There ought to be a law against such a garment! He disliked the sexuality of the Asarian robe she had imaged on him, but his Caledonian clothes highlighted his body in a way no Asarian attire could do. Liandra laughed, feeling for the first time as if a great weight had been lifted from her mind.

A crunching of gravel underfoot drew Liandra's mind back to the present. Half-turning, she expected to see Connal. Her smile froze on her face as she saw Jenna.

"The man is mine, *ban-druidh*! Mine - do you hear? I will be thanking you to keep your eyes and hands away from him. Or you shall answer to me!"

"I have no designs on your mate," Liandra said.

"'Tis not what I see."

"Please yourself, *Maera* Jenna. I have told you the truth."

"And I do not believe you."

"Excuse me," Liandra said, icily. As she turned to go, Jenna reached out and grasped her wrist, wrenching her back painfully.

The rose fell from her fingers and Jenna stepped on it, grinding it into the path.

"A final warning to you, alien bitch! Keep your distance from my lord, or you shall suffer the same fate as that rose. 'Tis a pity he has not the stomach to dispose of you, now that your usefulness is at an end. I cannot imagine why he insists on keeping you, like some exotic pet. You are much too thin and pale for his tastes!"

"I am pet to no one."

Jenna laughed. "In time you shall be. Connal can subjugate any creature to his will. Except me! That is why he favours me above every other."

"I understand -"

"Do you *ban-druidh*? For your sake I hope so! Should our paths cross again I will make you sorry you ever came to Caledonia."

"I was sorry the moment I first found myself on your world. I haven't any desire to remain here."

Jenna laughed. "Then jump from your window and end your miserable life. 'Tis the only way you shall be leaving Caledonia."

Liandra hurried away, retreating mentally and physically from Jenna's menace. Glancing back over her shoulder she saw the triumphant look on Jenna's face. Liandra fled to the castle, finally reaching the sanctuary of her apartment. Dougall was no longer there. His table and chairs had also been removed. Now, when she needed his protection, he had gone.

There was no doubt that Jenna would try every means at her disposal to rid herself of her imagined rival. Would she resort to murder?

No doubt at all. Jealousy had driven people the galaxy over to commit murder. Liandra had never thought she would gain first-hand experience of such emotional dysfunction.

"You have a lot to answer for Connal MacArran, for what I must endure!" she said to the cold walls.

Liandra locked her door, and leaning against it, summoned her strength and courage. No time to lose, the sooner she left Caledonia the better. First things first.

First she had to get a message to her father and then she would seek the protection of the Caledonian Council.

Alien invasions and a jealous woman's machinations! She was going to have to be careful ... very careful.

Chapter Ten

Having quickly disposed of his business with the Castellan, Connal returned to the garden.

Disappointment welled up inside, as he saw Liandra was no longer there. He wanted to talk to her, for he found her interesting. *More* than interesting. There was a lot to like about her. Her soft voice, for one. Sometimes she mispronounced the Caledonian words, a tutoring machine was not infallible, but he could understand her. He enjoyed the stamp of individuality her rendition put on his native tongue. Despite his initial disdain, he enjoyed hearing about the League and her home, her life. Did she have the right of it? Were Caledonians too insular? No! There were very good reasons why they remain hidden. The lessons of the past must not be forgotten.

Connal paused in mid-step as he saw the crushed flower. Sorrow, twisted his gut, as he bent to retrieve the rose. Damn! He had hoped the witch was mellowing. Earlier, she had chatted happily with him. She had accepted his gift, appearing to be genuinely admiring of it. The realisation that she had, again, deceived him made him angry, and desolate. He had thought he had made progress ... had wanted, very much, to put aside hostilities. *Damn you,* ban-druidh! *You make this harder than it need be.*

Connal glanced up at the windows of her apartment before he turned on his heel and stalked from the castle. He needed to be on his own, far from his troubles. From one particular trouble. Truly she be a thistle under his kilt! He saddled Dubhlan. Once mounted, he wheeled the horse around and headed out of the stable in a flurry of hooves and gravel.

Puzzled, Liandra drew the curtains together. She had watched Connal in the garden, and although he had been heading towards the castle, for some reason he had gone, instead, to the stables. With a mixture of fear and admiration she had watched the battle between Connal and his horse. Once mastering the animal, Connal had allowed it its head and it had galloped across the fields and was soon lost from view.

She shuddered. And he had offered to teach her to ride a horse? Not likely! She'd fall and break her neck If Jenna didn't get her first.

Grimly, she walked to the bed and studied Fianna. Her aura, although a little wan, had normal healthy colours. Liandra sat beside her friend, monitoring her for the remainder of the day.

In the evening Fianna awoke and stretched languidly. "Liandra ... I dreamed."

"I know. You've slept the day away."

"I have?"

"You needed to. I have refreshment waiting. The serving girls said these were your favourites."

Fianna sat upright in the bed, and Liandra put a tray across her knees.

"You are very kind to me, Mistress."

"Please, will you call me Liandra?"

"Aye, if you will call me Fianna."

Liandra smiled. "Thank you."

"I should be thanking you." Fianna frowned. "I said my farewells to my *gradhmhor*. I do not feel as bad ... The bed?"

"My bed enhances a person's natural ability to heal their own hurts."

"You sang to me."

"It's my way of treating you. All counsellors have their special techniques."

"Much better than Katrine's monstrous tonics." Fianna's smile was short-lived as she looked up at Liandra. "I am sorry for how things have worked out. Truly! If there was any other way, Connal would not keep you here against your will. He is not a cruel man."

"Oh, really?" Liandra smiled her disbelief.

"He loves his people. Perhaps too much. Otherwise would he have dared to risk so much to find Garris?"

"What do you mean?"

Fianna looked at Liandra over the rim of her teacup. "I have a loose tongue, that is my problem. Do not ask me to betray my *Tighearna*."

"I won't. Tell me, does Connal rule Caledonia as diligently as the people in his Castle?"

"Connal is lord and master of County MacArran. 'Tis a great pity, that he does not govern our world. The Council does."

"The Council?" Liandra forced her voice to remain calm, a facade of polite interest, though her heart and mind were in a frenzy.

"Aye. Each County sends their *Tighearna* and two other men to the Council. As Lord MacArran, Connal's place is at the head of the Council. However, no decision is made without a majority decision of those present."

"So your Council rules Caledonia? It's the same with the League Worlds. Representatives meet at Central. That's an artificial satellite in the exact centre of League territory."

"Our Council meets every new moon at a different Castle. From there laws are passed, judgments made, grievances heard."

"We have similar on every League World. We don't take it in turns, there's a chamber specifically used for planetary council. League Central is where all members meet."

"Truly? I should like to see that. The MacLachlan's have the Council next month and I know Connal does not like their castle. Too gloomy for his tastes. Besides which Mistress MacLachlan has always had an eye for our Connal. She wants him to wed her youngest daughter. The MacLachlan *Tighearna* is not well pleased, for Connal will have none of her."

"Why?"

"Alanna MacLachlan be a wilful brat."

"And Connal likes his women compliant."

Fianna laughed. "Hardly. My sister ... I speak too freely of what is the lord's affair. What were we discussing?"

"The Council. The MacLachlans."

"Aye. This journey to Council, Connal shall undertake reluctantly. 'Tis a fair distance and so close to winter, 'twill be freezing. That is clan MacLachlan for you. Never ones to think of any save themselves. One of the other clans would be willing to substitute their turn. But *Tighearna* MacLachlan drew his lot and cares not a fig for anyone's comfort, so long as he can swagger about and play the game of being host."

Liandra raised a quizzical brow.

"There has always been rivalry between the clans and counties. Though 'tis the truth, when I say, that none can compete with County MacArran for its wealth and beauty."

"So Connal always tells me."

Fianna smiled. "He is justly proud of his holding."

"I walked in the Castle grounds today. I've seen many worlds, many things, Fianna, but never anything so lovely as the rose garden."

"Connal's mother planted them. She had a way with nurturing. I am pleased to know that you no longer confine yourself to your chamber. Our world is not such a bad place. Maybe in time you will grow to love it. I would like to show you everything."

"Later," Liandra said. "I'm rather tired."

Fianna put the tray to one side. "I am sorry. Here I sit chatting, while you are exhausted. And no wonder, after all that has occurred."

"Where are you going?"

"Back to my own rooms. I have immersed myself too long in sorrow. Time moves on and I must, too. Only ... will there always be this hollow feeling inside for my Garris?"

"My mother has an old Terran saying. *Time heals all wounds.*"

Fianna nodded and took up the trays. "Rest for as long as you need, Liandra. I will see to it that no one disturbs you."

Liandra locked the door behind Fianna. Marshalling her thoughts she strode to her bed.

Problem number one. She had to find the missing crystals. Once in her possession she would undertake the dream-search to reach her father. Her duty, first and foremost, was to warn the League of the alien threat, and then help her friends in the dream-dimension. After that, if possible, she would look to her own rescue, by appealing to the Council.

After purging herself of all thoughts and emotions, she attuned her mind to the crystals, allowing their colours to invade her consciousness. Finally, she caught their vibrations. Finding them would be the easy thing. What lay ahead ... Never before had she been afraid of any aspect of her work. Once she entered the dream-scape, she would have no choice other than confront the aliens.

Before her courage failed her, Liandra left her room and hurried along the length of the corridor and up the stairs. Thankfully, she saw no one. No doubt it would be common knowledge that she was allowed the freedom of the Castle, so she did not run the risk of being challenged should she encounter any of his people. Though it might be a different thing if she was seen going into Connal's private apartments.

Liandra paused on the threshold of his chamber and mentally braced herself. She suppressed the images of what had occurred there. Her lips tingled anew with the memory of his kiss.

Holding her breath, she opened the door a fraction and peered in. Creeping forward, she located the wooden chest, and flung open the lid. Pushing aside the clothes, she grasped the crystals and stuffed them into her jacket. Their heavy, pulsing warmth settled reassuringly against her breasts.

With heart hammering, Liandra returned to her chamber. Quickly locking the door she hurried to her bed. She re-hung the crystals, each in their proper place and drew on the dreamer's cap. No time for her usual meditation, the prelude to entering her dream-state.

For a moment she felt turned inside out, then the rainbow hues spun her down, transporting her away. Tentatively, she probed outwards. All was as it should be in the dream-world. No aliens. No faint, mysterious emanations of any sort. Liandra quickly forced herself on and on, her mind reaching across time and space, seeking home.

She paused, turned a complete circle, trying to get her bearings. This was no ordinary dream-search where only she existed. It was a dream-sending and as such she usually encountered other consciousness using the dream-dimension to send messages. Yet, Liandra found herself alone. Totally.

She wanted to cry with exasperation. To have dared so much, only to fail. No, she would have to keep trying. She would find someone ... anyone ... and use them to send her message to her father. The mind she touched would remember her as a dream, its legacy, a compulsion to find Alleron Tavor. And once done, her father would know what to do to extract the subliminal message.

It bordered on the unethical, to use another being in such a way. What other choice did she have? She had to proceed, though her instincts told her she should not. Her father would understand and make the necessary apologies. Not one spark of consciousness appeared throughout all the space she roamed.

"Liandra!"

Gasping, she twisted around. Connal's voice, and nearby! She ran in the opposite direction, hoping against hope that he could not follow her.

Frantically, her fear and desperation adding strength to her sending, she probed outwards into the void, and slowly the mists parted. The Asarian star system loomed up ahead. Then, as she plummeted down, she saw her green and white world. Asaria, the planet of her birth. As she focused, she saw her father's estate. Then her house. Her mother working at her desk in the conservatory.

"Mother!"

Sarah Tavor turned and Liandra sent her the first few images of her message.

"Ban-druidh!"

The sound of Connal's voice so close to her, wrenched her concentration away. Her mother's image wavered and Liandra found herself back in the void.

She fled, knowing that he pursued her, knowing she could not hide, sooner or later she would have to return to the real world and Connal would be there waiting for her.

Liandra came to a skidding halt as the white mists parted and Connal strode out towards her. She twisted away and ran on. Moments later she felt him against her, bringing her to the ground. Though as they fell, Connal turned her, so his body beneath hers cushioned her fall.

"Return us. Now!" he hissed.

"Connal -"

"Now! Or, by Arran, I will make you sorry you were ever born!"

Shifting her focus, she awoke on her bed. Connal was not lying down beside her, but sitting. With a string of Caledonian expletives spoken so fast she could not understand, he threw off his cap.

Terrified, Liandra stared up at him. His ashen face was all harsh angles, his lips drawn to a thin line. "Connal, let me explain."

He stalked to the window and with his back to her, Liandra watched as he struggled for control. The battle lasted minutes. In that time, she had an eternity to consider what was going to happen to her.

He turned to her. "I should be giving you the spanking you so richly deserve."

"A ... what?" The image of what he had threatened came to mind as Liandra probed her subliminal tutoring. She gasped. "You wouldn't dare."

"Would I not?" His hands balled into fists as he took one step towards her.

Liandra eyed him warily. "Come any closer, Connal MacArran and I'll scream the walls down."

"Yet another challenge? You know how I deal with such. My people would not come to your aid, even if your cries did carry beyond these walls. They respect their *Tighearna* and will not interfere in my business." He drew in a long, steadying breath. "There are easier, more effective punishments for a woman such as you! I had hoped you were coming to terms with your new life, but 'twas only a ploy."

"I had a duty to warn my father, at the very least to let him know I was alive. You don't seem to realise there's more at stake here than one world."

"I understand only too well what is at risk. I will deal with this menace in my own way."

"How can you?" Liandra challenged. "And don't just say *'tis Caledonian magic*. I'm getting tired of that excuse."

Connal smiled grimly. "'Tis clan business, Mistress Tavor. We have ways and means of protecting ourselves and others, without League interference." He folded his arms and glared at her. "What you dared! You could have been lost -" He drew in a steadying breath. How easily she could have been lost to him! By Arran! He did not want the witch around ... he wanted to be rid of her. Did he not?

Liandra forced herself not to flinch, as his narrowed eyes bored into her. He was in a terrible state. Fear and anger were only two emotions she caught from him before he quashed all behind his impervious mask.

Connal stepped closer to her. "Was your dream-search successful?"

"I managed to reach my mother. She knows I'm alive. Nothing more. I was careful not to betray your privacy."

"Your actions have proved you untrustworthy. 'Tis a pity, *ban-druidh*! I was beginning to think that perhaps you and I might become friends. For defying me, for risking yourself and my people, your punishment is two-fold. Your crystal bed is confiscated and I will set you to work in my Castle. Your status is no longer one of guest. You will have to earn the right to be considered such again. And you have forfeited your privilege to call me Connal. Only my chosen friends and kinsfolk may call me by name. Henceforth, you shall address me as *Tighearna*, until you have proven yourself again in my eyes. *If* that is possible."

"You can't take my bed from me. I need it."

"You should have thought of that before you entered my chamber and stole the crystals. Surely you knew your action would not go unpunished?"

"I considered it my duty to warn my people. *My* honour, if you will!"

Connal regarded her in astonishment. Liandra stood tall and proud, not humbled and afraid. Her words amazed him, not her stance. To sacrifice oneself for a higher ideal, it was a quality of which any Caledonian would be proud. But hers had been a terrible gamble. Perhaps not unlike his when he had first decided to follow Garris into League space.

Was that the cause of his anger? Because they were alike in placing duty and honour before oneself? And that being so, he did not want to punish her - for in her place he would have done the same.

Connal sighed tiredly, steeling himself. "Do you accept the consequences of your actions?"

Liandra nodded. She couldn't have spoken,

not if her life depended upon it.

"Very well. Come here."

For a moment she panicked. Well, whatever he was going to do, he'd do it. Eventually. She swallowed and forced her shaking limbs to obey her. Slowly she came to stand before him.

Connal grasped her chin. He felt her flinch. He wanted her cowed, not terrorised. Deliberately he forced his fingers to gentle her cheek. "For one month you will carry out kitchen duties. For that month you will be deprived of your bed. After that time I will review your status. I might return your bed, without its crystals."

"I -"

He put a finger to her lips. "Argue with me and I increase the punishment by a month."

"Can I say one thing?"

He sighed. "Only one thing."

"I didn't betray you to the League, even if I had the time, I wouldn't. I respect your wish for anonymity. And if you take the crystals from the bed -"

"'Tis two things you have said, Liandra."

"Yes, but -"

"And now *two* months you work in the kitchen and lose the use of your bed."

Liandra opened her mouth to protest, and Connal's eyebrow raised a fraction.

"Do I make it three?"

She shook her head. What use in arguing? Besides, if her plan was successful, she wouldn't be on Caledonia for two weeks, let alone two months! *So much for his punishment, then!*

"I'd like to know one more thing. The terms of my punishment."

"Aye?"

"Am I confined to my chamber, or can I still have the freedom of the castle? I'd like to visit the garden."

"That surprises me, after I saw the evidence of your high regard for my roses."

"I don't know what you mean."

"Do you not? Normally, I do not pick my roses for any one. Think about what you did to my gift."

Connal's rose had been crushed by Jenna. He wouldn't believe her if she told him the truth - take the word of an alien witch over his woman? So she said nothing, though inwardly she cursed herself for being a coward. Coward for accepting Connal's punishment, for accepting Jenna's treatment. For everything. He was right, a League member didn't have the stomach for a fight.

"Your punishment begins as of now. Come with me."

Connal took her arm and guided her out of her chamber. In silence he led her down the many passageways and staircases.

Liandra smelled the aroma of cooking food. As Connal waved her ahead of him, he pushed open a door and paused at the entrance. The men and women working in the kitchen turned to her enquiringly. Then as they saw Connal they resumed their duties, the tension in the air tangible.

Wiping her hands on her long apron, a middle-aged woman strode up to Connal. "Good day to you, *Tighearna*. What may I do for you?"

"Good day to you, Amilia. I have someone for you to instruct. When it comes to cooking, the *ban-druidh* is a complete novice. I want her trained well."

Amilia's smile broadened. "Oh aye, on that you can be assured, *Tighearna*."

"Then I can leave her in your capable hands?"

"Aye."

Liandra turned to Connal, the entreaty dying on her lips the moment she caught sight of those steely eyes.

"Do not disappoint me, *ban-druidh*."

Liandra sighed and watched him stride away. Slowly, she turned to Amilia.

All those smells and oh ... *Seven Stars*! Raw meat hanging on hooks ... Despite the indignity and violence of a spanking, that punishment didn't look so bad. Work for two months with those blood-dripping carcasses?

She couldn't endure it. She couldn't. Panic welled up inside, followed by a dark, creeping tide. She fled the kitchen.

Chapter Eleven

"Are you coming to the *tiodhlacadh* tomorrow eve?" Amilia asked looking up from her roll of pastry.

"*Tiodhlacadh*?" Liandra frowned. "A funeral? Oh, you mean a life-severing."

Amilia cocked her head to one side. "A what?"

"A ceremony where friends and relatives gather to say goodbye to one whom has stepped forward to embrace the universal mystery." Liandra smiled.

"Hmm. The *Tighearna* has decreed that we must bid Garris farewell. Will you attend?"

"Yes."

She had only known Garris through the dream-state, but what little she experienced of him, she liked. She approved of Amilia, too. In the two weeks she had worked in the kitchen, Liandra had made new friends. Once the staff had grown accustomed to her, she had slowly been included their in banter. Her tasks were not difficult, at times even enjoyable.

Wrist deep in pastry, Liandra paused, realising that finally her opportunity to escape the Castle had presented itself. With all attention focused on the funeral, she might be able to slip away unnoticed. But so soon? She needed more time to plan. To prepare. Ill-conceived plans had a habit of ending in disaster. Dare she risk it? Of course she must. What other choice did she have?

The morning flew by as Liandra planned her escape, discarding every idea almost as soon as she gave it a hearing.

At mid-day, she sat outside in the kitchen courtyard to eat her lunch. She smiled at the people chatting and laughing about her, remembering a time not so long ago when the tables were deserted, save for Amilia and her kitchen staff. That had changed the moment word spread among the inhabitants of the Castle that she was there. Now the tables were filled to capacity, all eager to see and speak to the *ban-druidh*. Though none dared call her that in her presence.

"Your home-world, Liandra. Is it far from here?" Andrew asked.

Liandra smiled at the young kitchen boy. "I'm not sure. I don't know where *here* is."

"Then, what it be like, yer world?"

"Very different from Caledonia."

"Och aye?"

As she explained some of the obvious contrasts, his eyes grew round and disbelieving.

"You make a jest of me," he said, indignantly.

"No, I'm telling you the truth."

Andrew smiled his disbelief.

"I'll show you something." She collected seven apples and four large cherries from the fruit basket and returned to her table.

Liandra concentrated and Andrew gasped as the seven apples rose out of her hands and hung suspended in the air in a triangular configuration. Slowly the fruit turned on their axes. She sent the cherries in a staggered orbit around the apple which formed the apex of the triangle.

"The seven apples represent the seven stars which form the Asarian coalition. The apple which has the cherries in orbit around it, this is my star system. This is Asaria," she said pointing to the fourth cherry.

"How can ye do that? 'Tis magic."

"No, it's a skill I've learned. Others of my kind are more proficient."

The people clustered around her, gently touching the spinning fruit.

"What are ye doing?" Connal demanded.

Liandra's concentration diverted, people ducked for cover as the fruit flew in every directions. One diner, not fast enough, ended up with a cherry spattered across his forehead.

"I was showing Andrew my star system ... the seven stars ... the first star system to form the League."

"And hence your oath, Seven Stars." Connal nodded. He held out his hand. "A private word with you *ban-druidh*."

Nervously, Liandra followed him, feeling the

eyes of the people on her as she walked away.

Connal came to an abrupt halt and turned to her. "I do not want you telling my people about your blasted League, Liandra. 'Tis something no one needs to know. It would be better if you forgot it, too."

"Why, it's my home -?"

"Caledonia is now your home."

"It's where I live. I can never think of it as home. Home is here," she said touching her heart.

Connal frowned. "I thought your defiance of me had ended."

Liandra tossed her head. "If you want to think of memories as defiance, then that's your problem, not mine. I won't forget, just because you say I must. Would you forget if our positions were reversed?"

Connal folded his arms. "Probably not. No good will come of it, Liandra. If you insist on remembering, then you make it doubly difficult and painful to acclimatise yourself to your new life."

"Whatever I remember, or forget, I can never *belong* here. This life is totally alien to me."

He glanced down at her and before he masked it, Liandra saw the regret in his eyes.

"I am sorry 'tis so difficult for you. Do you not enjoy your work?"

"It was strange at first, until Amilia found me something I can manage."

"And what is your expertise?"

"I make fruit tarts."

"Do you indeed? Then I will ask you to make one for me. As you know I enjoy blueberry tart the most."

"I'm not qualified to prepare food for the *Tighearna*," she said, dryly.

"I will be the judge of that. I heard you were sick that first day in the kitchen. Are you recovered?"

Liandra swallowed against the memory. The cause of it was always there, on the periphery of her consciousness. "Your people still eat meat. I saw bodies of dead animals hanging in the kitchen. I couldn't face it."

"And now you no longer feel this way?"

"Amilia kindly gave me a work station farthest from the meat. I try not to notice, though sometimes the smell..." She shuddered. Though the kitchen was large, bright and airy, and the ventilators took most of the odours away, it still couldn't disguise the aroma of raw flesh.

Connal cleared his throat. "Well, you did bring your punishment down upon yourself. However, I am here to invite you to the *tiodhlacadh* for Garris tomorrow eve."

"I'll be there."

"Good. Fianna will have need of your support. Now you had best return to your work. I want evidence of your handiwork on my table tonight. A blueberry tart."

Liandra frowned at his retreating back. She'd

give him a fruit tart, all right, but not where he wanted it. She laughed as the image came to mind, of Connal's face covered in sticky fruit. Hastily she put it back where it belonged - in her imagination. If she dared to do what she wanted ... Seven Stars, he'd make her sorry. No doubt his retribution would be that threatened spanking. She grimaced. The pain and indignity of such a thing. Typical punishment from a barbarian.

While the kitchen staff broke for their afternoon nap in readiness for the demands of the evening, Liandra stayed at her station. Much better to work, than pace her chamber in nervous anticipation of her escape, she took out her anxiety on the dough, pummelling it over and over.

Jenna swept into the kitchen. "There you are." She smiled. "I was pleased to hear you were banished to a place that befits the likes of you. Though I will not be eating any of your concoctions, I hear Connal has asked for a sample of your handiwork."

News always travelled fast in the Castle. Liandra knew that much from listening to the gossip of the kitchen staff.

Jenna handed Liandra a glass container. "Here, you had best make sure you include plenty of heather-sugar in the tart. My Connal likes sweet things."

"I've never heard of it before," Liandra said, suspiciously.

"Rank has its privileges, it is only for the

Tighearna. Heather-sugar is not for the likes of servants."

"Why do you wish to help me?"

Jenna smiled, grimly. "Because my Connal has been in a fine temper since he returned from off-world. When you incite him, not only you suffer as a consequence, all of us do! Myself included. I want no more of his wrath!"

Liandra frowned. She knew about Connal's fury, no less his bed-mate, it seemed! "How much should I include?"

"Almost the entire jar."

Liandra stirred in the fine granules, her concentration focused on her work.

"You must ensure that only Connal tastes this tart. The last cook who served heather-sugar through incompetence, well, need I go on?"

"No, I understand. How can I make sure I don't make the same mistake?"

Jenna rolled her eyes heavenward. "Here." She snatched up a knife and quickly traced a design in the pastry lid. "'C' stands for Connal."

Liandra frowned down at the letter. As always, she felt that pressure in her head, a slight giddiness as her senses battled with one another to comprehend any form of writing. "Thank you, *Maera* Jenna for your help."

"My pleasure." Laughing, Jenna swept out of the kitchen, head held high.

"Well, *ban-druidh*? How goes it?" Connal asked.

Liandra glanced over her shoulder to see him leaning against the doorway.

Amilia clucked her tongue. "How frequent your visits are to my humble kitchen, *Tighearna*."

"Aye, I have been remiss in my regular inspections. I am trying to make amends."

Amilia smiled. "And how long will such occur? Two months?"

"Give or take a few days."

"As I thought."

Liandra glanced from one to the other, admiring their easy repartee. She knew the reasons for Connal's visits - checking up on her, making sure she didn't speak of her home world, nor cause mischief.

Surreptitiously the kitchen staff often plied her with questions, their curiosity insatiable. She told them what she could, though she knew, and so did they, that if Connal found out they'd all be in trouble. Secrecy was assured by their mutual regard of Connal's temper, by his uncanny habit of learning of any transgression and inflicting 'suitable' punishments.

"Is that mine?" Connal strode up to the pie sitting on its own on the work bench. "Please, cut me a slice."

Liandra did as she was bid and handed it to him on a china plate. "Have you made your final peace with the universe, Conna - *Tighearna*?"

He raised an enquiring brow.

"It might disagree with you."

He laughed. "I will take the risk."

Liandra watched in nervous anticipation. She and Amilia had tasted one of the other tarts, just to make sure. Both women had agreed it prudent to ensure that the other pies were edible, before allowing Connal to sample his own.

Connal bit into what promised to be a sweet, juicy dessert. *Ugh!* Such nauseating acidity, he almost gagged. Catching sight of Liandra's anxious face, he stopped himself from spitting out the piece of pie. The *ban-druidh* had tried her best, no doubt. Cooking was an exact science, she had little experience of it, after all. He chewed the mouthful as quickly as he could and swallowed it. "I ... I have not tasted its like before. But I will not have any more. I do not want to get as fat as Dougall."

"There!" Amilia said. "Told you our *Tighearna* would be pleased. She makes a fine pastry, my lord, even if, as her teacher, I do say so. May I sample some more of your handiwork, Liandra? I am afraid that I enjoy the berry tart. Too much, as you can see." Amilia patted her rotund frame. She bit into the slice of tart. "*Arran's Mercy!*" She spat out the food onto her plate. "Sorry, *Tighearna*. How did you manage to eat it, so calmly? 'Tis disgusting."

Liandra felt the colour drain from her cheeks. She looked from one to the other. "Let me try it." She bit tentatively into the tart. "It tastes odd."

"*Odd?*" Amilia gasped. "'Tis awful! What did

you put into the tart?"

"Heather-sugar."

"What?" Connal and Amilia demanded in unison.

"Heather-sugar."

"'Tis no such thing."

"There is. Look ... here." Liandra handed Amilia the glass container.

"Salt! You foolish girl. Whatever possessed you to include it in the tart?"

Liandra flushed, mortified to the depths of her being. She'd been so gullible. She should have suspected Jenna and her motives. Since when did her nemesis help her? If she hadn't been so pre-occupied with her escape plans, perhaps she might have been more suspicious.

"Was this on purpose, *ban-druidh*? Your revenge for my punishment?

"No!" Liandra cried. "Why do you always blame me for everything that happens?"

She looked at Amilia, then at Connal, seeing his disbelief and mounting anger. He'd never believe in her innocence, he'd never take her side over Jenna's. The final indignity, she'd be punished for something she hadn't done. Choking back her tears, she raced out of the kitchen.

"Liandra, come back here!" Connal called after her.

She raced up the stairs and down the corridor, colliding with someone.

"Liandra?" As Dougall steadied her, she flung

off his hands.

Connal strode around a bend in the passage. "*Ban-druidh!* Damn you, come here!"

"Mistress Liandra, I-" Dougall began.

"Let me alone, both of you!" She hitched up her skirts and left the two men staring after her, open-mouthed.

"What are ye' doin'?" Dougall demanded, his eyebrows bristling.

"Mind your own damn business!"

"Tsk!" Dougall hissed warningly at Connal's retreating back. The tight line of his mouth softened into a smile, then into a grin which cut his face from ear to ear. *The two of them were having a time of it, stubborn fools!* Whistling, he sauntered down the corridor.

Liandra reached her apartment and flung herself on her bed. She beat out her frustration against the pillow, muffling her sobs against it.

She could not endure Jenna's antics. No doubt her taunts would increase and intensify the longer she stayed at Castle MacArran. The sooner she was free the better. Even if meant a dangerous journey into the unknown to find the Council, better that, than face the demented animosity of Connal's mate.

Liandra paused in her misery. Connal had not been angry when he had first tasted the pie. He had hidden his disgust. To save her feelings? Unlikely! Perhaps the taste had temporarily overwhelmed him. Though his anger had quickly ignited with sudden suspicion that she had deliberately tried to poison him.

Seven Stars! Again, Liandra pummelled her pillow.

Connal could hear the muffled sobs, even from where he stood. Careful not to make a sound, he poked his head around the door, frowning as he saw her on the bed. Should he offer comfort or more punishment? He had no evidence that her act had been deliberate, and Amilia had told him Liandra was a fair cook - as good as could be expected given that she had no prior experience of it.

Then, what had happened? *Heather-sugar?* He stopped himself from laughing aloud. By Arran! He had never heard of such a thing, and had never tasted such a ghastly concoction, either! He sobered instantly as he sought answers.

She had not looked guilty of any mischief. She had readily revealed what she had put in the tart. Had someone deliberately tried to sabotage Liandra's work? Whom? He frowned. Who in the Castle was the witch's enemy? All knew she was under his protection. Who would dare raise a hand against her? He would make a few discreet enquiries and get to the bottom of it. If someone was harassing Liandra he would make him, or her, pay. *Her!* Connal felt cold fury race through his veins.

He berated himself for his slow-wit in lashing

out at Liandra. He should have known something was amiss, the moment he saw the 'C'
carved in the pie. Liandra could not read or
write. Someone had written it for her, ensuring
that it was he, and he alone, who sampled that
pie. Someone who knew him well. *Too well.*
Jenna would pay dearly for this escapade, for
that pie had damn near choked him. Yet, it was
the memory of Liandra's fear, on her face and
in her eyes, which upset him the most. No one
lived in terror of him. Least of all, his *ban-druidh!*

Liandra returned to the kitchen with a
headache. She had made herself sick with her
crying. Now she felt lethargic, almost hollow
inside.

If the others in the kitchen noticed her
swollen eyes and pale face they said nothing,
though Amilia made her sit at her desk and
drink several cups of strong tea before she was
convinced Liandra could carry out her duties.

Once the kitchen staff had left for the night's
revelries in the dining hall, Liandra set to and
baked another pie. She'd show Connal she was
neither inept, nor a poisoner.

Tentatively, she tasted the pie. Mm. Much
better. Cutting off a large slice, she placed it on
a plate and covered it with a cloth. Using the
back stairs, she reached Connal's apartment
and left the gift on his desk. Taking up a piece
of writing paper she concentrated and ran her
finger across the paper. A trail of colours etched

into the surface, her unique aura, her signature, which could never be duplicated by another being. She left it beside the pie and retreated to her chamber.

As always Fergus was there waiting for her. The dog spent every evening sitting with her before the fire. After the first night, he had moved his sleeping position from the hearth, to the foot of her bed. While Liandra had tried to budge the hound, Fergus remained unyielding. After a few nights of the battle in which she realised she had no chance of winning, Liandra admitted defeat, gradually finding his heavy weight a welcome comfort. Even when he shifted from the foot of the bed to lie next to her, back to back, she didn't try to move him. She'd never had a sleeping partner, and now she shared her bed with a shaggy monster. She had heard of strange bedfellows, hers the strangest of all.

Liandra awoke with a start. Restlessly, she tossed from side to side. Fergus rumbled low in his throat, as she climbed out of the bed, disturbing him.

Throwing a shawl over her nakedness, she stepped out onto the patio. Outside, the midnight air was humid and still. An almost ominous calm.

Without thinking, she glanced up one floor and far to her right. The light from Connal's apartment shone through a half open door onto his balcony. He was working late. *Working?* She smiled to herself. Working at what, or with whom?

He hadn't come to her to make his peace. Perhaps he hadn't seen the pie ... Liandra chewed her lower lip. Or maybe her cooking wasn't up to standard? No, if that was the case, she would have heard from him by now. She forced her gaze to the mountains, to the place where tomorrow night she would be travelling.

"My *gradhmhor* -" Jenna's whining whisper travelled down from above.

Liandra moved back into the shadows, intending to return to her chamber. Instead, something made her pause and look up.

Connal strode out onto his balcony. His long robe, unfastened, flapped around his nakedness. Jenna trailed after him, dressed only in her chemise, the flimsy material hiding very little of her voluptuous body. She pressed up against Connal's back. Angrily, he shrugged off her hands.

"I said no, Jenna. I mean it. I am tired."

"Tired ... busy ... not in the mood. You will be running out of excuses soon, My *Tighearna!* Why not be honest with yourself and me?"

With arms folded, Connal turned to her.

Definitely the stance of a man who did not want to be trifled with, even from the distance Liandra could see that much. Jenna, not to be so easily rejected, ran a hand through his hair, down his throat, to his chest, travelling lower with seductive smoothness. With an angry oath, his fingers stilled her hand. Jenna stretched up and kissed him, dragging his head down to hers, holding him prisoner. Connal groaned. Jenna laughed and shrugging herself out of her clothing, she arched her body into his. Connal swung her up into his arms and disappeared with her into his chamber.

As Liandra walked to her door, Jenna's shriek pierced the night. Now she knew why Connal had not paid her a visit. No doubt both of them were laughing over the pie incident. Irritably, she paced around her bed-room.

Connal glanced down at Jenna as she struggled out of the bath. The water had been in there for hours.

"No doubt that cold dunking will extinguish your ardour, Mistress MacLeod."

"Why you, bastard! You treat me shamefully."

"As you deserve. You have been causing trouble and I like it not. My people are under my protection and not to be harassed by you."

"What do you mean?"

"A little matter of heather-sugar I believe."

Jenna's face darkened. "What did that bitch tell you? It be only a joke."

"Was it that? Am I laughing? She told me nothing, though she might have implicated you. She kept her silence, which is more than I can ever say of you! At least by your confession, I have been spared the wasted time in wringing the truth out of you!"

Connal grabbed her wrist and dragged her from the water. Before Jenna could struggle he dumped her on his bed.

Smiling seductively, she raised herself on her elbow. "Not so tired, after all, My *Tighearna*."

Connal sat beside her and lifted her to him. As Jenna snuggled closer he flipped her over and across his knees.

She struggled and then laughed. "Do it, *ghraidh*. Why are you waiting? Please ... Do it, now!"

Connal frowned down at her. Jenna's tastes ran to the exotic. When and where he could he indulged her, though never once had he capitulated to her demands for rough treatment. Pain and violence were not things he considered as companions of his love-making.

This was not foreplay, but chastisement. His hand raised, poised, ready to strike. Though Jenna's actions deserved it, still he liked it not, what he must do. Why did he treat this woman so differently from Liandra? He had set the witch to kitchen work, yet for his own lover, he was about to do the unthinkable.

No, he could not. He had never done it in the past, though, to some wayward women, he had threatened it. The warning was always enough. Except for Jenna. She begged him to hurt her, to bring her pain amid the pleasure. Arran's Mercy! He could not now, not even as a much-deserved punishment.

He pushed her away. Jenna scurried backwards, her face red with fury and desire. He knew she burned with longing, for her sultry dark eyes swept over him. His stomach clenched, not with longing. With loathing. Of his Jenna!

"It was a wrong you did Liandra and tomorrow you shall apologise to her. I will let you know what other correction you are to receive for your conniving."

Jenna's lips tightened. "You go too far, even for you Connal MacArran. I will not apologise to that bitch for anything! Not for anything! No matter what you do or say to me!"

Connal reclined against the bed. "That sounds very much like a challenge, Jenna MacLeod."

She tossed her head. "Take it as you will. You have not been the same since that bitch came to Caledonia. Nothing I can say or do makes a difference. Never one to spurn me from your bed, now you have so many excuses, so not once in weeks, have I loved you. That witch's dreams have turned you. Surely not for good? Have a care, My *Tighearna*. Though I have kept myself exclusively for you, do not expect it of me in the future. Make your choice - the *ban-druidh*, or me. Do not keep me waiting. Others are eager to assume the place you once, so willingly filled -"

Connal smiled grimly. "That may be so. Will my successors satisfy you as I?"

Jenna flung her cloak around her shoulders. She reached the door and as her hand fastened on the knob, Connal's voice halted her.

"And tomorrow before the entire house you will make your apology to my guest."

Jenna cast a furious eye on him. "Try and make me."

Connal sucked in his breath. "I can and will. Much better for us both, though, if you do not force me to *make* you. Think on that tonight."

Jenna slammed the door with such force that the weaponry adorning his walls quivered on their mountings. Connal slipped off the bed and strode out onto the balcony. Leaning on the balustrade, he looked out across his lands.

Jenna did have the right of it. He had not *had* her since returning from off-world. Too busy. Well, that was one reason but there were others. How could he tell her that at the thought of bedding her, he felt nauseous. *Arran's Mercy what is wrong with me?*

His eyes, with a will of their own, glanced down to Liandra's dark apartment. *What am I going to do with you, My Lady Ban-druidh?* He smiled without humour. In his current state, he knew what he would like to do with her, to test whether the reality of loving her would be as intense as their dream.

No, he could not go to her. That would be base, no more than an easing of the ache in his loins and he would never use a woman in that way. Not even an alien whore. And Jenna. What was he going to do about her? In the past, he had found her jealous little tantrums intriguing, but this latest episode ...

He frowned. How could he once have found her so desirable? Jenna did not know it, though she soon would, that forevermore, she was no longer welcome in his bed.

Was Jenna right? Had Liandra cast some spell over him, sapping his manhood? Though still as hot-blooded as any man, his passions were not about to be assuaged. He could take another lover - What an appalling thought! The alternative - sleepless nights and cold baths, at least for the foreseeable future. Connal glanced down, again, at Liandra's apartment. So near, yet so far.

Damn! He retreated into his bed-chamber and ate the rest of the pie, all the while looking at the piece of paper with its strange mark of rainbow colours.

Chapter Twelve

Liandra shivered, not from cold, but with embarrassment as many pairs of eyes focused upon her. She glanced around the *tiodhlacadh* assembly. The flickering amber light from fires burning in huge braziers cast shadows about the field and upon the faces of the hundreds of men and women of Connal's household. Dotted about the field's perimeter were tall fluorescent light sticks. Fires and high tech. lights - another anachronism. Another mystery. She didn't like mysteries, she thought, drawing the long cloak closer about her.

"The people are curious of you, Liandra. They mean no disrespect," Fianna said.

"I know. I'm glad you insisted I wear this."

"Aye, if Connal sees your suit he will likely have a fit. 'Tis indecent." Fianna smiled.

"Is it?" Liandra laughed, her eyes sweeping the field.

Connal stood alone, beneath a large banner of MacArran tartan. Her heart quickened its pace as she saw him, resplendent in a new style of kilt that saw his body draped in elaborate folds, the plaid held in place by a wide, gem-encrusted belt. One end of the material had been drawn diagonally across his chest to form a sash that hung over his shoulder, down his back, to his knees. It was fastened at the shoulder by a large, circular brooch. Beneath the sash, he wore a ruffled shirt with a froth of lace at neck and wrists. A sword hung at his side. Every other man and woman also wore his or her best, bejewelled and girt with weaponry.

Across the arena Connal nodded to her and beckoned. Liandra hesitated.

"You had best go to him, else he will come to you," Fianna said.

"I don't want to leave you alone."

"I am all right. Do not make Connal angry. His mood has been awful for days."

"Don't I know it," Liandra replied.

"It seems only you can soothe him, Mistress, so best do it."

Liandra glanced back over her shoulder as she walked towards Connal. She was pleased to see several young women and an elderly man come to stand beside Fianna. In her time of need she was not alone.

"You requested my presence, *Tighearna*?"

Connal smiled. "Almost you sound like a Caledonian, though your accent betrays you."

"Perhaps it's because the word chokes me. You aren't *my* lord."

"Am I not? I thought I had already settled that misunderstanding."

As Liandra folded her arms, her cloak fell

apart, revealing her body-suit. Connal's gaze took all of her in. She saw the narrowing of his eyes in silent warning, and hastily drew her cloak about her. "What did you want me for?" she asked.

"Can a man not have company when he wishes it?"

"I thought you'd much prefer Jenna's intercourse to mine."

Connal laughed. 'Tis a strange way of putting it."

Liandra flushed, wishing time could go backwards, so she could retract that double entendre. The incident on Connal's balcony had both intrigued and unsettled her. After it, she hadn't been able to sleep. She found it frustrating that Connal and Jenna would have spent the night in each other's arms, when she was bereft of company, save for one hairy dog. And now, her comment sounded as if it was spurred by jealousy. Ridiculous!

Connal squeezed her shoulder, his hand warm and gentle. "I called you here to thank you for the pie. Without heather-sugar, 'twas most enjoyable." He laughed and despite herself Liandra managed to smile back.

"I am curious about that coloured swirl on the paper."

"My signature. It's the pattern of my aura."

"Ah, as I recall, you cannot write."

"No."

"Have you ever thought to learn? We have excellent teachers in the Castle, I could ask -"

Liandra shook her head. "It's not for want of

trying, Conn - *Tighearna*. It's because of what I am. Dream-weavers see things differently to other people. We think in colour and sound. That's why, to me, any form of writing is like gibberish."

He frowned, remembering the time he had accused her of being totally reliant on her mechanical servitors, even down to reading and writing, not understanding that she was incapable of it, because of what she was. Why had she not explained? He felt a flush of guilt - because he hadn't given her the opportunity to explain. And that knowledge made him ashamed. He cleared his tight, dry throat. "Yet, to read a book, from a machine's perspective, surely you would not catch the author's intent behind his every word?"

"I don't know."

"Computers are a poor substitute for the voice of a man, or woman." He stared down at her. "I also owe you an apology, Liandra. I too readily accused you of wrong-doing with that tart. I should have thought first. Will you forgive me?"

Liandra glanced up at him. His fingers ever so lightly kneaded her shoulder again, making it difficult for her to think. "Yes," she whispered. "I forgive you."

He smiled, with that gentle intensity he so rarely displayed. It made her stomach muscles clench. His eyes, catching the firelight, flickered amber grey. Warm and sensuous. She could only stare at him.

"I do not want to see you choke over the word, so an easing of your punishment. My way, if you will, of thanking you for that tart. Hence-forth you can, again, call me Connal."

"Thank you. Will you satisfy my curiosity?"

His eyebrow raised. "If I can."

"Your clothes, and those of your kinsmen, they're different. Why?"

"'Tis an ancient form of dress, the *breacan an fhelidh.*"

"A belted plaid. Why is Caledonian so unpronounceable?"

Connal's face reflected pure anguish. "You are going to have to practise your Caledonian. 'Tis quite appalling. We wear the belted plaid for ceremonial occasions, such as a hand-fasting, a funeral, new year, or for Council. 'Tis a mark of respect and honour. Twelve yards of plaid are wrapped around the body and held in place by a special belt."

"No other fastenings?"

"None."

"What keeps it from falling down?"

"The belt, and luck!" Connal grinned. "After the gathering, I have a surprise for you. Before the household, Mistress Jenna wishes to make amends."

"I -" Liandra recoiled in horror, as she heard the most awful blood-curdling noise.

"What is wrong?" Connal asked, his arm around her shoulders. He could feel the trembling of her body.

Liandra stared, terrified, as Connal's pax-man

entered the field. He carried a strange looking creature. Several long things extruded from its body, one of which had attached itself to Dougall's mouth. She had never seen such a symbiotic relationship. Why was the monster screaming?

"Dougall's being attacked! You have to do something!"

"He is - what?" Connal's hand strayed to his dagger.

"The creature on his body. Quickly!"

Connal chuckled. "They are bagpipes, Liandra. A Caledonian musical instrument."

"You call this screeching ... *music?*"

"Aye. Dougall and his band are famous for their skill. It takes many years to learn to play. Few can hold a candle to my pipers."

Behind Dougall, other men entered the field, each carrying a set of bag-pipes. Liandra felt a fool. Yet, who was the greater fool? She for being afraid of a musical instrument, or Connal MacArran for insisting that this piercing wailing was music?

"Now they begin the lament. Listen to it. In this way we mourn Garris."

Liandra heard the different tempos of the dirge. Slow and sorrowful. Fast and furious. Though she had attended many funeral services, this was the strangest and the most moving. Tears sprang to her eyes. Seeking solace, her body of its own accord leaned into Connal. In response, he drew her in front of him. His hard thighs pressed against the backs of her legs, her bottom moulded against his, his ... *Oh*... She swallowed, trying to concentrate on anything except his male warmth, his scent.

The lament ended abruptly, with one note straining high.

"I must speak the eulogy, now," Connal whispered against her ear. He set her from him. She retreated behind the tartan partition where, unobserved by the household, she could watch.

Liandra listened to his reminiscences. There was humour amid the sorrow, though all his words reflected his love and respect for Garris.

"You have taken the high road, *companach*." A faint tremor to his deep voice was the only indicator of his true feelings. "Garris, return home to us on the low road. This, from me, to light your way." Connal set a torch to the bier that was adorned with heather, and draped with a cloak. Upon it lay a great sword, similar to the one Connal wore, similar to the one which they had used as the dream-search focus. The roaring flames stretched high into the night sky.

With his eulogy concluded, Connal again drew Liandra to his side. Together they listened as others spoke about Garris. Liandra felt his body trembling with the effort to control his emotions. She rested her hand on his arm, but he didn't seem to notice.

"Will you explain to me, Connal, what is the high and the low road?"

"'Tis an ancient belief that if a clans-man

leaves his home, he does so by always taking the high road. If he dies away from his kin, then his soul will return by the low road. The road of death. Please, no more questions."

Occasionally Liandra glanced at Fianna. Throughout the ceremony, she stood proudly, her friends and clan-folk clustered around her.

With another wailing melody from the bag-pipes, the ceremony concluded. Instead of returning indoors, the gathering remained on the field. Servants brought out trestle tables upon which were heaped great platters of food and casks of drink.

"Dougall." Connal beckoned and his pax-man strode across the field.

"Aye, My Lord?"

"Liandra is curious about your pipes. Will you show her?"

Dougall's round face burst into a wide grin. "My pleasure, Lady," he said bowing.

Liandra touched the bag-pipes and almost jumped out of her skin as the air rushed out of the instrument with a sound almost like a snarl. "I haven't seen anything like it, not in all the League Worlds."

"Is that a compliment?" Dougall's eyebrows hackled.

"Yes. The League reveres the diversity of culture, no matter how outlandish."

"'Tis a back-handed compliment, Mistress," Dougall said, grinning.

"You have the right of it." Connal laughed.

"My piping has given me a thirst. I want to sample some ale before the others drink the barrels dry." He bowed to them both and hurried away, his kilt swinging high with his haste.

Connal smiled down at her. "Liandra, point out which pastries are your handiwork. I will sample each and let you know how your lessons are proceeding. I hope you are still finding your kitchen work a punishment?"

"I would be lying if I said I didn't enjoy it. I suppose now with that admission, you'll set me to work elsewhere?"

Connal frowned. "Thank you for your honesty. 'Tis precious little you find to like on my world, so I will not rob you of something that gives you pleasure. What sort of man do ye think I am?"

"That I won't answer."

"Will not? Or cannot?"

"For my own sake. *Will not.*"

Connal laughed and with a hand under her elbow, he guided her to a table. "Here, you must try this," he said, pushing a plate into her hands. 'And this. And of course, this leek pie."

"I can't, I'm not hungry. Please." She tried to evade the food he piled onto her plate.

"You will be fading away, Mistress Tavor. I insist you try a little. Just to please me."

"Very well." She spooned a mouthful to her lips and swallowed, forcing it down her throat. Anxiety knotted her stomach. Connal's doting, gentle presence, at odds with his normal brusqueness, coupled with anxiety to put her escape into action, made her so tense, she could hardly eat a thing.

The solemnity of the occasion soon became lost, no doubt due to the amount of wine drunk, Liandra thought. The laughter, the trilling of flutes and screech of bag-pipes was a cacophony of noise which made her senses reel.

"I will be away now," Connal whispered. "I must be seen to mix with my clan-folk, though I much prefer your company. Your silent company," he added, leaning closer, his breath tickling her cheek. "Have I your permission to leave your side?"

She frowned at him. "Yes."

Liandra wandered about the field, speaking to friends.

"Mistress Liandra, there you be!"

"Angas..." she began, uncertainly. Glancing about, she saw Connal in the company of kins women. They eagerly vied with each other for his attention and he sampled their offerings with great appetite.

"Later on this eve there will be dancing. Promise me a dance, or two. At least two, aye?"

"I - I have a head-ache, *Maer* Angas. Please, release my hand."

"I have just the thing for a head-ache. Do not call me *Maer*. Angas will do just fine. That it will."

"Please, let me pass." She used her counsellor's voice, and Angas stepped back.

"Aye, of course," he said. "When the dancing begins, I will find ye."

Liandra slowly slipped away from the mourners. If she had her crystals, she would have been able to glamour herself and leave undetected, but thanks to Connal for his confiscation of her property, that avenue was closed to her. Instead, she had to rely on stealth, and her cloak to make her indistinguishable.

With every step she took, her heart increased its frantic beat. Terrified of discovery, Liandra crept from one shadow to the next until she finally reached the main gate. She passed through the orchard, reached the outer meadow and began the long, arduous descent to the river's edge. Glancing back, she saw Castle MacArran silhouetted against the moon. From the distance, she could hear the sounds of revelry.

She bit her lip. Indecision and another sensation ... remorse ... flooded through her. Such an inappropriate time to escape, Fianna needed her. But when might another opportunity present itself? Besides, Connal had said that Jenna was going to apologise to her. Seven Stars! She knew for a certainty that her enemy would not do so unless coerced. And what would Jenna's future revenge be for the humiliation of a public apology? It didn't bear thinking about.

Liandra hurried along the riverbank, leaving Castle MacArran and its *Tighearna* far behind - in distance, but certainly not in thought.

All night Liandra struggled and stumbled along the riverbank, the ground so uneven and slippery underfoot, that many times she pitched forward, her knees and hands bearing the brunt of her fall. Her face stung with scratches where she had collided with branches and thorns.

The moon disappeared behind thick clouds and did not reappear. That made her task even more difficult, though if any pursued her, they would be similarly hampered by lack of light. Sometimes she stopped in mid-step thinking she heard stealthy footsteps following her. Her imagination, surely?

The lessening of the gloom told Liandra dawn had arrived, though the sun remained shrouded by dark clouds. Then the rain came. At first light drizzle, then as the storm hit, sheet upon sheet of rain fell, making the already spongy ground a morass of clinging mud. It caked her boots and trousers, weighing down her cloak. She flung it aside, leaving it where it fell. The thing was next to useless in keeping her body protected from cold, her enviro belt more than adequate for the task.

Jagged lightning ripped across the sky, temporarily illuminating the gloom. What a dreadful place. The forest crowded in on her. Sometimes she had to double back and crawl through the undergrowth in an effort to maintain her direct heading towards the mountains.

Finally, exhaustion sapped her determination. She could go no further. Squatting down against a thick tree trunk she closed her eyes.

"Hoooot!"

Liandra started upright. The noise came again, followed by another, answering. Something flew nearby, the chill current of its passage swept across her face.

Seven Stars! She had forgotten about the non-human creatures that inhabited Caledonia. As she thought about them a panorama of strange and frightening beasts passed before her eyes. Subliminal tutoring had its advantages, but now it frightened her: Wild-cats, boars, bears, any one of them might be stalking her at this very minute.

You'll soon be safe with the Council. Just think of that! Safe. Free of Caledonia. Going home!

Home. The thought of it momentarily renewed her sagging spirits, before hunger became her next tormentor. Her chance of escape had occurred so suddenly that she hadn't had time to slowly stockpile food. A rumbling stomach was a small price to pay to escape Caledonia. Liandra straightened her shoulders and pushed herself onwards.

It was night-time when the rain finally stopped. Mist swirled so thickly around her, she could hardly see an arm's length in any direction. The heavy rains had caused the river to become a raging torrent. Its churning speed threw water high into the air, drenching everything. While her enviro belt kept her warm, her saturated suit clung to her body.

Liandra crawled up the steep riverbank. Everywhere she looked, nothing but trees, darkness, and water. About her, she heard the furtive scurrying of wild animals. A pair of orange eyes focused on her, blinked once. Slowly, very slowly the beast crept forward, twigs snapping ominously beneath its weight. She caught its long, sleek outline against the trees.

Stepping backwards, Liandra screamed as the ground dissolved beneath her. She rolled down the steep embankment and came to rest, entangled in a thicket of reeds at the river's edge.

Slowly, Liandra came to her senses. So cold. She lay half in the river, the water lapping at her body. She reached down to her belt to re-adjust the setting.

Seven Stars! The enviro belt was gone!

On hands and knees Liandra searched the area. After more than an hour of digging in the mud, she had to admit defeat. With the belt lost, so too her last hope of survival. She shook her head against the thought. She must continue ... somehow ... *must*. She forced herself to stand.

So difficult to move. So cold! She shivered, hugging her arms around her body. Nothing for it, but to continue. It couldn't be much further. From memory she knew the river turned away from the forest before it disappeared into the mountains. She had only to follow it and she'd find the Council. In the warmth and security of her chamber it had been so simple. She hadn't bargained on losing her belt, nor this disgusting weather, nor the hunger, which left her nauseous and light-headed.

She steeled herself. She'd survive the cold and the hunger. She had to. For the only alternative was to admit defeat and return to Castle MacArran. Connal awaited her there. He'd be less forgiving than the monstrous wilderness.

Again struggling up the riverbank, she came to stand on the muddy ground. The trees were thinner and light glimmered in the distance, so she headed towards it.

Perhaps an hour later, she reached the edge of the forest and stared in disbelief at the wide chasm, its bottom obscured by fog. She hadn't seen this from her window! Where was she?

She wasn't lost. How could she be? Asarians had an unfailing sense of direction. Liandra turned back and stumbled through the undergrowth, twigs and branches jagging against her flesh, in her hair, hampering her. With her teeth chattering and her body shuddering in cold, she thought fondly of the cloak she had disdainfully discarded.

Finally, the cold and exhaustion undermined her will to continue. Sinking down to the ground, she leaned against a tree trunk. Hugging her legs to her chest, she rested her head on her knees and closed her eyes. Rest. Just for a few minutes.

Warm ... so warm. The bed on which she lay was so soft. Better than her crystal bed ... better than anything she had ever experienced ...

Liandra jolted from her sleep, shivering with cold. A low snarl came from the depths of the forest. Moments later she saw glowing orange eyes. She heard the sound of something rhythmically hitting the earth with dull thuds. The eyes retreated into the darkness.

The sound came closer, slower now. Alarmed, she jumped up, turning full circle, trying to locate their direction. More wild creatures? She heard a sniffing and growling. A massive shape streaked towards her. Liandra screamed and fled. Seconds later, she ran headlong in the body of a great, black beast. It snorted and reared.

"Dubhlan," Connal soothed. "Steady, steady."

Reeling away from him, Liandra felt something nip at her heels. She fell forward. Turning to look over her shoulder, she saw Fergus sitting back on his haunches, head cocked to one side, his tail wagging.

"Liandra, come here!" Connal jumped down from his horse.

"No!" Liandra pushed herself up and ran. Branches crashed against her, tearing at her clothes and body. She fell, picked herself up and stumbled on, only to fall again. And again. Each time it became more difficult to push herself to her feet. She could hear someone ... something ... following her, not quickly, just a slow, relentless pursuit. Connal, taking his time stalking her, knowing that inevitably he would capture her.

"Liandra, where are ye?" His voice behind her, sounded strange, muffled by the fog and the trees.

Filtering through the tree canopy, the wan yellow light from the moon cast eerie shadows about her. She crouched in the hollow of a dead tree, shivering with fear and exhaustion. Seven Stars, nothing was worth enduring this. Orange-eyes blinked at her through a parting of undergrowth.

Pushing herself to her feet, she edged away. In response, the creature slunk low to the ground, blocking off her intended escape. Again and again, Liandra tried other directions, with the same result. The monster knew its business. Slowly, ever so slowly, it circled her, the distance diminishing, until it revealed itself.

Numbly, she stared at the shaggy-haired creature. It opened its mouth to reveal large fangs, much larger and sharper than Fergus' formidable set. Perhaps she could turn it aside. Liandra closed her eyes and tried a gentle, soothing probe. Instead, the beast screamed and reared on its back legs, shaking its head, more crazed than before.

Another shape streaked out of the shadows. In answer, the creature twisted about swatting, its claws extended. With a pained yelp, Fergus arched away, but quickly returned to run back and forth in front of the beast, trying to lure it from her. Both animals snarled, hackles raised, tails bristled.

Connal drew his horse to a halt. Across the forest clearing his eyes met hers. "Stay very still, Liandra," he whispered.

As if in slow motion, she saw Connal reach behind his back and draw out a bow. His eyes never left the beast as he quickly threaded arrow to string.

Liandra edged backwards. In a blur of speed, with claws extended, the monster hurled itself at her. With a cry she flung herself sideways, not quickly enough, for something raked her shoulder. The beast howled in triumph and turned. With muscles bunched, it leaped. In mid-flight, an arrow shaft embedded itself in the animal's chest. Warm blood spattered over her as the creature fell beside her. She screamed once. Forcing herself to her feet, she stumbled away from the carnage.

"Liandra! Come back!" Connal called after her.

Monsters. Blood.. Death. Never had she encountered such. She had to reach safety. Run on. *Must.*

She came to the riverbank and before she could check her speed, she plunged over the edge, falling, tumbling before finally coming to a painful halt. She lay face down, half in the mud and half in the water. Her arm and side burned like fire. Blackness, tinged with red crept over her.

She heard the squelch of footsteps in the mud, and wearily raised her head. Connal emerged from the swirling mists, his blue-black hair plastered to his face and shoulders, his cloak flapping around his body. He looked like some winged monster. He stood above her, hands on his hips.

Liandra tried to push herself up. The

weakness and the pain were too much. With a small cry she fell forward, and allowed the soothing darkness to take her away from the frightening sight of Connal MacArran towering above her.

Chapter Thirteen

"The *Tighearna* will see you now." Dougall stepped aside as Liandra entered Connal's apartment.

He stood at the window looking out. The rigidity of his back, an ominous precursor to the reception she could expect from him.

Slowly Connal turned. She endured his perusal without flinching, her anxiety coiling inside like a spring. When would he vent his wrath? The calm way he studied her only made her more apprehensive.

Connal thought she looked much like her old self, though perhaps still too pale. At least the dark circles under her eyes were gone, so too the myriad of scratches, weals and bruises on her face and body. What she had looked like when he found her! Arran's Mercy! He still felt sick at the memory of her, lying as if boneless by the river. Before he had found the pulse beat, he had been certain she was dead.

Though ten days had passed since he had returned her to the castle, still he felt the legacy of his fear and exhaustion. And the people in the Castle bore the brunt of it, until he confined himself and his emotions to his private apartments. Only Dougall and Fianna braved his temper, to give him reports on Liandra's progress. It had been a near thing, Katrine had said.

He cleared his throat. "You look as if you are recovered. The wounds have healed? *All* over?"

"Yes. Thank you for what you did for me. Fianna explained."

"Thank Fianna, not me. She knows the workings of your bed. She was the one who monitored you and ensured your injuries were healed by that *infairrnal* contraption. What am I going to do with you, *ban-druidh*?"

"You could get rid of me by sending me home."

Connal smiled, grimly. "Quite out of the question. For the trouble you have caused, not only for me, but for everyone who went searching for you, I have to devise some suitable, lasting punishment. Though what you endured, by the look of you when I found you was chastisement enough. Do I have the right of it?"

"Yes."

"Next time I may not arrive in time to save you from the jaws of a javal-cat. Arran's Mercy! You fool!" He ran a hand through his hair. She had come so close to dying - from the cat, from exposure. The only thing standing between her and death had been Dubhlan's speed and stamina in returning her to the castle.

"You will not be tempted to brave the wilderness again?"

Liandra dropped her gaze to the floor.

"Liandra?" The first hint of ice tinged his voice.

"Once was more than enough. I want to go home, Connal. *P...please*."

P...please. The softly spoken word with its tremor, how it tugged at his resolve. He sighed deeply and came to sit on the edge of his ornate wooden desk. "Aye, I know. If I were in your position, I would have done as you. Your foolish actions would normally warrant a severe punishment."

He wanted to say more. How he admired her tenacity and courage for surviving and continuing where others would have laid down and died. How could he tell her that?

"Come here."

Liandra moved, woodenly, to him. She knew what awaited her. She'd been thinking about it for so long during the days of her recovery, that the thought of it was almost as bad as the punishment about to be inflicted.

He reached out and cupped her chin, his fingers surprisingly gentle. "I want to know what part Jenna played in your escape."

"She did not help me."

Connal shook his head. "That is not what I mean, Liandra. I have the right of it, do I not, that her taunts drove you to run away?"

"She was the final incentive."

He smiled grimly. "I know the games she has been playing with you. She can be very vicious. However, rest assured, Jenna will not trouble you again. She knows that if anything happens to you in the future, I am holding her personally accountable."

"Why do this for me?"

He raised a dark brow. "Every person in County Arran is protected by my laws. No less you. And if one of my people harms another, he or she answers directly to me. I am not a tyrant, Liandra. In your fever-delirium I learned where you were heading, and why. If you wanted your case decided by the Council you had but to ask. Every person on Caledonia has that right."

"I didn't know."

"You live on my world, now, so you have the same rights and privileges as any Caledonian. You also have the same responsibilities and reparations."

Here it comes. Mentally Liandra braced herself as Connal stood up and moved to his chair. He sat down upon it.

"Come here."

Her every nerve screamed a warning, her flesh shivering in terrified anticipation of what was going to happen. Somehow she would have to suffer the spanking, though Seven Stars ...

"Hold out your hand," Connal ordered.

"Pardon me?" Liandra whispered.

"Hold our your hand." He placed a set of heavy keys on her outstretched palm.

"For three months, each morning, you will rise an hour before dawn and prepare the main store-room for the demands of the day."

Liandra frowned. Again, that uncanny knack of his in finding a suitable punishment for her! When others in the Castle were bustling about, she was lying in bed, indulging her only vice, to sleep in. Now he had taken that pleasure from her.

"In the afternoon, so that your energy is diverted from thoughts of escape, you will be under Vanora's supervision and join the ranks of the cleaning staff. You are not to argue with her authority. If I hear of any difficulties-"

"I don't know how to clean."

Connal chuckled. "By the end of three months, *ban-druidh*, you will be an expert. Of that I am certain. You made a reasonable job of cleaning up that spilt tea, and my shirt not so long ago. Now you can hone your skills."

"I'm to be a flesh and blood servitor for you?"

He nodded.

"Is that all?" Liandra asked, coldly.

"Is it not enough?"

"I don't warrant any punishment for what I did, Connal. It was my right to escape -"

"That is as may be, but no right did you have to upset Fianna. When she realised you were gone, she had hysterics. And in searching for you, my people endured danger and hardship in that accursed storm. These are the reasons for my discipline."

Liandra ran her tongue over dry lips. "I didn't realise -"

"And now ye do?"

She nodded. "What happens after the three

months have expired?"

"That will depend upon you, Liandra."

"Am I confined to the castle?"

"After two weeks you may have the freedom of the grounds and the surrounding field. Not a day before. And during this time no one is permitted to speak to you. We call it shunning. It shall act as a stern reminder of what you have done and the trouble you have caused."

"Dougall is guarding my door again. He doesn't have to. I won't try and escape. I know I can't survive the wilderness."

"There you have the right of it. Closer to the mountains the land is already snow-bound. Spare a thought for me, as I have to journey there within the week to the Council meeting. If you still want me to petition them on your behalf then best prepare a document. The Castellan can assist you in this."

"You're being very equitable."

Connal smiled. "Am I not always?"

Liandra regarded him, uncertainly.

"You look as if the axe is about to fall on your neck, *ban-druidh*."

"I don't understand."

"You look like you are going to your own execution. All things considered I would say you got off very lightly. A warning to you. Should there be a next time, you can expect more from me, the least of which will ensure that you will not be able to sit down comfortably for a week. Do I make myself clear?"

"Perfectly."

"Then leave. Remember, if you want me to plead your case before the Council you have two days to prepare your arguments in writing."

Liandra nodded. "The Castellan will help me?"

"Yes."

"Thank you."

She closed the door and breathed a heavy sigh of relief. She saw Dougall outside, hovering in the shadows. As she walked down the passageway, he fell into step beside her.

"You survived that encounter remarkably well."

"Yes."

"I thought to get some liniment from the healer's stores, but do I have the right of it, Connal did not -?"

"He didn't. I have a more suitable punishment. House work."

Dougall roared with laughter. He drew Liandra to a halt, his huge hands on her shoulders. "You frightened us, Mistress. And the *Tighearna* most of all. When he brought you back to the Castle more dead than alive, more often than not it was he who tended you." He shook her once. "It was a foolish, wilful thing to do, without hope of success. Do we have your promise that you will not try such again?"

"You do."

Dougall smiled. "Arran be praised!"

"Did Connal truly tend me when I was sick? He said Fianna did."

"She helped. It was Connal who had your bed

re-assembled and it was he who sat beside you, soothed you while you were in fever. Though if he knew I told you, I would be set to house-work, too."

"I thought he'd be the first person to celebrate the loss of a troublesome alien witch."

"No one thinks of you as such."

"No one?"

Dougall grinned. "Well, Mistress Jenna may. However, for the moment she is of no account in the Castle's scheme of things. And I suspect her diminished status, as far as the *Tighearna* is concerned, will become permanent."

"What has happened to her?"

"For her harassment, she has been sent to the kitchens for four months. She loathes any work, and it is made doubly worse because she and Amilia are not ever on speaking terms."

"Then, I'm sorry for her, I -"

"*Sorry?*" Dougall's voice was shrill with disbelief. "I canna' understand ye! The woman is your sworn enemy, yet you sympathise with her plight." He shook his head. "'Tis a strange one you be. I want you to make me a promise, Mistress."

"Only if you'll call me Liandra."

"Aye," Dougall said. "If any man or woman in the County bothers you again, in any way, you tell the *Tighearna,* or me. Here, no one leads a life made miserable by the actions of another."

"Are you exempt from Connal's shunning?"

"He has done that to you?"

"Aye. I mean yes."

"I will speak to you as often as I wish. Until he orders me otherwise."

"Aren't you afraid of what he'll do to you?"

Dougall laughed. "Connal holds no fears for me. I have been his pax-man 'ere he was weaned from his mother. And truth to tell, when he was a boy, it was I who took a birch to his backside when he became unmanageable."

"You did?"

"Aye. He could be very wilful."

"He hasn't changed," Liandra remarked.

Dougall grinned. "Aye, he has. Whatever you may think of him, Liandra, he is not a cruel man. He listens to the wishes of others when he can, where the needs of the clan are not compromised."

"He doesn't listen to me."

"You are wrong. Connal tries to do his best for you, and for his clan. 'Tis all you can ask of any man. Now inside with ye. I have orders to see you locked in your chamber."

Liandra nodded and as the key scraped in the lock behind her, she walked to the door leading to the patio. It, too, was locked. She rested her forehead on the cool glass and closed her eyes. Now she truly knew she could never escape - unless the Council listened to her petition.

She didn't hold out much hope in that regard. Connal led the Council. She'd never acclimatise herself to this world. *Caledonia.* Almost a pleasant, lyrical name. But there was nothing poetic about this barbarous world. She had experienced its true nature. And nothing, no power in the universe, could induce her to risk another such encounter. *Nothing. Not ever!*

Chapter Fourteen

They deliberately made the work difficult for her, Liandra thought grimly. No matter how hard she tried, she could not please her new overseer. Unlike Amilia's placid nature, Head-woman Vanora found fault with everyone. With everything. Especially with her, Liandra knew only too well. Today, being no exception.

The other girls and women had finished their work for the day. Only she was ordered to remain and re-scrub and re-polish the floor that she considered spotless, though Vanora scathingly called it 'filthy'.

Liandra knew better than argue, for Connal's orders were quite specific. Vanora's word was not to be questioned. If she did so, then Connal would intervene. And she knew what would happen to her then! Dougall would have to fetch that liniment from the healer.

Seven Stars! And maybe Arran might show her a little mercy, too! Every bone in her body ached, and her muscles had given up protesting long ago. Even if she wanted to complain, the shunning meant she was neither seen nor heard by anyone, except Vanora.

Liandra paused in her work, her flesh creeping in warning. Someone was watching her. Casting about, she saw a small shape huddled beside the curtains. Under the guise of her scrubbing, on hands and knees, she edged slowly forward. The unknown watcher retreated behind a curtain, though two tiny feet protruded. Liandra touched one foot and heard a gasp. A girl peered at her between the parted curtains.

"Who might you be?" Liandra asked.

"Mind your work, *ban-druidh*!" Jenna hissed.

Liandra sighed. In Vanora's absence, Jenna was always at hand. The two women conspired to make her life miserable.

Liandra glanced up at Jenna, then frowned down at the trail of mud which had come from Jenna's boots. All along the passage ... her *clean* passage! Ruined!

Lightning fast, Jenna reached into the curtains and drew out the girl. "Be off with you, Bronnia. The one you spy upon is a witch. She will turn you into a beetle and squash you flat beneath her heel."

The child's eyes grew enormous in her pinched face. She fled down the corridor, crying. Jenna laughed maliciously.

Slowly Liandra came to her feet and threw down her cloth. She glared at her nemesis. "That was uncalled for."

"I thought I heard someone speak. Doubtless, 'tis my imagination!"

Liandra pursed her lips. "Shun me if you

want, but -"

"A warning, witch! Leave the child. She is quite unstable. Comes of her tainted blood."

"Oh?"

"She is a bastard. A by-blow no man laid claim to. Now, get on with your work! Or I will see to it that your duties are increased. No time then to play games with anyone. Connal is too soft with you, so it is left up to me to see to your punishment. And so I shall. Get to work!"

"I -"

"Ah, Mistress Vanora, good day to you," Jenna said, smiling sweetly.

Liandra turned. The tell-tale hands on Vanora's thin hips was her trademark, a precursor to a scolding, or worse.

"Look at the dirt! You can start again, witch! I do not care if you stay here until mid-night. I want this so clean and shining that you can eat from it. Do you understand?"

Liandra nodded.

"Get on with it, then."

Jenna smiled in triumph and with her head held high, she strode down the corridor, with Vanora laughing beside her.

Liandra blinked back the tears. They came easily to her these days, and she cursed herself for her weakness. No use crying. She had brought the punishment on herself. Not that she deserved any such thing. She could understand Connal's need to punish. He must maintain discipline over his household. That much she accepted. What she couldn't accept was her inability to help her friends against the alien menace. She had lain awake, night after night, planning and then rejecting every strategy. Marooned on a primitive planet, stripped of her crystal bed, she was rendered ineffectual. Her only hope, if it could be called that, lay in the sympathy of the Caledonian Council.

She dipped her brush into the bucket and scrubbed at the flagstones. Connal had been gone from the Castle ten days. By now, he would be at the Council meeting. What would the other clan-leaders make of her petition? Castellan Ranald and she had spent hours preparing the document.

She smiled as she remembered. A taciturn man, Ranald, he had been quiet and respectful of her, transforming her hesitant oral submissions into written form for presentation to the Council. He had even made some suggestions she had not considered. Daily, she worked with him in the store room, and although he could not speak to her, he made it plain in other ways that he was a friend. He left small presents for her on the desk they shared, so that each morning she would be greeted by a bauble or a flower.

Some of her other friends passed by her as she worked around the Castle. Ostensibly they appeared as if on routine duties, but they always made a point of stopping and smiling at her, before scurrying away. In such ways Liandra was comforted to know they were still her friends, though forbidden to have anything to do with her for the two weeks of her shunning.

Hours later, Vanora having finally approved her work, Liandra returned to her chamber, too tired to go to the kitchen to prepare a meal. When she entered her bedroom she found a covered tray on her desk. Lifting the lid she saw her favourite foods. More gifts, this time from Amilia and Fianna.

Liandra took the tray and sat before the fire. She shivered with cold. For the thousandth time she regretted the loss of her enviro-belt. Despite Fianna bringing her "suitable clothes", Liandra kept to her own suits, though over all she wore a heavy shawl. Whatever else, she couldn't get used to the cumbersome skirts which Caledonian women seemed to wear with ease.

Fergus planted a wet nose on her hand and absently she scratched his head. Like her, the hound had recovered from his mauling, though the fur would never grow again over the scars on his ears and neck. Liandra regretted his injury and pain. Every evening, the hound became her constant and only source of companionship, though how and where he spent his days she didn't know.

"Two weeks have passed, Mistress Liandra," Ranald said. "I have nothing for you to do this morning. Why not go for a stroll in the garden? 'Tis a lovely day."

Resisting the urge to hug him, Liandra flew to the garden. It looked brighter than usual, the scents seeming more pungent after her long absence. She sat in the sun and just drank in the sights, sounds and fragrances.

She wrenched her mind back as she heard the snuffling, like someone's muffled crying. Standing up, she followed the sound and parting a bush, stared down at the bowed head of a child. The little girl looked up at her, her violet-blue eyes brimming with more tears.

"Don't be afraid," Liandra said, holding out her hand. "You're Bronnia, aren't you?"

A slight nod of that tousled auburn head.

"Whatever Mistress Jenna said, I'm not a witch, and I won't turn you into an insect. Why are you crying? What's wrong?"

"Lost Heather."

"Heather?"

"My friend."

"I'll help you look for her, if you like. First you have to come out of there. Now, be careful, the bush has terrible thorns."

Even as she spoke Liandra saw the scratches on the child's thin arms, the rips in her clothes. Such pallor and with dark circles under her eyes, if she didn't know better she'd say that Bronnia was malnourished. Liandra tried a surface probing, recoiling from the illness and sorrow she read within the child. But that was all. Bronnia had around her an almost impenetrable mental shield.

Liandra gently brushed the dirt and twigs from Bronnia's clothing. "Now, let's look for Heather. Where shall we start?"

"Do not know. Lost."

"What does she look like?"

Bronnia held out her hands a foot or so apart. "Heather is this big. Got a bit of black hair and one blue eye."

Liandra gasped. "I've never seen any one like that in the Castle! Was she in some sort of accident?"

Bronnia looked up at Liandra, bewildered. "Dolly!"

"Pardon me?" Liandra asked.

"Heather is my dolly."

"What's a dolly?" Concentrating, Liandra caught the fleeting image from Bronnia. She laughed at her own stupidity. *A toy!* Heather was a child's toy, not some flesh and blood creature. She knew about toys, she had a room full of them back on Asaria. But of all her high-tech playthings, the one she had most cherished as a child was a cushion with eyes. The universe over, it seemed, a child's love was bestowed on the most unlikely objects.

"Where did you last have Heather?"

"In the orchard."

"Then we'll start there." Slowly Bronnia placed her tiny fingers into Liandra's outstretched hand.

By mid-afternoon, they both admitted defeat. Heather remained missing.

"I'll take you to the store room. I'm sure we can find another dolly."

Bronnia pulled away. "No! Want Heather!"

"Is she very special?" Liandra knelt before the sobbing girl.

Bronnia nodded. "Mama made it for me."

Liandra smiled. That cushion which she so treasured as a girl had been the handiwork of her own mother. "I understand. Maybe your mama could make you another one?"

"Mama dead."

"Oh, I'm sorry." Liandra wiped the girl's tears away. "You have other family in the Castle?"

Bronnia nodded slightly and looked down at her feet.

"Who?"

"Uncle Fraser."

"Then I'm sure he'll get you another dolly."

"He hates me."

Liandra gasped. "I'm sure he doesn't."

Bronnia snapped her head up to meet Liandra's eyes in a terrified gaze. "Please, not tell him!"

"Tell him what?"

"That I lost dolly. Clumsy ... I always lose things. He gets angry with me."

Liandra studied her deeply. She caught a hint, a whisper, of something that almost escaped the child. Bronnia's elfin face was gaunt, and her dress threadbare. As far as Liandra knew, everyone in the MacArran household lacked for nothing. Perhaps she'd missed something. For if a child was mis-treated, what other horrors might also have been hidden from her? Now, she'd keep a wary eye on them all!

Liandra put aside her foreboding and smiled down at Bronnia. "Heather is your special friend?"

She nodded.

"Would you like to be my friend?"

Bronnia glanced up at her uncertainly. "You be a witch."

"No I'm not. I'm a bit different to you, but that doesn't make me something you have to be afraid of. Off-world, I've got lots of friends. They can't visit me here. I'm always lonely. I'd like to have a special friend. Will you be mine?"

Bronnia nodded. "Tell me about your friends off-world."

"There's so many, perhaps I could tell you about one each day. Now, Telocthan is an Xadian ..."

They sat side by side under a large oak tree. By the time Liandra had finished telling her about Telocthan, Bronnia was gurgling with laughter. Her humour fled the instant a stranger strode into the garden.

"My uncle is looking for me." Bronnia cringed back behind Liandra.

With bated breath they both watched as the tall thin man swept his gaze around the orchard. But it seemed the shadows beneath the tree concealed them. He walked away, the swiftness of his gait reflecting the anger within.

"You'd better return. Tell your uncle where

you were."

Bronnia hunched over, terror radiating from her. "Cannot."

"He won't hurt you, will he?" Liandra frowned. "I'll look for Heather, but you must return home."

"Promise find Heather?"

"I promise. I have ways of finding lost things."

"Except our missing clans-man," Jenna snapped.

Liandra groaned inwardly. "How long have you been there?"

Jenna smiled. "Long enough. I wondered how long it would be before you and she joined forces. Like attracts like. Witch and brat."

Bronnia's thin fingers bit into Liandra's arm. What had Jenna done to her to make her so afraid? Liandra jumped to her feet. "I don't like it when you call me witch. I never have, in fact!"

"I am *so* sorry to offend you. Still, your presence offends us all, particularly me. Get inside brat! Your uncle seeks you."

Bronnia clung to Liandra's leg.

"Did you not hear me?" Jenna stepped forward, hand raised.

"If you touch her, I'll be very angry."

Jenna smiled. "What will you do to me? Turn me into a toad?"

"That wouldn't be so hard to do, given your disposition," Liandra remarked, dryly.

"Why you bitch!"

"Have a care, *Maera* Jenna. You may think I'm defenceless, but if you push me further,

you'll find out that you've underestimated me."
Liandra rarely used her best, most intimidating
counsellor's voice. It had the desired effect.
Jenna retreated a step.

"Go, Bronnia. Quickly. I'll find Heather and
bring her to you."

Bronnia scampered away and once she had
disappeared into the Castle, Liandra turned to
Jenna. "Understand this, *Maera*. If you take out
your anger upon that child, you'll be very sorry."

"When Connal returns this day, he shall be
the one making you sorry, for threatening me
and for consorting with that abomination."

"We'll see about that. Get away from me,
Mistress, before I put the sleeping-spell on
you!" Liandra hissed.

Jenna picked up her skirts and fled.

Liandra found the doll on the outskirts of the
orchard. It had taken her most of the day, as she
only had the faint remnants of Bronnia's aura
on which to focus. Simple surface probings had
yielded no result, so as a last resort, she had sent
herself into deep meditation.

Liandra stared down at the battered,
muddied doll, disbelieving that anyone could
covet such a monstrosity. It said much for
Bronnia and very little for her kinsman that she
was reduced to loving such a thing.

By the time she retraced her steps, it was
early evening, and cold. Her feet felt like ice,
and her saturated slippers squelched as she

walked across the dew-laden grass.

"There she be!" A shout behind her, and Liandra spun about. A party of men carrying torches intercepted her. Looking over their shoulders she could see other people, in groups of two or three, carrying light-sticks. In the distance there were others on horseback swarming over the countryside.

"What's happened?" Liandra asked.

"The witch is here!"

"Of course I am - "

Before Liandra could say more, one of the men grabbed her roughly by the arm. His comrades closed in on her as she was dragged along.

"What's -?"

"Shut your mouth, *ban-druidh*!"

"I won't."

The man's fingers bit into her arm, sinew scraped against bone painfully and as she went to protest the pressure increased. She kept silent.

Marched with military precision into the dining hall, Liandra saw Connal and several men bent over a table, studying a large piece of paper. Ranald, wringing his hands, stood watching the proceedings.

"Here she be, *Tighearna*."

As Liandra was pushed forward, Connal turned to her. "Did I not say that the next time you tried to escape the Castle, I would make you sorry? Come with me!"

Before Liandra could speak, Bronnia dashed out from a hiding place in the hall.

"Arran's Mercy, child -!" Connal flung out a restraining hand.

Ignoring him, Bronnia raced up to Liandra. "You come back!" she cried.

Liandra knelt down and drew out the dirty, bedraggled doll from beneath her shawl. "See, here she is. I promised didn't I?"

"Thank you, Mistress Liandra," Bronnia whispered.

"You and I are friends, aren't we? That means you have to call me Liandra."

Bronnia's eyes swam with tears.

Connal went down on one knee. He reached out and turned Bronnia to him. "What have you there, child?"

"My Dolly! Was lost! She found! See!"

He recoiled a few inches as the grimy doll was thrust to his face. "The *ban-druidh* found it did, did she?" Connal's voice and face were suddenly soft.

"Liandra, not witch. She *friend*."

Connal raised a dark brow as he regarded the child. "Och, I stand corrected, then."

Liandra stared at Connal's tender regard of Bronnia. What a revelation, that he could be so taken with a child.

He tousled the child's unruly locks. "Then best you look after your dolly more carefully in the future. The *ban-dr* ... your friend has more important things to do than search for lost property. Now away with ye!"

"Thank you for finding Heather," Bronnia said, smiling up at Liandra before scampering away.

Connal stood up. "Everyone, go about your business." He took Liandra's shoulder. "It seems I owe you an apology."

"Did you think I'd run away again?" She smiled grimly. "I'm not so enamoured of drudgery that I'd risk another of your punishments, Connal MacArran."

He smiled, his eyes warm as he regarded her. "Meet me in my chambers within the hour. I have the Council's response to your petition."

"Tell me now."

"All in due course, Liandra. Get out of those wet clothes before you catch your death. I have other business to attend to. So patience, please."

"Easy for you to say, *Tighearna*."

"Patience be a virtue, *ban-druidh*."

"Not one I'm well versed in."

"So I gather. The longer you stand here arguing with me, the longer it will be for you to have your news."

Liandra pursed her lips. *Insufferable! You're so insufferable - especially when you're right!* She turned on her heel and stalked from the chamber.

Liandra tapped lightly on Connal's door and waited for his command to enter.

"Connal -" she began and then halted as she saw he had the company of two other men, sitting at his desk. "I'm sorry, I didn't know you were busy." She turned to leave.

"No, enter. My guests are here to see you,"

Connal said.

Liandra stepped forward, suddenly nervous. The men, one of about Connal's age and the other of the same vintage as Dougall, regarded her with unfriendly eyes. She drew the heavy plaid shawl around her body, pleased for its thickness. Her suit offered little protection against such fierce perusal.

"Liandra, this is Douglas MacLachlan and Andrew MacTiernan from the Council."

She nodded to the older MacLachlan *Tighearna* before acknowledging the younger.

"This is the *ban-druidh*?" Andrew MacTiernan asked.

"*Counsellor* Tavor," Connal corrected, icily.

Liandra glanced at him. He was the first one to call her 'witch', now when someone else did, she saw he didn't like it.

"Will you sit, Liandra?" He waved her to a chair in front of his desk. Resuming his own chair, he drew out a rolled piece of paper from an official looking leather satchel. "We debated long and hard over your petition to us."

"Aye, wasting time with such when we had more important tasks before us!" MacLachlan hissed.

Connal shrugged. "The law is the law, no matter whom -"

"Or *what* petitions us?" MacLachlan regarded her angrily.

"I'm not a what, I'm a sentient being and -"

"Liandra, there is no question you are flesh

and blood. Here." Connal held out the parchment and she took it from him.

Her hands shook so much she could hardly unroll the paper. It was almost a work of art, with its long, flowery script and elaborate signatures and seals of all the men who had witnessed it. "You know I can't read."

"Study it in your own way, to see that every Council member has attested his seal to it. Understand well, Liandra, we did not take your petition lightly."

Andrew MacTiernan moved noisily in his chair and Connal's eyes narrowed as he glanced at him.

Liandra studied the paper. There were many auras attached to the parchment, Connal's the most vibrant.

"Will you read it for me, please, *Tighearna*?"

"I shall." Taking the document from her, he cleared his throat.

"*Castle MacLachlan, Twentieth day, Tenth month, Year 709. We the undersigned having duly considered the petition of Liandra Tavor do, hereby give the said applicant notice, verily, that her petition is dismissed.*"

"Dismissed, just like that? No reason -"

"Because, witch, this is MacArran business," MacLachlan said. "As head of the Council, Connal did argue most judiciously on your behalf. However, we agreed since you are under his protective custody for the reasons he has explained to you previously, it is he, and he alone who decides your fate. Understand this, if it were not for his guardianship, we would have been moved to dispose of you in a more permanent fashion. Connal assures us that he can look after you, and we know his mettle. 'Tis the only reason you still live."

Liandra stood up, her eyes never leaving Connal. "You'd kill me for being here, even though I didn't come willingly?"

MacLachlan waved his hand dismissively. "We gave due weight to the circumstances. Connal brought you here, so you are his responsibility. Should you leave County MacArran without your *Tighearna*'s leave, you have lost his protection. Anyone finding you has the right to execute you. Drowning is as good as any means to dispatch a witch."

"We want no witch contaminating our world," MacTiernan hissed.

Liandra looked from one to the other. "This is barbarous! You condone *this*?" she demanded of Connal.

He spread his hands. "You sought the determination of the Council. You now have it. If it is not to your liking, I am sorry. You cannot have it both ways, Liandra."

"This isn't fair. Not only am I a prisoner, I'm to be killed if I wander too far from home?"

Connal's heart skipped a beat. *Home* ... She had called his castle *'home'*!

"You have the understanding of it, *ban-druidh*," MacLachlan snapped.

"Don't call me witch, you accursed barbarian!"

"Counsellor Tavor -" Connal began.

"Spare me your pleasantries, *Tighearna* MacArran. I'm the *ban-druidh* and always I will be to everyone on your miserable, archaic world. Well, so be it. I have my answer, and thank you for the gentle eloquence with which you delivered my death sentence."

She turned on her heel and strode to the door. Taking a leaf from Jenna's book she slammed it shut, satisfied to feel the door jamb and surrounding corridor shudder with the force of her temper. Just for that moment she wished she truly was a witch. She would turn each man into an Olatian blood-worm, or something even worse!

Liandra returned to her cleaning with a vengeance, exorcising her temper on the wood, the stone work, anything. Keeping to the shadows and disappearing when any came by, her constant companion was Bronnia. Though often more a hindrance, the child assisted her with the work.

"Well, what a surprise! The two witches together!" Vanora hissed. "Wasting time as usual, Tavor! I see my duty list does not keep you fully occupied for you still have time to waste on that brat. Well, another task for you to complete before this day is out. You may scrub the entire length of this passageway."

Liandra pursed her lips. Two days ago, with her shunning lifted, she had protested the amount of work required of her, especially when it seemed, in comparison, some of the other women did very little. In retaliation, Vanora gave her the chore of cleaning out a top-most tower. A place untouched for years, it had become a haven to spiders and dust. Liandra had nightmares about those crawling insects ever since. She hadn't voiced any of her complaints again.

"Anything you wish to add, witch?"

Liandra shook her head, not trusting herself to speak.

"Then best you start. The sooner you do, the sooner you be finished."

Once Vanora had gone, Bronnia came out of hiding. Side by side they began to scrub the floor.

"She hates you, too. Why?" Bronnia asked, her eyes huge in her small face.

"Because I'm different. Some people find it hard to accept another who is not like them," Liandra said.

"Maybe that is why my Uncle hates me."

"No he doesn't."

"Does. Said I killed my mama."

In shock, Liandra dropped her scrubbing brush. "Who told you such a thing? Who are *they*, Bronnia?"

The child shook her head. Liandra saw she was too afraid to speak.

"That snivelling brat *did* kill Heather MacLeod," Jenna said, striding forward.

Furiously, Bronnia stood up, her small hands balled into fists. Jenna only laughed at her display.

"Why do you insist Bronnia killed her mother?" Liandra demanded.

"'Tis true! Heather was only eighteen when her belly swelled with that one. No man came forward to claim responsibility, though there were several who would have taken Heather as wife, thereby averting a scandal. But no! My kinswoman would have none of them, no matter what her father said, or did. And when she whelped the brat, she was much weakened, so that for almost two years after, she lay confined in her bed. She died from the strain of bearing this little bitch."

"Heather MacLeod was a kinswoman of yours?"

"Aye."

"And you treat her child in such a way? For shame!" Liandra said.

"There be shame - shame that such a misbegotten creature as Bronnia could carry the blood of MacLeod."

"You're a hate-filled woman, *Maera* Jenna."

"You are to blame for it! See here!" She held out her hands. "Red and raw from peeling the potatoes. Not to mention the other work I am given for simply having the courage to confront you."

Liandra regarded Jenna's long slender fingers. They didn't look too bad to her, not in comparison to her own sore and water-shrivelled hands.

"You are an affront to my eyes. Both of you!" Jenna towered over Bronnia and to her credit the little girl stood her ground. Liandra had to admire her courageous display.

"Still got a bit of spirit left, have ye? Your uncle knows how to treat such. Get you gone!

The witch and I have things to discuss."

Liandra came to her feet. "Go along, Bronni, I'm all right. Truly."

Reluctantly, Bronnia walked down the corridor, pausing every few paces to look back over her shoulder. Liandra waved her away. The confrontation had been long delayed. Too long, Liandra thought. Bronnia was not going to be allowed to witness it.

Eye to eye the two women glared at one another. Liandra folded her arms and regarded Jenna in the same infuriatingly arrogant way Connal often did to her. Jenna's face reddened, though she remained silent.

"Well, what is it you wish to say to me, *Maera* Jenna?"

"Only this -"

She stepped forward and before Liandra knew what had happened, she felt the stinging slap across her cheek. As she reeled back in pain in surprise, Jenna advanced, her hand raised to deliver another blow.

A flurry of robe attached itself to Jenna's skirts. Liandra could only stare in disbelief as Bronnia attacked the woman with all her tiny fury.

"Bronnia, no!"

The corridor echoed with the sounds of Jenna's cries and Bronnia's high pitched squealing. Liandra stepped into the foray, dodging fists and nails, trying to interpose herself between the two combatants.

"Arran's Mercy! What goes on here? What

deamhans are invading the Castle?"

The sound of Connal's voice restored a measure of order. Jenna sprang back, Bronnia after her, until Liandra managed to prise her from her victim.

Liandra knelt down and held Bronnia to her. The child sobbed hysterically against her chest.

"I said what goes on here? The screaming could wake the dead! I will not have fighting in my halls. Jenna? Liandra?"

"I-" Liandra began.

"Both the witches attacked me," Jenna whined. "I was walking down the passageway and that brat started on me. Connal ... *ghraidh*. " She burst into tears.

Connal folded his arms and frowned at Jenna.

"I witnessed the event, *Tighearna*," Fianna said, emerging from the shadows. "As much as it pains me to say, my kinswoman is to blame for this whole affair."

"You lying bitch!" Jenna hissed.

"Your tears are suddenly dry, Jenna," Connal remarked. "Continue, Fia."

"My sister taunted them both. They showed much restraint. In their place, I would not have kept silent. For what she said about Bronni's mama ... my little kinswoman attacked Jenna. Liandra tried to separate the two."

Connal's mouth twitched in suppressed laughter as he regarded Jenna. "The child attacked you?"

"The brat is a lunatic. She ought to be locked

295

up, Connal."

"Bronnia you canna' assault people just because of what they say to you. If you have a grievance, you must come to me and I will listen. Do you understand?"

Bronnia looked down at her feet and nodded. "*Tighearna?*" she whispered. For an instant she raised her tear-filled eyes up to Connal.

"Yes, *gradhag*."

"I am not a witch, Liandra is neither!"

Connal ignored Jenna's snort of derision. "That I know. Now you must apologise to Jenna."

Though her cheeks paled, Bronnia forced her chin up. "'Tis sorry I am, Mistress Jenna."

"And so you should be. You try that again and -"

"You shall do nothing. Henceforth, the child is under my personal protection," Connal snapped.

"As all witches are, it seems," Jenna said, tartly.

"I see your stint in the kitchen has not mellowed your temper. You can have a further three months there to consider your place in my household."

"You cannot be serious? I am no kitchen-maid. I am your -"

"There is nothing between us, Mistress MacLeod."

"Connal -"

"As you so rightly pointed out to me some time ago, a cold bed is not a pleasant state. Your side of the bed has been chill overly long. Think about why."

"I do not have to! 'Tis the witch! She has

shrivelled your manhood!" Jenna screamed.

Connal's face flamed red, as he stepped towards her.

"Please, Connal," Liandra interposed herself. "She doesn't know what's she saying. She loves you."

He glared at her. "This one has hurt and taunted you, yet you intercede on her behalf."

Jenna stepped forward. "I need none of your sympathy, witch! Mark my words, Connal MacArran, your bed will be comfortless for months to come."

"Aye, I know it. Do not seek to warm it ever again."

Jenna gasped. "My Connal -" Clapping a hand to her mouth, she picked up her skirts and fled down the corridor.

Connal sighed. Dragging his fingers through his hair, he winced from the dull throbbing at his temples. He glanced over his shoulder, and only then did he notice members of his household gathered to witness the confrontation. He saw their shock and amusement, and surprisingly, fierce approval for what he had done. Dougall, at the fore, nodded to him.

"Have you nothing to do?" Connal shouted. Immediately, they disappeared into rooms, down corridors. A silent, hasty retreat.

Connal laughed grimly to himself. The clan would revel in the intimate details of what had just occurred, gossip amplifying it out of all proportion. And why? Because, for once, his temper had gotten the better of him. Instead of dealing with the women in private, where he could maintain some dignity and secrecy, his personal life had become a public spectacle.

With Jenna gone, he felt a weight lift from his shoulders. Still, it had been a cruel way to break the news to her. They had shared many pleasurable nights and days bringing comfort to one another. When his humour improved and Jenna was in a receptive mood, he would apologise. A severing of lovers should never be done in such a callous way. *Arran's Mercy!* That dull throb in his temples had become a full-blown headache.

Sighing, he glanced at Fianna. "I am afraid, *ghraidh*, your sister will not forgive you for taking the side of another."

"Jenna and I are not close, that you know. I made my choice, Connal, Are you all right, Liandra? You look sick."

Connal swung on her immediately. "Aye, you do look pale. Even more so than usual. What ails ye?"

"Nothing." As she went to collect her bucket and cloths, Connal restrained her.

"Fianna, see to Bronnia. Liandra, I need to speak to you privately," Connal said.

"More punishment?"

"No *ghraidh*." Connal took her arm and escorted her along the corridor.

"Where are you taking me?"

"To my chamber."

"Why?"

"I have matters to discuss with you. I do not want to be disturbed."

"What do we have to talk about?"

"Patience, Liandra."

"I'm through with being patient!"

Opening the door for her, Connal ushered her inside his apartment. He motioned her to a seat before the fire. Going to the sideboard he poured two goblets of wine. He brought them to the fireside and handed her one. She sipped the drink gratefully, he noticed, though her hand trembled. From fear, fatigue, or something else? He wished he had the power to read her mind. She kept so much from him, that it was difficult to know what she was thinking and feeling.

By Arran! He sucked in his breath. No Caledonian ever wanted to be a mind-reader. And he was *wanting* to? He had allowed her to touch his mind once, to save their lives. Maybe the witch had tainted him, more than he knew! He ran a hand across his eyes. That pounding in his skull was now like a hammer hitting an anvil.

Chapter Fifteen

"What would you say to me, Connal?" Liandra prompted, after the silence between them had lengthened into minutes.

"I am sorry. All the screaming has brought on a headache, I canna' concentrate."

She cocked her head to one side, reading him. "I can help to get rid of the pain. Will you let me?"

"Aye, just this once you can practise your witchery on me."

Laughing gently, Liandra stood up. "How can you, a big, strong man, be afraid of one small counsellor?"

"Do not provoke me, *ban-druidh*. Headache or no, I can best you, if you force the issue."

"Mm."

"Why is it I feel so uneasy with your acquiescence?"

Liandra saw how he forced himself to smile. His eyes as dark as midnight were narrowed with pain. Standing over him, she found the position intolerable. She knelt at his feet.

"What are ye doin'?" Connal frowned down at her as she wriggled about.

"Trying to get comfortable. I can't work on

you unless I'm in harmony, body with mind."

She tested several positions, and to his consternation the one she seemed well pleased with had her kneeling before him, between his legs. Connal swallowed against an accursed dry, tight throat. A trickle of perspiration ran down his spine.

She cupped his face in her hands, her fingers across his cheeks up to his temples. Carefully, she pressed her finger-tips to the temple points, gently massaging.

"What are ye doing?"

"Close your eyes, Connal. Relax, I'm not going to do anything terrible to you."

Chuckling, he closed his eyes and leaned against the back of his chair. "It is like heat flowing from me," he whispered.

"I'm drawing out the imbalance."

At first the softness of her fingers on his face was very welcome. Her skill soon took away the throbbing in his skull, though in its place, was the growing longing to have her hands on other parts of his anatomy. And at that idea, his body tightened, hardened. Pain of another, more familiar, and of a much less welcome kind replaced his headache. His body pulsed with the hot flush coursing through his veins. Faster and faster, hotter and hotter.

It was with the greatest difficulty, he opened his eyes and cleared his throat. He took her hands from his temples. "My thanks, Liandra. Your healing is very swift and certain."

"I haven't finished -"

"Aye, you have. Now back in that seat, so we can talk." *Because if you kneel at my feet and continue to touch me, I will not be able to think clearly, let alone ... talk.* Connal smiled, grimly. "My Castellan speaks highly of you, and that is praise indeed, for Ranald can be reticent. He also tells me things which I am ashamed to discover occur in my Castle, behind my back. I must also talk to you about your petition."

"They said you spoke eloquently on my behalf."

"Did you think I would not support your application?"

"It is you who keep me here."

"Aye, but I can understand how you feel. Believe me, Liandra, I would release you if I could. Therefore, I am responsible for you and your comfort. If I was stranded on some League world, I would be sick to my stomach. Is that why you are ill and pale? Is that it, *gradhag*?"

Liandra looked up at him. Those softly spoken words ... *a dear little one*? She wasn't any such thing to him, was she? Perhaps his endearment was a ruse to subdue her?

"*Ban-druidh*? Answer me."

She flushed and dropped her eyes.

"Have you spurned our food again?"

"No. Fianna successfully tempts me with the foods Amilia insists on personally preparing for me."

"Then why do you look as if you be ailing for something?"

"Because I worry about -"Liandra bit her lip.

"What do you worry about?"

"The aliens, and my friends trapped in the dream-state."

"They may be free by now."

"They may not."

"Worrying is only hurting yourself, Liandra. You must learn to accept that you cannot right every wrong. This takes wisdom and courage. We each do what we can. Hard lessons have taught Caledonians to know when we cannot undo a wrong."

"You sound like a counsellor."

"Do I?" Connal's smile faded. "The aliens have not invaded our world, Liandra, so it gives me hope that all is as it should be."

She regarded him intently. "You know more than you're telling me, *Tighearna* MacArran."

"Aye. Ask me no questions, for I canna' answer them. Just trust me." He paused. "Closer to home, I know of some wrongs that need to be righted. Henceforth, you are relieved of your cleaning duties. From what I am told you have carried the burden of cleaning almost single-handed. I am sorry for that. Vanora can be a vicious woman. I thought I had cured her of her disposition with my last punishment."

"I don't understand her -"

Connal snorted."Nor do I. The problem I have, Liandra, is that normally Lady MacArran would oversee the domestic arrangements of this Castle, and ensure that none is set upon, that no person of authority perverts his or her responsibility. I have no wife to do this task, so it falls to me. I cannot be everywhere, see all. Fianna tried, but she is too gentle to control the household." He regarded Liandra's downcast face, and a sudden thought came to mind. He smiled. "I need someone who is used to dealing with people in a professional, dispassionate way. In short, a trained counsellor."

Liandra gasped and snapped her head up. "Me? I cannot!"

"You have the expertise. I want this of you, Liandra. Please."

Liandra sighed. That word *please* - he used it, oh so well, to his advantage. How he purred and spoke softly when he wanted to, with a voice which stroked her senses, made her stomach flip. So many things ...

"It will be a task to keep you busy, though not so much that you cannot find time to relax and enjoy yourself. Besides, I have the feeling the house will run that more efficiently with your skills."

"And what will your wife say when she comes to Castle MacArran? Surely then I'd become redundant."

Connal laughed. "I run the castle as I see fit. If I should take a wife, I can keep her busy with other things than my household. Henceforth, Liandra Tavor, you will be Chatelaine of Castle MacArran."

"Have I no say in the matter?"

"Do you truly object?" He paused and regarded her deeply. "Well?"

"Vanora and the others will not accept my position -"

Connal's eyes turned steely grey. "You leave them to me. Make no mistake, Liandra, my people shall know that when you speak, it is my voice they hear! Your detractors will be subdued."

"I'm not certain it'll be that easy."

"You underestimate me, I think."

"No, you underestimate them," Liandra said. "However, I would prefer it if you allow me to build my own authority."

Connal frowned. "Understand, Liandra, their domination of my household is at an end. You may try it your way, but if you have difficulties, then I will intervene. Now, go to my desk. In the top shelf there is a set of keys on a ring. Bring them to me."

Liandra did as she was bid. Rummaging in the desk, she was shocked to discover her enviro belt. She brought the keys to Connal and dropped them and her belt on his lap.

"Fergus found first your cloak and then your belt. I had forgotten about it."

"What a convenient memory you have! Well, at least I can now have it back and wear -"

"No, Liandra. The belt stays with me, for the time being. No arguments! It shall be returned to you eventually."

"What possible use can you have for it? I need it."

"You do not."

"Without it, I'm always cold."

"Then wear proper clothes, as befits a lady. Indeed, now you be the Castle Chatelaine, I insist you dress accordingly. No more of your off-world indecencies."

"And I told you before, I find Caledonian clothes suffocating."

"Then you have a choice. Dress appropriately, or suffer the cold. The belt stays with me. And do not seek to find it, as you did the crystals."

Liandra folded her arms and glared at him. "How long must I lose the use of my belt?"

Connal shrugged. "For a week I want you to rest. Then you will be presented to the household in your new capacity. Here."

He drew her forward, and pushing aside the heavy folds of her shawl, he fastened the ring with its heavy jangling sets of keys onto the flimsy belt around Liandra's waist. A waist that his two hands could span. He rested his palms against her hips.

"Connal, is something wrong?"

He drew his mind back to the present. "The keys mark you as my Chatelaine. Only you and my Castellan have such. Now sit, we must talk further."

Liandra assumed her seat, and sipped her wine.

"The Council was divided in what they saw as their duty to you. We argued long and MacLachlan, as always, the most unyielding. If you had reached the Council, Liandra, before it was convened, he could have disposed of you as he saw fit."

"You would have let him kill me?"

Connal's lips clamped tightly together at the thought. "So far distant, how could I protect you? By the time I reached the Council, it would have been over. Naturally, I would have sought satisfaction for the wrong done to you, and me. Cold comfort for us both! In the circumstances, the terms given you are fair. You have the freedom of County Arran. If you wish to travel farther afield, then you may, in my company or in the presence of one of my pax-men. Venture forth alone, however, and you will be treated like any invader."

"I am not an invader -" She caught the faintest whisper from him ... a slip from his mind. "Connal. I sense something. You have known alien invasion before? Is that why you fear outside contamination? Is that it?"

"Somewhat of the truth, Liandra." Connal glanced down at his goblet and twirled it in his fingers. "Let us say we have known such long ago and leave it at that."

"Then -"

"No! I canna' tell ye! Maybe one day in the future, but for now, ask me nothing more."

"Connal, please. I'm trying to understand -"

"I know. 'Tis something of which we do not speak. And do not try to interrogate my people. Your questions will upset them, and I do not like my people worried. Do you understand?"

"Oh yes." Liandra sighed.

"There is one more thing. As I said your cleaning duties are finished, save for one place. I want you to keep my private chambers in order. Your task is supervision only, save for my bed-chamber. That I, solely, want you to tend."

"You're tormenting me!"

"How so? I do not want the castle alive with gossip. For weeks, no woman has warmed my bed, though Vanora has looked for evidence of it. I am told there has been much speculation. You do not gossip, so I know I can trust you to keep my secrets. Will you do this for me, also? Please."

Liandra nodded. "If I must."

"Now be off with you. I have work to attend."

Standing up, she walked to the door.

"Remember, *ban-druidh!* I want you to rest and eat, and when you change your mind about wearing suitable clothes, then you know where the store-room is to be found."

Liandra eyed him murderously, and closed the door sharply against his laughter.

Chapter Sixteen

"And for two days the castle was swarming like a hornet's nest," Dougall said. He laughed and sipped more wine.

"But 'tis settled down now?" Connal asked.

"Aye, though at first Katrine was besieged with every manner of complaint. *I am too sick to do any extra work* - that was a favourite. Katrine's remedy for such was a dose of fish-liver oil. After that, none complained of imaginary illness."

Connal grimaced. As a child, he had suffered liberal doses of that bitter, unctuous tonic. Now just the thought of it made his stomach churn. Hastily, he gulped down his wine, without savouring the vintage. "And the *ban-druidh*? How does she fare?" He had not interfered with Liandra's new duties, though he had sent Dougall to discreetly monitor.

"Well enough," Dougall said. "When Vanora heard the news she was to be replaced, her face would have curdled new milk. Ranald, at his most eloquent, took great delight in the telling. 'Tis a pity you missed it! Vanora and Jenna are busy peeling vegetables under Amilia's supervision. Every second day they form part of the cleaning detail. The new roster sees all in the household sharing the domestic duties. Even Liandra lends a hand, though she keeps well out of the way of Vanora and her cronies."

"Truly? Liandra cannot abide house work."

"Aye, you have the right of it. She told me she will not ask any to do a task she, herself, is not prepared to undertake. An exceptional woman, our off-worlder."

Connal grunted. "Liandra already has her fair share of cleaning, she tends my chambers. What is she about?"

Dougall grinned and shrugged. "She has not enlightened me in this regard. However, I well know that given half the chance, many women would gladly take up the task of seeing to your apartments, more particularly, your bed-chamber. A rare opportunity -"

"Spare me!"

"'Tis what is said," Dougall replied. "I only repeat it for your edification."

"Then do not. I prefer to remain in ignorance."

Dougall chuckled. "And I heard your chamber was the scene of a few tantrums?"

"Some grumbled about their change of duties. When they sought my ruling on the matter, I suggested that if they could find the time to complain, perhaps they needed more work to fill their days. They kept silent after that. With this new roster, there seems to be a lighter attitude around the castle. Do I have the right of it?"

"Aye. At first there was much dissension, but 'tis hard to fight with someone who will not argue back, or lose her temper. Mistress Liandra makes a fine Chatelaine."

"*Mistress* Liandra?" Connal asked.

Dougall blushed. "She deserves the title and respect of us all," he said, pointedly.

"I agree."

"Why give her the role which normally belongs to the wife of our *Tighearna*? She has the lady's apartments, and 'tis rumoured you have no one to share your bed. What say you to this conjecture? Is there something you are not telling me?"

Connal grimaced and shrugged his shoulders. "You read more into it than there is. Truly! My *ban-druidh* needs something to occupy her time, and I need someone on whom I can rely to run my house. The two problems are solved in Liandra. 'Tis all."

Dougall raised a red brow. "Och aye? I think it more than that. Especially since you call her MY *ban-druidh*."

It was Connal's turn to blush. "You *think* too much, old friend."

Inwardly Connal was pleased. He had not mis-placed his trust. Another in her position might have sought revenge, not so Liandra. The only people who criticised the new arrangement were those who had been accorded special favour by Jenna or Vanora. Now all were treated equally, he believed that in time, the Castle would go about its business as if nothing had happened.

Pity I cannot do the same. Ever she reminds me of ...

Connal closed down that thought. Of late his mind had turned more and more to that empty bed of his. It had never long remained so in the past. Jenna saw to that, and before her there were others, always discreetly ensconced in his arms, but always someone to share the cold, lonely nights. Now, the only women to grace his chambers were Liandra and her cleaning detail.

They polished and cleaned dutifully. He often found an excuse to be in his rooms when they arrived. Often he watched the way Liandra moved around the apartment. She kept to her off-worlder clothes, the tight trousers encasing her comely legs, before the tantalising sight disappeared up under the heavy folds of her shawl. It drove a man to distraction, to glimpse a little of what she kept hidden. Still, that was the way he wanted it, was it not? And to his chagrin he found more than a few of his men, both old and young, following her passage around the Castle with smouldering, speculative eyes.

Be damned! He would not return her belt. If he did, then doubtless she would dispense with that shawl and gallivant around in next to nothing, in that thrice accursed Asarian robe of hers, or worse still, in that body-hugging pant suit. And that thing was worse than wearing nothing at all! How it highlighted her figure, hugging her curves ... *Arran's Mercy!*

Connal slammed down his goblet and strode to the window. He glanced back at his pax-man to see him watching in silent amusement.

"What be so funny?" he demanded.

"'Tis you. Ye like a caged wild-cat pacing up and down."

"Damn your hide!" Connal said, and stepped out onto the balcony. He leaned on the balustrade. Below, the gardeners were trimming the lawn. He could smell the fresh cut grass. Further on, others were collecting fruit from the orchard. Between the trees, he saw a flash of robe and smiled. Many people made the shadows beneath the trees their trysting place. He never had. He preferred privacy. Besides which the ground would be next to impossible with stones and twigs digging into one's flesh. Call him old, he much preferred the comfort of a warm, soft bed for his liaisons.

His smile turned to a frown as he saw Liandra emerge out of the shadows, and a little behind her, Angas. Connal sucked in his breath. He had noticed Angas on several occasions, following her, waiting for a kind word or gesture.

"Damn you, boy!" Connal's hands throbbed in pain as he gripped the stone balustrade. He watched Liandra dodge Angas' outstretched hands before she scurried into the orchard. Arran's Mercy, he would ... Then he sobered. He had imprisoned Liandra, forcing her to endure a life which was foreign to her. It suddenly occurred to him that perhaps one day she would seek out the company and pleasure from a man. *Or men, more like!* One lover would not be enough for her exotic alien tastes. In the future she might even look for marriage and children. Something that all Caledonian women sought, perhaps an alien witch also? If she wished to take a lover, how could he deny her?

Connal swore and dragged a hand through his hair. What they had shared together ... the memory of her slender beauty still haunted him and woke him at night in a fevered longing.

"I will not be sharing ye!" Connal gasped, as he heard his words. *What he just said!*

"Something amiss, Con?" Dougall asked, casually. Too casually.

He glanced sideways. Unnoticed, sometime, Dougall had joined his side. How long had his pax-man been there? *Long enough*, if Dougall's grin was any indication.

Connal strode from the chamber, all but running by the time he reached the orchard.

Following the sound of Liandra's voice, it took no time to find them. Angas had her trapped against a tree.

"Good morning to you, Angas," Connal said, tightly, noticing that Liandra looked almost relieved to see him.

With a face as red as a beet, Angas turned to him. "Good morning to you, *Tighearna*."

"What is it you do here?"

"I was ... uh ... discussing -"

Connal folded his arms and scowled. "Off with ye! I want a word with my *ban-druidh*.

Angas's lips drew down at the corners. *My*

314

ban-druidh - the possessive endearment hung heavily in the air between the two men. Angas retreated.

"My thanks for that, Connal." Liandra drew the shawl tighter around herself. "He pursues me everywhere."

"And why not? You entice him with your clothes."

"I do not! Connal, it says little for your men, if I'm not free to dress as I choose and then walk without fear of being accosted."

He raised an eyebrow. "The blame lies entirely with you, Liandra. A flirting woman -"

"I don't flirt."

"Perhaps not as you understand it. On this world we do not flaunt our lovers before all eyes. Caledonians do not live a celibate life, merely a circumspect one. As long as both parties are consenting, and old enough to be aware of the consequences of their actions, and no clan affiliations are compromised ... If you wish to have a man, then do so a little more discreetly.

"I don't want a lover!" Liandra snapped.

Connal flicked back her shawl, his eyes smouldering as he took in her curves. "Look at yeself. The way ye dress is a tease in itself."

Liandra retrieved her shawl. "Get used to it, because I won't wear anything else."

"I have watched how my men follow you about with their eyes. Their curiosity shall cause you trouble. I will not have you behave like a wanton. Henceforth, in public, you will wear only Caledonian clothes."

"I won't."

"You shall, *ban-druidh*! If you fail to obey me in this, I will dress you myself. Your choice."

Liandra folded her arms and glared up at him. "Why are you so intractable? I don't understand you."

"As *Tighearna*, my word is law. My clan knows they must obey me. It is their duty."

"I once read that absolute power can corrupt absolutely."

"Am I corrupt?" Connal grinned. "Then, another order for you, *ban-druidh*. I want you to take your meals with me each night in the dining hall. No more skulking in your room."

"Anything else?"

"Not that I can think of. I will tell you if anything further comes to mind."

"Damn you, Connal MacArran!"

He laughed.

Still with his laughter ringing in her ears, Liandra stalked away and stormed into her chamber. She sent cushions flying about the room.

"And then he said I was to dress appropriately and join him for dinner. *Every* night!" Liandra kicked a cushion aside and paced up and down. Fianna watched patiently, then returned her attention to her knitting.

"Why are you smiling?" Liandra demanded.

"Indeed, you must see to your wardrobe, and

you should join us in the hall. 'Tis only the right thing to do."

"I thought you'd be on my side."

"So I am, Liandra. So I am. Connal has the right of it. The men do ogle you! Besides, you must be cold in those thin clothes. When winter comes, you will be freezing to death if you do not see to your attire."

That halted Liandra's furious pacing. "It gets *colder*?"

"Aye. When the frosts and snow come, we do not venture outside, sometimes for days. Weeks if we become snow-bound. You do not have to wear clothes you dislike. You can alter them to your own tastes. Only, show a little discretion."

"That's what he said. *Discretion*! Still, he did say I could wear any Caledonian clothes ..." Liandra smiled.

"What are you intending?"

"Nothing ... everything."

Fianna laughed. "'Tis always dangerous to allow a man to have his way too often. Our *Tighearna*, no exception!"

They exchanged conspiratorial grins.

Silence descended on the diners the moment she strode into the hall. For the amount of trouble she had gone to, Liandra had the satisfaction of seeing the choked, pained look on Connal's face, as she joined him at the high table.

From the store-room, Liandra had appropriated a boy's kilt which, after a little alteration, moulded itself to her figure. Over all she wore a blue velvet tabard, and around her neck, a trailing silk scarf. Velvet slippers and fine hose completed the outfit.

Liandra smiled sweetly at Connal as he stood up to greet her. He pulled out a chair next to his and helped her to be seated, before resuming his place. The dining hall began to return to normal, as more and more people resumed their conversation and laughter.

"Is something wrong, *Tighearna*?" Liandra asked, thinking that Connal looked as if he was fit to explode.

"Nothing," he ground out.

"You look feverish. Should I send for the healer? That fish-liver oil does wonders. Cured some of your kin-folk of their recent malaise." She laughed. If anything Connal looked even sicker at her suggestion. Hastily, he gulped down a great mouthful of wine.

He glanced at her. "Those clothes were not exactly what I had in mind."

"You did say I must wear Caledonian clothes when I venture out of my room. These are such."

"They are men's clothes."

"But Caledonian."

"Aye. Well, then let me make it plainer to you then, *ban-druidh*. You are to wear Caledonian *women*'s clothes."

"I see."

"I do appreciate your effort, however."

"Thank you."

"I am certain you will look even more fetching in proper attire. 'Tis best to leave something to a man's imagination, for if 'tis so easily satisfied an admirer may quickly lose interest."

"I have no desire to interest any!"

"Ensure it is so, then, by your choice of clothing when next you come to my table. However, whether you like it or not you are the object of lust from at least one quarter I could name."

"Don't be ridiculous. If you're going to torment me -"

As Liandra went to stand, Connal's hand around her wrist restrained her.

"I have not finished. Besides which I did not give you my leave to depart."

She tore free from his grasp. "I don't need your permission to come and go."

"Do you not? You sit at my high table, so 'tis only courtesy to ask leave of your host. Or do you have so little regard for our ways you would flout the tradition?"

"No, I cannot defy your convention."

"Good, now sample treats from my table. Amilia has accomplished wonders, tonight. Besides, you are still much too thin."

"I am not."

"Why are you always so contrary?" He sighed and shook his head in exasperation.

"Because you're always so domineering."

"I?" Connal chuckled. He held out one of the silver plates. "Try this. I like peace and quiet when I dine, so if you are eating, you cannot argue with me."

Insufferable barbarian, arrogance and logic. "I'm not hungry."

Unperturbed, Connal placed food on her plate. She stared at it. The aroma made her mouth water. Glancing sideways at him, she watched as he ate neatly and quickly. He smiled at her between mouthfuls. Liandra looked away, studied the diners in the hall, anything to take her mind far away.

Sometime later, with hunger gnawing at her, she eyed her plate, longingly. Why was she starving herself to spite him? She was the one suffering, not him. *Not ever him*. She would be light-headed from hunger if she continued with her childish display.

Tentatively, she raised the fork to her mouth and bit into the pie. Seven Stars! Its taste was like nothing she had ever savoured, not in all the League Worlds! She swallowed and ate more, as quickly as she could. Only after she had begun her second course did she look sidelong at Connal. That infuriating triumphant smile on his lips ... She placed her fork on the table and half turned from him as he laughed.

"It was good enough to tempt even you, Counsellor," he said. "Admit it."

"It's amazing how one becomes less discerning in the face of starvation."

Connal threw back his head and roared with laughter. "You will come to enjoy our way of life, of that I am certain. Weeks ago you would not even touch our food. You called it poison, as I recall." He regarded her over the rim of his goblet.

Liandra glared at him. Now, the thought of eating was out of the question. Connal had won that round. She was determined it would be his first and last victory!

And how many times had she thought that? Connal had a way of undermining her resolve. Had a way of unsettling her, so that sometimes it was difficult to think, to know what to do. So much for being a professional counsellor! She couldn't even check the outrages done to her by one conceited barbarian.

Chapter Seventeen

As Liandra rounded the corner, she heard the strange sound. A ringing, clashing noise coming from the end of the corridor.

Curiously, she walked forward and peered over the balcony. In a hall which ran the entire length of that part of the Castle, she saw men practising with weapons - swords, daggers, shields and lances. In stunned horror she watched them, her gaze resting on Connal. Stripped down to only his kilt, he circled and sparred with a kinsman in the centre of the hall.

The two men lunged at each other and Liandra gasped as their swords and bodies crashed together in a ferocious display, before they sprang away to again circle and taunt one another. Almost like a ballet, they moved sinuously, rhythmically, in a deadly dance where sword and body moved as one in a flurry of graceful speed and balance. She watched, enthralled, despite her disgust. Though Seven Stars, why such barbarity should hold any interest for her, she did not know.

Oh really? She smiled grimly to herself, her eyes riveted upon Connal. He was beautiful, and for a man his size, surprisingly graceful. That body of his now glistened with a fine sheen of perspiration. As he moved, muscles bulged and rippled along his torso. And that kilt rode higher, swaying, giving a glimpse of upper thigh. *Too intriguing*.

The battle between Connal and his partner intensified. Shield crashed against shield. Their swords arced and parried in defence. Around and around the room they traded blows.

Liandra flinched at every ring and clash of steel against steel. Any moment someone would lose an arm ... or worse ... be killed.

With a flick of his wrist, Connal managed to disarm his opponent. The sword clattered onto the floor. Bowing low, Connal's partner acknowledged an end to the contest and laughing, the two men embraced.

Connal turned away, bending down to collect a towel. Wiping the perspiration from his face, he glanced up and saw her, saw the disgust, and other emotions on her face, in her eyes. What he read demanded clarification.

He signalled to her to remain where she was, but instead she withdrew. Cursing beneath his breath, he took the stairs three at a time, and pursued her down the corridor.

"A word with you, Liandra!"

She paused, glancing back over her shoulder. With long strides he came to her side. As she tried to evade him, his fingers clamped down on her wrist, drawing her close.

"How long have you been watching me?"

She raised her chin. "What makes you think you are so important that I'd waste my time watching barbarians trying to kill one another with swords?"

Connal grinned. "Oh aye? This is our exercise. A sport. Men enjoy such."

"Only *you* could consider it a *sport*."

"And women enjoy watching it, too, judging by the look of you. Am I correct?"

"No," Liandra said, indignantly.

"Then what were you doing standing there open-mouthed, if not *enjoying*?"

"There's a difference between observing and enjoying."

He raised a disbelieving brow. "Truly? One day you must explain such distinctions."

"A barbarian would not grasp the subtleties between the two."

Connal grinned. Curling a finger under her chin, he raised her face. "I am not a barbarian, Liandra. Have I not proven that to you, yet?"

That voice had taken on a husky timbre, and as always at its sound, she felt her body pulse. Her heart thudded against her ribs. So close, Connal's naked chest, his flushed skin glistened with perspiration. Instead of feeling disgust at such a dishevelled state, her nerve endings spiralled into her, tightening and warming her core.

Her gaze lifted to a safer height. Or so she thought. His hair was tied back severely from his face, yet tendrils had escaped to curl against his brow and cheeks, giving him a roguish appearance. A barbarian rogue - that was what he was! Liandra smiled.

"I like not that smile of yours. It bodes ill for any man. And me in particular, I think." Laughing gently, he stepped closer.

Liandra swallowed against the tight dryness in her throat as his musky male scent washed over her.

Connal stroked her cheek. "You be blushing, Liandra. How so? I think I should leave you to regain your composure." He smiled mischievously. "Good day to you, *ban-druidh*. Next time your curiosity of a man becomes aroused, take a cold bath."

"W...why you -" Liandra stammered her outrage.

Laughing heartily, he strode down the passageway, his mind awhirl. So, Liandra was not immune to the stirrings of passion in the real world. Did her blood race for him? Or for another? One of the men in the exercise hall - who? Which of his clans-men?

He halted in mid-stride, shocked at the jealousy and anger coursing within his body. Jealous that she found one of his clans-men stimulating? And why anger? Why?

Perhaps it was he who needed that cold bath. And at that thought, he groaned. *Too many cold baths of late, you have had, Connal MacArran! Any more and ye will be catching your death!* He strode down the hall, determined to put as much distance between himself and Liandra as he could.

In silent fury, Liandra watched him depart,

mortified to the depths of her being that Connal MacArran indeed had the right of it. *Again!* She did really need to cool off - that sensation within her was one thing, and one thing only. Desire! She cursed it; herself. How she'd fought to dispel it, because every time he was near her resolve was completely undone. Did he do it to her on purpose? Was it some alien chemistry of his which affected her so? Her meditations had always worked in the past, but not so of late when it came to Connal.

That was it, she decided. Alien chemistry undermining her. She breathed a sigh of relief. So simple an explanation she'd missed it entirely. Now she understood, she would be able to deal with him, but even so, she would have to be careful. Avoid him when and where possible. Not so easily accomplished. Liandra shook herself from her musings. For a moment she couldn't recall where she had been going before the noise had diverted her. Then she remembered and hurried along the passageway.

Pausing at the entrance to the solar, she smoothed down her hair, trying to regain her composure.

As one, the women looked up at her noisy arrival, smiling in welcome as she joined their sewing circle.

"You are never late, what have you been doing? Your face is flushed," Fianna remarked, returning her concentration to her embroidery.

Liandra took her customary place in the

solar. The group met every second afternoon, ostensibly for sewing, though as they worked, they gossiped and drank tea and ate the tiny cakes which Amilia baked with her own hands. The small gathering had grown ever larger with more and more women and girls coming to the solar.

Theirs was an easy camaraderie which Liandra enjoyed. Despite her many attempts, she could not master the intricacies of the embroidery which every Caledonian female learned from a young age. Even the sewing was beyond her, though she could knit clumsily. Her first efforts ended in disaster, but no one laughed at her. Fianna had written out the knitting instructions in picture form, so she could follow a simple pattern.

Bronnia sat beside Liandra. "See, look what I did." She held out a small embroidered patch. Some of the stitches were askew.

Liandra hugged her small friend. "That's very good, Bronni. Much better than I could ever do."

"Need to practice more," Bronnia replied.

"She has the right of it," Fianna said, and the sewing circle laughed.

"Tell us about the women of the League, Liandra," Anya said.

"Aye, do!" several voices chorused.

Liandra smiled at their insatiable curiosity. She was always besieged with questions. "There are many different female species."

"Well, what about their clothes? Are they like yours?"

Fianna chuckled, and Liandra cast her a stern gaze.

"Yes, they mostly prefer a suit, such as I - I used to wear, for it can accommodate many different shapes. It allows for easy movement, unlike your stifling garments." She flicked her fingers disdainfully over the robes she now wore. Though she had the dress-maker adapt them for her by raising the hem to ankle height, and had panels of fabric removed to allow her greater mobility.

"'Tis only for your own good, Liandra, that Connal insisted you wear our clothes. If you kept to your flimsy suits, you would freeze to death." Fianna giggled. "Though some of the other men are *most* disappointed by your new attire."

The women laughed as Liandra grimaced.

"And you paint your face as we, only I never see you touch your make-up. How so?"

"My styling servitor tints my skin with special treatments every three months. It can also change the colour of my hair."

"It was green when I first met you," Fianna remarked.

"I alter it according to my mood."

"And how long does it take?"

"An outrageous amount of time, because I have older servitors. Five minutes."

The women roared with laughter.

"What's so funny?"

"It takes you five minutes, once every three

months. For us, daily, it takes at least twenty."

"*Daily?* Seven Stars! What a business! It's so *primitive!*"

"Primitive is it? When after three months, here, Liandra, you will also have to -" Fianna gasped. "Oh, I am so sorry, I did na'-"

Liandra smiled sadly and touched Fianna's wrist. "I'll manage."

For a time they concentrated on their sewing. Liandra became aware of several of the younger women whispering together, prodding each other.

"Go on, Esme, ask her!"

Esme's face flamed crimson as the women looked at her.

"Go on!" An elbow to her ribs made Esme flinch, though she still remained silent.

"What would you ask of me?"

"Tell us about off-worlder men."

Liandra smiled. She wondered how long it would take for someone to dare raise that question! "I -"

"Oh aye, *do!*" Connal drawled.

Liandra turned in her seat to see him with his arms folded, leaning against the door frame. He was dressed in fresh clothes, she was relieved to see. No bare flesh to torment her, though in his hip-hugging kilt and chest-clinging jerkin, he may as well be unclothed. Because his presence had the same tantalising effect on her whether he was nude, dishevelled or immaculate. Blast his alien chemistry!

"Well, Counsellor, do inform us. You are blushing again. Surely you are not shy? You have been asked a question, so best answer it."

Though his words and their delivery were done in a light-hearted manner, Liandra had a feeling he was baiting her. She was trapped. Again.

The women bent to their sewing, eyes firmly on their swiftly moving fingers.

Liandra cleared her throat. "There are many male life-forms. Though they aren't as barbarous as the men of this world. Here women are treated as slave -"

The sewing circle erupted in laughter, and denials.

"MacArran clans-men are renown for their tolerance of their women," Fianna said. "They are mindful of the honour they must accord us. Stubbornly mindful!"

"Stubborn is right!" Liandra agreed, directing her gaze to Connal.

"You were telling us about League men. Do continue!" he said.

"League men are civilised. They allow women to share government, for instance. They regard women as equals in all ways."

"And I presume such extends to the bed-room? Do they prefer a position above or beneath?" Connal laughed to hear the shocked gasps of his women-folk. Needles flew even faster through fabric.

Liandra felt her face redden. "That depends

on the species and personal preference."

"Further enlighten me, *ban-druidh*. It must be very entertaining to have so many positions at one's finger-tips. Or perhaps I should say tentacle? Or claw?"

Liandra shrugged. "Claw, tentacle, hand. It makes no difference to me."

"Of that I have no doubt. Come with me. Please." That last, added hastily, and somewhat mockingly, she thought as she put down her knitting.

Following him along the corridor, he opened the first door he came to and drawing her inside the room, he closed the door sharply behind her. She stepped back as Connal turned to her.

"I have asked you before not to tell my clan about the League."

"I only tell them about the people, not the science."

"You make them wonder and perhaps yearn for things like your servitors. We have no need of such. Our world works well without such baubles."

"So you say! You keep your people in servitude and drudgery."

"Would you prefer it that we became as you? Enslaved by machines and unable to wash one's own hair unless aided by a mechanical servitor?"

"I can tend, quite proficiently, to my own needs."

"Practice makes perfect, does it?" He eyed her warningly. "Keep your world to yourself. My people enjoy honest work, they are not slaves to any creature, or thing."

"Technology is not evil, it's what a man does with it that makes it so."

"Exactly!" Connal snapped.

"Do you have so little faith in your ability to control machines that you spurn them completely?"

Connal frowned. That remark hit home, but he could not let her know. "We do everything a machine can, and more!"

"We have had this argument before."

"And with the same result," Connal remarked dryly. "Caledonia survives well enough, even if it is primitive by your standards. 'Tis our choice. You always tell me the League offers choices. This is ours."

Liandra stared up at him, stunned. "Very well, I accept your right to live by your own code. I may not approve of it, but to deny your right to choose, it's one of the worst crimes in the League Worlds Charter. I have lived by that Charter all my life." She paused. "You've taken from me my right to live as I choose."

"Aye. I have tried to make allowances."

"Very small concessions."

"At least I have tried. And my world is not as barbarous as you once believed."

"I'm surprised by your level of sophistication. It's contrary to what I know of primitive cultures."

"We are not what you expected?"

"No."

And it was true. The more Liandra came to

see the workings of the castle, the more it didn't make sense. They weren't primitive, choosing instead to use natural, non-mechanical alternatives when and where they could. Power was obtained from solar panels. Barbarians pillaged and polluted their world, yet Connal's people respected it and used only what was necessary. Most of their wastes were re-cycled.

"Do you admit you were wrong about us, then? This is a rare occasion! Perhaps I should sit down before I faint with surprise!"

Liandra bit her lip to stop from laughing. "Savour the moment, Connal MacArran."

Connal chuckled. "Liandra, this concession to you. I know how difficult it must be for you to keep silent when so many question you about the League, so I will trust you to be selective in what you tell them. Besides, does not the remembering cause you pain?"

"Sometimes. Though often it is a comfort to share remembrances."

Connal raised her chin. "Aye. I remember something very pleasant, and would experience it again. Solely to satisfy my curiosity, you understand."

Before Liandra could stop him, he had taken her into his arms and kissed her. A soft kiss which electrified her every nerve. She struggled against his embrace. That only made his kiss more intense. Though he held her gently, she could not escape. She made a token effort to break free, before she breathed in his scent. That unique exotic mixture of male arousal tore at her resolve to remain detached from his caress. She was vanquished by him. She clung to him and parted her lips, allowing his tongue to enter her mouth.

Deeper and deeper, she allowed him to drink from her. She felt herself edged back against the door. His thigh between hers, half lifted her from the floor. As loin pressed to loin, she felt his tautness. In response, her nipples hardened and throbbed. With a will of its own, her body tightened in anticipation. Sweet tension spiralled from her feminine core to race through her. She ran her hand up his spine, knotting her fingers in his hair, holding his head to hers, so she could explore his mouth leisurely. She wanted more of him. Her body clamoured for it. Against her mouth, he drew a deep, ragged breath. It was the worst form of desolation, when moments later, she was lifted gently, but firmly, away.

"Ye see what ye do to a man?" he asked, his husky voice trembling. "Even now properly attired, ye still -" Connal shook his head as if to clear it. "I find the reality of you, now, even sweeter than when we first met, Counsellor." His hand cupped her shoulder, gently kneading.

Liandra ran a finger over her lips, shocked and surprised at her own reactions. Her body wanted this barbarian, though intellectually she must reject him. Seven Stars! She suppressed every feminine urge within her, in an effort to regain control. She must fight this attraction. For

Connal MacArran was a man who could never be the lover she needed. She had to tell him that, even if her body played traitor to her mind.

"I find your kiss just as disgusting as the first," she hissed.

Connal's amusement and desire fled, leaving in their place anger and ice. Cold fury swept through his body. "Disgust? It was not from *disgust* that ground your body against mine. Am I mistaken? Dare you tell me you prefer Angas's embrace to mine? Well?"

The savagery of his voice was terrifying. Shocked, she saw the murderous gleam in his eyes.

"By your silence, I have my answer! 'Tis a pity you prefer a boy when you could have a man. But you have made your choice. I hope you are happy with your scrawny bed-fellow, *ban-druidh!*" He wrenched the door open and strode down the corridor.

Liandra watched, relieved, as he all but ran from her. If he had continued to kiss her like that, no telling what she might have done, or what he might have asked of her. And her answer would have been ... she knew only too well. At the thought of having him love her, she trembled. From desire? Fear? A mixture of the two? She was too confused to be certain. Safer to let him think her affections were elsewhere, than run the risk of him forcing himself upon her.

Force himself on her? Liandra laughed. Connal would not have to coerce her. One kiss from him and her body thrummed with fire. She was ready to give all to him. But she could not, dare not, for he was incapable of giving her the love she required. Yet if that was so, why did she feel such pain? Such regret?

Unaccountably, tears came to her eyes and she rested her forehead against the door. If only, Connal. *If only ...*

Chapter Eighteen

Liandra heard a muffled voice, followed by a shrill wail, coming from inside the empty storeroom. Pushing open the door, she froze in horror to see Bronnia crouched in a corner. Her uncle stood over her, holding in his raised hand a thin whip.

"Stop this at once!"

Fraser MacLeod glanced over his shoulder. "'Tis nothing you need be concerned with. She is punished for hiding from me."

"Little wonder she hides from you, if you whip her."

"Mind your own business, else I will take the lash to you." He raised his whip.

Liandra strode up to him, wrenching his arm back. Deflected, the whip flicked across her chest and shoulder. She gasped in pain.

"'Tis all right, Liandra -" Bronnia whimpered and buried her face in her hands, again curling in a foetal position awaiting the next stroke.

"It is not all right!" Liandra dragged Bronnia to her and shielding the child with her own body, she stepped backwards to the door.

"You bitch!" Fraser MacLeod propelled

himself across the room. Before he could reach them, Liandra scooped up the child in her arms and ran as fast as she could down the corridor, down a long flight of steps. She rounded a corner and ran headlong into Vanora and a party of women cleaning the hallway.

"Hold the witch and the brat!" Fraser's cry echoed about the walls.

Hands reached out, but she wrenched herself free, and putting Bronnia behind her, Liandra confronted her enemies. Two women detached themselves from the main group and ran away.

"Time, witch, to sample the punishment Connal denies you. And I will be just the one to give it to you!" Vanora hissed.

Liandra tossed her head. "Have a care. I'm a witch and I'll cast a shrivelling spell on the first one to lay a hand on me, or Bronnia."

Vanora laughed. "Spare me your cursing. You have no such power."

"Do I not?" Liandra glared at her. "Try it and see."

Indecisively, Vanora and the women clustered together.

"Give me the brat. She will take her punishment now!" Fraser held out his hand.

Liandra felt Bronnia cower behind her, her body pressed painfully into the backs of her legs. The terror radiated so strongly from the child that for a moment Liandra felt overwhelmed by it. Finally managing to block it from her senses, she found that in her preoccupation, Fraser MacLeod was now within arm's reach. Hastily, she retreated a few steps.

"No matter what a creature does, it cannot justify any act of brutality," Liandra said.

"Is that so? I caught her in the stable again. She knows not to be there, and then she defied me and ran away."

"Not hurting, just reading," Bronnia snuffled.

Fraser snorted. "Lies! Ye be too stupid to read. Ye canna' make sense of even the simplest word."

"Neither can I," Liandra said.

"There you have it!" Vanora said, triumphantly. "Like attracts like."

"Come here, brat! If you do not, when I catch ye, I will make ye thrice sorry."

"I have to go," Bronnia whimpered, emerging from behind Liandra's legs.

She gripped Bronnia's shoulder and shoved her back behind her. "No. Over my dead body."

"That can be arranged, witch! There are many in the Castle who want to see an end to your spells."

At that, her enemies surged forward. Without conscious thought, Liandra reached out, and grabbed one of the ancient claymores decorating the wall. She stared down in disbelief at what she had done. Desperate times required desperate measures!

"One step closer and - !" With difficulty, Liandra waved the sword in front of her. If the circumstances had not been so desperate she would have laughed at herself. The sword trembled in the air before its weight tore at her wrist. She lowered it, its tip resting on the floor.

For a moment her enemies measured her, before they stepped forward en masse. Again, with difficulty she raised the weapon and swept it in a clumsy arc in front of her, while retreating. With Bronnia's fingers clutching at her skirt, Liandra could hardly move.

Her pursuers followed her slowly down the corridor, gaining on her, but always keeping out of range of the sword.

Out of the corner of her eye, Liandra saw one woman lunge forward. As quick as she was, Bronnia was even quicker. Squealing, she darted out and grabbed a pot from its stand, and hurled it, before returning to her place of safety behind Liandra. The projectile slammed against the woman who fell back against her comrades sending them sprawling onto the floor in a flurry of skirts, thrashing arms, legs and much cursing.

Fraser MacLeod flung himself at Liandra, and at the last moment she managed to lift the claymore. With a cry of pain he jumped back. Horrified, she saw the slit in his arm where the blade had cut. Blood dripped down onto the floor. She stared at her own handiwork, sickened to her stomach.

"Ye shall pay for that witch!" He pounced on her, his fist connecting with her jaw.

Liandra reeled backwards, the sword flying from her grasp. Every bone in her body jarred as she crashed against the wall. Furiously, Fraser dragged her to him. She tried to prise his fingers from her. He would have none of it. Her blouse tore as she twisted away from him. She scratched his hands with her long nails, and although she hurt him, not for an instant did his hold lessen.

"Now we have the witch ..." He raised his fist.

"Touch her again, and be assured it will be the last thing ye ever do!" Connal's chillingly quiet voice froze Fraser instantly.

Liandra saw Connal in the hallway, sword in hand, several kins-folk gathered about him.

Striding up to Fraser, Connal wrenched him away from Liandra and flung him back against the wall. With his arm across Fraser's throat, he held him suspended inches above the floor. Connal's sword was poised to strike.

Liandra saw the fury in Connal's face, the throbbing tic in his clenched jaw.

The silence in the hallway was terrifying. Dougall shouldered his way through the crowd. He paused a few paces from Connal. "*Tighearna?*"

"Stay out of this, Dougall!" Connal's gaze never left Fraser's face. "I will not have any of my women abused." He drew in a ragged breath and stepped away. No longer supported, Fraser slid down the wall and sagged onto his knees. Connal stared down at him. "Well, no words to me? You were very vocal moments ago."

"Con," Liandra used her most soothing counsellor's voice. "Do not harm him. He deserves your pity."

Connal swung on her, the unbridled fury in his eyes impaling her. The tic pulsed anew in his clenched jaw as his gaze rested on the torn blouse, the scratches in her flesh. "Pity? For what he was about to do to ye?" He swallowed down hard, trying to master the rage burning through him like fire. "What happened here?"

"I intervened when I found him whipping Bronnia."

Connal's grim face turned ashen. He turned to Fraser MacLeod. "Beating a child? What a *man* you be, MacLeod!"

"The brat be unmanageable! I have to take her in hand, else she will bring shame down on the clan like her mother. A *man* must control a wayward woman!" He glanced sidelong at Liandra and that look was not lost on Connal. He dragged Fraser to his feet and hurled him back against the wall. Again, his arm pressed against Fraser's throat until he gasped for air.

"As for shaming the clan, that you have done already by your actions here today. I will have no one beaten in this Castle, least of all a child. You are expelled from my house. Get you gone from my sight!" He flung Fraser away.

"And what of my niece?"

"You have forfeited any right to lay kinship to her. Understand this well, everyone here. Bronnia MacLeod is now foster-child to Connal MacArran and no one, *no one*, touches her without my permission." He rounded on Vanora and her women. "Get out of my sight, too, before I cast out the lot of you. Now leave. All of ye!"

The household scurried away in silence. Connal drew in a deep breath and turned to Liandra. He held out his hand. "Give me the sword, *ban-druidh*!"

Liandra retrieved the sword from where it lay on the floor. She held it out and Connal stepped back as the tip wavered in front of him.

He smiled grimly. "Please, hilt first! Or do you intend to blood me, as well?" He took the sword from her. "Dougall, have the sword cleaned before it is returned to the mounting."

Dougall collected the sword and Connal's own claymore and stalked down the corridor.

Connal crouched down to where Bronnia cowered against the wall. As he reached out, she screamed. He snatched his hand back and looked up at Liandra.

She was shocked to see tears glittering in the steel depths of his eyes.

"What is wrong with her?" Connal whispered.

"She's hysterical."

"Bronnia." Connal gently touched the child's head. "You be safe. Come with me."

"Want ... Liandra."

"Liandra can come, too."

A slight movement of her head, Bronnia looked up at him doubtfully, one swollen eye blinking from behind a wild tangle of hair. Connal caught his breath as he saw the bruise on the child's temple. "Seven Stars!" he whispered.

"How long has this been going on?"

"I don't know," Liandra said.

"Awhile." A woman stepped out of the shadows. Liandra recognised her as being among the group who had fled the moment Vanora and Fraser had began their assault. "We considered it his business, since she be his niece. We thought you knew, *Tighearna*."

"And ye think I would condone such? Since when have any of my people been thus treated?" He caught her frightened look, and clamped his hand over hers. "I am not angry with you. You did well in coming to me, Magda. If you had not done so ..." He shuddered with the thought of what might have been. What Fraser might have done to Bronnia. And to Liandra.

Connal raised Bronnia's limp form into his arms and grimaced as she planted a tear-wet face against his neck. "Mistress Tavor, please come with me," he said, coldly.

She had to trot to keep up with the brisk pace he set. Breathless, she followed him into his chamber. Moments later the healer joined them.

"Dougall said you have need of me?" Katrine asked, quietly.

"Aye, see to the child." Connal said, placing Bronnia onto his bed. She cringed away as the healer went to touch her.

"NO!" Bronnia wailed. Liandra gently ran a hand through the child's matted hair and sent soothing thoughts to her. Finally Bronnia relaxed enough to allow the healer to remove her torn clothing.

Connal stared at the battered flesh on her small body and turned away, sickened to his stomach. "There are so many bruises! Will she recover?" he asked.

"Aye, bodily, in time," Katrine said, hoarsely.

He shook his head in disbelief. "What sort of *Tighearna* am I to allow such brutality in my Castle?"

Liandra glanced at him, shocked to see the pallor of his face, the desolate pain in his eyes. She drew him away from Bronnia. "You didn't know, Connal," she said, gently stroking his arm.

"And that makes it right? I am master here, I should know all."

"You can't be everywhere at once." She frowned down at the little girl curled in a tight ball on his bed. "I suspected something amiss. But then she seemed so happy coming to the sewing circle that I forgot my suspicions. Connal, it's my fault!"

He reached out and stroked the back of her hand. "No, 'tis mine. I am *Tighearna*, and I havena' made your life so easy that you can spare much of a thought for others. No! The blame lies with me!"

Liandra swallowed back her tears. "Bronnia has suffered more abuse than I realised. I would like to monitor her and heal her mind and body -"

"With your crystal bed?"

"Yes."

"Very well." Connal strode to his desk and drew out a key. He went to a side door and opened it. "I have kept your bed here."

Liandra had often wondered what that room contained. Even when she came for the daily cleaning of his chamber, the door remained locked. None of her keys would open it. The other women did not know what lay behind the locked door, either, their curiosity led to ribald speculation. Their inventive suggestions had made Liandra blush.

Glancing at her bed, she saw that it was deactivated. No wonder she had not been able to catch any of its emanations. He had been very clever in securing her property.

Connal rummaged through various cupboards and returned to her, carrying the crystal prisms. Taking them, Liandra hastily prepared her bed.

When Katrine had finally finished her ministrations, Liandra returned to Connal's bed-chamber and went to lift Bronnia.

"Allow me," Connal said, carefully raising the child into his arms. "Lead on, Counsellor."

He gently placed Bronnia on the crystal bed and covered her with a quilt. The crystals came to life as Liandra joined with the bed, going deeper into her meditation. She activated the healing crystals and attaching the dreamer's cap to Bronnia's head, she stepped back.

"Like Fianna, Bronnia will dream. She'll be healed as she sleeps."

"There be no danger from the aliens?"

"I'm only using a healing frequency."

"What of Bronnia? Will there be permanent scars on body and mind?"

"The bed will heal all, though she'll retain some memories. I'm a counsellor, so if you'd allow it, I can tend her daily. I'm optimistic of a full recovery."

"Aye, do what you must as often as you like. I want her mended."

"She will be, I promise."

"My thanks for that, *ghraidh*." Connal ran a hand over his face. He felt so old and tired. Never had the responsibilities of clan-leader weighed so heavily upon him as they did now. "Some times I *doona'* know what I would do without ye."

"Your life might be more peaceful if I wasn't here."

He laughed harshly. "Peaceful? Maybe. Though certainly not as interesting. Now, turn to me."

Liandra did as he commanded. While one hand cupped her chin, the knuckles of his other hand rubbed her cheek where Fraser had struck her. She flinched with pain. His gaze dropped down to her shoulder, the torn blouse revealing the whip mark in her flesh. She saw his frown, the angry tic playing along his jaw.

"You did not escape unscathed, Liandra," he

said gently. "I have some liniment to help."

"You do?"

He smiled. "For bruises and small hurts when one of my sparring partners is too boisterous."

Liandra frowned. What did he mean? A few thoughts raced through her mind - bed-mates mostly. Did he, did they, enjoy violent couplings? The thought terrified her.

Connal returned from the dresser and opened the jar of salve: its pungent scent, a mixture of lavender and rosemary. He gently massaged the cream onto her bruised cheek. She flinched and choked back a cry.

"Stop your squirming, *ban-druidh* and take your medicine. The stinging will ease in a few minutes." He turned his attention to her upper chest. Carefully parting the rents in her blouse, his fingers caked in lotion, gently stroked the lash weal.

His face was a mask of pure concentration as his warm hand gently swirled over the swell of her breast.

Liandra gasped, not from the biting, burning pain of the liniment, but from the heat of his tender touch. Her stomach muscles cramped sharply in a pain that was almost a pleasure.

"Do your partners enjoy such delicate ministrations?" she asked, huskily.

"My ... *partners*?" He studied her in shocked silence, then slowly he smiled as he continued to rub in the salve. "You do me a great dis-service Liandra Tavor. I can assure you no woman ever leaves my bed bloodied or bruised. 'Tis often I who bears the mark of their passion on my body. I do no such in return. My abrasions come from the exercise field."

"Oh," Liandra said. Satisfaction raced through her.

"There." Connal stepped back and smiled. "How does that feel?"

"Better. My thanks for your care. You are very gentle, for a barbarian, of course."

Connal grinned. "Of course. You and I must talk, if you feel up to it."

"Yes."

"In my sitting-room. Come." Gently taking her arm, he guided her to a seat before the hearth. He joined her side after handing her a goblet of wine. Stretching out his feet to the fire, he stared at the flames for so long that Liandra wondered if he had forgotten her presence.

"Con?"

He glanced at her and their gazes met and held. He smiled, his eyes and face aglow from something more than the reflected firelight.

"I'm sorry, I didn't mean to call you that."

"No, it pleases me that you do." He took a sip of wine. "In my house no one has the right to raise sword against another. Except in defence of another, even I, as *Tighearna*, must abide by this law. Only on the exercise field may a man unsheath his sword, and even there, to draw blood is considered clumsy. A man who does is held in little regard. But such sentiment in modern. In times long past we were a barbarous people. There were clan feuds. Now we rival one another in different, more peaceful ways."

"I don't understand -"

"Patience, Liandra. I be recounting some Caledonian history. I thought you might be appreciative of that fact."

"I suppose I should be thankful for small mercies."

Connal chuckled. "Blood-letting is a very serious matter. For over one hundred years, no sword has been drawn in my Castle."

Liandra studied her lap. She didn't like the sound of this. "I suppose as punishment, I can look forward to months of housework, or ... worse?"

"Look at me, *ghraidh*."

When she did dare raise her eyes to his, she saw many things in his steady gaze, anger and revenge not among them.

He frowned. "Bronnia is but skin and bone. It fell on to your shoulders, to protect her. To do my duty for me. I should have -"

"Connal, you can't be everywhere. You can't see all. Bronnia has places in the castle, known only to herself, where she plays alone. How can you see someone who prefers to remain hidden?"

Connal smiled tightly. "There will be no punishment for you, though you drew sword against my kinsman. In times past you would have been challenged for that."

"Challenged?"

"Aye. Honour satisfied. No woman can be challenged, but your nearest male relative would have answered for the consequences of your actions. Generations ago, blood feuds were started over less."

"I have no wish to start any feud."

Connal shook his head. "The matter is ended. For your defence of a child, everyone will overlook what you did. If a wrong needs to be righted, do not, ever, take up sword again. Tell me and I can deal with the matter in a civilised way."

"You are not civilised."

Connal returned her smile. "You are deliberately trying to provoke me."

"I?"

"Perhaps instead of calling you *ban-druidh*, I should re-name you *ban-laoch*."

Ban-laoch ... "What is an amazon?" Liandra asked.

"A woman warrior."

Liandra shuddered. All this talk of blood and feuds and warriors, and what she had done ... She put down her goblet and strode to the window. She closed her eyes against the memories; the sight and smell of Fraser's fear, the metallic taint of his blood.

"*Ban-laoch?*"

She turned to him, finding to her surprise, that he stood behind her.

Instantly, he felt the smile freeze on his lips. Her face was so pinched and pale. Her sapphire eyes which normally fascinated him with their flash and sparkle were now dull and pained.

"Don't call me that! *Please!* I'm not a warrior. What I did was a terrible thing."

"Fraser deserved more besides for his actions."

"He must have deep reasons for his behaviour. Let me counsel him."

"I have banished him, in disgrace, back to his clan. Within the week, he will be far from here. How can you wish to help a man who did what he did to you and Bronni? 'Tis a strange woman you are, Liandrrra."

"I am what I am" She ran hands through her hair. "Seven Stars! I used a weapon against another creature. I could have killed him!"

"That I doubt. You have not the strength to use the claymore to proper effect. 'Tis not a woman's weapon."

Liandra turned away and pressed her forehead against the window. The cool glass brought some relief to the pounding in her head. She felt sick to her stomach ... so small, so afraid - so lost in this world of blood-letting and swords ... What she had suppressed for weeks was finding its release through her lack of control, a legacy of the events just occurring.

"You are trembling," Connal whispered against her ear. His hands rested on her shoulders, gently kneading.

She turned and pressed her face into his chest. Tears came to her eyes and rolled unchecked down her cheeks.

Connal gently stroked her hair. "Hush, *ghraidh*. What is wrong? Tell me."

"Can't!"

Sighing, he lifted her into his arms. Liandra did not protest, nor did she say anything when he sat once more in his chair before the fire, and brought her down onto his lap.

As more emotions began to well up inside, she began to struggle. She had to get away and relieve her misery in private, away from him. She couldn't let him see her fragility. *Couldn't.* "Let me go, please."

"No! You stay! Does not a friend console another in time of pain? Allow me to do this for you."

Liandra tried once more to escape, but found his embrace intractable. The struggle was over before it truly began. Her emotions were out of control. She needed the closeness of another creature to sustain her through her misery. He was offering it. His presence so welcome. So very welcome.

How long she cried, Liandra did not know. Throughout, Connal silently cradled her in his arms.

He cleared his throat. "Would you prefer I sent for Angas to ... console you?" His voice was a tight whisper.

Couldn't he bear to be near her, or did her hysteria disgust him? It sobered her instantly. As she brushed her cheeks with the back of her hand, Connal produced a strange square of linen from his vest pocket and with infinite gentleness, wiped the tears from her face.

"Send for Angas? Why?"

"For you," Connal said, tightly. *Arran's Mercy how it hurt to say that!* When he wanted it to be he, and he alone, whom she turned to for comfort.

"Angas means nothing to me," Liandra murmured.

Connal felt the knot in his stomach unravel, just for an instant. Then the churning returned. Different, more intense. *Angas meant nothing to her!*

It was as if something long supressed within him suddenly sprang to life. His body was suffused with a heat that lit every nerve ending, then it fled, replaced by a pleasant heady warmth. A nerve twitched uncontrollably at the base of his spine.

"Seven Stars!" Connal ground out.

Liandra tried to smile. "Again, you use a League oath, *Tighearna.*"

"That I do. Maybe you have contaminated me beyond hope of redemption." His smile faded as Liandra shuddered. He tightened his arms around her. "Is there anything I can do for you?"

"Will you just hold me? What you're doing is the best thing for me."

"I do not understand."

"Normally I would seek the aid of another Asarian. In times of great stress we give comfort to each other."

"By holding? By joining minds and bodies?" There was just a tinge of ice to his voice, coupled by a sudden tensing of muscles beneath her. Was Connal afraid she would ask him to share with her? And at that thought something stirred within her, tensing her muscles. How she wanted him to share! But she couldn't, dare not ask.

"I ... If you can hold me just a few minutes longer. Can you manage that? I don't want to disgust you."

"'Tis no hardship for me. You can never disgust me, Liandra." Connal rested his cheek on her head and gently rocked her in his arms. *No, 'twas no hardship, My Lady Ban-druidh! Far from it. 'Tis my pleasure to do so ... if you but knew it!*

"I should return to my room," Liandra whispered.

"Why?" Connal asked. "Do you not trust me?"

"I need to heal myself. Today's events were very -"

"Aye. Mark me well when I say Liandra, you shall never again be treated so by any of my people. Can I make some recompense? Allow me to heal you."

Liandra laughed, gently.

"Is that so amusing?" Connal whispered against her temple.

"You aren't Asarian."

"No, but we men of Caledonia have ways and means ... what would an Asarian do that I cannot?"

"One of my kind would sing to me, or think in music to soothe my nerves."

Connal laughed. "If I were to sing to you, My Lady, your nerves would be much abused. My voice is little better than my ability to play the lute. I have a better idea."

Still holding her in his arms, he eased himself out of the chair and walked across the room. Gently depositing her on his bed, he removed her slippers and tucked the quilt around her.

"Con -"

"My word as *Tighearna* you are safe ever with me."

"I know that."

He smiled. "Perhaps now that you concede you can trust me, maybe you will learn other things."

He strode out of the room and returned moments later carrying a book. Kicking off his boots, he swung himself onto the bed and covered himself with part of the quilt.

Liandra was too amazed to protest, and more than a little curious as to what he intended. When he drew her against him, allowing her head to rest on his shoulder, she snuggled against his warmth. An arm enfolded her to him.

"This was my mother's favourite. 'Tis called *Fire on the Heather*. Such a ridiculous title, it can only be a woman's book." He chuckled as he turned to the first page. Liandra glanced at it. The jumble of letters and words swirled around and hastily she closed her eyes against the queasiness.

She listened to the story, a romance, full of magic and love, betrayal and reconciliation. She laughed and almost cried as his narrative brought the story to life. He used a different tone of voice when each character spoke. She had never experienced anything like it, not in any of the serials played on the 3-d image screen, nor when her language servitor read to her. Perhaps it had something to do with the narrator. She smiled dreamily. With her ear pressed to his chest she listened to the slow, steady beat of his heart, and felt the vibrations through his body as he spoke.

You are such a man of contrasts, Connal MacArran. Fierce like a wild beast, yet so gentle with Bronnia. And now you heal me in a way no Asarian could. *My Connal ...*

She was too content to struggle against the realisation ... *My Connal.* It wasn't wrong, or dangerous. How could it be? It felt so right.

Liandra had not moved for some time, Connal realised, nor had she spoken. Perhaps she was bored. He was probably a poor substitute for her reading-servitor. He glanced down and saw her asleep, her hand curled against his chest, a slight smile on her lips. Vulnerable. So fragile, his *ban-druidh*. What had occurred in his halls, would never be repeated. If any man, or woman, dared raise voice or hand against her again, he would kill them. Arran's Mercy, he would! And be damned to the consequences.

He put the book to one side. He would finish reading it to her another time. Shifting in the bed, he eased cramped muscles. In response, she snuggled against him, throwing one leg casually across his thigh. Connal sucked in his breath, for in that unconscious act she had touched parts of his anatomy ... and as a result he felt the familiar tightening begin in the pit of his stomach, then coil downwards.

He stroked her hand and her fingers entwined with his. She murmured something against his chest ... some alien word he presumed. He gritted his teeth. He should not be doing this! For now, his body clamoured for a deeper intimacy. His fingers traced up and down her arm. Desire and delight coursed through his veins. Delight of having her in his arms, on his bed. The mere holding of her gave him so much pleasure. And so much pain. He tenderly kissed the top of her head, breathing in the sweet, floral scent of her hair. He groaned against her temple as his body flamed hot and ready, taut and painful, insisting on its customary release. Well, he had started this dangerous journey, so now he would have to endure it, however much discomfort it caused. He had promised her she was safe in his bed.

He closed his eyes, drew her tighter against him, stroking her body, taking so much enjoyment from the feel of her against him. His arousal passed through another phase, he was shocked to discover. Something which had never occurred. His comfort, his fulfilment, came by the simple satisfaction of just holding her as she slept in his arms, obliviously. Trustingly. That was a greater fulfilment than any coupling.

Chapter Nineteen

"Ten days ago, you undertook Bronnia's restoration. And your progress?" In his chamber, Connal sat beside the fire opposite Liandra.

"She's young and strong, so physically, she's mended quickly. Mentally, there are still wounds. She remembers the brutality, though she doesn't dwell upon it. That's a good sign. I will see to it that she puts it behind her. Now free of her uncle's cruelty, she's started to blossom. Thanks to Fianna, she has begun to read."

"I thought her incapable."

"Because no one understood. Dyslexia is a rare complaint."

"Dyslexia?" Connal grimaced. "Is it contagious?"

Liandra laughed. "It's not a disease. It's an inability to properly see the written word. The brain jumbles and confuses what the eye sees. I can help her a little, though I'm not a trained educator, and I can't read anything."

"I am certain you will do your best, Liandra. My thanks for your interest in my fosterling. And what of Fianna? How does she fare? She never speaks of Garris."

"Fianna has taken over the role of mother to Bronnia. It gives her someone to focus upon."

"I had noticed. The two heal one another. Bronnia takes Fianna's mind away from her loss. And you, Liandra. What about your loss? Who consoles you?"

"I have many friends in the Castle. I have to believe that my father has dealt with the dream-scape problems, otherwise I'd go insane with worry." She paused. "And it is my hope that in the future you might relinquish my captivity."

Connal folded his arms. "You are a MacArran clans-woman, not a captive."

"I'm kept here against my will. Though the conditions of my imprisonment are far from intolerable."

"Do not look to my change of heart, Liandra. Such has no future." Connal glanced away, his eyes lingering on the bed which they had shared. And that memory had sweetly haunted him ever since. He had left the bed while she still slept, not trusting himself to have the strength and courage to leave her when she was awake. It had been the hardest thing in his life, to leave, when he wanted to stay beside her and wake her. To... Connal suppressed the thoughts and forced himself to his feet. Returning from his desk, he held out a small sporran to Liandra.

"I thought you might like to have this."

"Thank you," she said. Not made of customary leather, instead it was fashioned from velvet, embroidered and tasselled with gold beads and thread. "It's very beautiful."

Connal smiled. "There be something inside."

Liandra opened the catch and drew out the delicate crystal and silver filigree necklace.

"'Tis my way of thanking you for your hard work in running my household. The Castle has never been so efficient. Too long there has been need of a lady's hand about the place."

Liandra smiled. "It isn't a hardship, I enjoy it." She ran her fingers over the crystal necklace. They were of a high quality, their resonance clear and strong. "These are local?"

"Aye. Near the southern boundary of my County, there is a network of caves, some of them made up entirely of these crystals."

"The League would -" Liandra glanced at him nervously.

Connal raised an enquiring brow. "Aye? Finish what you started."

"Asarian traders roam the star systems for quality crystals such as these. We need them for our work, in ever-increasing quantities. Our own supply is almost exhausted."

"Too many crystal beds and the like?"

"Aye ... I mean yes!"

"You speak more like a Caledonian each day."

"I'm being contaminated!"

"I prefer the word *civilised.*" Connal laughed as Liandra grimaced. "Here, allow me." Taking the crystal necklace from her, he gently brushed aside her hair and fastened the catch. His eyes with their own volition roamed down to where the gems rested against the swell of her breasts. What he would not give to rest against her like ... Damn those crystals for their good fortune! He smiled to himself, putting aside his impossible thoughts.

"Tonight we are holding a special celebration to mark the commencement of winter. Will you attend?"

"Is that an order, or an invitation?"

Connal frowned. "I was *inviting* you."

"Then I'll be there."

"And as always, properly attired." He waited for her explosive reaction, disappointed when it did not occur. "Why are you smiling?" Connal asked.

"Just ... nothing."

"Hmm. Why do I not like the way you smile? It alerts me to your conniving." He chuckled. "Then I look forward to your company at my table tonight, suitably attired in Caledonian women's clothes."

Liandra strode to the door. "Until tonight then." She paused and looked over her shoulder at him. "Thank you for your gifts, Connal. I shall treasure them."

"My pleasure, *ban-druidh*." His smile made her heart beat that much faster and with a shaking hand she turned the door handle.

Liandra paused at the entrance to the dining hall, filled to capacity, the laughter and talking a deafening roar. Tonight the cavernous chamber had been decorated with flowers and vines and in the centre, hanging from one of the massive light frames, she saw a strange spiky bush of red and green. Trinkets and ornaments hung from its many branches. She noticed that the people avoided walking under it. Wasn't it safe to walk beneath it? If so, why did Connal allow it to hang there?

As Liandra slowly made her way to Connal's table, many people hailed her in welcome. Finally reaching the high table, she smiled at Fianna and Bronnia and then at Connal.

"I thought I requested you wear a suitable woman's gown. A Caledonian gown," he said icily.

Liandra smiled, projecting what she hoped was a picture of pure innocence. She had fashioned her clothing from a length of black brocade velvet. It was the most beautiful fabric she had ever seen, its patterned surface embroidered with tiny flowers and leaves. She hadn't been able to bear the thought of cutting it, so she had wound it around her body and pinned it, so that it left her arms and one shoulder bare. The remainder of the fabric hung down her back to her ankles. Her only jewellery, her crystal necklace and a pair of earrings borrowed from Fianna. Instead of wearing her hair loose, she had coiled it on top of her head. Her make-up was highlighted by the subtle addition of more coloured shading on eyelids and lips. It felt strange to have such on her face, but she would have to get used to it.

"Liandra?" Connal's voice intruded and she drew her thoughts back.

"Don't you like my clothes?" she asked.

As she went to take her seat, his fingers gently, but firmly, held her shoulder. "Your gown resembles a *breacan an fhelidh*. Was such your intent?"

She smiled. "Fianna said welcoming the winter solstice was an important occasion, so I dressed appropriately."

"Your interpretation is quite fetching."

"I'm glad you approve."

"I did not say I approve, merely that on you it was becoming." Connal held out her chair and helped her to be seated.

For a time, they ate in silence. She studied Connal sidelong. In stark contrast to the simple severity of his hair braid, he wore an elaborate shirt with voluminous sleeves. At his neck and wrists, layers of lace, the delicacy of which only highlighted, rather than detracted from his potent maleness. Truly, a man of contradictions! But a man unlike any other she had known! Her blood began to race.

Hastily, she dropped her gaze and it fell to his kilt. Lower to his bare knees. Lower to his long, hose-covered legs. He shifted in his seat, his kilt parting at the side, to reveal a muscle-contoured thigh. She drew in a shivering breath. Tension coiled itself in the pit of her stomach. She ran a tongue over suddenly dry lips. Glancing up at him, she saw his attention full upon her.

"Something be wrong?" he asked casually, a mischievous glint in his eye.

"Nothing," Liandra replied, not recognising the husky tremor of her own voice. She returned her concentration to her meal. There was no danger in looking at food!

The servants brought all manner of delicacies to the table, Liandra content to eat her usual meagre, simple fare.

"You are passing up Caledonia's finest foods," Connal said. "Here, try some of this. 'Twill put some meat on those bones, Liandra. You are still much too thin."

"Don't be ridiculous. I've put on weight. Soon I won't be able to fit into any of my suits. Is that your plan?"

"You wrong me woman."

"I have the right of it, Connal MacArran."

He laughed. Following which, he teased and cajoled her into eating more food than she would ever have imagined possible.

The dining concluded, the trestles and benches were removed. Men seated themselves on the floor, and unravelled the sash of their kilts to form a covering on the floor beside them. Sitting on the strip of tartan, women joined their men folk. The household formed a circle about the floor, leaving the centre of the hall empty.

Four men, dressed in belted plaids, entered

that circle. On the floor, they placed swords at right angles and each stood still and erect, hands on hips, waiting.

Liandra cringed as the raucous noise from the bag-pipes echoed around the hall. She would never regard that screeching as music - not in a million years!

She watched as the dancers leaped over and across the swords, the tips of their toes touching the spaces between the blades. Faster and faster they moved, their kilts swinging high with the energetic motion of their dance. Without a break in tempo, more men took over, and for at least an hour the concentration of the hall was focused solely on the dancing.

More entertainers followed one another in quick succession. A woman with a harp sang a haunting lay, while others presented humorous tales, a mixture of song and narrative that had their audience screaming with laughter. Then a lone musician walked around the gathering, changing the style and content of his song as he stopped before each person.

Liandra decided he must be empathic. How else could he do what he did so skilfully, to guess the mood and interest of each man or woman for whom he sang? When she glanced at Connal she saw he watched the musician with obvious pleasure and pride.

He turned to her suddenly and smiled. "Have you such in that League of yours, *bandruidh*?"

"No."

"Think you a servitor could do such?"

"No."

Connal smiled. "*No* arguments?"

"None."

"Glad I am to be sitting down, else the shock of your agreement would knock the legs from under me." He laughed as Liandra eyed him warningly.

The musician approached her. The music he played for her was lilting, slow, rhythmic. Sensual. Beside her Connal shifted in his seat.

Then the music changed its rhythm, as the entertainer stood before Connal. Once again the tune reflected the focus of his piece. Strength and passion exuded from the lute's every note, though interspersed were moments of calm, not unlike the music he had played for her, Liandra thought.

Then the musician bowed to Connal and exited the hall to the thunderous applause of the gathering. Other entertainers entered the circle. A juggler, acrobats, more harpists and dancers.

"Each of my people performs tonight. In this way they make a gift for the *Tighearna*, and his household. What about you, My Lady *Ban-druidh*?"

Liandra drew her attention away from the harper.

"I can't sing and I certainly can't do a balancing act."

Connal laughed. "Now that would make an

interesting spectacle. Counsellor Tavor the acrobat!"

"You've drunk too much mead."

"I have hardly touched my goblet all night."
He grinned. "I do insist you entertain me with
some of your alien magic. If you please."

"If *I* please?" She smiled at that. "I might
corrupt you."

"I am prepared to risk it."

Once the people realised that Connal had
requested Liandra to perform something from
her own world, they clapped and cheered and
called on her to enter the entertainer's circle.

"Very well. I will need the use of one of my
crystals."

Connal raised a brow. "Which?"

"The pyramid-shaped one."

Connal left the hall and quickly returned.
Liandra was already seated on the floor, cross-
legged. He placed the huge crystal into her
cupped hands.

Liandra bent her head and concentrated
onto the crystal surface. Slowly it glowed with its
inner fire. The lights played across her face and
arced around the room in a spinning
kaleidoscope of colour. Then the coruscating
energy coalesced into a single shaft of light a few
feet from where she sat. Slowly, it took on the
shape and form of two dancers, a man and
woman, wearing the flowing robes of Asarians,
their faces painted in the traditional way of a
bonded couple. Laughing, they circled one
another, their finger-tips just touching, their

gowns joining sinuously in the bonding dance. Embracing in a shaft of pulsing light, they rose into the air, their robes and long silver hair flowing around their bodies. The faintest music emanated from the crystal Liandra held.

Some minutes later, she finished the projection, certain everyone in the hall would know what followed in real life. As tradition decreed, the couple would eventually consummate their love, privately and passionately as only fully bonded Asarians could do.

The audience was deathly quiet as Liandra stood up. Uncertainly, she glanced around. Had she offended them? Then they burst forth in laughter, clapping and cheering. As they called for more, she shook her head.

"Later, perhaps. It's quite draining." She gratefully sipped the goblet of wine Connal handed her.

"That was very enlightening," he said huskily.

"You enjoyed it?"

"Most assuredly."

She regarded him in a mixture of suspicion and surprise. Beads of perspiration dotted his brow. His eyes smouldered with that inner fire she now knew so well. There were other such reactions in the hall, she noticed, for some couples slipped surreptitiously away, no doubt to consummate their own love privately in Caledonian fashion.

"The hall numbers have thinned somewhat since that entertainment of yours, Liandra,"

Connal said.

"I didn't know the bonding dance would have that effect."

"The -?"

"Bonding dance. An Asarian couple wears the traditional robes and performs the dance to show their love for the other, before they join mentally and physically."

"The man had his face painted like the woman."

"In his own aura colours, as his partner wore hers."

"And he was dressed in that same robe in which you imaged me, when we dream-searched. Why?"

Liandra shrugged. "I had no reason. It just came to mind."

Connal's eyes were steely and his jaw clenched. Then he laughed. "Aye, well I suppose that is how you see things. The joining of a man and woman can indeed be potent magic."

It was Liandra's turn to regard him sharply. In response he smiled enigmatically.

"What's happening now?" she asked, noticing that on the floor, men and women were lined up facing each other and from the alcove above the hall, flutists and pipers began a stirring tune.

"We will be dancing the night away, I think. Care to join me?"

"I ... I don't know how to dance."

"I can teach you. Come along, *ban-druidh*!"

Taking her elbow, he escorted her to the line

of dancers. Although Liandra tried to follow the intricate and fast moving dances, sometimes she, and others, became hopelessly entangled. Everyone laughed as they tried to weave a path through the sea of bodies.

Then, a slowing of tempo and Liandra followed the sedate moves, the clasping of hands and fingers, as men and women circled their partners. Most couples took the opportunity to caress, a meeting of hips or more. Connal did try to tease her in such a way, and Liandra found it difficult to elude him. Though occasionally they could not help but touch bodies in the pressing throng of people about them.

Connal took her into his arms and swung her about as the music changed pace yet again. She clung to him to keep her balance, and he lifted her off the ground.

"Not like your Asarian dancing?"

"More primitive."

"More enjoyable?" he asked.

"I prefer the other."

"Do you? That is not what your eyes and laughter tell me."

Liandra frowned. It was true. She did enjoy this way of dancing - uninhibited and sexual in a more conspicuous way than any Asarian dance.

Still carrying her, Connal manoeuvred her into the circle of dancers.

"Aren't you going to release me?"

"No." He laughed.

Liandra squirmed against his inescapable embrace. Connal drew her closer and she put her arms around his neck. He glanced up and Liandra did the same.

"You are now under the kissing bush. As your *Tighearna*, I claim a kiss from ye."

About them the people laughed.

"Wha -"

Connal's mouth swallowed her protests. She felt his arms tighten around her, and one hand snagged in her hair, holding her head. His tongue touched her lips and she gasped, too late realising her mistake. Seizing the opportunity, his tongue plunged into her mouth, entwining sinuously with hers.

She knew she ought to object, but could not, for her every cell hummed a resonant warmth. Faster and faster the blood raced through her veins, and soon it was she who clung to him in order to drink more deeply from him. On and on. She felt the taut expectancy of his body against her. In response to his arousal, her own body pulsed. Slowly, she began to reach out to meld body and soul with him.

Laughing, Connal tore his mouth away, and set her down on her feet. People around them clapped and cheered and laughed. He drew her away, so that other couples could take it in turns to stand beneath the kissing bush.

Liandra breathed in deeply, trying to still the quaking of her body. Connal, too, she noticed had reacted to their kiss. His face was flushed and the tension in his body radiated outwards, merging with her own. She stepped back, so she could gather her wits. To understand, to decide what, if anything, she should do about this reaction to him. This was more than his alien chemistry arousing her ... It was ...

She half turned away and across the hall she saw, *sensed* it. When she tried to focus, it was gone and in its place she saw Jenna's furious, horror-filled face.

Liandra gasped and staggered against Connal.

"What is it, *gradhag*?" His fingers on her shoulder traced a fiery path to her neck. He cupped her chin and made her look at him.

She glanced back. While Jenna had gone, in her place she caught an outline. A green-black shadow. Liandra gasped. And in that instant, she knew. It was the alien presence from her dream. Only now it was not a dream. Somehow it had found a path into Caledonia.

"What is wrong, Liandra? You look as if you have seen a ghost."

"Connal, they're here!"

He frowned about the room and tugged her playfully closer. "Who be here?"

"I saw an alien."

He sucked in his breath. His fingers bit into her shoulders. "What did ye say?"

"Just after the kissing bush. I sensed something ... someone. When I focused, I saw an outline. Just a lingering presence."

Connal smiled and cupped her chin. "Maybe

your senses are awry from my kiss." His fingers traced over her bare shoulder.

"Stop that, please!" Liandra batted at his hands. "Connal be serious! I'm telling you what I saw. I didn't imagine it. Are you so drunk that you can't understand?"

Connal's smile faded rapidly. "I am not drunk!" Taking her shoulder, fiercely, he spun her about, and clearing a path through the throng of revellers, he led her out of the room to the corridor. "Tell me, again, exactly what ye saw."

Liandra painstakingly recounted her experience, her feelings. "How it could reach here, that I don't understand."

"Nor do I. I made certain, unless -"

As he turned away, Liandra gripped his forearms. "What aren't you telling me?

"I canna' tell ye. No questions! I must look to this menace. If any aliens be here, then we must prepare our defence."

"You need help, Connal."

"Help?"

"League help, or at least Asarian."

"No!"

"Con, you don't understand!"

"I understand only too well."

"If these creatures have penetrated real-space, then every world is threatened! You must let me reach my father."

"Caledonia will defeat this enemy, Liandra. The League will not be involved."

"Listen -"

"No! And I know I have the right of it when I say that the moment my back is turned you will be seeking out your bed, defying me."

"Connal -"

"Liandra I understand your loyalty to the League. I can even admire it, truly! But we want no more of your kind on this world. Come."

He took her arm in a grip that would have been painful if she struggled. She glanced at him, saw his determination in the clench of his jaw, the glint of his eyes.

He opened the door of her chamber and ushered her inside. "I will not ask for your word in staying to your apartment. You will only break it." Connal strode to the balcony door and after locking it, he put the key in his sporran.

"You intend to imprison me?"

"That I must. Have no fear. These creatures if indeed they are here, will not remain so for long. Trust me."

He strode to the door and Liandra raced after him. Too late, it shut in her face and the final indignity, she heard the key scrape in the lock. Locked in like an errant child! Liandra paced the confines of her room, venting her frustration on everything in sight. She tried to pick the locks, without success. She even tried a probing to see if somehow she could warp the metal and thereby escape. Not that she had any chance of success without her crystals, but she felt as if she had to do something. Nothing she tried worked. She sat down on the edge of her chair, thinking furiously, discounting every plan that came to mind.

Hours passed and when the wan light of dawn filtered into her apartment Liandra heard the door opening. Jenna crept forward.

Although she wanted to retreat from her enemy, Liandra stood her ground. Jenna regarded her, then stepped backwards, her gaze averted.

"You and I have had our differences. The cause of such, well you know. I am here to help you," Jenna whispered.

"I remember the last time you *helped* me, *Maera* Jenna. I won't be deceived again."

She dismissed Liandra's words with a wave of her hand. "I heard we are in danger from an enemy not of Caledonia. You have ways and means to help. My Connal is a stalwart man, but even so, he may not be able to defeat this enemy. He will not entertain the idea of help from your kind. I think we need it. I have a way for you to reach your people."

"My bed -"

"No. Something better. I can help you leave Caledonia."

"How?"

"Come."

As Jenna tugged at Liandra's arm, she wrenched it free "I know better than to trust you!"

Jenna smiled bitterly. "Before you came here my lord had eyes only for me. Since your arrival he has watched you as he once did me. With you

377

gone, he will, again, look upon me with favour. I am a woman fighting for her man. That is why I help you."

Liandra frowned. She could understand. If things had been different, maybe she would fight to retain the love of such a man as Connal MacArran ... Seven Stars!

"What about Connal? If he finds out you've helped me -"

Jenna smiled. "I can weather his temper and punishments. Come."

Liandra chewed her lower lip. She had to take the risk of believing Jenna for the chance of reaching home, for the chance to help Caledonia. She followed Jenna down the corridor.

Using the network of narrow backstairs, they descended to the lowest levels of the Castle. Liandra felt as if the air was alive, it prickled at her, making her skin itch.

Jenna led her down another stairwell. The passage of many feet had polished the stones, rounding the edges of each step. Finally they emerged into a darkened chamber.

"The dungeon is the oldest part of the Castle. The foundations were laid by Arran himself." Jenna's voice echoed in the gloomy cavern. She took up a light-stick, and held it out, the blue light almost suffocated by the dank oppressive chamber.

Liandra cast about. Age was certainly there. And other things. Strange sensations and energy vibrations.

Jenna pushed against an iron-studded wooden door. Slowly, it creaked open. Liandra, following closely behind, frowned as the light revealed the chamber. At its centre she saw a metallic device, a metre tall, shaped like a pyramid. About the corners of the room were similar, but smaller structures. All were black and no light or contour marked their smooth surface. She sensed something, a familiar resonance.

Then she remembered. The machine-thing which she had encountered in the dream-search. "I know this. What is it?"

"This be the source of all our trouble. The trans-mat. It brought you to Caledonia."

"It *what*?"

"When Connal went off world seeking Garris, he took this machine with him."

"He reached League space with this thing?"

Jenna shook her head. "He used the MacArran star-ship."

Liandra stared at the woman, open-mouthed. "You have no such!"

"Aye, that we do, *ban-druidh*. He journeyed to your space in our ship and from there he used the trans-mat to reach your apartment, kidnap you, without any being the wiser. Connal said it was so easy."

"Are you telling me this machine can transfer people from place to place?"

"Aye."

"How?"

"I care not. The person wishing to be transferred stands against that device in the centre and after a few moments the light appears and dissolves the person. They are no longer there. This machine shifts them to a pre-determined destination."

Liandra shivered. "I don't like the sound of having my molecular system destroyed and then reconstructed elsewhere."

"Nor I. But 'tis the only way you can reach the star-ship above Caledonia. Then you can get home."

"Won't there be any on board the ship to stop me? And how will I reach the League? I don't know where I am."

"'Tis the easy part. The ship is deserted. Every warrior is hunting the alien you claim to have seen. As for finding your way, there is a guidance system. You have but to tell it where you wish to go and it will take you there."

"I'm not certain about this trans-mat. Is there is no other way?"

Jenna shook her head. "Do you not understand, *ban-druidh*? This chance will not present itself again. Connal plans to destroy the trans-mat."

"Why?"

"Get you gone! There is no time to waste." Jenna pushed Liandra towards the machine.

"No. If there's trouble, I'm not going to desert my friends! I only need send a message to my father. I can quickly reach him through my bed."

"Connal has that under lock and key."

"We can find it."

"No!" Jenna screamed. "You have to go!"

"I -"

"Do as I say, bitch!" Jenna shoved her back forcefully, her nails catching in Liandra's gown, ripping the fabric.

Liandra fell against the machine, and struggled to maintain her balance. Before she could right herself, she felt the trans-mat erupt into life, holding her immobile in some sort of stasis field. From each small pyramid structure a network of lights extended and melded before more rays erupted from the main console. Her whole body was bathed in a glowing red light that tingled against her skin.

"Stop, Jenna!"

The light intensified, then everything went black. When her consciousness returned, she found herself in a place that was cold and dark. Silence all about.

Where am I? Shivering, she wrapped the remnants of the velvet gown around herself.

At last! The one we must have. It is here!

The alien minds pounced on her. Liandra screamed as the gathered consciousness violated her.

Chapter Twenty

How long their assault lasted, Liandra did not know. When their minds finally withdrew from hers, she curled herself into a tight ball, sobbing with pain. And fear.

She was trapped in a dimension bereft of everything. Light, sound, colour, smell, touch: she floated in dark nothingness. They had even taken her gown and crystal necklace, her only sources of comfort, a focal point on which to anchor her sanity. She would not long survive their imprisonment. They knew their business of torture only too well.

What had Connal called her? *Ban-laoch*. She was no amazon-warrior. She was incapable of fighting her captors, at least for any length of time.

And Jenna? Had she deliberately sent her to the aliens, or was it just a mistake? Did they control the trans-mat's destination? Had the machine somehow infiltrated between the dimensions and caused the rift, such as she had sensed in the dream-search?

Finally, she closed her mind to her many questions. They'd get her nowhere and they were consuming her strength. She must reach help before she was too weak. Liandra forced herself into the dream-trance and focused outwards. On and on she pushed, fighting against the confines of her prison.

Hours later she returned to her body, shuddering with fatigue. She had touched nothing out there. Just a void so dark and silent it was terrifying. Liandra rested her head in her hands. She'd try again later. She wouldn't give up.

Do you admit defeat yet? The aliens probed sharply.

Liandra refused to answer and in retaliation the creatures sent a bolt of pure agony into her. As her nerves exploded she fainted.

Slowly she dragged herself back. How long had she been unconscious? Liandra tried to move. Too cold. She remembered the time before in the dream-state, Connal had warmed her then, his cloak about her, his arms pressing her to him.

"Connal," she whispered into the darkness.

Was it her imagination or did the void truly shimmer?

Connal? Again, she called. Nothing in response. Just her imagination after all. She closed her eyes. Unbidden, images of Connal came to mind. She relived their experiences together. All the bad times and the good Though of late she had found him entertaining and ... yes, she could admit it to herself. Now she was alone, and no one to witness her capitulation. She desired him. Wanted him in reality as she had in her dreams.

In her dreams he had been the gentle, sensual lover who ignited her body to levels of desire she had not known existed within her. But perhaps, in reality, he might be violent. He was capable of it, she knew only too well. Yet, only once had he hurt her and when he realised what he had done in his ignorance, never again did his strength abuse her. Might he then be able to love her in the ways she needed to be loved?

She would be willing, more than willing to try. She focused on him, weaving her dreams, and fantasies. Renewed life flowed through her, the blood pounded in her body, as her emotions and senses took control, as she imagined them together. No need to suppress such now. No one was near to read them, anyway! Except the aliens and she didn't care what they thought.

Connal. She tried to image him there with her, and his shadowy form did appear briefly before being snatched away. She tried over and over, with the same result. The aliens were too strong for her. Finally, she let go. Instead, she internalised her dreams, allowing them to take her where they willed. And always Connal was at the centre of her thoughts.

What would her father say if he knew she wanted a barbarian for a lover? Might he approve? Though concerned by her desire to remain unpartnered, he could understand her reticence. He had been slow in seeking a life-mate, too. Her mother had told her there had been incredulity from his family, when he had soul-partnered with a Terran woman.

And what would her parents make of Connal MacArran? Her barbarian? The only man to elicit any response from her, was the same one who challenged her and her way of life. Made her forget who and what she was. Only all that mattered for her was the having of him! Because somewhere - somehow - she had bonded with him.

She realised it, now. She had ignored all the signs, fighting daily against the attraction, but it was a battle she could not win. He had touched her soul with his own. And that being so she would forever love him. Be his ... always his.

He was beautiful, her Connal. She remembered the way he had moved in the exercise yard, and so strong were the emotions kindled by that memory, she saw him again before her, almost real, his body shining with perspiration, muscles flexing, sword in hand. Yet that was only one facet of the man. The memory wavered, to be replaced by the memory of their time together on the bed when he had read to her. Connal, gentle and tender. He made her laugh and cry! One moment she was furious with him, the next her body burned with the heat of passion. Images of him coalesced and layered one on top of the other.

By Arran and the Seven Stars! What would he say and do if he knew? Would he be repulsed, or incensed, that she, an alien witch, loved him? Or would he also respond with desire? There were times, of late, when she sensed a mellowing in him. His gentleness towards her far outweighed his intervals of anger. If only she had not been so stubborn, she might have known Connal in other ways. And now it was too late to tell him, because she was trapped here and would die, her secret dying, too.

Oh my Connal.

"Ban-druidh?"

Liandra started awake "Connal?" She'd been dreaming again! There was nothing here for her but dreams and nightmares. How ironic that in her final hours she could only think of Connal MacArran and tell him the many things she should have and now would never be able to.

"Liandrrra!"

"Go away you ... *deamhan-coimheach*. You won't be taunting me. I know who you are.

She closed her mind against their assault. 'Demon-aliens' she had called them, cursing in Caledonian. Would Connal be proud to know that her last fighting words were in his own tongue, rather than League Standard?

Connal battled against the darkness. It clung to his body like a horrible second skin. It smelled of fear, pain and death.

"Damn this to the Seven Stars!" At his fury,

the void parted. He saw her.

It was the way she lay which made his heart stall. He strode forward, afraid to the depths of his being. He bent down and rolled her carefully over. At her throat, his hand sought a pulse beat. Nothing.

Frantically, his hands ran over her body. There was just a little warmth left, and the faint tremor of her heart beneath his hand. He flung off his cloak, wrapped it around her and lifted her into his arms.

Had it truly taken him hours to find her? No telling how much time had passed until he had heard her first call, then a little while later, another sending, a feather-soft whisper. So weak. After that, nothing but silence. Terrible silence.

Dougall should be activating the device soon, Connal thought. His pax-man had wanted to accompany him into the void. The resulting argument had been brief, but bitter. In retaliation, Dougall had severely limited the time Connal would spend in looking for Liandra. That or nothing: as pax-man, Dougall had been his most obstinate.

Connal hated the machine like nothing on Caledonia, or on any League World. Once home, he would destroy the trans-mat as he should have done long ago!

"Now, Dougall. Bring us home. Now!" Connal called into the void. But of course Dougall could not hear.

On the periphery of his consciousness he felt the aliens racing towards him.

Something clutched at Liandra. It began to drag her away. He held on with both hands. He wished for his claymore, to fight the monsters as he done once before in the dream-state. Only this was no illusion. And if he fought them, he would have to relinquish his hold on Liandra. And that he would not do, not for all the universe!

The enemy's assault began in earnest. Minds plunged into his, while something grasped him, spinning him about, trying to tear Liandra and he apart. Throughout the battle, she lay like one dead in his arms. He glanced down at her face, thin and pale, with dark circles under her eyes. She'd only been gone a day. What had they done to her to make her look so? Fury rose up inside, and like a bolt he hurled it outwards. The enemy retreated. He sensed their measuring.

As one, they attacked him again and it felt like something was biting him all over, scratching and clawing with fangs and talons. Gasping in pain, he bit down hard to stop from crying out. He tasted his own blood on his lip.

Arran's Mercy! He breathed in relief as he felt the familiar prickling over his flesh, the tingling beam of light before he was wrenched back into more darkness.

Connal sensed the aliens' pursuit. Something brushed against his body. What was in the trans-mat with him? There was little time. It was out of the question to willingly lead any invader to his Castle. Balancing Liandra in one arm, he dug into his sporran, fingers clasping on the trans-mat homing signal. He de-activated the switch just as he saw the ghostly outline of the machine in the castle dungeon. For a moment, he hovered in that terrible place between dreams and reality.

Moments later, with an awful gut-wrenching turning inside out, he sprawled face first on long, wet grass. Liandra lay a few feet from him.

Seven Stars and Arran's Mercy ... where am I?

It took him some minutes to recover his wits. Slowly, he crawled to Liandra. Turning her over, he drew her against him and lifted her up into his arms. Shakily, he rose to his feet.

"C ... Con?"

He almost dropped her in surprise. As he looked down at her, her eyelids fluttered open a moment before closing again.

"You're here, truly?" she whispered.

"I am here, *gradhmhor.*"

"I'm dreaming?"

"No."

"How did you find me?"

"The trans-mat."

"The enemy?"

"Gone." *I hope,* he added to himself. He stared about. Was this another illusion? He frowned and concentrated, trying to image another landscape. It remained solid. Real.

Was it truly Caledonia? It was so dark, so silent. Not like anything he had ever experienced. Ominous dark clouds overhead were laced with shimmering green. Something was terribly wrong!

If this was Caledonia, then he knew where he was. Behind that range of hills and beyond the valley lay Castle MacAarran. A good day's walk, if one was able to walk. Liandra certainly could not make the journey - not in her present state. He glanced down at her before shifting her in his arms. He brought her close against his body and rubbed his cheek against hers.

She stirred slightly. "Where are we?" she asked, hoarsely.

"Safe. There be a cottage nearby. We can rest."

"Must warn ... Father."

"Worry about that later. I have to get you to safety. 'Tis a storm heading this way."

Long before the stone cottage came in view, Connal was drenched to the skin and Liandra was a cold weight in his arms. Beneath the saturated folds of her cloak, she shuddered violently. He knew she was unto death.

Chapter Twenty-One

Connal cursed his shaking fingers. He was so damn cold and the thrice-blasted fire was slow in catching hold. He should have had this *bothan* replaced by a modern cottage, but it was one of the last remaining from the old days. A touch of nostalgia had stayed his hand when he had overseen the modernisation of his estate. Now that sentiment was likely to see he and Liandra freeze to death.

Outside the wind howled, buffeting the cottage so that the walls and roof shuddered. Hail beat incessantly against the shingles, the relentless pounding echoing inside the cottage. He had never experienced such a tempest.

Connal fanned the fire, coaxing it to life, adding more logs to the now blazing hearth. Satisfied, he turned back to Liandra. She still shuddered beneath the thick quilt. Gathering her up into his arms he placed her before the fire on a pallet of lambs-wool rugs. Briskly, he again massaged her body, forcing warmth into her chill flesh. He tucked the quilt back around her.

Taking a few moments for himself, Connal stripped off his sodden clothes and wrapped a blanket around his body, all the while shivering in the dankness of the cottage. Slipping beneath the quilt, he pressed against Liandra, giving her the warmth and strength from his own body. Gradually her convulsions abated. Slowly ... so slowly, her body lost its iciness.

Hours later, satisfied she was a little recovered, he left the safe haven of the hearth and rummaged through the ration cupboard. He returned carrying a flask of whisky. He forced the bottle between her lips and made her swallow a mouthful.

"Don't, Con ... " she protested, batting at his hand, pushing the flask away.

"'Tis my best whisky, *ghraidh*."

"It's horrible!"

If the circumstances were different he would have laughed at the grimace on her face. He forced her to drink a little more before he swallowed several gulps. The whisky blazed through his body, warming and invigorating. Drawing her closer, he let her cheek rest against his chest. Gently he stroked her hair, his hands falling away, to trail down the length of her, rubbing over and over, trying to banish the last of the cold from her.

"C...Con?"

"Aye, *ban-druidh*?"

"Where are we?"

"In a cottage at least a half day's walk from my Castle."

"Safe?"

"For the present."

"How did you find me?"

"Fergus led me to the dungeon, where I discovered Jenna hiding, with remnants of your gown. I forced the truth from her. Then, I followed you into the trans-mat, using your *sending* to guide me to you."

"You heard me?" she asked.

"Most strongly. How I know not."

"I'm thankful you did. I nearly died in that place. I never want to be in the dark or cold again."

Connal enfolded her tightly against him, and gently kissed her forehead. "By Arran, Liandra, you will not suffer such again." He glanced down at her. The firelight flickered across her face. There was a little colour to her cheeks now, and the dark shadows had diminished. He had almost lost her! And in that realisation come another thought, if she had died ... That he did not want to think about! Not now, not ever! "How do you feel?" he asked.

"A little better."

He ran a trembling hand up and down her arm. In response she snuggled into the curve of his body, her knee pressed across his legs, inadvertently touching his maleness. He drew in a sharp breath. Now no longer afraid she would die, other considerations flooded his body. Connal gritted his teeth, vainly trying to ignore the heated blood swirling in his veins.

"Hold me closer, Con."

"There is some danger in that, Liandra. You

can surely *feel* the evidence of it?" He smiled grimly as she raised her gaze to his.

Closing her eyes, Liandra rested her cheek against his chest. She heard the thumping beat of his heart, and its rate increased the longer she listened.

"I know what I'm doing," she said.

"Do ye?" he answered, gently lifting her so that she lay on top of him. His arms held her close, as his legs wrapped around her. "For if we start, Liandra, I am not certain I can stop."

"I'm not afraid of you, Connal MacArran," she whispered.

It felt as if his every nerve electrified at her words. He kissed her gently, half expecting she would pull away. Instead she parted her mouth to the tentative probing of his tongue tip. Connal groaned against her mouth. He had wanted this. Wanted it for so long it had been such a sweet agony, keeping him awake night after night. And when he could snatch a few moments of sleep, the erotic intensity of his dreams made him start awake, heart and blood racing, his shaft thick and aching with such need, not even cold baths in the middle of the night could quell his torment. Being in such a state of arousal and not being able to do anything about it, for no other woman held any interest for him, his temper had been foul for as long as he could remember.

Fear sliced through his euphoria. Fear that this might be yet another dream to bedevil him.

If this be another dream ... Arran's Mercy, let me wake up when it is finished, not half-way through as I always do!

His kisses, lazy feather-soft caresses, traced a slow, sensual teasing journey across her mouth, throat and cheek, to reassure and to intoxicate. He revelled in the feel of her against him, drank in her femininity. Teasingly, his palms massaged her body, cupping and stroking every inch of her curves.

Liandra rolled onto her back, drawing Connal over her. The heat of their bodies merged. Her heart thudded so fiercely her breasts quivered. She explored him, marvelling at the contrast of his whipcord muscles and satin-smooth flesh. The spicy musk of his male heat permeated her every cell, driving her to new heights, to greater daring. She cupped his male rigidity, drawing a ragged gasp from him.

"Did I hurt you?" she asked.

He pressed against her. "Do not stop, *gradhmhor*," he whispered huskily against her mouth. "Do that. Oh, yes! Oh ..." Her nails carefully raked his swollen flesh.

Gently his fingers snagged in her hair, tilting her head back, exposing her neck to his mouth and tongue. His lips traced a blazing trail down her neck to her breast which he teased into a rigid peak. His fingers slowly stroked down her leg, teasingly returning along the inside of a silken thigh to find the centre of her. He heard her gasp and in response his blood pounded, its epicentre in his groin, a rhythmic throbbing that travelled his entire body. He drew in a ragged breath. Almost he felt a virgin, a callow youth trembling with the need to bed his first woman.

Liandra writhed beneath his touch. Never had she dreamed it could be like this ... feel the things this man was invoking. She opened her eyes and he smiled down at her, the gentlest lover's smile that drove a thrill deep into her soul. His gaze held hers as his fingers teased her, parting, stroking, swirling in and out, over her cleft, returning, retreating, inexorably building a pressure within her. She watched the play of firelight across his face, lighting his eyes so that they glowed a beautiful combination of gold and grey.

"Please ..." she murmured.

"Please ... what? My Lady *Ban-druidh*?" His hoarse whisper caressed her senses as his hands claimed her body. "*Please* ... that I stop? Or ... *please* that I continue?"

Shaking her head, slowly she reached out with her mind, coming up against his instinctive mental shielding. She heard him draw in a quick, trembling breath. Had he sensed her presence? She had almost done the unthinkable in forcing a meld. Connal was not ready to mind-share. She was going too fast for him, though she wanted that exquisite joining more than anything. But she could not force him. Instead, she traced a finger over his flushed face. She sensed the strength of his desire and longing. He held himself in check, so much so that his body trembled with the effort to maintain control, in order to pleasure her, to bring her to fulfilment, considering her needs before his own. She loved him in that moment with such intensity it frightened her. She arched her body to his and kissed him. Slowly his mouth left hers, travelling lower and lower.

At his daring, she gasped with shock. "Con!"

He would not be dissuaded, even as she curled her fingers in his hair to still his questing mouth. Undaunted, he continued his sweet plundering. So easily, so expertly he carried her far beyond anything she had ever experienced in her dreams ... in her wildest imaginings. Mouth and tongue knew their teasing art ... oh so well. "Connal ... please!"

His fingers again stroked her hot silken texture where moments before he had shared with her the most intimate kiss of all. Liandra's body convulsed as his caresses brought her so close ... His hand stilled, deliberately holding her at the brink, letting her regain a measure of sanity before easing her again, on and on inexorably to that pleasure-border, delaying it for so long that she writhed like a wild thing against him.

His hands under her hips lifted her tenderly. Liandra felt the gentlest probing, the tip of his flesh begging entry. Smiling against his mouth, she opened herself in welcome. Tenderly, he thrust forward, his searing penetration branding her as forever his. His mouth stifled her cry of pleasure and pain.

Slowly, so slowly, retreating and returning, savouring inch by slow inch, he finally rested deep inside her. As his hips rotated gently, her body spasmed against his, sending waves of pure delight through him. "*Gradhmhor,*" he whispered huskily. Resting on his elbows, he cradled her head in his hands, his fingers entwining with the silver silk of her hair. "My *gradhmhor.*"

She opened her eyes to see his triumphant smile. Holding her gaze captive, he undulated against her, his long, slow strokes teasing, retreating and returning, a languid thrust and drag. His tongue darted inside her mouth, mimicking the rhythm of his body in hers.

She rested her palms on his hips, her fingers fanning over his taut buttocks. Muscles flexed and contracted beneath her hands as he loved her.

His pace quickened, becoming more urgent with every thrust. She matched his speed, the tempo binding them together. Enjoined, faster and faster they climbed to that peak where reality became suspended in a painfully sweet explosion ...

Liandra came to consciousness to hear him whispering her name against her ear. She lay atop him, his arms about her, one of his legs curled across the back of her thighs, cradling her to him. She reached out a trembling hand to brush away the strands of matted hair from his face.

"You were crying. Why, *gradhmhor*? Are you all right?" Connal asked.

"I'm wonderful."

Grinning crookedly at her, his hands feathered over her body. Liandra moaned and wriggled against him. "Con! Con. Please don't stop!"

His witch wanted him again, he could read it in her eyes. And he wanted her, too. Never an easy man to satisfy, now so quickly after the first, he was again quaking with almost uncontrollable expectation and need. He shuddered and groaned in anticipation, as she ran her hand down the length of his body. At her touch his every nerve tingled.

"*Doona'* stop, Liandrrra!"

"You like this?"

"Aye, oh aye!"

"And this?"

Connal moaned a response. Smiling down at him, Liandra straddled his body. His hands cupped her hips, raising her, seeking, guiding them both. She arched her body and Connal held her waist, hands fanning over her back to cleave her to him, in one swift, sweet stroke.

Gently, he tugged her down, so that she lay against his chest still intimately united with him.

"Much better," Connal said.

"I was lonely, too," Liandra whispered.

"I was just thinking that, *ban-druidh*. I wanted

you against me. It almost seems as if I am not entirely myself."

Liandra caressed his cheek with her tongue. "It's a legacy of our joining, Con. I can't help it. For a time we are going to be closely attuned. We may sometimes think the same thoughts. It will pass, have no fear."

"I am not afraid of you."

"Perhaps you should be!"

"Of a skinny witch? I think not!"

He laughed and nudged her over and once again they neared that pinnacle before he teasingly halted their motion, then continued again, postponing the inevitable for as long as they both could.

Resting on her elbow, Liandra watched Connal, drinking in the sight of him as he stretched out before the hearth. His body glowed with the light from the fire, and from his own inner furnace. She went to reach out to him. Her hand stalled as she saw the scratches and weals on his body.

"Con, you've been hurt! Did I do that?"

"The aliens, not you, are responsible."

"Damn them!"

He raised a brow. "You curse like a Caledonian."

"It's no laughing matter."

"No." His eyes lingered on her body and she made no move to cover herself. As he reached out to draw her to him, she wriggled out of range. Throwing a quilt around her shoulders, she went to the cupboard returning, minutes later, with a cloth and salve.

"Sit up, I have to see to your injuries."

"What -?"

"Don't argue. I'm not in the mood."

"So I perceive."

She knelt before him and carefully touched the liniment to the first scratch.

"Ouch! 'Tis stinging me!" He squirmed beneath her hands.

"Be still. Some of these wounds are deep."

Despite the gentleness with which she tended his injuries, his occasional sharp intake of breath alerted her to his agony. Throughout he remained immobile. Again, his strength and courage amazed her.

"You should have told me you were hurt ... before."

Connal chuckled. "With you beside me, *ghraidh*, I did not feel any pain. Besides, I have endured far worse."

Liandra frowned at him. She leaned forward, her leg brushing his thigh. He drew in a ragged breath as his body tightened and throbbed at her closeness.

"Where did I hurt you?"

He laughed gently.

"What is it?"

Connal shook his head, still chuckling.

Liandra crawled behind him, kneeling at his back. She brushed away his hair and kissed the nape of his neck.

"I much prefer this latest medicine," he said hoarsely.

Liandra traced her lips up and down his spine, before continuing to salve his wounds.

Connal sucked in his breath. As she worked, her breasts, with their taut nipples, brushed across his back. Beads of perspiration broke out over his body. Arran and the Seven Stars, he could not take much more of this. "Have you done yet, woman?" he ground out between clenched teeth.

"Almost." She ran her hands gently over his back, making sure every injury was tended. "I will not forgive them for doing this to you." She kissed his shoulder, let her mouth trail over the length of his neck. She slipped her hands beneath his arms to cup his chest. She felt the muscles contract beneath her fingers. Arran's Mercy ... he was magnificent, her Connal! Beautiful, Magnificent. And all hers. She silently laid claim to every inch of him, before Connal turned and pressed his body to hers once more.

Liandra rested under the quilt, watching Connal as he moved around the cottage. He wore a blanket draped around his waist, not from modesty but through necessity. For only a short distance from the fire, the cottage interior was icy cold. Outside the storm still raged against their shelter and she shivered at its ferocity.

"Do you often have weather such as this, Con?"

Crouching before the cooking pot hanging in the hearth, Connal ladled food in two bowls. He looked back at her over his shoulder. "No. 'Tis unnatural -"

Their gazes met. Liandra watched his eyes turn dark and cold. They both knew the aliens were to blame.

"I fear what might be occurring in my absence," Connal said. "But it would be folly to even think of leaving our shelter. I must entrust the safety of my clan to others."

"Yes. Our duty is frustrated by this accursed storm!"

"Aye, 'tis. We must make the most of it."

"I think that's what we've been doing."

Connal forced a smile. Returning to her side, he placed the steaming bowls on their bed and added more logs to the fire, before returning to sit cross-legged before her.

"Are you well?" he asked, studying her face, noticing the high colour in her cheeks, her eyes, fever bright.

Liandra laughed and reached out to stroke the back of his hand and wrist. Connal shivered as he felt that caress invoke again a heady fire which if left to its own devices would lead them far from the cottage ... to another reality of their own making.

"Be that my answer?" he asked. Chuckling, he shoved a bowl into her lap. "Eat. Restore your strength, for My Lady *Ban-druidh* is very strenuous in her demands."

"Are you shocked by how much I enjoyed you?"

Connal nearly choked on his porridge. Damn the witch! She behaved as if she had been his lover for years, instead of hours. There was no embarrassment or shyness from her.

He reached out and caressed her cheek. "I did take pleasure from you. Still, I am a man not easily pleased."

"I know." Liandra glanced down at her food. Porridge with dried fruit. She wasn't hungry, but she spooned it into her mouth. She would be ravenous later when the effects of her joining with Connal had abated ... if that was possible. He had awakened her as only a lover could. Already she felt the rising need within her, and glancing at Connal, she could read the kindling of passion in the glowing depths of his eyes. She averted her gaze. They both needed a respite, though she sensed it would be only a brief one, knowing Connal. Knowing herself.

Liandra frowned. Now that she was thinking more clearly, this setting looked familiar.

"What is wrong?" Connal asked.

"This place. Do you remember it?"

"I have been here before. My people use it as a journey station."

"No. It's from our first dream-sharing. Surely you haven't forgotten?" She smiled as Connal flushed.

"That I could not forget." He laughed. "How is it that in our dreams we were in this place?"

"It's very rare, though not unknown.

Sometimes dreams can traverse time and space and merge with the past, or the future. It's never happened to me before."

Connal smiled. *That makes two of us, Liandra Tavor!* What they - what he - had experienced in the cottage was far more potent than any dream. Would he ever be the same again? No. He had loved her but thrice. Now he knew that no other woman would do for him. He wanted her again and again. Today. Tomorrow. Perhaps ... forever. The infatuation he felt for her, from the first moment he met her, had that somehow, sometime, been transformed into something more than desire? He had not been able to love any woman since meeting her. What witch's spell had she cast over him?

Liandra took the bowls away and Connal watched, laughing as she hopped from one foot to the other as her bare feet met the freezing stone floor.

He reclined on the bed, smoothing out the coverlet in preparation for her return. His hand stopped and he drew in a deep breath.

Blood. He frowned, and checked his wounds. They were not bleeding, Liandra's gentle ministrations had ensured that. Then, what? Had he been too rough with her? She was an alien woman. She had cried out with his first taking of her -*First taking ... Arran's Mercy! NO!* Connal's flesh goosepimpled. Fear and joy coursed through him.

Liandra knelt beside him, taking his palm to

her cheek. "What's wrong, Con?"

"When I took you, I hurt you, *gradhmhor*."

Not a question, a statement, Liandra felt her blush extend all the way to her toes. When she tried to drop her face, he reached out to cup her chin, his eyes searching hers.

"Answer me!"

"The first loving can be difficult. Isn't it the way of your women, Connal?"

He swore beneath his breath. "Och! Did I hurt you ... badly?"

"You were very gentle. There was some pain. That's to be expected."

"But why, Liandra? Why me? And not one of your kind who could understand your needs -"

She put a finger to his lips. "With me, you were perfect, Connal."

He snorted. "Why -?"

"'Tis a long story."

"I am listening," Connal muttered.

"I'd rather not talk."

"I rather would," he said, stilling her questing fingers. "I dare not take you again, so soon, *gradhmhor*. You need to recover -"

"Asarians are a resilient species."

"That as may be, but you have yet to answer my question."

"Very well." She twisted a lock of his hair around her fingers. "You once berated me for changing the colour of my hair, only Asarians have hair such as I -"

"What has this to do with -?"

"Everything, Con. I hid my heritage, for my own sake. Because ... because of what I am. Dream-weavers can be pursued by the curious and the deranged who wish to live out their fantasies with one such as I. When I was a child, a man ... accosted me."

"Arran's Mercy!"

"Physically, I wasn't hurt. And for my mental recovery, my father counselled me most skilfully. Maybe a legacy of that time has remained, because up until I met you, I never wanted a man."

Connal groaned and closed his eyes. Another explanation of hers that made him ashamed. He had accused her of being a vain woman, not realising she camouflaged herself for her own protection. *Why am I always wrong about you, ban-druidh?*

He fell back against the covers. Liandra followed him down, pressing her body to his. He moaned as her fingers inched over his body, sapping his will. Not that he had much of that where she was concerned. Her gentle laughter invaded his already overloaded senses.

"No, I must not, for I will hurt you, so soon -" he protested.

"Hush, you won't."

She drew him, once more, into the circle of her arms.

Connal stared into the fire. Pressed back against him, Liandra lay sound asleep, her hands holding his arms as tightly as he held her.

Her soft woman's bottom curved into his groin. One of his legs was thrown casually over her, so that even in sleep she was part of him - he a part of her.

By Arran! He could not understand. She was a woman common to all ... a whore. Or so he had thought. The evidence on the coverlet, testimony enough that he had been wrong. He had been her first lover.

That discovery brought pain amid the joy. He had never had a virgin before, such was a complication he had not wanted. Ever. He had thought she was well versed in love and seduction. She responded to him with such familiarity ...

He closed his eyes and swore silently. He had taken all from Liandra, and still he was not satisfied. His turgid body throbbed for her again. But he dared not. She had made no complaint the last time he had reached for her, despite her earlier protestations that Asarians were resilient - yet he had seen the apprehension in her eyes. She was tired and sore, she had every right to reject him, but she had not. So he had called a halt to their lovemaking and she had fallen asleep, while he remained on fire. How many times would it take to exorcise her from him?

Did he truly want to be free of her? *Could* he be free of her?

He had bedded a woman who was an alien. Yet that did not matter. Honour demanded he be accountable, and so he would. For on his world, the taking of a virgin was not done lightly. Whether he liked it or not, he had obligations. Responsibilities. The honourable way. The only way. And in his loving of her, he had given her the gift of his body, as she had done to him.

And what of Liandra? Her innocent responses to him had been a joy. *Innocent.* An innocent woman was not likely to be protected. He had not taken precautions. He had never gone to a lover without safeguards, but with Liandra the need had been so strong, burning. He had been so desperate - they had both been so desperate - that nothing was in his mind but to love her. And she him, it seemed.

Might a child have been conceived from their moment of lost control? Physically she was very like the women of his world ... might it be possible? Arran's Mercy! He did not want to think about that. But he had to. And would it matter if it was true? Dougall, and others, had been vocal about him finding a wife. What if that wife was an alien witch? *Seven Stars!* And what of Liandra? How would she feel -?

"Con? Something worries you?"

"I thought you were asleep."

"Only resting." She glanced back at him. "What troubles you?"

"You were a virgin, Liandra."

"Yes." She smiled. "I was."

He frowned at her, unsettled by the

directness of her response. "I always thought you were common to all. A whore."

"I was common to all, but only in my availability as counsellor. I did tell you I wasn't a sensualator. You didn't believe me."

"And do I take it that as a professional, there will be no consequences to our night of folly?"

Creeping cold coiled inside her, quashing the inner glow which Connal had ignited. In his eyes, their joining was folly! Something was wrong.

"Well?" he demanded.

"What do you mean?"

"A child, *ban-druidh*. Might I have given you a child?"

"Con, is that what's worrying you?" Relieved, she laughed. When she turned to him, the smile froze on her lips. He had retreated from her. Those lover's eyes which had burned and caressed were now distant and as chill as ice. She stroked his cheek. "Dear Con. You don't have to worry. In order to qualify for my licence I must carry within me a contraceptive implant. Even though I'm not a sensualator every one of my calling must take this precaution."

"So, always the *professional!*"

"Of course. Why are you angry?"

"I am not."

"Con?"

"Go to sleep, Liandra. We have a long day ahead of us."

As she pressed back against his chest, he could feel the tension within her, mirroring his own.

Worried for nothing, it seemed. She had even laughed at his fears! And the hurt of it was tinged with regret, for what he had imagined might be in the future. She found the thought of a child amusing, because when bedding down with him, she knew she was protected by some *infairnal* League device.

And worse, a hundred times worse, she had been unperturbed by the loss of her maidenhead. *Yes. I was* she had said. What she had done meant nothing to her.

Why had she accepted him, when she had spurned League men? There must be more to it than that childhood incident. Liandra often called him an 'ignorant barbarian'. That being so, why did she take the gift of his body?

Desperate times, desperate measures - the thought savagely intruded, making his blood run cold. She accepted his loving merely as a means to regain her strength. Their joining, as far as she was concerned, had nothing to do with love. For her it had merely been a renewal, a taking. Nothing more. He had been used. Realisation was like a knife twisting in his gut and sundering his heart.

Now the memory of their coupling was bitter-sweet. How could he explain to one such as she that what they had shared, what he had taken from her body, was considered a gift on his world? Such was not squandered for the sake of a moment's easing. What they had shared, at least for him, was more than just a night's pleasuring. He could never explain, for she would neither understand, nor care.

He had wanted more, so much more, the world had been bright with possibilities in one insane moment of love, forgetting that she was who she was. She was a product of her environment, when all was said and done. An alien, a member of the League. That organisation valued nothing. And he had thought, for just a moment, she was different. That in bequeathing her greatest treasure to him, she had hinted the promise of a future together. Disappointment, pain, a hundred other regrets cut into his soul. How could he have been such a naive fool? Arran and the Seven Stars!

"Con?"

"I told you to go to sleep! If you are not tired, then keep silent for my sake. I need to rest."

She frowned up at him. Once more he assumed the facade of the taciturn barbarian. Had she offended him in her wild reactions to his loving? Perhaps she should have been more circumspect. But she was Asarian, and she could not respond to him less ardently.

Or perhaps ... had he taken her gift of love without understanding, or caring? She blinked back the tears. Had he only taken her to ease his own cold and pain? Or to ease hers, in the only way he knew? That and nothing more? Arran's

Mercy!

Was it possible his only concern now was that he had bedded someone who might fall pregnant to his seed? And if there was a child he'd have to face the responsibility, and the probable condemnation by his people for his actions - for his one night of illicit pleasure with an alien witch!

That was why he was so angry! And now he knew she was safe, he free of obligations and recriminations, he turned from her in bitterness and loathing.

But he had called her his *greatly beloved*. And then almost in the same breath he'd used another epithet for her. *Witch*. She felt ill with the realisation that they were all just words to him, interchangeable to suit his mood and the circumstances. His tender words spoken in that husky voice of his were meaningless, a part of his well-rehearsed pillow-talk, and nothing more. Liandra's eyes burned with unshed with tears.

How could she have been so wrong about a man?

Chapter Twenty-Two

"The storm is over, Liandra. We must go!"

She started upright from the bed, to find Connal standing beside her, already dressed.

"Your porridge is on the hearth. I have some wood to cut while you eat. Hurry! We must get back to the Castle."

"If you're in so much of a hurry, why waste time cutting wood?"

"Because this is a journey station. Our law requires that I replace the wood we used last night. If the one who stayed at the cottage before us had not done so, we would have frozen to death. That is why."

Liandra frowned as he strode away. Taking up her bowl, she stood at the doorway, watching as he chopped wood into shards, using a great axe which he swung with all his might. The harsh planes of his body radiated tension. He swung the axe furiously, splintering each log in one swift stroke. So different this morning, this man who had, the night before, been such a tender lover. *Our night of folly,* he had said. She swallowed the porridge though it settled like a lead weight in her stomach, choking her with every forced mouthful.

Confused, afraid, she returned inside the cottage and found the clothes laid out for her. A shirt and kilt, a pair of old shoes.

Outside she heard the splintering of more wood, followed by his cursing. Hastily, she dressed in her clothes, adjusting the belt around her waist, so that the kilt would not fall to her ankles. She tucked in the voluminous shirt and folded back the sleeves. The boots were a little large and clung heavily to her feet. Better than nothing, but only just.

Connal stalked into the cottage. Liandra turned to him, momentarily disorientated by the sight of him dressed only in his kilt. He used a scrap of towel to wipe perspiration from his body. Jealously, her eyes followed the path of that fabric. Not long ago it was she, her tongue, hands and body which had traced over him.

He shrugged himself into his shirt. "Are you ready to leave?" He turned away.

"Wait. Connal?"

He paused mid-step, the rigidity of his back a silent affirmation that something was terribly wrong. Worse than last night. He was so tightly withdrawn from her that no emotion escaped him, though she tried a surface probing. Inside herself, she felt the first spirals of real fear. "What's wrong, Con?"

He shrugged off her hands as she touched his back. "Business, *ban-druidh*. I want no more of your diversions. We have many miles to cover before we reach home. If you are ready, let us away. Now!"

Liandra followed him, blinking back tears of anguish. Gone was her sweet, gentle lover. Now, a new Connal, a stranger more than ever, someone who frightened and hurt her with his brusque indifference. What had she done to drive him from her? The man she loved ...

Well, in the cottage she had pierced his facade to discover the gentle man beneath the barbarian's mantle. Surely she could do so again? First, though, they must meet on neutral ground, to re-build their relationship from where it teetered, on the verge of extinction. Liandra swallowed against the thought and the fresh, scalding tears it brought.

"Connal will you tell me about the trans-mat?"

"What about it?"

"For decades, League science has been trying, unsuccessfully, to build a machine which transports living things. How did you manage it?"

He glanced back over his shoulder and then hastily returned his eyes to the path ahead. Damn the witch! Even in an oversized shirt and kilt she still provoked his blood.

"The machine was a gift," he ground out.

"From whom?"

Connal sighed, waiting until she drew level with him. "Every twenty-five years each *Tighearna* is gifted with something from the ancestors."

"Your ancestors?"

"Aye. They were an advanced race, before calamity struck them down. Only a few survived. So that their achievements were not lost, they bequeathed their technology to us, a little at a time when they considered we are ready to receive them."

"Some still live?"

Connal paused. "The ancestors died long ago, although their presence lingers on." He shrugged. "I do not know how they deem when the time is right to give us their gifts, only that it has always been appropriate. My gift was the trans-mat, my grand-father's the MacArran star-ship."

"Do all clans have these gifts?"

"Star-ships, aye. The trans-mat is the gift only for MacArran. Would that it were otherwise."

"It's a marvellous thing. Why do you hate it?"

"Because, *ban-druidh*, 'tis the root of all our problems. Garris entered it, when I would have, but for clan reasons, he took my place. He returned somewhat confused. Two days later, he left Caledonia. The rest you know."

"That first time, he didn't tell you what he saw, or felt?"

Connal shook his head.

"I always wondered how your people remained, socially, in such a primitive state, yet had the alternate technology of a civilised world. Why didn't you tell me the real reason?"

"I said it was Caledonian magic. So 'tis, in a manner of speaking. Clans never reveal their secrets to strangers. And you be an off-worlder!"

"So your science was never learned, just attained through gifts?"

Connal laughed without humour. "We have paid a heavy price for such, I think."

"I-"

"No more. We have a long journey ahead of us. Save your energy for walking, not talking. Are you able to continue?"

"Yes."

"Let me know if you cannot. You nearly died of exposure before, I want no such burden around my neck again."

Stung, Liandra stared at his retreating back. That knot in her stomach was now a slicing pain. He had rejected her, this time viciously. Though she tried to engage him further in conversation as they walked the long, lonely miles back to the Castle, Connal remained silent. She had found love, only to lose it within the space of a day. Why, she did not understand.

"The Castle is under attack!" Connal shouted. Liandra staggered up the hill to join his side.

From their vantage point they could see Castle MacArran. An eerie, green glow emanated from foundation stones to top-most tower. The taint shimmered in and out of existence. Liandra could sense the alien contamination. It made her stomach churn. When she glanced at Connal he looked sickly.

"The aliens have not a firm hold yet. See how the light wavers? We must hurry," he said.

Connal raced down the hill. She tried to keep up as best she could, arriving in the courtyard a minute or so after him.

They ran into the hallway. Men stood in formation, girt with sword, dagger and shield. An horrific screeching tore into her mind and tortured her ears. She reeled back in pain.

"*Tighearna!*" A man called. As one the warriors turned.

"Arran's Mercy! Ye both are alive!" Dougall strode forward, hand out.

Connal waved aside his friend's embrace. "No time. What is happening?"

"This started late last night. We were monitoring the machine, trying to find you. Three creatures came. We could not stop them, so we shut down the trans-mat in case more tried to invade. Ever since, we have been fighting the aliens. With little success."

"They can't be fought like flesh and blood. They have no substance. I need my bed," Liandra cried.

"I forbid it!" Connal shouted above the din in the hall.

"The time for forbidding is over, Con. I have to reach my father. You're being invaded by creatures who have no compunction about whom they hurt. We need League help, or we'll

419

be taken over completely. Is that what you want? To become as they? They intend to merge with you, that much I found out in my time of imprisonment."

The faces of the men turned ashen.

"Truly?" Connal asked.

"They'll violate you as they did me, and you'll lose yourself in that union. I can't protect you all."

With Connal at her heels, she raced to his apartment and tore open the door. He grabbed her wrist and spun her about, dragging her close.

"Is there no other way? What about you? Is there danger?"

"No time to argue! Where are the crystals?"

Connal fitted them to her bed and Liandra drew on the cap. Lights distorted about her, a rainbow shot with green and black. She screamed, flinging off her cap.

"They're controlling my bed!" She snatched the pyramid crystal from its mounting. The gem seared her hand. Despite the pain, she forced herself to keep a firm grip on it. She would need it in the battle ahead.

Connal dragged her back. "Watch out!" A shaft of green light erupted from the bed. He ducked for cover, dragging Liandra behind him, protecting her with his own body.

The light scorched the floor, where they had been standing a second ago. Lightning fast, Connal hurled himself across the room.

Drawing his sword from its sheath he hacked at the bed, breaking the crystal alignments with the claymore. Connal dropped his sword as blistering heat raced through the metal into his arm. The sword lay in a smoking, melted mass on the floor.

The crystals shattered with a terrible, high-pitched squeal. Liandra staggered back as her connection with her bed was severed painfully. Green smoke coiled upwards and spread across the ceiling.

"*Seven Stars!*" Connal cried.

Hand in hand, they fled the chamber. Reaching the landing above the hall, they saw people running in retreat. Warriors formed a last line of defence against the shimmering light that shot all about, bouncing off the stone walls, sending sparks to the floor. Using anything to hand, people beat at the tiny flames.

"Stay here, Liandra!" Connal ordered and bounded down the stairs. "Kins-men, form a barrier!" Shield beside shield, one slow step at a time, the warriors pushed forward, while the alien light crashed against the metal and then retreated.

Liandra crouched in a corner and focused on her crystal. She might be able to weave a psychic barricade to protect the men. It wasn't much, but it might help.

The pain of her forceful sending seared her brain. She wrestled for control of the hall and almost had it, when she was torn out of her trance.

Something collided with her head and she was lifted to her feet. The crystal fell from her hands and broke into a thousand shards as it hit the floor. Still linked to it, she screamed as she felt its death.

When she came to her senses she saw Fraser MacLeod. His hands were around her throat, squeezing the life from her. She fought him furiously. Looking into his eyes she saw the green taint, the alien hue exuded from every pore of his skin.

"Look upon your last of this, *our* new world." His voice, like his features, was distorted by the alien possession.

"No!" Liandra clawed at his face. His fingers dug into her throat, stifling her cries of pain and fear. She twisted about in his grasp, lashed out with her feet, but Fraser's hold was inexorable. Little by little her vision clouded as his throttling took effect.

Connal! She sent the thought clear and fast to him, hoping that from their recent intimacy, a lingering rapport still remained. Just enough for him to hear her, as he had done before.

"Let her go, damn you!"

Connal's fist connected with Fraser's jaw and sent him reeling back. Liandra dropped to the floor, gasping for breath.

"I banished ye from the Castle, MacLeod!"

"I had a task to complete. To kill you and your bitch!"

MacLeod grasped one of the swords from the

422

wall adornment and lunged forward. Unarmed, Connal had no choice other than to retreat down the corridor as Fraser advanced confidently.

Liandra staggered to her feet. Dodging past Fraser, she tore a sword free from its decorative mounting. "Con, here!" With all her strength, she hurled the claymore. Connal caught it, and in one fluid movement, he met the slash of Fraser's sword with his own steel. Sparks flew.

Warily, they circled one another.

"Come on, Connal! See -" Fraser held his arms apart. "Kill me if you can, you witch's lap dog!"

Connal pursed his lips, his gaze riveted on green eyes which wavered between normal human-green to alien green-black.

With a snarl Fraser charged. His sword sliced through the air, missing Connal's stomach by a hair's breadth.

Liandra cried out and stifled another, seeing that the sound of her alarm distracted Connal, made him glance at her, instead of focusing on his enemy.

The two men clashed again and again, swords ringing, air swishing as steel sliced, arced, parried. Liandra focused on Connal, sending him strength. Willing him to victory.

Connal brought all his strength to bear on Fraser's sword and the man staggered backwards. Over and over, he attacked mercilessly and each time, against his attack, Fraser's sword was feebly raised in defence.

Fraser staggered to his knees as Connal's claymore crashed down. With a movement too fast to follow, Connal flung aside Fraser's sword.

Connal raised his claymore to deliver the death blow. "It ends here and now!"

Liandra raced forward, interposing her body to protect Fraser. "Stop! He's been possessed by the aliens. You can't kill him."

Connal tried to push her out of the way. "He be a coward and a traitor!" He glanced down at Fraser who was curled in a ball, moaning pitifully.

"You can't Con. You mustn't. Please." She gripped his sword arm. Finally, she saw the madness leave his eyes and reason return.

He ran a hand over his face, smiling grimly. "He meant to kill you, *gradhmhor*."

"I know. Oh - " Liandra spun around.

"What is it?" Connal gripped her shoulder.

"They're here!" She turned and ran down the corridor. Connal caught up with her at the top of the stairs.

"Who is here? Oh - by Arran!" Connal stood frozen in shock as he stared down at his hall.

It was full of aliens. Asarian and ... monsters! Huge reptilian monsters, eight feet tall, walking erect.

And Garris, leading them all.

Chapter Twenty-Three

Deathly silence descended on the hall, but only for a moment. Quickly the warriors realigned themselves, brandishing their weapons, ready to face the new invader.

Liandra bounded down the stairs. "Wait! These are my people!"

Recovering from his shock, Connal was only moments behind Liandra as she raced across the hall.

Sobbing and laughing, she flung herself into the arms of one Asarian. Connal was close enough to see the surprise on the older man's face.

"No time for this now," the Asarian whispered, his gaze resting on Connal. "Show me the machine. Quickly!"

Connal stepped forward, appalled. The off-worlder spoke Caledonian, like a native!

He did not have time to think more of it, for a green light crept up the wall and over one window. It rattled the glass before sweeping over the hall. People dove for cover as the taint swept around them. Immediately, three Asarians, with Garris at the fore, aimed rod-like devices at the alien presence. Coloured light, emanating from the rods, battled against green-black. People stood transfixed as the confrontation ensued.

With their rod-devices focused on the green haze, Garris and the Asarians drove the alien into a corner. It flared once before it was drawn into the cylinder Garris held.

"Quickly, before they can escape, we must reach the trans-mat." The older Asarian gripped Connal's arm.

"Dougall take charge here!" Connal called over his shoulder. Signalling to some of his men, he ran from the chamber, leading them swiftly to the dungeon.

About the glowing trans-mat, Connal saw his elite warriors shivering with the strain of their guard duty. With faces grey-gaunt, they looked unto death, much the same as Liandra had done when he had found her in the alien prison.

"Let us through!" demanded the older Asarian.

Connal and his warriors were swept aside as the League contingent raced into the chamber. The Asarians formed a circle around the trans-mat and again using their rod devices they aimed a stream of rainbow-hued light at the machine. Sparks flew and colours flashed. Slowly, slowly, the trans-mat became encased in a beam of light.

Connal felt the hair on the back of his neck rise, not from fear, but from the powerful emanations in that room. The battle was silent, yet deadly. The Asarians were not having an easy time of it, if the expressions on their faces were anything to go by. Glancing down at Liandra, she, too, had that strange far-away look, combined with pain. He liked it not that she fought the invader when he could not.

"Quickly! The Stasis!" In response to their leader's command, two Asarians at the side of the chamber placed a silver box on each trans-mat console. A shimmering luminescent screen sprang into life, instantly blanketing the trans-mat. The electric tension in the room vanished and Connal let out the breath he had been holding.

Liandra turned to him. "It's over."

"It is?"

"The trans-mat is held in a stasis field. Nothing can escape it, nor can any use it again."

"I will have the accursed thing destroyed."

"You mustn't do that," Liandra said.

"*Doona'* tell me -"

The older Asarian stepped forward. "You will not. The aliens are trapped in the dimensional rift that your machine created. You must take some responsibility for what has occurred. You have to help find a way for them to be returned to their home. Therefore, you can't destroy the machine. I won't allow it."

Connal folded his arms and regarded this man. "And just who be you to order me about in my own Castle?" he demanded.

"Con. This is Alleron Tavor. My father."

Connal felt his face flush as the Asarian stepped forward, finger-tips outstretched. It was not the greeting which worried him. This man was Liandra's *father*! A hundred thoughts rushed through his mind. How much did he know?

Liandra's hand rested on Connal's arm, her fingers searing his flesh, further discomfiting him.

"Since you be her father, I do owe ye an apology for what has been done her," Connal said, stiffly.

Alleron Tavor made a curious hand gesture. "Your clansman Garris has explained much. I feel I know you already." He smiled at Connal and then at Liandra. That smile unsettled Connal even further.

For a moment the eyes of father and daughter became remote. Connal caught a faint whisper. Alleron Tavor knew everything in that instant of psychic sharing, of that he had no doubt! Damn mind-reading aliens! Connal turned on his heel and stalked back to the hall, Liandra, to his chagrin, hot on his heels.

Connal paused. People had come out of hiding and although still distressed, they were setting all to rights. Pride surged within him for the steadfastness of his household. He scanned the crowd, seeking his *companach*.

Garris met his gaze, and in long strides the two men met in the centre of the chamber and embraced long and hard.

Connal held him out at arm's length. "I thought I would never see your ugly face again!"

"I missed you too, Con!" Garris laughed. "It was a near thing for me, I owe everything to Alleron, if -"

"Garris!" Fianna flew into the hall and flung herself between the two men, laughing and crying. She kissed Garris and then slapped him hard across the face.

"Ouch!" Garris put a hand to his stinging cheek.

"That for going off-world without me. Oh my *gradhmhor*!" Sobbing, she threw her arms around him.

"*Maer* Garris. At last we meet," Liandra said, joining Connal's side.

Garris extricated himself from Fianna's embrace, and bowed low before Liandra. "Aye." He touched her finger-tips in the traditional Asarian greeting. "I owe you much, *Maera* Liandra. But ... Con! By the Seven Stars! The wonders I've seen! You won't be believing me when I tell you."

Connal raised an eyebrow. "You speak like a damn off-worlder!"

One of the huge reptilian creatures joined their company, its claws on Liandra's shoulder. To Connal's horror and amazement she pressed her forehead to the monster's massive, scaly chest.

"Elexxessrr. I'm glad to see you," she said.

The reptile answered in a noise that sounded very much like the hiss of a snake. Connal's fingers twitched, wanting a dagger or sword in his hand, just in case the monster turned nasty.

"We'll sweep the Castle and lands. Make sure no other aliens are trapped. I've got med-tecs ready to see to the injuries of your people," Elexxessrr said, his slitted, glowing gaze resting upon Connal.

"Thank you," Connal said. What else could he say to such a creature?

"Anything else, Garris?" the reptile asked.

Garris grinned. "Best ask the *Tighearna*."

The creature bowed. "*Maer*? How can we be of assistance?"

For the first time in his adult life, Connal felt dwarfed, finding it necessary to crane his head back to meet the eyes of another. Only that someone was a thing ... a giant lizard-thing, eight feet tall.

"Please, just carry on as ye have been. Will ye excuse me? I have personal business to attend," Connal said.

Liandra watched as he stalked away, soon lost from view amid the swarming crowd in the hall.

With a squeal Bronnia launched herself into Liandra's arms, laughing and sobbing. "They said you were dead. I not believe! *Not!*" she cried, and then with the resilience only a child could display, Liandra thought, the little girl half turned and stared up at Elexxessrr, wonder and delight shining in her huge eyes.

"What be you?" Bronnia asked.

"My name is Elexxessrr. I'm from Saurus." The reptile bowed formally to her.

Bronnia allowed him to lift her, so they could regard one another, eye to eye.

"You be quite a creature," Bronnia said. She reached out to gently stroke the blue-scaled hide.

"Elexxessrr and I are old friends," Liandra said. Turning away, she froze as she saw Connal and her father in deep conversation. What they were saying to each other? Connal had the air of a man sorely discomfited. Well, he probably had every right. Her father knew exactly what had occurred from the time of her abduction to the present moment. Even if she hadn't told Alleron he would know. She could never disguise from him the flood of emotions spiralling through her body every time Connal was near.

"Bronnia, Fianna, please come with me. I have someone for you to meet."

Liandra went to her father. "Excuse me a moment, Con." She smiled at him, ignoring his frown at her interruption. "Bronnia, Fianna, this is my father, Alleron Tavor. Father, my friends Bronnia and Fianna MacLeod."

Her father bowed to Fianna. "Garris has spoken often of you, *Maera*."

Liandra saw Fianna flush deeply as Alleron's eyes held hers in his perceptive gaze. He knelt before Bronnia and they exchanged the traditional Asarian greeting.

"Little *Maera*, it's my pleasure to meet you." His eyes widened in surprise as her gaze met his. "She's an empath! A very strong one!' he said.

"She is?" Liandra asked. "I hadn't noticed."

Standing up, Alleron Tavor laughed. "She blocks herself very skilfully for one untrained. *Sensing* never was one of your strong points, daughter. Besides, perhaps you had ... distractions?"

Liandra blushed and Connal coughed as Alleron Tavor turned his piercing blue eyes on him. Connal felt himself blush all the way to the roots of his hair.

"Are many of your people empathic?" Alleron enquired.

"No," Connal said.

"I'm not so certain," Liandra began. "Some have faint traces of it, I've sensed that much."

"Come with me, *Maera* Bronnia, you and I must talk." Alleron Tavor held out his hand and Bronnia slipped her hand in his. Side by side, they left the hall.

"Now, *companach*, 'tis an explanation you owe me." Connal began, turning to Garris.

Like a man coming out of a deep trance, his kin-brother regarded him with heavy-lidded eyes. Exasperated, Connal swore beneath his breath. Always the same, when Garris was with Fianna, he could get little sense out of his friend.

"What did you say, *Tighearna*?"

"I want to know what happened to ye! Why you brought these aliens to Caledonia. That for a beginning -"

"Once they freed me from that alien prison, I had no choice other than to lead them here," Garris said. "Forgive me for that Con. Either I showed them the way, or doom Caledonia."

"You have betrayed the sacred trust put upon us by Arran himself."

"I don't think Arran would have minded, all things considered."

Connal pursed his lips. He felt like throttling Garris, but the damage was done. Somehow he had to salvage something out of the accursed mess he and his clan-brother had caused.

"How did they pierce the planet-shield?" Connal asked.

"That was the easy part. Alleron mind-linked with me -"

"He *what*?"

"Mind to mind, it wasn't unpleasant. The planet-shielding isn't breached, we merely bent it for a time." Garris grinned. "Through another of Alleron's mind-links, that's how the rescue party learned Caledonian. He's an amazing individual ... what he can do!" Garris grinned lop-sidedly. "Though having his daughter here as your guest, I've an idea you might have an inkling about Asarians."

Connal folded his arms and glared at his kinsman. "You have changed somewhat, brother."

433

"Aye," Garris laughed. "I'm not the only one to change, so have you, *Tighearna*."

"I do not know what you mean."

"Is that so? Then you surprise me."

"Not half as much as you have surprised me. Walking in here as bold as day leading these aliens to our home."

Garris' smile faded. "It was that or have the aliens invade the League, starting with Caledonia. Our world for hundreds. Besides, 'twas meant to be."

"It what?"

"You remember when you received the gift of the trans-mat? As *Tighearna* it was your place to use it first, as instructed. Only I entered it in your stead, and because of that I received a message that was meant for you. It came from Arran himself."

Liandra looked from one man to the other, thankful that her presence had been forgotten for so long. Now, she was getting some answers.

"Arran? Arran has been *dead* seven hundred years."

"That's right. But the message was there. He told me that we must come out of hiding. We had our place in the galaxy, it was time for us to take it. That's why your grand-father received the star-ship and you were gifted with the trans-mat. The message was that, in secret, we must seek out Alleron Tavor. He would help. I guess for a message that's been hanging around for seven hundred years, it was bound to go a bit awry. I got the name Liandra Tavor from somewhere. I couldn't tell anyone, even if I wanted to. I was compelled to do this by Arran. I couldn't fight it .. I didn't much enjoy his mind-control! So I used the trans-mat to reach the ship, only I never made it. The aliens intercepted me. And the rest, you know." Garris shrugged.

"Are ye telling me that this *infairrnal* mess was a plan?"

"Yes."

"How could Arran guess the events of the future?" Connal asked. A dull throb pulsed at his temples. He was going to get a headache out of this. *He just knew it.*

"Alleron and I've talked that one over, Con. We believe that for any species who can build a trans-mat, or shield an entire world from discovery, looking into the future wouldn't be difficult."

"I can hardly make out your Caledonian, 'tis so tainted. And ye look like an Asarian in that blasted robe."

Garris scratched his head and laughed. "Aye, well the clothes I had on me when I was rescued were near to indecent. They loaned me this thing, though I'll be glad to get back into my kilt. Or perhaps ... not so soon." He glanced down at Fianna who blushed crimson. "Now, if that's all, will you excuse me? Fia and I have some catching up to do." He and Fianna left the hall arm in arm.

"I suppose you heard everything?" Connal asked, looking down at Liandra.

"I did, and some of it makes no sense."

Connal ran his hands through his hair. "Nothing today makes any sense. And now I have a headache."

Liandra smiled and stroked his arm. "I have just the thing for that."

"No you do not, My Lady *Ban-druidh*." Hastily, he stepped back from her, away from the bitter-sweet memories of the time she had wrought her healing upon him. He could not let her touch him again. No telling what might happen if he did! "I have work to do and people to tend."

Confused, Liandra watched him stalk away. As she went to follow, her father's hand on her shoulder restrained her.

"Our arrival here was not planned. They're bound to feel over-loaded. They need time to assimilate. And no less that man of yours."

"He's not *my* man," Liandra said.

"Is that so? You can't deceive me, Liandra. Ever you have been easy for me to read when you are emotional. In that respect you are very much like your mother."

"How is she?"

"Worried sick. Especially after your message."

"I tried to reach you many times."

"I know, we tried to contact you, too. We searched and searched and that's how we found

Garris. We dragged him, and the other survivors out of the dimensional rift. No easy thing, it took a circle of minds to do it and Garris was more dead than alive after it was over. This man of yours, Liandra. You and he have bonded?"

"Not fully."

"Will you?"

"I don't know."

"Do you want it?"

Liandra blinked back the tears. "Of course I want it! But he does not want me!"

Alleron Tavor's eyes darkened as Liandra raced from the room.

Chapter Twenty-Four

With Fianna, Garris and her father at her side, Liandra tapped on Connal's open door.

"Aye, enter." Connal turned from where he stood at the window. He closed the curtains against the view of his people outside, swarming over the League ship. He ushered his guests to a semi-circle of chairs arranged around the hearth. "All is set to rights?" he asked, and listened in silence as they made their reports. "And my people, the ones who were controlled by the enemy?"

"Jenna, Vanora and Fraser are quite recovered," Liandra said.

"I find it a strange coincidence that your worst tormentors, Liandra, were those under alien control."

Alleron Tavor spread his hands in a gesture, almost Caledonian. "Their natural dispositions made them susceptible to domination."

"How did they come to be infected?"

"Jenna was the first," Liandra said. "Unfortunately, she can remember very little."

"*Tighearna* MacArran, many of your people have telepathic abilities. Some in greater measure than others. When the rift occurred, the aliens reached out and touched the first mind able to help them escape their prison. They chose Jenna, because her powers, although untrained, are quite powerful. Through her, others were enticed into the alien web. Now, Elion has made it his special life assignment to act as her mentor, among other things." Alleron laughed.

Connal frowned. It was incomprehensible to him that Jenna and that pale-faced Asarian had become mutually besotted the moment they laid eyes on one another. Still, his former lover was never backward in certain respects. She always knew what she wanted! He wished her happiness.

"What is to be done with the alien invaders?" Connal asked.

"For the moment we have contained them in the trans-mat rift. We have appraised them of the situation. They have agreed to wait while our people devise the necessary means to return them home. However, it will require the use of the trans-mat, with your permission, *Tighearna* MacArran."

"There is no risk of further invasion?"

"None. They understand their predicament perfectly. Now that we are aware of them, and know how to combat them, they are only too willing to return to their dimension."

"Why were Asarians kidnapped and killed?"

Alleron shook his head, sadly. "We were the

only creatures who could sense their presence, understand their intent, and combat their desire to merge. Invasion of another species, whether mental or physical, goes against our code. We would fight long and hard against any creature who dared try impose itself on another."

"You should have been there, Con." Garris' eyes shone. "The enemy refused any peaceful resolution, so the Asarians launched an offensive. The battle for the dream-dimension was relentless. It saved Caledonia."

"Aye?"

Garris nodded. "The aliens were powerful. If they had been able to concentrate all their forces for an assault on Caledonia, they would have won through. Their strength was divided. Almost all faced the Asarians."

"So you kept the enemy off our backs?" Connal asked.

"Yes," Alleron said. "The instant we withdrew from the dream-scape, they launched their attack on Caledonia."

"I wondered why there was no sign of the aliens after our second dream-sharing, Con. You had the right of it. You said my father was dealing with them," Liandra said.

"And the trans-mat? Once you have finished with it, you can destroy it?"

"If that's your wish. Some of my people believe the machine has been damaged, for its emanations *feel* wrong. A little fine-tuning and it should be operational without the risk of tearing space-time. The machine is too valuable to be destroyed, *Tighearna*. We could safe-guard it for you."

Connal sighed and ran a hand through his hair. That headache was back, only much worse than before.

"I will consider it. Thank you for your help." He handed them each a goblet of wine.

Alleron Tavor sipped his tentatively. "Why it's very good. Almost like Verian juice."

"But twice as potent, father. Be careful."

"Are you talking from experience, daughter?"

Liandra blushed. "Yes."

"I have sent word to the Council. They are on their way here," Connal said tightly. "I need to know what you intend with my world."

"That depends upon you, *Tighearna*. We have never foisted ourselves upon any species that does not want us. You have that choice. Liandra has explained some of your misgivings to me. They are unfounded."

Connal grunted. "You are but the first ship -"

"No, Con." Garris said. "The ship's crew came in blind, the navigation systems were off. The only way I would agree to bringing the League to our door was if Alleron swore that only he would know the location of Caledonia, hence our mind-link."

"Star-farers know the patterns of the constellations," Connal began.

"Yes, but your anonymity will be ensured.

My promise to you, *Tighearna* MacArran. The ship's automatic navigation recorder has been rendered inoperative, and each of the crew has agreed to undergo a debriefing once home, to ensure that no one has inadvertently figured the location," Alleron said.

Garris nodded. "We've covered every aspect, Con. Caledonia is safe."

"Safe? With the League swarming over my halls, poking and prying!"

"It will be wrong for you to stand in the way of progress," Alleron said, gently.

"Progress? Is that what ye call it?"

"I don't believe it would be in your best interests to close yourself off from the League."

"*Best interests!* Whose best interests are we talking about here?" Connal sipped his wine. "Garris has explained much to me. Perhaps in some respects my fears are groundless. I am not wholly convinced. As to why, let me tell you a story."

Connal heaved himself out of his chair and paced up and down the room. Liandra watched him, sensing his foreboding. Seven Stars! She wished she could go to him and hold him, kiss and love away his fears, open her mind to him, so that he could read the truth ... everything. Except she knew it would be the greatest mistake of her life, turn him completely from her with no hope of salvaging any of their former intimacy. He was a man coming to terms with the loss of everything he held sacred. She looked down at her hands linked tightly in her lap.

Connal cleared his throat. "Seven hundred years ago my ancestors arrived here. Not through choice, but abduction. There had been a terrible battle on their home-world. As a conquered people, they were subject to such tyranny that they were in peril of losing their identity. Their culture was forbidden them. Many perished because of the hardships inflicted upon them. Help arrived, from an unexpected quarter."

He ceased his pacing and glanced at his audience. His smile to them was forced, bitter.

"The home-world of my ancestors was often visited by star-farers. One such race took pity on the vanquished, and over three hundred people from among the sundered clans were brought here."

"Which race dared do such a thing?" Liandra demanded.

"A people who were desperate. They are long gone, *ban-druidh*, we are all that remain of them."

"I don't understand."

"If you keep interrupting, then your questions are not going to be answered," Connal said. "The aliens were an old, dying race. They had lost their ability to reproduce. For one last chance at survival, they needed younger, vibrant creatures with whom to merge, mentally and physically. Since my ancestors were captives, they were not given the choice when this process was inflicted upon them."

"This is why you loathe the mind-touch of an alien so much?"

"Aye, Liandra. We retain a memory of that time so long ago."

She went to question again, but Alleron put his hand on her arm.

Patience, daughter. Let him speak without hindrance. This is difficult enough for him, as it is!

Connal frowned at her, catching her frustration. Almost he laughed, but caught himself in time. This was no laughing matter. What he told these League *coimheach* was never spoken of. Remembered, only. Now he had to reveal the deepest secrets of his people to foreigners.

"When the merging was completed there were unexpected results. The people re-learnt many things, so long forgotten. Even to love. They were no longer sterile, and from their unions came a new race, a blending of the two. Their off-spring were cherished, so much so that this world was shielded from discovery. And so it has remained. Until now."

"I don't understand," Liandra began. She glanced at Garris and Fianna. Their faces were downcast. "There's so much which doesn't make sense. You say you are a hybrid race. Whom do you resemble? Your ancestors, or the aliens who abducted them?"

Connal ran fingers through his hair, wincing as his temples throbbed. "The original blood of my ancestors was too strong to dilute! Ours is a very stubborn race. Little by little we have reclaimed ourselves, though certain taints of that alien breed still remain. The telepathy for one. And every generation, each *Tighearna*, is given a gift. Such appears at a pre-designated time and place. Eventually, we were given devices with which to view our solar system, and then later, other monitors to watch the League. We know what is out there."

"Then you know you have nothing to fear," Liandra said.

"On the contrary. Caledonians do fear it, perhaps with some justification. We do not want to run the risk of losing our identity, again, to some alien culture. Fate has determined otherwise. Seven hundred years ago, Arran and the other eleven clans made this their home. Now I am the last in the line of Arran. 'Tis ironic to realise that this last son of Arran is also the first to return to the stars."

"And do you know the original planet from where your ancestors were abducted?" Liandra asked.

Connal smiled bitterly. "That I do, *ban-druidh*! Only too well. We were called Highlanders. We are from the land of the Scots. Scotland. In the poetry of our ancestors they called their land Caledonia, the name which we bestowed on this world, when it was transformed to resemble the Highlands. Our ancestors were from Terra."

Liandra gasped and looked to her father. He

nodded a silent confirmation.

"Garris explained a little of this, though he kept the secret remarkably well from me," Alleron said.

"The time for our isolation is over," Garris said. "There's no going back, Con. We can't ignore what's out there!"

"That is for the Council to decide."

"Blast them! They can't deny us. They *can't!*"

Connal raised a quizzical brow. "That sounds very much like an ultimatum. What if the Council refuses to open Caledonia to the League?"

Garris's face twisted with pain. "I hope I'm not forced to make a choice. I can't forget. Caledonia will always be my home, the place of my heart, but I would see other worlds."

Connal glanced at Liandra and she caught the meaning of that glance.

It said - *I told you so!*

"To confine your people to one world when they have glimpsed the endless possibilities of the universe, *Tighearna* MacArran, in the end it will destroy your world."

"That I know, *Maer* Alleron. As I see it, my world is doomed whichever way you look at it. Already I know the mind of the Council. Not a unanimous decision by any means, still, Caledonia will enter your blasted League, whether I like it or not. Our ancestors foresaw these events. They prepared the way by the gifts of the star-ships, and the trans-mat. All their machinations have been to this end, for us to join the League. We would have been found eventually, even if I had not gone off-world seeking my missing kinsman!" He threw up his hands in resignation. "However, this world shall have restricted access. If Caledonians travel off-world that is their affair, but numbers visiting here will be controlled. I want you to ensure this, *Maer*."

"Of course, it will be my honour."

Connal smiled bitterly. "I hope my trust in alien *honour* is not misguided."

"It won't be, that I promise. I'll contact the League and ask for a delegation of envoys. They can handle the negotiations." Alleron stood up.

"All this talking has given me an appetite." Garris rose to his feet, drawing Fianna with him.

Alleron Tavor laughed. "Caledonians have an amazing capacity for food."

"Aye, for *real* food!" Garris grimaced. "Con, they tried to feed me with concoctions somewhat like milk. 'Tis a long time I've been weaned from my mother, I told them. I thought I'd starve to death on their fare, before I got back home. Good night to you."

Connal smiled. "Wait a moment, Liandra, please. You and I must talk."

Liandra remained seated as the others left the room. She watched Connal lean back against the door. He looked exhausted.

"So *ban-druidh*. Now you have the answers to your questions."

"Yes." *Oh yes, but no answers to those questions I can't ask.* Those silent ones which hurt, that kept her awake at night. "I understand why you don't like mind-touching aliens, Connal."

Was that why he had become so cold and distant to her in the cottage? Had he sensed what she had tried to do? Had she, in her passion, irretrievably lost him when she had reached out with her mind as well as her body?

"Because of the events triggered by the transmat you were forced to relive those things you hated the most. Little wonder..." Liandra bit back the rest of the words. *Little wonder that you hate me so!*

She could not look at him, afraid she would see the loathing in his eyes. She'd remember the way he regarded her in the cottage: lover's eyes, glowing amber-grey from the flickering firelight.

Connal came to stand at her side and looked down at her bowed head. His fingers stirred, desperate to touch her. Despite their differences, despite what had happened in the cottage, he needed her, wanted her ... badly.

How he wished he could caress her silver hair, take her into his arms and love her again and again ... and again! But he could not. Even if, somehow, she accepted him, what did he have to offer her?

It would be years before his world was completely opened to League technology. There would be controls and only the best of what the League had to offer would ever enter Caledonia. As MacArran it was his duty to see to it. Liandra had made it perfectly plain that she loathed the primitive conditions on his world. She would not be happy anywhere else but with the League. And he?

His place was on Caledonia. Responsibility, obligations before his own needs. *Again!*

"The years ahead will be difficult for Caledonia," Connal said, huskily.

"My father's diplomats will help you. They've done so in the past, and no world or its people have suffered."

"For that I will be grateful. Tonight the household plans a celebration to formally welcome the League. Will you attend?"

"Of course."

The silence stretched between them.

"We have come a long way you and I, Liandra Tavor. If I had the chance to do it all over again, I would not change a thing."

"Nothing?" She dared not raise her gaze to his.

"Your father tells me he will be leaving in two days. You will go with him?" He asked, evenly. *Arran's Mercy! How it hurt to say that!* Connal swallowed against the tightness in his throat, while his stomach contracted painfully.

Liandra stared down at her lap, tears pricking her eyes. He hadn't asked her to stay. Wouldn't. He knew something of her needs and he couldn't fulfil them, even if he wanted to. He had always found her a nuisance ... *I'd send you off-world so fast your head would spin* … he had said that not so long ago. She marshalled her strength. She had to maintain her mask for her sake as much as his.

"Yes, I'll go home. I have my work to do."

"Aye, your work is very important to you, as mine is to me." He strode to his desk and returned, dropping her enviro belt into her lap, along with her Asarian ring. "These I return to you. Jenna found the ring among your things when I first brought you to Caledonia. She kept it hidden from us all. Now she is recovered, she tries to make amends. It is disconcerting to have her so eager to please."

"I've always missed my ring."

"Aye. I know that. 'Tis sorry I am that my kinswoman stole it."

"You must forgive Jenna, for she was not herself. You will not punish her?"

Connal shook his head.

"There is still one thing which puzzles me, Con. You said your grand-father received the first of the star-ships. Before your gift of the trans-mat, how could you get from the surface of Caledonia to your orbiting ship?"

He smiled. "I wondered how long it would be until you considered that. My grand-father received three flier-craft, not dis-similar to the League contraption sitting on my field. That way we transported from surface to space."

"And where are these ships?"

"I have a storage hangar not an hour's ride to

the south."

"You kept that secret, like so many others."

He chuckled. "'Tis true. For I understand you only too well, My Lady! That if you knew I had flying craft, even if I chained you to the dungeon walls, you would have defied me and found a way to escape, and stolen one to get away from me. You can be very determined. Do I have the right of it?"

His gentle teasing tore at her insides, she felt the tears brimming in her eyes. "Aye, you have the right of it, Connal MacArran." Liandra stood up, shakily. "I should go now, as I've got a lot to do before I leave."

"Aye," Connal said, quietly.

She did not look back as she fled the chamber.

Connal silently watched her departure and slumped down onto his chair. He twirled the goblet in his fingers and gulped down the wine in one mouthful.

"Damn it to the coldest hell. Why canna' I be free to go with ye?" He hurled the goblet into the fireplace. Heaving himself to his feet, he stalked up and down the chamber. Fury. Sorrow. Desolation. The sensations whirled around his mind and body.

If only ... *if only* he were not *Tighearna*. If only the responsibilities of the clan rested with some other. He would leave the world so fast all heads would spin, not just his. He smiled grimly, remembering his angry words to Liandra. Always so much anger between them, so little gentleness, so little love.

He wanted to see for himself the wonders which Garris had described. Experience what Liandra had ... How could a man stay confined to one world in the face of the hinted wonders out there?

And the greatest wonder of all, his love for that alien witch. His beautiful *ban-druidh*. A dozen women had tried to ensnare him. He had been amused by their vying and conniving to gain his title. To no avail. He had been totally vanquished by Liandra the moment she had walked out into her living-room, green hair and all. He smiled to remember that day.

Yet despite everything, he could not leave. Always, duty and loyalty to his people, before any personal consideration. He could not renounce his obligations. Not for anyone. He and Liandra had shared a night of intense loving. For the rest of his life, that memory would have to sustain him. She had gifted her body to him, for her own reasons, and love not among them. While he - he had been ready to do anything she asked. Be all for her ... in time. And time they did not have. She was eager to leave, to return to her place in the League. And he would stay. Alone. That was that.

But by the Seven Stars, he had never imagined it would hurt this much to let her go.

Liandra flung herself on her bed and cried until she made herself sick. He hadn't asked her to stay. Did he loathe her that much? She was but the last in a long line of telepathic aliens. The horror of mind-touching was an in-bred thing, from the time when Arran had suffered such.

And if Connal asked her to stay? In what capacity? As counsellor to his people? As someone to warm his bed? She wanted - needed - much more than this from him. Yet he could give her nothing else. She knew that from his reaction to her in the cottage. He could not share his mind, though he had shared his body, loving her with such intensity it pained her to remember. Even if, somehow, she could convince him to mind-link, it would be something he would find abhorrent, given his heritage. He might come to resent her insistence, and resentment led to anger ... to hatred. She would have to go, for both their sakes.

Connal would find a woman on this world whom he could love, who would be everything for him.

And you, Liandra? What will you do? She asked herself. She had touched his heart and soul, just for a moment in the cottage. It had not been a complete bonding, but it was enough for her to be forever his. Only half-joined, there would always be an emptiness within her which no other man could ever appease.

Liandra sobbed into her pillow, agony slicing her every cell. Somehow, she must survive. Inside, she felt ill and frightened. And inside, too, the little life she had touched that morning, would grow and grow. Their child, from their *night of folly*.

How had it happened? Against all understanding and against the hormone implant, the best of League science, she carried his child. Even if she had foreseen the consequences, nothing would have stopped her from joining with Connal.

And Connal, how would be regard the fruit of their union? - an alien telepath. No doubt he would spurn it. As he had spurned her.

Chapter Twenty-Five

Liandra sat silently next to her father at Connal's high table. Neither the food nor the entertainments especially planned for the night held any interest for her. Her heather-coloured velvet gown was the best the store-room had to offer. She kept its Caledonian style. Her effort was in vain. After a curt nod of greeting from Connal, he ignored her completely.

She watched the interaction of Connal's people with the Asarians and Saurians. As she knew, Jenna had taken one look at Elion Feyr, and from that moment, the two had been inseparable. Elion was remaining behind on Caledonia, ostensibly to commence healing training, but already he and Jenna had bonded. On her cheek, Jenna wore the colours of his aura alongside her own. Liandra was happy for them, though their joyous bonding, only made her sorrow the more acute.

"There is one thing I need to ask of you, *Tighearna*," Alleron Tavor said.

"Aye?"

"Bronnia has a strange form of empathy, something I haven't encountered before. Have you never wondered why she was so clumsy? The other little things which were considered abnormal? She needs special training. I would like to take her home with me."

Connal nearly choked on his wine. "She is fosterling to MacArran. Are you certain she is telepathic? I was told she was slow-witted."

"Her abilities have been misunderstood and stifled," Liandra said.

"Please allow her to accompany me. She wants to go very badly. Bronnia says she has no real family on Caledonia. Except her uncle ..." Alleron shook his head. "Did you know her parents?"

Connal shrugged. "As for her father, I know not. Heather MacLeod kept herself aloof from every man. 'Twas such a surprise to learn of her bairn. No man came forward to acknowledge the deed. Or its consequences." He glanced at Liandra as she coughed. "Are ye well, Mistress?"

Liandra nodded, her gaze averted. Connal frowned at her, again, as he watched her take a long gulp of wine. What was wrong with her?

"Bronnia's strangeness, then, was due to this empathy, and the abuse she suffered at the hands of her uncle?" Connal asked.

"Yes. Even if she had not suffered so, she would be different. It's because of who she is; a person with special abilities. What Bronnia requires isn't available on Caledonia. At least not yet," Alleron said.

Connal glanced across the hall. The child was sitting on the lap of that horrific looking lizard. "She wants to leave?"

"Very much."

"And where will she live? With whom?"

Liandra smiled. "She will be in good hands, Connal. My mother and father will take her in as fosterling. She can come home to Caledonia any time she wishes."

"I will keep you appraised of her progress. We can visit often," Alleron Tavor said.

Connal winced. *Visit.* Other kin-folk had said much the same to him. They'd come back home to visit, but for them, home was no longer Caledonia. Home for them was amongst the stars.

Home for him was where his heart would be, also amongst the stars! Even Garris would be leaving soon, with Fianna. And Liandra, too. All those whom he loved the most. *Seven Stars!* Loneliness and sorrow cut deeply into his soul.

"Very well, if that is what she wishes, then she has my leave to go."

Liandra steeled herself, mentally and physically, before she knocked on the door to Connal's chamber. Moments later the door swung open.

"*Ban-druidh?* What an unexpected pleasure. "

It won't be for long, when you hear why I've come. "I need to speak to you Con."

"Then come in, unless you want to stand in

the passageway." Connal stalked to his desk and
fidgeted with a stack of papers. "What would
you say to me, Liandra?"

She swallowed down hard. "It concerns
Bronnia."

He turned to her suddenly. She could not
understand the play of emotions in his face,
they reached her in swirling confusion, so
tightly bound were they, she was unable to
identify a single one.

"Bronni?" he said, hoarsely. "Go on."

"She begged me not to come to you, even
though I explained I must, since you are her
foster-father."

"What has happened?" He took a step
towards her, then halted.

"When I helped her to pack, I noticed her
doll was torn. Fianna began to mend it. We
found this hidden inside." Liandra held out her
hand and Connal took the brooch from her.
Inscribed on its back were the words *Rob* and
Heather.

"This device is of clan MacLachlan," Connal
said.

"That's what Fianna said, too."

He frowned down at the brooch, thinking
furiously. Rob and Heather? Rob! Was it
possible? He brought back the long-suppressed
memories of his friend. Rob and Heather in the
garden ... arguing. The two always fought like
cat and dog. Sometime love must have
overcome anger... He closed his mind against

that painful thought. Too close for comfort. He ran a finger over the brooch.

"Now that I have my wits about me, I realise that Bronnia's eyes very much resemble Rob's."

"You knew him?"

"Oh aye. Very well. He died ten years ago."

"Bronnia is almost that age."

Connal nodded. "Do you remember when I told you of my father's accidental death? Several clansmen were killed in the same accident, along with Rob. They were returning from space in one of those *infairrnal* air ships. Trusting life and limb to a machine!"

"Hence your obsessive hatred of technology."

"'Tis any wonder? In that one day I lost my father and my best friend." Connal smiled bitterly. "*Tighearna* MacLachlan was beside himself with grief. The only thing which stopped him from calling out his clan against mine, was that my father died in the accident which also killed his son. Up until that time our two families had been friends."

"Why wouldn't Heather name Rob as Bronnia's father?"

"Because after the accident, there was much bitterness. The hostility is mellowed somewhat since then, but so soon after, MacArran was not a name mentioned in MacLachlan's halls. Heather was wise to keep silent. Rob was a good man. Had he but lived ..." Connal shook his head sadly. "Well, now I must tell MacLachlan he has a grand-daughter. And the child is more

MacArran than she will ever be of his clan. He is not going to be pleased."

Liandra drew herself up to her full height. "That's what I want to talk to you about, Connal. You promised you'd allow her off-world."

"That was before I knew her pedigree."

"What little I saw of MacLachlan, it was enough to convince me he won't be the right sort of guardian. Just Fraser MacLeod in another guise."

"MacLachlan is her grand-father."

"She is your fosterling. But if that isn't enough, she's also a League citizen."

Connal's face went deathly pale. If those eyes were swords, she would have been cut to pieces by the intensity of his gaze. She stood her ground, with difficulty.

"What did you say?" Connal's voice was low and deadly.

"She has taken out League citizenship."

"Your suggestion, no doubt?" Connal folded his arms and frowned.

"No. You can thank Elexxessrr for his foresight."

"That scaly monstrosity? I will have his hide! This is clan business!"

Liandra laughed without humour. "Neither MacLachlan, nor even MacArran could stand up to a Saurian. They're warriors and defend kin and property to the death. Elexxessrr has *named* Bronnia. That's something like adoption. As she is his adopted, he'll tear anyone to pieces who might try and harm Bronnia."

"Is that so? I would cut that reptile down to size, for his interference, citizen of the League or no! Bronnia is of clan MacLachlan. Her heritage cannot be denied."

"She does not want it, at least not yet. Please, Con!" Liandra took a step towards him, hand outstretched. "Please try and understand. She is only now learning not to be afraid, to trust people. MacLachlan terrifies her. Bronnia needs much training but above all, love. She won't get anything from MacLachlan. She was sick with fear when she knew I was coming to speak to you."

"She was?"

His voice was quiet, almost gentle, and before he dropped his eyes, Liandra thought she caught a flicker in those steel-grey depths, which might have been a trick of the light, or a tear.

"Why did you come to me, then? You could have escaped off-world and none the wiser."

"I trust you to do the right thing for Bronnia."

Connal closed his eyes and ran his hands through his hair. "And what did Bronnia say when she knew her grand-father is *Tighearna* MacLachlan?"

"After I calmed her hysterics, she told me in no uncertain terms that she won't be going to MacLachlan, no matter what, because her allegiance is to the MacArran household."

Connal smiled in spite of himself. "Wilful brat! I suppose you taught her that."

"As citizen of the League, she has choices. She exercises her right to decide her future."

"I presume you informed her of *all* her League rights?"

"As counsellor I thought it my duty to advise her of her options."

He sighed. "I will tell MacLachlan. He arrives here, with the others, in less than a day for our Council meeting. It might be prudent to ensure that when he reaches my Castle, Bronnia is nowhere on Caledonia. Do you understand?"

"Yes. Thank you." She touched his arm. Beneath her fingers she felt the warmth of his body, though he was shivering. "Con, you've chosen wisely. Thank you for trusting me."

He snorted. "I will be the one to face MacLachlan's fury. Again!" He smiled grimly. "Well, I suppose I could agree to marry his daughter. MacLachlan would forgive me anything to have me as son-in-law."

His words were like a bucket of ice, chilling, tearing her breath from her. Liandra gasped and turning away, she all but ran out of his chamber.

Connal frowned and after watching her race down the corridor, he kicked the door closed. Striding to the window, he looked out. *Marry Verana MacLachlan!* He shuddered at the prospect. He would marry no woman. And clan duty be damned! He would find another way to placate MacLachlan. Arran's Mercy! Why was his life so complicated? And ever he knew the answer. Liandra.

He should not have agreed to her scheme. But how could he deny Bronnia her chance of a new life, a chance of happiness, such as was denied him? He leaned forward and rested his forehead on the cold glass of the window.

Fianna threw her arms around Liandra's neck and sobbed.

"I thought you would stay with us awhile longer. Can you not?"

Liandra winced from her friend's embrace. "It'd be very difficult."

"And Connal?"

Liandra turned away. "He's said nothing."

"He has *said* nothing. It doesn't mean he is wanting you to go."

"He has his duty and responsibilities, as do I."

"I thought he ... cared for you."

"There's a difference between caring, and what I need from a man."

Fianna bit her lip and nodded. She wiped her hand across her eyes. "Aye, well you can blame his father for that. Connal would deny it, but the treatment he received from his father when he was a child, has always made it difficult for him to say what's in his heart."

"Not so, Fianna. I know he is fond of me."

"Only fond? I thought it more. 'Tis sorry I am." She shook her head. "See here. I have gifts for you, from Garris and me, from others in the household. You must promise to come back one day."

"I will."

Liandra ran her hands over the gifts arrayed on her bed. The tartan shawl, the cook book, a kilt, yards of fabric, a set of bag-pipes, a brooch. Each gift represented the personality and interests of the giver.

"And Bronnia will be all right with your family?"

"She'll want for nothing, as I did when I was a child. My parents will delight in having a child in their home again."

Liandra looked down at her shaking hands. Not just one child ... soon there would be two children in her parent's house. She swallowed against the tears.

"What's wrong, *gradhag*? You look sick," Fianna whispered.

Liandra smiled. "You talk more and more like an off-worlder."

"Garris's influence." Fianna blushed. "But are you sick?"

"Aye ... yes. I hate good-byes."

Fianna burst into tears again, but she brushed them angrily aside as she pushed Liandra's farewell gifts into a bag made from MacArran tartan.

"Garris promises me that we'll visit you off-world. I long to see the stars, Liandra. I even look forward to seeing some more of those outlandish beasts which Bronni is so taken with."

"Saurians might look frightening. They're very gentle."

"But they have such long claws and teeth."

"They're vegetarians." Liandra managed a weak laugh.

The two women stepped out into the corridor. Dougall was waiting there and he took the bag from Liandra.

"Truly you be leaving then? 'Tis a shame. Fianna can you not convince her?"

"She promises to come back, and you can always go off-world and visit."

Dougall grimaced. "I be too old to go gallivanting around the galaxy."

Liandra and he stared at one another. She had the distinct impression he was trying to say something which he found very difficult. His eyes glistened with tears.

"You will come back to Caledonia, or I shall go off-world and bring you back!" he choked out.

"I promise to visit."

"'Tis not what I meant, I - *Tighearna*!" Dougall's stricken face was suddenly bright.

Liandra turned to see Connal striding stiffly down the corridor, his face set, that square jaw of his clenched formidably.

"So 'tis farewell, My Lady *Ban-druidh*?" he said, softly.

Dougall took Fianna's arm and ushered her down the corridor.

"A word in private Liandra, if you will." Connal drew her inside her chamber and closed the door. He looked at her for so long and so hard that Liandra fidgeted beneath his steely stare.

He handed her a small velvet case and a tartan satchel. "I brought you these gifts, Liandra. Though I see by the bag Dougall carried, others have also given you farewell tokens."

"Yes."

Opening the satchel, she gasped in shock as she drew out a small dagger, its hilt decorated in an intricate leaf and star design. A tiny, glittering crystal lay at the centre of each star.

"I know you are not overly fond of weaponry, but I thought this might remind you that all the science of the League is no match for loyalty and love. Our weapons symbolise honour and friendship."

Liandra smiled, blinking back her tears. His words cut like a knife - how ironic that his gift should be a dagger.

"And now the other," Connal said.

Opening the velvet case, Liandra drew out a necklace even more beautiful than the one he had given her before. From the silver band, a tier of perfect crystals formed the shape of an inverted pyramid. At the apex of the design hung one large crystal, multi-faceted and sparkling with every hue of a Caledonian rainbow.

"It's very beautiful, Con."

He smiled. "When you wear it, think of us. I hope you will forgive me the way I treated you when we first met. I was quite a beast. A ... barbarian!"

Liandra smiled. "That you were Connal MacArran. I have forgiven you - long ago."

"And this, also for you." He pushed a book into her hands. "I never did finish reading *Fire on the Heather* to you. Perhaps you can train one of your servitors to speak Caledonian."

"Con -" She reached out to him.

He took her hand and raised it to his lips, a tender caress which turned her inside out. He held her hand between his own and stared down at her. "Farewell My Lady *Ban-druidh*," his whisper was barely audible.

"Con," she said, shakily. "I want you to have this." She slipped her Asarian fire-ring from her finger and taking his hand, she placed it on his palm, closed his fingers with hers. "When you look at it, remember me ... fondly. If you can!" Liandra did not look backwards as she sped away.

Connal watched as she hurried down the passageway. *I will remember you more than fondly, gradhmhor, for you are my heart and soul!*

No! This was not how it should end. Perhaps he could persuade her to remain, just for awhile longer. He took a step after her.

"*Tighearna* MacArran!" MacLachlan's voice called and Connal turned to look over his shoulder. Beside the older man, as always, was the young shadow, Andrew MacTiernan. The two men strode quickly forward and came to stand on either side of him.

"We have been seeking you, MacArran. MacEwen is disputing our agreement of the land transfer. He looks fit to draw blood. You had best come quickly!"

Connal frowned at the older man. MacLachlan's hand on his shoulder propelled him forward. He glanced back at the now empty corridor, torn between duty and Liandra. Still, if there was to be blood spilt in his halls ... Business always before his pleasure ... ever it had been so. Only now, he would give it all up just for a few words to the witch! Although what would be the use? She wanted no more of him and his world.

"Connal?" Andrew MacTiernan asked.

"Aye, I am on my way. 'Tis a sorry day indeed when a man cannot have peace in his own house! Lead on Andrew. 'Tis I who might be doing some blood-letting, I be just in the right mood."

MacLachlan roared with laughter. "Twice in one day, Connal, you and I agree on something."

Liandra slowly walked the silent, brooding corridors. Never had she felt so alone in her life.

Crossing the grass to the scout-ship, she paused to see the crowd gathered on the field. At her approach, Dougall and his pipers started up their bag-pipes and began a tune which was so mournful, she knew it was his way of bidding her good-bye.

After the lament, she was kissed and embraced by the whole household. The whole household, save one. And it was that one whom she wanted more than anything to be there, to farewell her above all others. Angas, she saw, stood at the back of the crowd. Clustered about him were several young women. Notorious Angas. He returned her smile with a lop-sided grin.

A high-pitched yelp made her spin around. Fergus! The hound strained forward. She tried to mask her disappointment that at the end of the leash was not Connal, but Dougall. Liandra dropped to a knee and fondled Fergus' massive head.

"Take good care of him, Dougall," she said, pushing herself to her feet.

"Aye," he replied. Their gazes locked. The unspoken thought between them. *Take good care of Connal.*

Liandra glanced back at the Castle, delaying the inevitable until a member of the ship's crew ushered her inside. With a low hiss, the hatch sealed behind her. Slowly she sat beside her father.

He glanced at her sharply. "You're coming with me?"

"Yes."

"I thought you would stay," he said.

"I wasn't asked."

Alleron raised his eyes heavenward. "You're always so stubborn. Your greatest failing, as it is with your mother. Why do you think he didn't ask? Maybe you gave him no encouragement."

"Don't be ridiculous."

"A man does not have to speak the words. You have only to look in his heart and soul."

"He doesn't allow me to."

Alleron Tavor smiled, sadly. "He might have, if you gave him a chance. Stubborn! Both of you!"

"Please don't say anything to me."

At the subtle increase of cabin air pressure, she gripped her seat with both hands. Minutes later she forced herself to look out the porthole. The green and purple world of Caledonia hung in the velvet of space, one jewel in a shimmering midnight tapestry. She closed her eyes against the sight.

"Goodbye my *gradhmhor*," she whispered.

Chapter Twenty-Six

Connal twirled the goblet between his fingers. Sitting at his feet, Fergus eyed him mournfully.

"*Doona'* look at me like that, ye blasted hound! 'Tis nothing I can do!"

As Fergus whined, Connal swore in exasperation. The dog had been a misery for weeks, and off his food. Much like his master in both respects. He absently stroked the ring on his finger. It looked as if it were dying. Was that possible? Night after lonely night, he had come to know its every hue and ever since Liandra's departure, twenty days ago, it had begun to lose its vibrancy. Now it was a pale, lustreless thing. Perhaps it reflected the inner pain of its new owner?

Connal cursed himself. He was behaving like a boy, when a man ...

*A **man**, Connal MacArran, would not have allowed her to go!* Again, Dougall's words returned to haunt him. Connal smiled grimly. Dougall had never been backward in coming forward, an invaluable trait over the years. Now the man's candour was infuriating. Another reason to stay away from the hall, that and the silent condemnation of his friends - Liandra's friends.

Connal closed his eyes. Exhaustion nagged him, making him feel sick. He no longer sought his bed. Too damn cold and lonely. A chair beside the fire was as good a place as any to try to sleep. Again, he stroked the ring. *Ban-druidh ...* He closed his eyes.

Across the vastness of space, she turned and smiled. As she ran to him her long strapless gown billowed out around her. They met in an embrace that took his breath away. As he bent to kiss her, he sensed the difference. Two souls greeted him, not one.

He frowned and she smiled up at him, placing his hands on her stomach. He smiled, too, as he felt the life within her, which together they had created.

My Lady Ban-druidh! What other surprises do you have up your sleeve?

My robe does not have sleeves. She laughed.

He swept her up into his arms and ...

Connal jolted upright in his chair. The pain of memories and longing tore him asunder. By Arran and the Seven Stars! He breathed in a shuddering, ragged breath, and flinched as perspiration ran down his spine. Yet another dream to bedevil his nights! He ran a hand through his damp hair. How long *will* this continue?

As long as it takes, MacArran, to make ye come to your senses! an inner voice rebuked.

By his reckoning he had two choices. Stay on Caledonia, alone, and go quietly insane, or head off-world and bring the witch back. Abduct her again, if necessary. Even if she rejected him, argued with him the rest of his life, it would be a thousand, a million times better than not having her with him at all.

And the bairn? What a ridiculous dream! As a professional counsellor she was incapable of conceiving. She had told him that in the cottage. Besides what were the odds of making a child with an alien woman when they had bedded down only ... Connal closed his eyes, willing that memory away.

A bairn could be planted at the very first loving, every Caledonian boy knew that. And as for odds, were not the odds even more unlikely that Connal MacArran would fall in love with a green-haired witch? Connal flung himself out of the chair and strode to the door. Wrenching it open, he stared in disbelief.

"Dougall?"

"Aye my lord?"

"What are ye doing sitting out there?"

"Waiting for ye to come to ye senses and give me the appropriate orders."

Connal snorted. "Get on with it, then!"

"About bloody time!" Dougall muttered, as he raced down the corridor.

No sensors squealed in alarm as the door swished open. Garris' *phonnic* lance worked well … too well. If he could break into her home this easily, then so could another. Connal strode into the apartment, stopping in stunned amazement. If he did not know better he would swear he was in the wrong place.

The colours were still the same, the swirling opalescent rainbows, but about him, he saw all the artefacts she had taken from Caledonia, and more besides. Hanging on the wall, two claymores crossed over each other, the dagger he had given her at the centre. Strips of MacArran and MacLeod tartan hung around the display. Why had she decorated her quarters in such a way? She hated everything about his culture.

He drew out one of the claymores and tested it. Perfect balance, a man's sword in every respect. That being so, what was it doing in Liandra's lounge-room? Was it possible that she had a man, or men, living with her? By Arran he would wring the neck of any man who touched his woman! If he found evidence of it, they would be sorry and so would Liandra! *Seven Stars she would!*

He stalked about the chamber. On the table, held in a stasis field, was a sprig of heather. Next to it stood a 3-d image of Bronnia dressed in Asarian robes. The child looked healthy and happy, a far cry indeed from that forlorn waif he had adopted as fosterling. Bronni was doing just fine - unlike himself!

Two sofas, draped with MacArran tartan rested against the far well, near the view-screen. It had changed, too. No longer the underwater antics of those creatures he had watched before, now it was a duplication of the scene from her Castle apartment. As he stepped closer to it, he heard, as if from the distance, the faint wail of bag-pipes. He breathed in the scent of heather. The illusion was so real ...

"What can I do for ye?" a voice behind him droned.

Cursing, Connal twisted around, hand reaching for his dagger, too late remembering he had left it behind on the star-ship. Garris had insisted that he come unarmed, otherwise he would not pass through any security sensor, no matter what tools he had at his disposal.

Connal stared at the owner of the voice. Although the silver thing was man-shaped it had no face, just a semblance of a head and two glowing orbs for eyes.

"Who are ye?" Connal asked. With narrowed eyes he regarded the creature.

"I be Dougall, Mistress Liandra's butler-droid. At your service, Master."

Connal glared as the machine bowed. *Dougall*? What would his pax-man say when he learned he was name-sake to an electronic gadget?

"Where is Mistress Liandra? I demand to know."

The butler-droid was silent.

"Can ye not understand me, ye rusty bag of bolts?" Connal asked.

"I am programmed in a thousand languages. Caledonian is my speciality, Master."

Connal grimaced. He liked it not that a machine could speak his tongue. No doubt, though, as things now stood it was something he would have to get used to!

"I am looking for Liandra Tavor."

"Mistress Liandra is not at home."

"That I can see, ye electronic monstrosity." Connal ran a hand through his hair. He hadn't expected this, not any of it. Not in a million years. "Dougall, how long will Mistress Liandra be away?"

"The Mistress is out shopping."

Connal swore beneath his breath. What little experience he had of women's shopping, he could be in for a long wait. Why had she not used her computer dispenser? She had no reason to leave her apartment to do something as mundane as shopping.

"Can I offer you some refreshment while you wait Master?"

"Aye, I suppose. Do you have whisky?"

"The finest malt in the galaxy. Would you prefer Terran or Caledonian?"

"Terran whisky, if you will."

"Aye, right away, Master. Please be seated."

If the circumstances had not been so desperate, Connal might have laughed. What would they say back home if they could see him now? That a metal servitor was waiting on him, bringing him a draught of Terran whisky. By Arran! He really had lost his mind!

Dubiously, Connal accepted the proffered drink from the 'droid. It bowed to him before moving away to stand in a corner. Truly, an amazing machine. Perhaps Liandra did have the right of it. Machines and technology were not the problem. It was how they were used. And by the actions of the League members in his castle, it appeared they utilised their science for the purest of motives. Perhaps the measure of a man was not whether he had machines, but in the way he used them. Still, any day he would prefer flesh and blood servants to a silver 'droid!

He sat down on the sofa, his position strategically chosen. Half hidden behind an iridescent, crystalline screen, he could watch the door. When Liandra entered her apartment, she would not see him. Not until it was too late.

Connal eyed the whisky and tentatively took a sip, almost choking in surprise. It was damn good! If Terrans could make such a passable whisky, then surely as a race, they could not be so bad? He had a sudden urge to see the land of his ancestors. To see, if it still stood, the castle of the enemy from where the suit of armour - Liandra's 'robot' - had been seized.

Two glasses of whisky later and Connal's

nerves remained taut. If anything he felt worse now than he had before he entered the apartment. The waiting was getting on his nerves and the worst of it, Liandra's aura clung to everything, tormenting him further. Connal swallowed the last of his drink.

"Can I bring you another whisky, Master?"

"No thank you. Dougall, when the Mistress returns, I do not want you to announce me. I want my visit to be a surprise."

"My Mistress likes surprises."

Connal grinned wolfishly. "Then you will keep silent about my presence?"

"Aye Master."

Connal pushed himself to his feet and paced around the chamber. The wall shimmered open and he stepped into her bedroom. Her crystal bed, now repaired, stood in the centre, as before. Metal cases lay strewn over the floor. Some were half full of her clothes and other possessions. Where was the witch thinking of going? Not anywhere without him, that was for damn certain!

He heard the swish of the outside door and stealthily returned to his hiding place. In amazement he watched two golden balls, which he had assumed were wall ornaments, leave their perches and fly across the room chiming an electronic greeting.

"Be welcome home, Mistress. We have missed you," the silver man-droid said.

"I've missed you too, Dougall."

Liandra stepped into the lounge-room. Although dressed in her usual body-suit, over it she wore a short cloak made of MacArran tartan. She shrugged off her coverlet and Connal drank in the sight of her sweet curves. He had been a fool to have allowed her to slip away so easily!

"Be welcome home, Mistress. I have missed ye," Connal drawled.

Liandra gasped and turned. She stared in shock to see Connal leaning against the wall, arms folded just staring at her. *By Arran*! Her whole nervous system flared at the sight of him. She closed her eyes. She must be dreaming again. Though when she opened her eyes, he was still there.

"C ... Con? Is it truly you?"

"Aye."

Liandra took a tentative step forward, her hand outstretched and then she steeled herself. She must not make a fool of herself, or embarrass him with any display of emotion that he could not requite.

Then something prickled her memory. Connal was wearing his belted plaid. Surely his visit was not an occasion which warranted his traditional costume? Unless ... Something ominous was just going to happen - she just knew it.

"What brings you to my home, Connal MacArran?" she asked lightly, trying to alleviate her foreboding. "How did you gain access to my home? You're not using the trans-mat again?"

Connal smiled without humour. "The

479

infairnal machine is under lock and key. When I left the Castle it was being studied by a group of League scientists. They were swarming over it like bees around the honey pot. As to why I am here, I have unfinished business with ye."

"Ye ... you do?"

He pushed himself away from the wall. "Aye, *ban-druidh*! If ye be thinking I would allow my child to be raised in this alien menagerie ye be *vairry* much mistaken!"

Liandra gasped. "You know! But how?"

Connal smiled grimly. "I had a dream about you. I did not know for certain until now, when you confirmed it. Why did ye not tell me?"

"I would have, when the time was right."

"By Arran! By those blasted Seven Stars of yours, Liandra Tavor! The *right* time for telling me was *before* ye left Caledonia! And how long did you intend to keep me in ignorance of my own child?"

"Eventually I would have brought Alaric to meet you. It would be unthinkable to deny him his heritage."

"*His? Alaric?*"

"Our child. He and I have touched consciousness. His name is Alaric."

Connal felt numb. He had been prepared for anything. Or so he had thought. But this ... "A son?" He smiled tentatively.

"Yes, a son."

In an instant his smile was gone. She drank in the sight of that steel-grey gaze of his, the clench of his jaw, and its all too familiar throbbing tic. Even angry, he was still beautiful, her Connal. How could she have ever left him? Now having him here enraged was better than not having him with her at all! She swallowed down hard, marshalling her frazzled nerves.

"But a son, how ... how...?" Connal asked.

"The cottage, if you remember."

"Aye I remember our joining well enough. Too well, in fact! Ye said ye couldna' conceive. Yet ye have!"

"Father said it was because of the trans-mat. The machine has an in-built safety feature to screen out any harmful substances, or viruses. It removed the chemical implants from me when you and I used it to transfer."

"How ironic. You have been caught out because of your reliance on League technology!" He laughed, yet there was no humour in the sound. "My son will be raised as a true MacArran. How fortuitous that you have been packing, for I be here to take you back to Caledonia. Both of you!"

"Have I no say in this?"

"That depends upon you, *ban-druidh*! Return to Caledonia where we can discuss this -"

"We can discuss it now. Or are you going to abduct me again?"

"If I must, to make you see reason."

"Why is it that *your* reason is the only viewpoint? You're so stubborn! You can't just come barging in here and demand this or that from me. What about my life? My work?"

"Understand this now, Liandra. My woman shall never work like that again. I will not have you sharing with another man."

"Physically, I have never done so! You of all people should know that. My dream-weaving was always just that. Never anything more."

"But it was enough for you, was it not? I understand you only too well. You were always afraid of real love. And not just because of that childhood incident, either! You lived out your fantasies on your *infairrnal* bed. And when you had a real man, for a change, you ran the first moment you could!"

"Con -" Liandra closed her eyes as the room pitched and spun. That dizziness was back to plague her. She put a hand to her temple.

Connal jumped to her side, supporting her, leading her to the sofa. "What is it? What's wrong?" He knelt in front of her, taking her hands between his own. "You be thin and pale You should not be upsetting yourself."

"*You* were the one shouting at *me*."

"Aye for that I'm sorry. I forget your condition. Your nature, 'tis so contrary."

Liandra closed her eyes. His fingers, stroking her hands, made it difficult to think. Almost she thought she caught a faint sending from him. She wished she could open herself to him so that he could see all and know all. He wouldn't shout at her then.

But maybe, though, if he saw the extent of her

love for him, he'd just run, as she had from him!

Connal stared at her, taking in her every detail. Angrily he berated himself. Had he learned nothing of her in their time together? Surely he remembered that the more he ordered and dictated, the more obstinate and defiant she became. Infuriating though her stubbornness could be, it was one of her traits that he loved the most. She kept him guessing at her moods. He never knew what to expect. Such a challenge to coax and coerce her, but until she had gone he had not known how much he had enjoyed their sparring. Now, by acting the arrogant barbarian again and storming into her apartment, he had forced her into a corner. Of course she came out fighting. In her place, he would do the same.

Connal raised her hand to his cheek. Her eyelids fluttered open. He was almost lost in that brilliant sapphire gaze of hers. "Forgive me, *ban-druidh*! I didna' mean to come charging in here like some wild beast." His smile was gentle, tender. "Truly, sometimes, you are a thistle beneath my kilt," he added huskily.

"I didn't expect to see you here, ever again. It was such a shock. And seeing you in your *breacan an fhelidh*, I feared you might be here to take Bronnia back to MacLachlan."

"No. For my attire I have my reasons. As for MacLachlan, he be subdued. My gift of a strip of land, which he has ever coveted, proved an irresistible inducement to renounce his kinship to Bronnia."

"And his daughter? When do you marry her?"

Connal grimaced. "Did you truly think I could have another woman after you? She marries Andrew MacTiernan. The two are well suited."

Liandra smiled and took his hand and rested it against her stomach. "Con, send greetings to your son. He'd like that better than your shouting at me."

Connal frowned and though he went to snatch his hand away, her fingers held his prisoner. He was not able to do this ... he was no mind-reader. And he was afraid. *Of your own bairn, MacArran? What a coward ye be!*

His fingers fanned over her stomach. "By the Seven Stars!" he whispered. "I ... I felt a spark ... I'm not sure."

Liandra smiled. "You sensed our son. Deny it if you want, but like most Caledonians, you have a remnant of your ancestors' empathy. I always considered it uncanny, your ability to devise appropriate punishments for your people. I now know why."

Connal pushed himself to his feet, staring down at her while she gazed up at him. Liandra watched the change occur in those beautiful eyes of his. No longer ice and steel, now they were softer, gentler. Almost lover's eyes, like those of the man she had cherished in the cottage. Then, even as she watched, they altered yet again to become dark as space and full of pain.

"I want you with me willingly. I shall not force you, Liandra." He turned away. *I love ye too much,* he thought as he all but ran to the door.

He did not reach it. The two ball servitors flew around him, barring his way. They crashed into him, trying to force him back. Connal swatted at them with his hands.

"What did you say, Connal?"

"Call off your servants, Liandra. *Ouch!* Stop that! *Ow!*" Although they poked and prodded him, he would not budge an inch.

Laughing, Liandra stood up. The servitors flew back to hover beside her. "What did you just say, Connal?"

He turned to her and their gaze met and held across the room. "I asked you to call off your servants."

Liandra shook her head. "No, before that. Something about love, or am I mistaken? Is it so difficult for you to say? Why didn't you tell me before I left Caledonia?"

"Why did you not tell me about Alaric?" he countered.

"I know how much you hate the idea of a mind-touching alien. I'm both these things. That being so, what would you have thought about our son? Perhaps something to loathe - an alien who has the same powers and needs as his witch-mother."

"I would never think that of you, or the bairn.

You wrong me, woman!"

"Do I? When you and I joined in the cottage I reached out to you with my mind. There was a block there I could not, would not, break through. To me, the joining of our minds is more important than our physical union. I needed more than you could ever give me, Connal. I would never force you to be something you did not want, or do something you found repulsive."

Connal strode up to her and she gasped as his hands curled over her shoulders. Fire raced through her at his touch. He shook her just once, a gentle caress, not meant to chastise.

"Liandra, how do you know what I can give unless you ask it of me? When I joined with you, it was not just for a night's easing. I gave you the gift of my body. When I knew I had taken your maidenhead, I was full of joy. On Caledonia, such is considered a special treasure. The woman does not give it lightly, nor the man receive her gift with little regard. Yet you seemed uncaring, even laughing at my concern. I truly thought you a whore. I was furious with you for thinking so lightly of what you gave me."

Liandra stared at him. "I gave you the gift of my body, too. After, I thought your only concern was that I might be pregnant."

"I was. Then, I thought you had just used me, as a means to revitalise yourself, the loss of your maidenhead a small price to pay -"

"Dear Con, I would never use any creature in any way, especially you! You wondered why I was a virgin, and I told you about my childhood experience. Yet, as you have perceived, the real reason has nothing to do with the man who tried to hurt me."

"Aye?"

"Why is it, do you think, that I allowed you - an insufferably arrogant barbarian - to love me as no other man had ever done? Because no man had ever awakened me as you did. As you will always do!" Her voice caught in her throat.

"Then the greater fool I! I should have listened with my heart, not my ears. Ever it has been so. I won't be making the same mistake, again. Why didn't you tell me this before?"

"We Asarians are very passionate. I was afraid I'd frighten you with the way I felt."

"Aye. You could've trusted me. Was nothing we shared worth the risk?"

"The greater risk to drive you from me in hatred or loathing, if I told you of my needs. I hoped in time to return to Caledonia as your friend, though I wanted so much more. And now the only reason you seek me out is because of the child."

Liandra half turned away. Connal still held her. Gently, but firmly, he turned her back to face him.

"For a trained counsellor, Mistress Tavor you have mis-judged me."

"Have I?" She raised her chin. "You who kept your thoughts and feelings to yourself, except when angry? For a short while in the cottage you were different. Then I thought all things were possible. But in the morning you were, once again, the stranger. I thought you were revolted by your joining with me. If I told you about the child, before I left Caledonia, you would have made me stay only for him. I wanted you to ask me to stay just for me. Now all your words are just for the sake of Alaric."

Liandra bent her head, so he could not see her tears. He held her head tenderly between his hands.

"Do not cry so, *ban-druidh*. 'Tis not good for you, or the bairn. Hush, listen to what I have to say."

He drew her back to the sofa and gently took her onto his lap and held her, rocking her like a child as he had done weeks before in his sitting-room. "I have come across the galaxy for ye, even before I knew for certain about our bairn. I need you. I would give up all for you, Liandra, if I could. And therein lies our greatest problem. As the last son of Arran, I have my clan duty. If it were not for that fact, I would leave Caledonia forever to be with you."

"I would never ask that of you, Con."

He smiled sadly. "I know that. A man or woman who asks their lover to forsake all, that love will not last. If you return home with me, I'll ensure your comfort and happiness. You'll want for nothing. Any contrivance of the League which you desire, you have but to name it. If you want the whole damn Castle filled with servitors who answer to the name of Dougall, then so shall it be."

"You hate mechanical things."

"I was wrong about machines, Liandra. Besides which I hate the loneliness more. Come back to Caledonia with me. And any time you need to go off-world, the MacArran star-ship will be at your disposal."

"Truly?"

He gently dried her cheeks with his kisses and then cupped her cheek with his palm.

Liandra took his hand and kissed each fingertip.

"You wear my ring," she said.

"Aye," Connal said. He glanced down at it, and stared. The colours were brighter. He cleared his throat. "You mentioned before that I wear my belted plaid. As I told you before, we men of Caledonia wear such only on special occasions; funerals, clan-gatherings." He raised her chin gently, his eyes full upon her. "And hand-fastings." Connal drew a ring from his sporran and held it out to her. "On my world when a lover gives their partner a ring, it's considered special. A betrothal ring. I wear my plaid to honour you, *gradhmhor*. For I formally ask you to become My Lady."

Liandra stared in stunned silence, shocked by Connal's words, his gentleness, by the beauty of the ring he was holding out to her. A perfect crystal surrounded by purple and green stones held in a delicate silver filigree setting.

"I will do everything for you, Liandra. Be everything you want and more, if you'd just let me. Give me the chance. Don't be so stubborn! Arran's Mercy! Do you accept the ring, *ghraidh*?"

"Aye, with all my heart."

He smiled then, and placing the ring on her finger, he kissed her hand. Liandra ran her fingers over his cheeks, gently brushing away his tears.

"I know how important your work is to you," Connal whispered. "Now that Caledonia is opened to the League, you can practice your counselling from the Castle. Only I'll not have you sharing your bed with anyone but me! In other respects you are free to perform your work -"

"You'd do that for me?"

"All that and more for you, *ban-druidh*, you have but to name it."

"Con ..." She took his head between his hands, and ran her fingers through his hair. "Counselling is no longer a joy for me. I was preparing to return to my father and help him act as League liaison to the Caledonian Council."

"What about your therapy-work?"

"I can't do it any more. Besides I have Alaric to consider."

"Yes, Alaric ..." Connal paused.

Liandra frowned, almost caught his thought, before it was suppressed, buried behind a veil of fear and silence. "What is wrong, my *gradhmhor*?"

He tried to avert his face, his eyes, but she

held his chin firmly. This time his anguish washed over her, he made no effort to hide it.

"Dear Con. Alaric remains within me until *he* wishes to be born."

He smiled, tentatively, tracing a finger over her stomach. "You're not disgusted by the result of what I did."

Liandra laughed. "How could I be? Besides, you can't take all the credit for Alaric. I did play a part in his conception, too, you know! You insufferably conceited barbarian!"

"That's not what I meant. You told me once how revolted you were at the thought of physically conceiving and bearing a child. The pain ... the other things, I will not force you to endure something you find abhorrent, but the thought of Alaric in some *infairmal* mechanical contraption ... Liandra, are ye certain?"

"I am a trained counsellor. Pain holds no fears for me, Connal MacArran."

"Truly you are a *ban-laoch*! I will do everything I can to always ensure your comfort."

Liandra nodded. "Medi-bays will be one of the first League contraptions I insist on importing to your barbarous world. Not just for me, for every Caledonian. There's much work to be done. I have a feeling I'm going to be kept very busy with the demands of the Castle. And other things. Do I have the right of it?"

"Aye." Connal grinned. "I can be very demanding. I intend to keep My Lady MacArran fully occupied. My promise to you."

"Connal, truly?" Liandra frowned.

He studied her, shrewdly. "Why are you still afraid? Tell me." He kissed her gently.

"How can you forget your aversions so readily? I need more than you know or understand, Connal."

"My fears belong to the past, Liandrrra."

"What am I going to do with you, barbarian?"

Connal laughed. "Anything your heart desires."

"Anything?"

"Aye. Look wherever you need to find your answers. I'm not afraid of your witchery."

"Do you truly mean that? Do you understand what it is you're telling me? I gave you my body, but for an Asarian, the greatest gift we can give is our mind-touch."

As she looked into his eyes she saw them turn a turbulent grey-black. Not through fear, with longing, with burning desire. *How* he wanted this bonding. Wanted it as much as she.

"Aye, I understand, *ban-druidh*. I will give you this gift, too. Look into my very being to read the truth. To know my words are not false, that I don't trick you solely because of the bairn. I want you with me on Caledonia. Not afraid. Not a prisoner. But as my wife. I need your love."

"Do you remember when I told you about the risks Asarians face if they fully bond with another? That if something should happen to one, then the other partner can die from loneliness."

"You're worth any risk, *gradhmhor*. Death does not frighten me, Liandra. What does terrify me is to be apart from you. I'll not lose you again. I have no wish to abduct you, again, but *Seven Stars*, woman! You don't give me much choice!"

She stroked his cheek and laughed. Throughout their confrontation, she'd noticed how his speech had changed: word contractions, amid his formal Caledonian.

"Aye," he said. "I talk like an off-worlder."

"You've just given voice to my thought."

"Aye, I can read you a little. I fought very hard against your contamination, little realising I'd lost the battle before it had started. If I had any wit, then, I could have saved us both a lot of heart-ache."

"Come." She tugged him to his feet.

"Where are you taking me?"

"To meet an old friend."

"I am not in the mood, Liandra."

"Don't be so stubborn. That's my prerogative."

He bit back the words as Liandra drew him into her bed-chamber.

"It is high time I found out if there truly is a thistle beneath your kilt!"

He laughed gently. "More than a thistle, I assure you, *ban-druidh*! Or have you forgotten?"

She unlaced his shirt, and drew it over his head. She pressed her lips against his bare chest, bringing each nipple to a taut peak.

Connal groaned as her mouth teased his body. His ornate leather belt fell onto the floor, his plaid hung loosely over his nakedness. He kicked off his ankle boots.

"What does My Lady MacArran ask of me?" He captured her mouth and tongue in a deep kiss.

"Nothing you are not prepared to give me, *gradhmhor.*"

Connal held her out at arm's length. "There is one thing I want you to do, Liandra."

"Name it."

He laughed. "So easy to agree? Why do I think this will be only a temporary thing? Do you remember the time you imaged me in the Asarian bonding robe? Image me in this way again, so that I can be the man you want. If you want, I'll even do that dance for you."

Liandra put her fingers to his lips. "I don't need to dream-image you, for you are exactly how I love you."

She tugged at his hand, to lead him to the bed, but Connal swept her up into his arms and placed her gently against the covers. He lay beside her, cradling her body against his. She moaned as he kissed her tenderly.

"Mistress! Mistress!" Dougall-the-droid called.

"Damn it!" Connal swung around to confront the silver creature.

"The man is in close proximity to you, Mistress. Do you allow it?"

Liandra laughed. "It is allowed, Dougall."

Connal picked up a pillow and hurled it at the

'droid. It ducked elegantly, but refused to budge from the doorway.

"Understand this well, you metal monstrosity! Henceforth you keep your distance, or I will melt you down. Leave at once!"

"Do as you're told, Dougall."

"Aye, Mistress."

Liandra laughed again and put her arms around Connal's neck. She kissed him gently. "Dougall is only protecting me."

"'Tis my duty." His tongue traced along the line of her lips and as Liandra drew in a sharp deep breath he invaded her mouth.

With one arm holding her firmly against him, his free hand unravelled his kilt and sent it flying into the corner of the room. Liandra's fingers teased off his hose.

Carefully he drew the jewelled clasp from her hair, and now free of any restraints, her tresses flowed like molten starlight over his hands. He rubbed his face against the silver river, breathing in the heady perfume of her hair.

"I thought you would have changed your hair to green," he whispered.

"I no longer hide what I am to others. To myself. You taught me that much, Connal."

"I can teach ye much more if ye desire it."

"Aye."

Liandra's clothes proved an infuriating obstacle, Connal found. Laughing, she helped him work the pressure seals. He peeled off her clothes, his fingers teasingly slow. Finally she pressed her nakedness to his.

As his hands fanned over her, he trailed kisses down the length of her body. His mouth came to rest against her belly. "You say his name is Alaric?"

"Yes. It's Asarian."

"Welcome Alaric MacArran. Be welcome. For truly do I love ye and look forward to the day I can hold ye in my arms," he whispered against her skin.

Liandra closed her eyes, her heart turning in her breast. Unable and unwilling to control her love, she let it flow out to him. As her sending touched him, she heard him gasp. He raised himself on his elbow and stared down at her. Their gazes merged. She saw the glimmer of his tears amid the love and passion.

Lowering himself, his mouth travelled across her body, to each breast which he loved and teased before slowly retracing his path, to rest his lips at her throat. Against his cheek, he felt the wild beat of her pulse points and the blood pounded in his body in unison with hers.

Liandra wrapped her legs around him, crossing her ankles at the base of his spine.

Connal paused at the threshold of her femininity. "Alaric won't be disturbed by my loving you?"

Liandra laughed gently. "He welcomes you, as I."

With a cry of delighted triumph, Connal entered her. His motion slow and smooth, he withdrew teasingly when her body arched upwards to meet his, to try to fully capture his turgid flesh in her woman's warmth.

"Patience, My Lady *Ban-druidh*. Patience." He laughed above her. He cupped her head and as he did, he caught sight of the Asarian ring on his finger. The gem glowed and pulsed with life. Colours swirled and coalesced within the stone. Its vibrancy mirrored the blood singing in his veins.

The crystals on the bed came to brilliant life, sending a rainbow of colours spinning about the room. To his amazement, he was lifted, Liandra with him, and held by some force, suspended weightless above the bed, warm light wrapping around them.

"Con - please ..." her whisper against his ear made him shudder anew. "Let me join with you."

"Aye, my *gradhmhor*."

His hips undulated, he came to rest deep within her. He felt a feather-soft probing of her mind and caught his breath. It didn't hurt, his shock came from the intimacy of her melding. The sensations were so much more pleasing than their physical joining. He closed his eyes tight against the intense, exquisite fulfilment.

Liandra waited patiently, letting him become used to her presence as he had done for her in the cottage. She had been an innocent then, now their positions were reversed. In this new form of loving *he* was the virgin.

She caught Connal's laughter as the thought echoed between their minds. Images, and feelings merged. Then she probed deeper, more intimately and Connal opened himself to her questing. She sent him love and warmth. The colours of her aura caressed his. At first he clumsily returned her imagery, but as he grew accustomed to the sensations and learned how to reciprocate, he sent to her clearly.

Liandra gasped and writhed. His hold, both tender and strong, teased her with the expertise of an experienced mind-lover rather than a novice. He withdrew a little and returned, his mind and body working in unison to torment and delight her, to drive her to the brink, to hold her there before retreating, so that he delayed her release.

"Oh Con ... my *gradhmhor!* Please! I can't stand it!"

Then their shared passion took them far away. Colours spun faster and faster in the room, as their bodies and minds finally became one.

Connal shivered in ecstasy, as his overwhelmed senses exploded. In one instant he was the one below and above. He experienced all of Liandra, and she, of him. On and on the colours wove around them, warming, lifting. They floated in a sultry cocoon of pulsing light.

There came the moment of release, a time of suspended awareness when they entered a realm where dreams and reality were joined in a mixture which was blissfully, almost painfully intense.

Connal burned from the inside out. He pulsed, exploded, and cried out with the sweet agony of it. He would lose everything, life itself if the feeling continued, but if it ended, he would surely die.

Minutes, or maybe hours, later he opened his eyes. Liandra was atop him smiling down. Her silver hair flew around them her, tendrils tickled his skin. He glanced about. They were still weightless, held suspended by the bed's mantle of light. It tormented his flesh and he moaned with pleasure.

He wriggled in delight as she caressed him from the inside out. "Ooooh," he groaned. "I cannot stand it. Please."

"Please what? *Please* ... that I stop? Or *please* ... that I continue?" Liandra asked sultrily.

"Arran's Mercy! *Doona* stop! What did ye do? Och! What are ye still doing?"

"My Connal, now you know what it is like to be loved by one such as me. You see the bed and I are one. Are you shocked?"

"No, *ban-druidh*." He squeezed his eyes shut. Seven Stars! He was losing his mind! How could a man survive such exquisite torture? "Is this what sensualators do?"

"Oh no, this is Asarian loving, Con. Only for you. Asarians only ever share this form of loving with a soul-mate."

"'Tis just as well! If I ever thought you had, or will do this with another man, I'd dispatch him to his ancestors. And you, I'd give you that spanking you have often deserved, but have always managed to elude. Answer me one thing, *gradhmhor,* while I still have my wits about me -" Connal swallowed down hard as he felt her hands and fingers, and her mind working in tandem to fondle his tortured flesh. "I wasn't able to lie with another woman after our dream-sharing. Though I burned with the need. All I could think of was you. Did you be-spell me?"

Liandra laughed. "Not exactly. But the result was the same. Somehow in that first dream-sharing, you and I forged a tentative bond. You were ever aroused and unable to do anything about it, because you wanted only me."

"And you? Did you also feel like this?" Connal asked.

"My heart and body warred against each other. I was as be-spelled as you."

"I'm glad you suffered, witch!"

"That I did, Connal MacArran."

He laughed. "Just now, I heard you singing and felt the bed's vibrations ... so many things I cannot put into words. You spoke to me in your language. I want you to teach me Asarian. Not by subliminal tutoring, you can personally introduce me to a new word every day."

"Aye, My Lord."

Connal grinned. "Didn't I tell you long ago that one day you would say *Aye My Lord* to me as sweetly as one of my own people."

"I'm not tamed to your hand -" Liandra said, testily.

500

He laughed. "Be at peace, Liandra! I never want you compliant. My Lady *Ban-druidh* is expected, no, commanded, to maintain, forever, all the fire and passion of that green-haired witch I fell in love with."

"Then I'll be happy to obey your command. Still, I should warn you about one thing. My Terran half is no longer restrained. I'm going to be difficult to live with. Terrans can be very temperamental. Just ask my father."

"Don't forget, I also have Terran blood in my veins. So we shall have some interesting encounters. Besides, I've endured your stubbornness before and not been defeated. I enjoy a woman with spirit."

"Too much could be tedious."

He grinned. "I think I have ways and means to ease you out of your contrary moods."

Still weightless, Connal gently nudged her over, bringing her to rest beneath him, his body covering hers. He wrapped his legs around her and they slowly spun in the pulsing light. His fingers explored ... this was so easy, so enjoyable ... every part of her accessible without hindrance or effort, and he didn't have to worry about crushing her beneath his weight. By the Seven Stars and by Arran! He loved the bed already!

Liandra wriggled as his fingers began a more sensuous, intimate stroking. Connal and she laughed, as their lips and tongues sought and found one another's love-points. Minds joined together to tease and arouse from inside out.

"There are fifty words for love in Asarian," Liandra whispered. She curled a strand of his raven hair around her fingers. "If you truly want me to teach you Asarian, it will take a long time. A life-time, in fact."

Connal smiled gently. "My Lady, such was my intention when I asked it of you." He ran his hands up and down her back, stroking and cupping her curves.

"Our lessons in Asarian begin now. *Eo-enoil-anallen*, my Connal."

He smiled against her lips, knowing what she had said. So closely attuned were they now with their mind-joining he needed no translation.

"I love you, too, my Liandra. My Lady *Bandruidh*." He was going to enjoy their lessons in the privacy of their bed-chamber back on Caledonia. He laughed and Liandra drew his head back so she could study him. "The first item I will be packing for our return to Caledonia is this bed. It has infinite potential and I intend to explore its every possibility."

"Only if you will finish reading *Fire on the Heather* to me. My servitor couldn't do it justice."

"We don't need that book, Liandra. We'll create our own fire on the heather, that I promise you. However, today, we shall finish here as we began so long ago ... on your crystal bed. I -"

Liandra laughed and kissed him. "Oh no, my Connal MacArran. My *gradhmhor*.

We are only just starting you and I. In the future I will show you what I can truly do when we share our crystal dreams."

A note from the author

I hope you have enjoyed reading *Crystal Dreams* as much as I enjoyed writing it. Despite the advice that in today's market it is 'impossible' to sell a book, I am thrilled to have my first novel published by an Australian publisher. I Dared to Dream. So did JB Books.

My books-to-write file is overflowing with ideas, but 'sometime' in the future, I would like to write Alaric's story as a *Crystal Dreams* sequel. And Bronnia? Here is an interesting tale to tell too.

But first, another book very different from the one you have just read, will be released in 1998. If you enjoyed *Crystal Dreams*, then I am sure you will enjoy this one too.

Readers may write to me: PO Box 211, Henley Beach, South Australia. 5022.

Or contact me through the JB Books web page, the place to watch for new releases.

http://www.ozemail.com.au/~jabauer

I will answer all letters, but please enclose a stamped, self-addressed envelope, so I can forward an autographed bookmark to you.